4/99

READING THOMAS HARDY

Also edited by Charles P. C. Pettit

NEW PERSPECTIVES ON THOMAS HARDY

CELEBRATING THOMAS HARDY: Insights and Appreciations

THE THOMAS HARDY SOCIETY

(President: **The Earl of Stockton**)

The Society welcomes anyone interested in Hardy's writings, his life and his times, and it takes pride in the way in which at its meetings people come together in a harmony which would have delighted Hardy himself. Among its members are many distinguished literary and academic figures, and many more who love and enjoy Hardy's work sufficiently to wish to meet fellow enthusiasts and develop their appreciation of it.

Members receive copies of *The Thomas Hardy Journal* which is published three times a year and is regarded as the leading source of Hardy studies. Lectures, guided tours and walks in Hardy's Wessex, and other events take place throughout the year, and there is a biennial conference in Dorchester which brings together students from all over the world.

For information about the Society please write to:

The Thomas Hardy Society
P. O. Box 1438
Dorchester

Reading Thomas Hardy

Edited by

Charles P. C. Pettit

First published in Great Britain 1998 by
MACMILLAN PRESS LTD
Houndmills, Basingstoke, Hampshire RG21 6XS and London
Companies and representatives throughout the world

A catalogue record for this book is available from the British Library.

ISBN 0–333–68283–1

First published in the United States of America 1998 by
ST. MARTIN'S PRESS, INC.,
Scholarly and Reference Division,
175 Fifth Avenue, New York, N.Y. 10010

ISBN 0–312–21299–2

Library of Congress Cataloging-in-Publication Data
Reading Thomas Hardy / edited by Charles P. C. Pettit.
p. cm.
Comprises papers presented at the Thomas Hardy Society's Twelfth
International Conference, held in Dorchester, Dorset, 1996.
Includes bibliographical references and index.
ISBN 0–312–21299–2
1. Hardy, Thomas, 1840–1928—Criticism and interpretation-
-Congresses. I. Pettit, Charles P. C.
PR4753.R43 1998
823'.8—dc21   97–32312
                                                    CIP

This book is printed on paper suitable for recycling and made from fully managed and
sustained forest sources.

10   9   8   7   6   5   4   3   2   1
07   06   05   04   03   02   01   00   99   98

Printed and bound in Great Britain by
Antony Rowe Ltd, Chippenham, Wiltshire

Contents

List of Illustrations

Helen Paterson's illustrations for *Far from the Madding Crowd* (serialised in the *Cornhill Magazine*, 1874)

Preface

Like its two predecessors, *New Perspectives on Thomas Hardy* and *Celebrating Thomas Hardy, Reading Thomas Hardy* brings together the papers given at one of the Thomas Hardy Society's biennial Conferences, in this case the Twelfth International Conference which was held in Dorchester, Dorset, in the summer of 1996. Yet again, the Society succeeded in attracting a team of lecturers which can be described without hyperbole as a selection of the world's leading Hardy scholars, and for the first time we have been able to include all twelve of the main lectures in the subsequent book. There is no overall theme to restrict the contributors, and the variety of approaches and topics form an appropriate response to Hardy's own range and versatility. What the papers have in common, apart from a keen understanding of their subject, is accessibility: the origin of the book in lectures delivered to an audience largely composed of Hardy enthusiasts (rather than academics) ensures that even those papers whose new research makes a real contribution to Hardy scholarship are eminently readable. It can be said of the book, as of the Conference itself, that it contains something for anyone interested in Hardy, whether student, academic or enthusiast.

The volume opens with four papers which concentrate on specific Hardy works, then moves out to consideration of key Hardy themes (love, tragedy, death) and out again to Hardy and other artists (Yeats, Elgar). Finally the focus is on Hardy the man, the volume rounding off with Harold Orel's 'The Wit and Wisdom of Thomas Hardy'. However, these loose groupings are no more than an attempt to give the book a helpful shape for the reader, and each paper is strikingly and stimulatingly individual. The arrangement is well exemplified by the first four chapters. While all are concerned with specific Hardy works, Pamela Dalziel's fascinating contribution examines the influence of *Far from the Madding Crowd*'s first illustrator (with reproductions of some of the illustrations), Robert Schweik perceptively assesses recent critical writings on *Tess of the d'Urbervilles*, John Doheny focuses illuminatingly on Hardy's characterization in *Jude the Obscure*, while Charles Lock's major piece on *The Dynasts* is a challenging reassessment of the entire work. And so the volume continues, in variety and in quality. Small wonder that the lecture programme was welcomed so warmly by those attending the Conference; it is now a pleasure to make the papers available to all those who could not be in Dorchester that week.

In view of the large number of editions of Hardy now available, chapter references are given for all citations of Hardy's novels, and the edition used by each contributor is identified in the end-notes to each chapter.

I would like to thank Macmillan Publishers Ltd for permission to quote from Hardy. The credit for assembling such an impressive array of Hardy scholars belongs rightly to James Gibson, who created the lecture programme for the Conference before he handed over the role of Academic Director to me; I am most grateful to him. I would also like to take this opportunity to thank my family for all kinds of support throughout the period of Conference organization and book editing (not to mention at other times!): my wife Judith, my children Richard and Claire, and my parents.

CHARLES P. C. PETTIT

Notes on the Contributors

Joanna Cullen Brown studied at Oxford and Cambridge Universities, and after some years spent bringing up three children and in various forms of teaching she published three books on Hardy: *Figures in a Wessex Landscape* (1987), *Let Me Enjoy the Earth* (1990) and *A Journey into Thomas Hardy's Poetry* (1989). She leads various summer schools on Hardy and is a Tutor for the Department of Continuing Education of the University of Bristol.

Raymond Chapman is Professor Emeritus of English at the University of London, and Lecturer and Academic Adviser at the London Centre of the Institute of European Studies. He has written a number of books on Victorian literature and the language of literature, including *The Victorian Debate* (1968), *Faith and Revolt: Studies in the Literature of the Oxford Movement* (1970), *The Sense of the Past in Victorian Literature* (1986), *The Language of Thomas Hardy* (1990), and *Forms of Speech in Victorian Fiction* (1994), and was an associate editor and contributor to the *Oxford Companion to the English Language* (1992). He was a contributor to *New Perspectives on Thomas Hardy*.

Pamela Dalziel is Associate Professor of English at the University of British Columbia. She lectured at the Thomas Hardy Society's Tenth International Conference (1992). Her publications include numerous articles on Hardy and editions of *Thomas Hardy: The Excluded and Collaborative Stories* (1992), *Thomas Hardy's 'Studies, Specimens Etc.' Notebook* (with Michael Millgate, 1994), *An Indiscretion in the Life of an Heiress and Other Stories* (1994), and *A Pair of Blue Eyes* (1998). She is currently completing a book on the visual representation of Hardy's works.

John R. Doheny is Professor Emeritus of English at the University of British Columbia. He has written on D. H. Lawrence, Herbert Read, the philosophy of anarchism and the education of the poor in the nineteenth century. His work on Hardy includes essays on *Far from the Madding Crowd* and on Hardy's Swetman ancestors, and two biographical monographs: *The Youth of Thomas Hardy* (1984) and *Thomas Hardy's Relatives and their Times* (1989).

Ralph W. V. Elliott is Visiting Professor in English and Honorary Librarian at the Humanities Research Centre, the Australian National University, where he was Master of University House for thirteen years. He has also taught at the Universities of St Andrews, Keele, Adelaide, Flinders and the Australian National University. He has published numerous articles and reviews in his main fields of interest, which include the history and character of the English language, medieval English literature, runes, and Hardy. His books include *Chaucer's English* (1974), *The Gawain Country* (1984), *Runes: An Introduction* (1959, 1989) and *Thomas Hardy's English* (1984). He is a Vice-President of the Thomas Hardy Society of North America.

Samuel Hynes is Professor Emeritus of Literature at Princeton University. His books include *The Edwardian Turn of Mind* (1968), *Edwardian Occasions* (1972) and *The Auden Generation* (1976), and editions of T. E. Hulme, Arnold Bennett and Conrad. His most recent publication is *The Soldiers' Tale*, a study of twentieth-century war memoirs. His work on Hardy began with *The Pattern of Hardy's Poetry* (1961) and has culminated in his authoritative five-volume edition of *The Complete Poetical Works of Thomas Hardy* (1982–95). He is an Honorary Vice-President of the Thomas Hardy Society.

Michael Irwin is Professor of English Literature at the University of Kent. His chief academic interest is in the area of fictional technique, and he has written a study of Fielding's novels, and *Picturing: Description and Illusion in the Nineteenth-Century Novel*. He has also written two novels, translated numerous operas and written the libretto for an oratorio about Jonah which was performed in Canterbury Cathedral. He has recently completed a book provisionally entitled *Reading Hardy's Landscapes*.

Charles Lock is Professor of English Literature at the University of Copenhagen, and has held teaching appointments at the Universities of Karlstad and Toronto. He has published on John Cowper Powys, Hopkins, Dostoevsky, Bakhtin, iconography and petroglyphs. His study of the critical reception of Hardy, *Thomas Hardy: Criticism in Focus*, was published in 1992.

Phillip Mallett is Senior Lecturer in English at the University of St Andrews. He has published articles on various authors, and has edited collections of essays on Kipling and on European satire. He edited (with Ronald Draper) *A Spacious Vision: Essays on Hardy* (1994), to which he also contributed a paper. He is currently working on a study and anthology of Ruskin.

Michael Millgate is University Professor of English Emeritus of the University of Toronto. Although most of his early work was on William Faulkner, his principal contributions in more recent years have been to the study of Hardy – among them *Thomas Hardy: His Career as a Novelist* (1971, 1994), *The Collected Letters of Thomas Hardy* (7 volumes, co-edited, 1978–88), *Thomas Hardy: A Biography* (1982), *Thomas Hardy: Selected Letters* (edited, 1990), *Thomas Hardy's 'Studies, Specimens Etc.' Notebook* (co-edited, 1994) and *The Letters of Emma and Florence Hardy* (edited, 1996). His editing for Macmillan of Hardy's ghost-written *The Life and Work of Thomas Hardy* (1984) led to the wider exploration of authorial deaths and literary estates which formed the subject of his *Testamentary Acts: Browning, Tennyson, James, Hardy* (1992). He is an Honorary Vice-President of the Thomas Hardy Society, and was a contributor to *Celebrating Thomas Hardy*.

Harold Orel is University Distinguished Professor of English Emeritus at the University of Kansas, and has held teaching appointments at the Universities of Michigan and Maryland, and in Germany, Austria and England. He is active in the study of Irish literature, and has published on a wide variety of authors, including Synge, Browning, Byron, Wordsworth, Edith Sitwell and Rebecca West. His extensive work on Hardy includes *Thomas Hardy's Epic-Drama 'The Dynasts'* (1963), *The Final Years of Thomas Hardy 1912–28* (1976), *The Unknown Thomas Hardy* (1987) and *Critical Essays on Thomas Hardy's Poetry* (1995). He has edited Hardy's *Personal Writings* (1966) and *The Dynasts* (1978). He is an Honorary Vice-President of the Thomas Hardy Society, and a Fellow of the Royal Society of Literature.

Robert Schweik, an Honorary Vice-President of the Thomas Hardy Society, is Distinguished Teaching Professor of English Emeritus of the State University of New York, and has been Visiting Professor at the University of Trier, and at Stockholm University. He is editor of the Norton Critical Edition of *Far from the Madding Crowd*; author of *Reference Sources in English and American Literature* and of *Hart Crane: A Descriptive Bibliography*; a contributor to fourteen other books; and author of over sixty other studies of Hardy, Tennyson, Browning, Mill, analytic bibliography, language and rhetoric, and cultural history in the nineteenth and twentieth centuries. He is currently writing an analysis of the rhetoric of twentieth-century art criticism.

1

'She matched his violence with her own wild passion': Illustrating *Far from the Madding Crowd*

PAMELA DALZIEL

First to my title, for which you will search the text of *Far from the Madding Crowd* – I dare say that of the entire Hardy oeuvre – in vain. It comes from a poster for John Schlesinger's 1967 film version of *Far from the Madding Crowd*. Peter Lennon, Hardy collector and proprietor of Casterbridge Books in Chicago, sent me a photograph of it some years ago, with the comment that it would have 'befuddled Hardy'.[1] Indeed. Headed "Zhivago's" Lara meets "Georgy Girl's" guy … in the love story of the year!', the poster contains four colour illustrations. One is of a rather smudgy-faced Julie Christie (Bathsheba) clinging tightly to an even smudgier Alan Bates (Gabriel Oak) as they escape from a raging conflagration: the caption reads, 'She was sure of his love … in spite of her other men!' In another illustration a coquettish Christie permits a worshipful Peter Finch (Boldwood) to kiss her hand; in a third a windblown Christie runs through a field, her cleavage prominent and knee-length skirt riding high up stockingless thigh. Finally, the caption that has supplied me with my title, 'She matched his violence with her own wild passion', accompanies the image of Christie, distinctly *déshabillé*, in the arms of a certainly shirtless and possibly naked Terence Stamp (Troy).[2]

The ludicrous aspects of the poster are obvious enough, and by invoking one of its captions in my title I am of course drawing deliberate attention to a distorted reading of Hardy's novel – and indeed of Schlesinger's film. It is significant that the poster's images are 'artists' impressions' (as they say), not photographs or stills: none of these scenes in fact occurs in the film, nor does Julie

1

Christie – who was never so buxom – ever appear in it with bare shoulders and legs. And if you are looking for scenes of bodice ripping such as those verbally and visually suggested by 'She matched his violence with her own wild passion' and its accompanying illustration, you will have to look elsewhere.

The film does of course possess a powerful sexual dynamic, but for most viewers it is dominated by its pervasive pastoralism – or so at least the numerous commentators on it (both Hardyan and non-Hardyan) would suggest.[3] The judgement reached by the *Daily Cinema* critic is typical: 'Bound to evoke the nostalgia for the simple life of the countryside which nestles in the hearts of the most unlikely of city-dwellers.'[4] If such an assessment seems unsurprising, that is because it reiterates a perception of *Far from the Madding Crowd* as rural idyll which has dominated the novel's visual representation from the very beginning, to the point that my own instinctive response to the film poster as a misreading of Hardy may itself have been conditioned by the prevalence of book covers implicitly positing the narrative as some kind of Arcadian romance. Many editions of *Far from the Madding Crowd* are adorned with images of picturesque cottages and country churches,[5] and if rural swains lounging in idyllic landscapes have in recent years largely given place to representations of rural labour, the idealization none the less remains, as do those indispensable mainstays of traditional pastoral idyll, sheep.[6]

In one respect, this predominance of the pastoral is scarcely surprising: the novel is, after all, called *Far from the Madding Crowd* and set in rural Dorset, and one of its principal characters is a shepherd. Moreover, as recent critics such as Peter Widdowson have demonstrated, the production of Hardy as the nostalgic chronicler of a vanished rural world is very common,[7] and leads naturally to sheep-filled covers, even for novels such as *The Return of the Native*[8] in which there is not so much as a whiff of the ovine to be caught (unless it is attached to Diggory Venn's clothes). Even so, what is unusual about *Far from the Madding Crowd* is the consistency with which it has had this particular visual reading imposed upon it. Other Hardy novels – with the notable but predictable exception of *Under the Greenwood Tree* – are represented variously on book covers: sometimes as rural idylls, but on other occasions as novels of sensation, as tales of the tormented psyche, or, most frequently, as passionate love stories somewhat of the Mills & Boon variety.[9] But *Far from the Madding Crowd* never seems to change, even though it, too, contains passionate love, psychological torment, and sensational action – to a greater degree, indeed, than many of Hardy's other novels. This supposed pastoral idyll does, after all, contain everything from life-threatening natural disasters to a coffin-opening and a murder.

To recognize the presence of such elements in *Far from the Madding Crowd* is inevitably to call into question my original response to the film poster: for all its over-heightened emphases and obvious departures from the actual film (let alone from the novel), it is perhaps not quite so absurd a reading of Hardy as I initially assumed. In many respects *Far from the Madding Crowd* – Hardy's version as well as Schlesinger's – can quite appropriately be called (to quote the poster) a 'dramatic love story'. One of the contemporary reviewers of the novel said that it could have been called 'Bathsheba and her Lovers',[10] and 'Bathsheba Everdene and Her Lovers' was in fact the title given to a dramatization of scenes from the novel performed by the Hardy Players in 1919.[11] Bathsheba can – again to quote the poster – be 'sure of [Gabriel's] love', even if it is difficult to imagine them in quite such a passionate embrace. Critics have long drawn attention to Troy's violence and Bathsheba's passion (to return to my title once more), and many would doubtless agree with the poster's caption to the Bathsheba–Boldwood illustration: 'She could destroy this man obsessed with love for her.' Above all, perhaps, the backgrounds of the poster frames point to a more complex representation of the novel than can be suggested by pastoral imagery alone: Bathsheba and Troy have an as yet unrumpled bed immediately behind them; gathering storm clouds darken the ostensibly idyllic English countryside as Boldwood courts Bathsheba; and the lurid conflagration from which Bathsheba and Gabriel have escaped is suggestive of that violence of nature ignored by so many of Hardy's illustrators but never by Hardy himself.

If the film poster, for all its exaggerations, constitutes in some respects a less distorted reading of *Far from the Madding Crowd* than the conventional visual representation of the novel as pastoral idyll, a question inevitably arises as to why that convention has established such a tenacious hold. The answer, as I believe and hope to demonstrate, can in part be found in the convention's original source: Helen Paterson's illustrations for the January–December 1874 serialization of the novel in the *Cornhill Magazine*.

Hardy's own response to the first of these illustrations (see Figure 1) was evidently positive, though doubtless he would in any

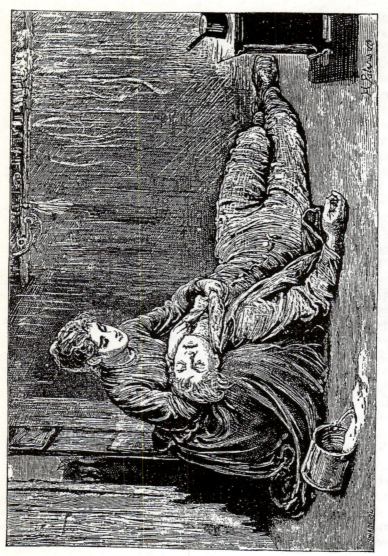

Figure 1 Hands were loosening his neckerchief. *Cornhill*, January 1874.

case have been relieved to be spared the ravages of someone like J. A. Pasquier, the illustrator of *A Pair of Blue Eyes* for *Tinsleys' Magazine* (September 1872–July 1873) and the only artist who had previously illustrated Hardy's work. More than forty years later, in the autobiographical *Life*, Hardy wrote:

> returning from Cornwall on a fine December noontide (being New Year's Eve 1873–74), he opened on Plymouth Hoe a copy of the *Cornhill* that he had bought at the station, and there to his surprise saw his story placed at the beginning of the magazine, with a striking illustration, the artist being – also to his surprise – not a man but a woman, Miss Helen Paterson. He had only expected from the undistinguished rank of the characters in the tale that it would be put at the end, and possibly without a picture.[12]

The illustration is 'striking', not least because it is quite sensational. There is nothing of the rural idyll in this image, though the rural itself is suggested by the overturned bucket of milk. Gabriel would seem to be dead – the potential horror of the situation being undercut only by the serenity of Bathsheba's expression and by the caption, 'Hands were loosening his neckerchief', which posits Gabriel as the originator of the thought, hence as a conscious, or at least semi-conscious, being. Also of significance in this opening image is the representation of Bathsheba as attractive in a conventional 'womanly' way. Her face suggests both tenderness and innocence, and she is appropriately occupied in a caregiver role. At the same time her depiction as literally (physically) above Gabriel effectively emphasizes her dominant ('unwomanly') position in relation to him at this time (she will soon refuse his marriage proposal). Such visual reinforcement of the nature of Bathsheba's shifting relationships with her lovers is, throughout the serialization, one of the consistent strengths of Paterson's illustrations.

Paterson's vignette initial for the first instalment depicts Bathsheba alone (see Figure 2), though the first-time reader of *Far from the Madding Crowd* could be forgiven for not recognizing this figure, with her rounded face and dark hair, as the same character depicted in the facing full-page illustration. The differences may be attributable in part to poor engraving – Paterson complained throughout her life of having 'suffered agonies from wood engravers (even from the best) all the years [she] drew on wood'[13] – but more significant, in any case, than the physical discrepancies

Figure 2   *Cornhill*, January 1874.

are the implicit differences in character. Sweet innocence has given place to saucy self-satisfaction: the Bathsheba of the vignette is the Bathsheba whose 'bright air and manner ... seemed to imply that the desirability of her existence could not be questioned' (Ch. 3).[14]

If these opening illustrations suggest different aspects of Bathsheba's personality, both none the less fall well within the range of what the conventional Victorian reader would have labelled 'feminine' – and the same can be said of all those aspects of

Bathsheba that Paterson chose to represent. Paterson ignored, on the other hand, those elements of Bathsheba which would conventionally have been designated 'masculine': for example, her independence, energy, and athleticism. Thus Paterson does not depict Bathsheba lying 'flat upon [her] pony's back, her head over its tail, her feet against its shoulder, and her eyes to the sky' (Ch. 3) – admittedly a somewhat indecorous image, hence probably unsuitable for a 'family magazine'. But neither does Paterson illustrate Bathsheba in the Corn Exchange or even Bathsheba paying her workers or sharpening the sheep shears.

It is true that in the illustration to the second (February) instalment (see Figure 3) the caption, 'Do you happen to want a shepherd, Ma'am?', suggests that Bathsheba is mistress of the farm; even so, there is no indication that she has in any practical sense moved into the 'male' domain – indeed at this point she has not, at least not in terms of work. In replying to Gabriel she tells him (through her 'workfolk') to speak to the bailiff, and in the facing vignette illustration she is engaged in 'woman's work', dusting bottles with Liddy. In that main illustration, however, her ascendancy over Gabriel – now economic as well as social – is again signalled by their relative positions. She is seated on her pony, literally above him;[15] he is on foot, his bowed head indicative of humility. They are entirely separate – at no point does Gabriel's figure even overlap with hers – while their clothes further emphasize the difference in their social status.

Equally significant in the present context is the background to the drawing. The meeting of Gabriel and Bathsheba occurs immediately after the fire, yet – in contrast to the film poster – there is no indication of that fire or indeed of Gabriel's less than Arcadian appearance, 'his features black, grimy, and undiscoverable from the smoke and heat, his smock-frock burnt into holes, dripping with water' (Ch. 6). In some respects the illustration functions in the same way as the previous month's representation of a sweetly serene Bathsheba bending over a possible corpse: the scene is idealized as much as possible to create an attractive, even 'prettified' image, rather than a dramatic or naturalistic one. This specific image, indeed, was probably reproduced on one of the items of ceramic 'Wessex ware' produced and sold in Dorchester, evidently with Hardy's approval, in 1910. Each of the chosen scenes from the novels was accompanied by a couplet 'selected' by Hardy – which presumably means written by him – and, according to a report in

8

Figure 3 'Do you happen to want a shepherd, Ma'am?'
Cornhill, February 1874.

the *Dorset County Chronicle*, on one 'specimen of the ware' Gabriel stood 'cap in hand before Bathsheba', while the couplet read:

> To his scornful love comes Gabriel Oak,
> And asks to be one of her shepherd folk.[16]

Not exactly Hardy at his poetic best.

If it seems surprising that Hardy in later years should have written such doggerel, it may seem no less surprising that he should ever have approved of the *Far from the Madding Crowd* illustrations, sentimentalized as they are and sometimes unnaturally stiff – as in the third (March) instalment (see Figure 4). Bathsheba seems much too serious for someone who has 'bounded' from her seat in her eagerness to try the Bible and Key divination (Ch. 13), and I have often wondered if Paterson was introducing an element of self-portraiture here. Certainly the representation of Bathsheba rather strikingly resembles the somewhat grim-faced photographs of Paterson herself in her early and middle twenties[17] (hence approximately contemporaneous with her work for *Far from the Madding Crowd*).

Some of Paterson's other *Far from the Madding Crowd* drawings are decidedly weak from an artistic point of view, especially those for the final two instalments (November and December; to be discussed below). Still others, such as that for the fourth (April) instalment,[18] seem inadequate because they so simplify Hardy's text, evading its complexities through idealization. The April illustration is in fact an engaging example of Patersonian sentimentality: an attractive Bathsheba holds the reins of her white horse as a beseeching Boldwood leans forward and says (to quote the caption), 'I feel – almost – too much – to think.' Once again, positioning functions as a visual marker of personal relationship: as social equals Bathsheba and Boldwood stand on level ground, but her bowed head suggests the guilt which requires her to listen to unwelcome protestations, while his highly stooped posture indicates the humility and abjectness to which his passion has reduced him. Paterson's Boldwood is a pathetic figure: so, in part, is Hardy's, but Hardy's also contains elements of the tragic – and of something darker. Paterson's representation includes no suggestion either of the original Boldwood 'pre-eminently marked ... [by] dignity' (Ch. 12) or of the disturbed, and disturbing, Boldwood obsessed by a valentine.

Figure 4　'Get the front door key.' Liddy fetched it.
Cornhill, March 1874.

In the following month's illustration (see Figure 5) even the pathetic Boldwood has disappeared, replaced by a handsome, young-looking Boldwood lounging at his ease in seemingly confident proprietorship of Bathsheba. This is the most idyllic of the illustrations, complete with a flute-playing shepherd and birds flying across the serene sky of a summer evening. It is also the illustration that Hardy would have seen immediately before he met Paterson for the first time; among the 'few points' he gave her on that occasion[19] one or two may have had something to do with the representation of Boldwood, since Paterson's drawing suggests that she had assumed Boldwood was to be the hero of the story – an understandable enough assumption at this stage in the narrative.

The May illustration was also Paterson's first substantial attempt at depicting the labourers. The previous month's vignette had portrayed the old maltster[20] (who continued to lend a hand on the farm during harvest-time), but with the illustration of the shearing-supper Paterson faced a more substantial challenge. Before the novel began to appear in the *Cornhill* Hardy had written to Smith, Elder in an attempt to control the visual representation of the labourers: 'With regard to the illustrations perhaps I may be allowed to express a hope that the rustics, although *quaint*, may be made to appear *intelligent*, & *not boorish* at all.'[21] The substance of this directive was presumably passed on to Paterson and she would seem to have carried out Hardy's intentions in this respect. Her labourers are certainly not boorish and some of them have intelligent faces, most notably the man reclining on his elbow. Each of her labourers is also individualized – a rare enough event in itself in Hardy illustration.[22] Moreover, in Paterson's drawing only the excessively timid Joseph Poorgrass – the figure seated nearest the window – is presented comically, and even he escapes the reduction of caricature. The moment captured is one not of comedy but of timeless idyll, a moment present also in the novel, where the shearers are described as reclining against each other 'as at suppers in the early ages of the world' (Ch. 23). In Hardy's text, however – as so often in his work – the ostensibly idyllic moment is at least partially subverted, in this instance both by the presence of the thieving bailiff Pennyways and by Gabriel's painful jealousy of Boldwood.

There is no visual suggestion of such subversion in Paterson's representation and indeed this illustration combines with the facing vignette illustration of a man shearing a sheep[23] to sustain the

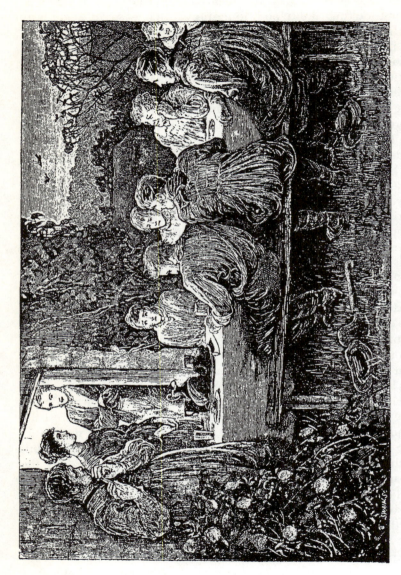

Figure 5   She stood up in the window-opening, facing the men. *Cornhill*, May 1874.

general tendency of the illustrations towards a distortingly idealized interpretation of Hardy's text. That Paterson should have
chosen to privilege the pastoral aspects of the novel is hardly surprising, since under her married name of Helen Allingham she was
to become the most successful of the so-called Idyllist school of
watercolourists, strongly influenced by Frederick Walker. Paterson
studied briefly with Walker at the Royal Academy Schools in the
early 1870s and much of her early work recalls his painting in both
its style and choice of subject matter, as indeed does her vignette
illustration of a young woman in a hayfield for the June instalment
of *Far from the Madding Crowd* (see Figure 6) and especially her
watercolour *The Girl Harvesting*,[24] based upon it. *The Girl Harvesting*

Figure 6   *Cornhill*, June 1874.

is undated, but the 'H. Allingham' signature indicates that it was painted after Paterson's marriage in August 1874, presumably as one of the watercolours she worked up in the middle and late 1870s from earlier woodblock illustrations. The best known of these is *The Young Customers*, the painting which in 1875 gained her admission to the Royal Society of Painters in Water Colours and the approbation of John Ruskin;[25] its 'original' was a woodblock illustration for J. H. Ewing's children's story *A Flat Iron for a Farthing*, published in the *Aunt Judy's Christmas Volume* for 1871.

While Paterson's tendency to rework her early illustrations has long been noted,[26] no one has hitherto remarked on the connection between Paterson's June *Far from the Madding Crowd* vignette and *The Girl Harvesting*, or indeed between her September illustration of Fanny asleep beneath the haystack (see Figure 7) and her watercolour *Tired Out* (1875), which features two young girls beneath a haystack, one sitting upright in a position similar to Fanny's, the other with her head in the lap of the first.[27] It also seems probable (I have not succeeded in tracking down the works themselves) that *The Milkmaid*, one of Paterson's two paintings accepted in 1874 for her first hanging in a Royal Academy exhibition, was based on the opening *Far from the Madding Crowd* vignette illustration of Bathsheba carrying a bucket of milk,[28] and that the 1873 painting *Far from the Busy Haunts of Men*[29] represented a reworking of one of the early *Far from the Madding Crowd* illustrations or of an unused sketch for such an illustration.

Although I have persisted, and shall for clarity's sake continue to persist, in referring to Paterson under the name she bore when doing most of the drawings for *Far from the Madding Crowd*, it was of course as Helen Allingham that she became well known in her later career – and has become, if anything, even better known in the closing decades of the twentieth century. Her reputation derives, however, as it always did, not from her work of the 1870s but from the watercolours she began painting in the 1880s – watercolours of country cottages and cottage gardens now familiar from their frequent reproduction on greeting cards and calendars and in gift books. As Paterson moved away from book illustration – and from Frederick Walker's influence – her figures became smaller and the 'landscape' more prominent. What remained consistent was the idealistic treatment. As Laura Dyer observed in an *Art Journal* article in 1888:

Figure 7 She opened a gate within which was a haystack, under this she sat down. *Cornhill*, September 1874.

In Mrs. Allingham's Art there is no trace of sympathy with the stern realism to which we have grown accustomed in the works of so many modern painters. For her there would be little attraction of a pictorial kind in the marks of grime and toil on rugged hands and bronzed faces. ... Still less is it Mrs. Allingham's province to portray the sadder phases of child-life – the pale faces in crowded city streets, the boisterous and grim pleasures of such young urchins and romps.[30]

Dyer is in no sense critical of Paterson's choice of subject matter: quite the reverse. In her opinion,

Mrs. Allingham deservedly ranks with the best water-colour painters of to-day through her appreciation of the simplest beauties of nature, and her persevering endeavours to delineate truthfully all that is picturesque in the fields and hedgerows, the cottages and lanes, the meadows and woodlands, and the daily toils and pleasures of humble dwellers in some of the most charming rural districts of England.[31]

There is, however, little suggestion of 'toil' in Paterson's paintings, even when the figures are engaged in some kind of task, and the assertion of the 'truthfulness' of her representations is highly problematic. Although she can perhaps be said to have painted in a 'realistic' mode, she is known to have used considerable artistic licence in her compositions, restoring thatched roofs and lattice windows to cottages which had been modernized, removing evidence of surrounding buildings from the background so that the cottages appear in isolation, and replacing vegetable gardens with exuberant displays of old-fashioned flowers.[32]

Of particular interest in the present context is the extent to which Paterson's idealized views of rural life have come to be associated with Hardy – not through the *Far from the Madding Crowd* connection but because of Hardy's own alleged idealization. For example, Ina Taylor in her 1990 book *Helen Allingham's England* remarks:

Without doubt Helen idealized the countryside in her art, depicting a way of life which never really existed. The sun-bonnets on her models were freshly laundered props from the painting cupboard as women no longer wore them in real life. Much as Thomas Hardy did in his Wessex novels, Helen Allingham looked back nostalgically to a mythical pastoral age set sometime in the 1840s. The days were always sunny, the rosy-cheeked cottagers lived close to nature, did an honest day's labour and rested, well fed and content.[33]

If few critics, even in the late twentieth century, have viewed Hardy as quite so extreme an idyllist, some contemporary reviewers of *Far from the Madding Crowd* certainly saw the novel much as Dyer in 1888 was to see Paterson's paintings. As Paterson's watercolours ignore the 'grime and toil on rugged hands', so in Hardy, observed the *Academy* (2 January 1875), 'The country folk ... have not heard of strikes, or of Mr. Arch; they have, to all appearance, plenty to eat, and warm clothes to wear.' As Paterson's paintings delineate 'all that is picturesque ... in some of the most charming rural districts of England', so what the London *Echo* (28 November 1874) called Hardy's 'chronicle of Arcadia' lingers, according to the *Saturday Review* (9 January 1875), 'in the pleasant byways of pastoral and agricultural life', and was seen by *The Times* (25 January 1875) as rising 'to the dignity of both an idyl and a pastoral'.

It is precisely my argument, in fact, that the real link between Paterson and Hardy consists not in any essential similarity in constructing 'An Idyllic View of Rural Life' (to quote the subtitle of Taylor's *Helen Allingham's England*) but rather in Paterson's doing with the English cottage what she had done earlier with Hardy's novel – and in the readiness of Hardy's critics and subsequent illustrators to follow her lead. It is important to remember that the serial illustrations were included in the two-volume 'first' edition of *Far from the Madding Crowd* (Smith, Elder, 1874) and therefore exerted their visual influence on both reviewers[34] and readers – as indeed did the two illustrations blocked on the cover of each volume. The first of these cover illustrations, situated above the novel's title, here elaborately decorated, reinforces that title's allusion to Gray's 'Elegy' in its representation of a country churchyard where the bird-filled sky, abundant summer foliage, and leaning tombstones emphasize the tranquillity of life 'Far from the madding crowd's ignoble strife'. The second illustration, located in the lower segment of the cover, draws attention to the narrative's more sensational aspects by reproducing the opening serial illustration of Bathsheba supporting the unconscious Gabriel. Smith, Elder were clearly hoping to attract a variety of readers by this visual combination of the idyllic and the sensational. By 1877, however, when the first one-volume edition of the novel appeared, the reviewers had re-inscribed the dominant interpretation of Hardy's text projected by Paterson's illustrations, effectively defining *Far from the Madding Crowd* as pastoral idyll,[35] and the cover of the new edition featured only the country churchyard.

As the inheritors of this representational convention, both nine-teenth- and twentieth-century illustrators and critics have for the most part continued to interpret the novel within the established framework. The front cover of the 1887 Sampson Low 'yellowback', for example, depicts Gabriel, shepherd's crook in hand, walking with Bathsheba through a cornfield, while the Henry Macbeth-Raeburn and Hermann Lea frontispieces for, respectively, the 1895 Osgood, McIlvaine edition and 1912 Wessex Edition both repro-duce idealized images of 'Weatherbury' village. Interspersed among all those sheep-filled dustjackets and paperback covers of more recent years are the illustrated editions by Agnes Miller Parker (Limited Editions Club, 1958), Leonora Box (Heron Books, 1970), and Peter Reddick (Folio Society, 1985) – various in their styles and choices of subject yet consensual in their basic reading of *Far from the Madding Crowd* as pastoral idyll.[36]

It is necessary consciously to distance oneself from preconceived notions in order to appreciate how very unidyllic this novel in fact is, even though a number of revisionist critics have recently been arguing the point.[37] The Gray quotation which gives the novel its title clearly has an ironic component. Physically far from the madding crowd these characters may be, but, unlike the imaginary inhabitants of Gray's hamlet, they are by no means exempt from ignoble strife: more episodes of melodramatic conflict – between individuals as well as between the individual and nature – in fact occur in this Hardy novel than in any other. To recognize this is immediately to realize how directive Paterson's illustrations were in a negative as well as a positive sense – to register how few of such scenes she chose to represent, in spite of the fact that the con-ventions of serial illustration, even in the 'upmarket' *Cornhill*, nor-mally mandated a focus on the most dramatic episodes. There are no Paterson illustrations, for example, of any of the natural disas-ters: the sheep driven over the cliff or bloated with clover, the fire, the storm. The only image which comes close to representing nature's dangerous aspects is the November illustration of Troy caught in the current, but any dramatic potential it might have pos-sessed is undercut by the cartoon-like depiction of a minuscule

Troy, arm upraised in a wide expanse of sea – a figure who, to reverse Stevie Smith's famous line, seems to be 'Not drowning but waving' – and especially by the reader's knowledge, provided at the conclusion of the preceding instalment, that Troy is in fact rescued.[38]

Paterson's avoidance of the more sensational aspects of Hardy's text can also be seen in the virtual absence of any representation of Boldwood's emotionally and physically violent encounters with either Bathsheba or Troy. The illustration for the July instalment[39] does show Bathsheba immediately after her highly emotional confrontation with Boldwood on the road to Liddy's sister's, when (to quote the caption) she 'flung her hands to her face, and wildly attempted to ponder on the exhibition which had just passed away' (Ch. 31). In the illustration itself, however, any impression of wildness is dissipated by the fact that Bathsheba's hands are not placed over her face as one might expect: her right hand rests on her forehead, her left is hidden behind her cheek. Paterson's intention was presumably to create a more attractive image by permitting an unobstructed view of Bathsheba's face and indeed of her curvaceous figure; the unintentional result is that Bathsheba seems to be suffering not from the violence of uncontrolled passion but from a crick in her neck.

The only image containing any substantial suggestion of the novel's darker side is the August illustration (see Figure 8). This Boldwood, lurking in the background, bears little resemblance to the earlier Boldwood of the shearing-supper – or even to the Boldwood of the proposal scene. The glint of despairing madness in his eyes and the tension in his clenched fists are stock markers of soon-to-erupt passion, so stereotypical in fact as to suggest that Paterson may have tended to avoid dramatic representation because she simply was not very good at it.[40] The strength of this illustration lies (once again) in the symbolic positioning of the characters, which emphasizes not only the supplanting of Boldwood but also the surrender of Bathsheba: Troy is visually in control of the situation as she leans against him in a conventional 'womanly' fashion. Interestingly, removal of Boldwood from the picture leaves behind the most sentimental of images, unrivalled by any of Paterson's other illustrations. It was presumably this image (sans Boldwood) which was painted on another piece of that Wessex ware, 'a vase bearing a representation of Sergeant Troy and Bathsheba Everdene', together with the couplet:

Figure 8   'There's not a soul in my house but me to-night.'
Cornhill, August 1874.

Far from the Madding Crowd,
Where lovers' hearts beat loud.

Even the original illustration is not particularly disturbing, given that Boldwood is relegated to the background and Gabriel is reassuringly present in the vignette on the facing page, 'leaning over Coggan's garden-gate, taking an up-and-down survey before retiring to rest' (Ch. 34).

For the final (December) illustration Paterson did choose a highly dramatic moment, that of Troy's unexpected appearance at Boldwood's Christmas party, but squandered its potential through the stiffness and artificiality of her drawing. The difficulty of portraying Troy's expression is avoided by presenting him from behind, while Boldwood stands in an unnatural pose, arm outstretched to welcome the as yet unidentified stranger. The faces of the 'workfolk' do register surprise and some concern but only Bathsheba's tiny pinched face suggests that anything is seriously amiss.

The most effective of the illustrations are those for the June and October instalments, which depict Bathsheba at, respectively, the moment of Troy's conquest and the moment of her recognition of the consequences of that conquest (see Figures 9 and 10). Both suggest the complexity and depth of Bathsheba's character far more strongly than do any of the more conventional, idealized representations. The Bathsheba of the June illustration, unflinching beneath Troy's sword, prefigures the Bathsheba who, after the confrontation over Fanny's corpse, will exhort Liddy: 'Liddy, if ever you marry – God forbid that you ever should! – you'll find yourself in a fearful situation; but mind this, don't you flinch. Stand your ground, and be cut to pieces. That's what I'm going to do' (Ch. 44). The Bathsheba of the October illustration, clutching the coffin as Troy bends down to kiss Fanny's corpse, has already progressed beyond tears. (The *Cornhill* caption incorrectly reads, 'Her tears fell fast beside the unconscious pair'; the error – presumably a consequence of Leslie Stephen's editorial deference to Mrs Grundy – was corrected in the two-volume 'first' edition to 'Bending over Fanny Robin, he gently kissed her'.) Paterson effectively portrays Bathsheba as seized by that intense yet childlike pain which will cause her to exclaim from 'the deepest deep of her heart': 'Don't – don't kiss them! Oh, Frank, I can't bear it – I can't! I love you better than she did: kiss me too, Frank – kiss me! *You will, Frank, kiss me too!*' (Ch. 43).

22

Figure 9   She took up her position as directed.
Cornhill, June 1874.

Figure 10 Her tears fell fast beside the unconscious pair. *Cornhill*, October 1874.

In these two images Paterson does successfully move beyond pastoral idyll to provide glimpses of the passion and disturbance which figure so prominently in Hardy's text. Yet they do not displace the dominant impression created by the illustrations as a whole, in part because they are so distinctly in the minority but also because their very attractiveness serves in itself to negate somewhat their potential for disturbance. In them Bathsheba is at her most beautiful – and her most sexual. In the June illustration, indeed, having (to quote the caption) taken up 'her position as directed', she stands beneath Troy's (phallic) sword as a willing object of sexual desire – almost as if she were a shepherdess of pastoral, entertaining the approaches of her yearning swain.

Remarkably, the attractions and dangers of sexual desire hinted at in these two illustrations are erased entirely from the representations of Fanny, where they might most have been expected. Fanny appears only twice, in the March vignette illustration and in the September full-page illustration. The former, depicting Fanny with one hand drawing her shawl tightly around her wind-buffeted body and the other outstretched to throw a snowball at Troy's barrack-room window, effectively captures her coldness. The latter (see Figure 7), showing her sprawled asleep beneath a haystack, no less effectively creates a sense of her weariness. Neither, however, gives any indication of the utter isolation, degradation, and suffering she endures. When Troy and Bathsheba meet Fanny on the Weatherbury–Casterbridge road shortly before she seeks rest beneath the haystack, the 'extreme poverty' of her garments and the 'sadness of her face' are plainly visible even in the autumn evening gloom (Ch. 39). Neither is apparent in Paterson's illustration; nor is the cause of that poverty and sadness – Fanny's advanced state of pregnancy – in any way indicated.[41] Potentially the bleakest of the illustrations, Paterson's drawing emerges as another instance of idealization, a representation of Fanny not as a destitute young woman overwhelmed by her physical struggle for survival, but simply as a weary traveller finding rest against a sturdy haystack, overlooked by a serene night sky. That Paterson herself read the image in such terms is suggested by her using the drawing as the basis for *Tired Out* (see above), an unambiguously idyllic representation of two young girls weary from the delights or labours of country life – or indeed from the 'delightful labours' so often emphasized in Victorian representations of rural life.

Both positively by their imagery, therefore, and negatively by their selectivity, Paterson's illustrations to the serialization of *Far from the Madding Crowd* effectively defined that novel as pastoral idyll. That definition was then reinscribed for the British reading public by the inclusion of all twelve full-page illustrations in the 1874 two-volume edition and by the selection of six of those illustrations for the 1877 one-volume edition. For the latter edition the choice of the idyllic churchyard scene as the sole cover illustration is endorsed by the presence as frontispiece of the overtly pastoral illustration of Gabriel asking Bathsheba if she wants a shepherd. The other five illustrations – Bathsheba loosening Gabriel's neckerchief, Boldwood's proposal, the shearing-supper, Bathsheba embracing Troy, and Troy's return – are also predominantly idealized (not included, unsurprisingly, are those potentially disturbing images of the sword exercise and the coffin scene). Subsequent illustrators of the novel, as has already been indicated, have continued to reinscribe this visual reading of the novel as pastoral idyll.

An interesting question, hinted at earlier, still remains. If, as I have argued, Paterson's illustrations were the originators of this one-sided interpretation of *Far from the Madding Crowd*, why did Hardy hang in his study a framed collection of eight of their woodblock proofs?[42] Why, indeed, did he consistently praise them in terms amounting to virtual authorization, as when he told the publisher James Osgood in December 1888, 'The best illustrator I ever had was Mrs Wm Allingham'?[43]

One reason could have been a recognition on Hardy's part that, limited though Paterson's work might be, what she did do she did well. It was important to him, for example, that Bathsheba be depicted as an attractive woman, not 'punished' visually for her unconventionality by being rendered physically unattractive – the fate that had befallen Elfride in *A Pair of Blue Eyes* and that would befall other of his heroines in the future.[44] It was also important to him that the details of rural life in the illustrations be accurate – and Paterson's were. Before the *Far from the Madding Crowd* serialization began, Hardy had written to Smith, Elder offering to forward sketches from his notebook of 'smockfrocks, gaiters, sheepcrooks, rick-"staddles", a sheep-washing pool, one of the old-fashioned malt-houses, and some other out-of-the-way things that might have to be shown'.[45] A sketch of a milking bucket and a shepherd's crook, signed 'T. Hardy/Bockhampton/Dorchester', does survive,[46] though it is not known when it was sent or indeed whether Paterson even received it. With or without the benefit of the sketch, however, she seems to have had little difficulty with either buckets or sheep-crooks. Even her vignette illustration of a sheep being shorn has a certain authority. Hardy must also have been pleased by her competent handling of architectural details: her September vignette illustration, for example, is a free but effective rendering of the east front of Waterston Manor, Hardy's 'original' for Bathsheba's house.[47]

Another, more fundamental, reason for Hardy's approbation of Paterson's illustrations may perhaps be found in his awareness of the exigencies of serial publication. It was with respect to *Far from the Madding Crowd* that he made his now-famous statement to Leslie Stephen about wishing 'merely to be considered a good hand at a serial', and he was clearly willing to make considerable concessions in order to ensure the novel's publishability.[48] Hardy would have realized that Paterson's visual reading of *Far from the Madding Crowd* was eminently 'safe' – not in any sense threatening to his audience, unlikely to deter any potential reader, and actively appealing indeed to many who (then as now) nostalgically yearned for some kind of timeless rural idyll. Given his arguments with Stephen over the acceptability for a 'family magazine' of some of the incidents in his narrative, he may even have perceived the idealizing tendency of the illustrations as helping to ward off threats to his already qualified authorial independence.

Clearly, however, there was also a significant personal element in his endorsement of Paterson's work. Dour as Paterson might appear in her photographs, it is evident that Hardy was charmed by her when they first met in May 1874, in the midst of the *Far from the Madding Crowd* serialization. More than thirty years later he whimsically recalled her in a letter to Edmund Gosse:

> The illustrator of Far from the Madding Crowd began as a charming young lady, Miss Helen Paterson, & ended as a married woman, – charms unknown – wife of Allingham the poet. I have never set eyes on her since she was the former & I met her & corresponded with her about the pictures to the story. She was the best illustrator I ever had. She & I were married about the same time in the progress of our mutual work, but not to each other, which I fear rather spoils the information. Though I have never thought of her for the last 20 years your inquiry makes me feel "quite romantical" about her (as they say here), & as she is a

London artist, well known as Mrs A. you might hunt her up, & tell me what she looks like as an elderly widow woman. If you do, please give her my kind regards; but you must not add that those two almost simultaneous weddings would have been one but for a stupid blunder of God Almighty.[49]

This letter (of 1906) was of course written years after Hardy had become disillusioned with his own marriage and it is difficult to know to what extent those 'romantical' feelings were present when he first met Paterson – or even to what extent he originally admired her illustrations. In the *Life*, an even later writing than the letter to Gosse, Hardy recalled that on first meeting his 'skilful illustrator' he 'gave her a few points'; Paterson's own memoir records that Hardy was 'fairly complimentary' on that occasion, although her qualifying comment, 'he said it was difficult for two minds to imagine scenes in the same light',[50] perhaps hints at reservations on his part. Hardy's letter to Paterson of 7 May 1874, presumably written shortly after their London meeting, seems to combine genuine respect for her work with a modest sprinkling of gallantry: 'I send a few particulars of the story, which may or may not be of use to you. Should you require any other information, or any sketch, I will if possible forward it, though I am afraid my drawing will be a somewhat melancholy performance beside yours.'[51]

Six years later, Hardy again wrote to Paterson, then of course Mrs Allingham:

Would you be willing to illustrate a serial story of mine [i.e. *A Laodicean*] that will begin in the Autumn of this year in a prominent American Magazine – Harper's Monthly... . The payment would be liberal; & my great admiration for your drawings induces me to address you in the hope that you may be able to undertake the work.[52]

Paterson declined his 'flattering invitation', explaining that she had 'entirely given up book-illustration'.[53] Hardy then approached Frank Dicksee and William Small before coming to an arrangement with George Du Maurier,[54] who had illustrated *The Hand of Ethelberta* for the *Cornhill* in 1875–6. That Hardy's first choice should have been Paterson indicates that he was indeed satisfied with her work; that his second and third choices should have been artists who had not previously illustrated his novels indicates his dissatisfaction with his other illustrators – not only Pasquier, but also Arthur Hopkins, whose Eustacia for *Belgravia* (1878) had been so disappointing,[55] John Collier, whose *Trumpet-Major* drawings for *Good Words* (1880) would remain the worst of all the Hardy illustrations, and even Du Maurier himself, whose work for Hardy fell well below his usual standards.

If it seems unremarkable that Hardy should have considered Paterson the best among these illustrators, it is more surprising that he should have continued, throughout his career, to rank her ahead even of the very capable artists with whom he worked in later years – most notable among them, perhaps, Robert Barnes, who so powerfully illustrated *The Mayor of Casterbridge* for the *Graphic* in 1886. Something, perhaps much, must surely be attributed to the fact that Paterson was the only female illustrator of Hardy's serialized fiction, and that – like Florence Henniker and Agnes Grove later on – she was a handsome, intelligent, and obviously talented woman to whom Hardy was strongly attracted. In feeling 'romantical' about the artist he seems to have allowed himself to feel a little 'romantical' about her work, subduing any aesthetic or interpretational reservations he may have had about the illustrations to *Far from the Madding Crowd*, and throwing over them a nostalgic, idyllic glow of his own.

Notes

1. Lennon to Dalziel, 25 November 1993.
2. In delivering this paper at the International Thomas Hardy Conference I was of course able to project an image of the film poster and of all the other visual representations to which reference is made. The impossibility of illustrating this printed version to the same extent has resulted in numerous revisions and compromises, but I am none the less grateful to both the editor and the publisher for allowing some representative images to be reproduced.
3. A number of reviews are quoted in Peter Widdowson, *Hardy in History: A Study in Literary Sociology* (London: Routledge, 1989) pp. 103–14; see also Nancy J. Brooker, *John Schlesinger: A Guide to References and Resources* (Boston: G. K. Hall, 1978) pp. 18–19, 73–7; Rita Costabile, 'Hardy in Soft Focus', in *The English Novel and the Movies*, ed. Michael Klein and Gillian Parker (New York: Ungar, 1981) pp. 155–64; and Roger Webster, 'Reproducing Hardy: Familiar and Unfamiliar Versions of *Far from the Madding Crowd* and *Tess of the d'Urbervilles*', *Critical Survey*, V (1993) 143–51.
4. 20 October 1967, quoted in Widdowson, *Hardy in History*, p. 114.

5. See, for example, the 1960 Fawcett Premier World Classic edition, reprinted throughout the 1960s and early 1970s with different (but equally idyllic) cover illustrations, and the 1986 Norton edition.

6. Most of the cover images of rural labour are details from paintings: see, for example, the 1978 Penguin English Library, 1993 Oxford World's Classics, 1993 Everyman, and 1994 Penguin Popular Classics editions, which reproduce, respectively, Joseph Farquharson's '... *The sun had closed the winter day* ...', George Clausen's *Sheepfold at Early Morning*, R. Whitford's *Mr Garne's Cotswold Sheep*, and Adolf Ernst Meissner's *Bringing in the Sheep*. The 1985 Papermac New Wessex edition reproduces a Gordon Beningfield painting (from *Hardy Country*) of sheep on a narrow path between hedges, while the 1995 Pan New Wessex edition uses an H. P. Robinson photograph of two young women passing by some grazing sheep. Sheep also dominate cover drawings: see, for example, the 1932 Cottage Library dustjacket and the 1965 Papermac and 1967 Airmont Classics paperback covers. One of the few sheep-less covers is the 1993 Wordsworth Classics edition's, which none the less reproduces an idyllic rural scene from George Vicat Cole's *A Surrey Cornfield*. A more significant exception is the dustjacket for the 1929 Macmillan Two-Shilling edition: printed entirely in red, it depicts a rather stark landscape in which two small figures huddle together to watch the sun rising/setting. Also interesting because of its complete departure from the pastoral convention is the 1974 New Wessex edition cover with its twentieth-century photo of a young woman in 'period dress' looking out of a window.

7. Widdowson, *Hardy in History*, *passim*.

8. See, for example, the 1985 Penguin Classics cover, which reproduces a sheep-filled detail from James Aumonier's *The Silver Lining of the Cloud*.

9. For each of these categories dozens of examples could be cited. Some of the more extreme include: the 1892 Sampson Low 'yellow-back' of *A Laodicean*, depicting Dare pointing a revolver at Havill; the 1966 Harper & Row Perennial Classic edition of *Jude the Obscure*, picturing the suspended corpses of the three children in the background and in the foreground Jude's head established in multi-coloured quasi-anatomical swirls; and the 1952 Pocket Books Cardinal edition of *Tess of the d'Urbervilles*, representing Angel carrying an unconscious Tess, whose figure is displayed to full advantage in a 1950s dress, low-cut in its bodice to draw attention to her cleavage and sufficiently short in its skirt to reveal her shapely calves, bare feet, and painted toe-nails.

10. *Saturday Review*, 9 January 1875.

11. Based upon an earlier dramatization, 'Bathsheba Everdene and Her Suitors', by Harry Pouncy; see Keith Wilson, *Thomas Hardy on Stage* (Basingstoke: Macmillan Press, 1995) pp. 55, 106.

12. Thomas Hardy, *The Life and Work of Thomas Hardy*, ed. Michael Millgate (London: Macmillan Press, 1984) p. 100. Hereafter cited as *Life and Work*.

13. Letter to Harry Furniss, quoted in H. Furniss, *Some Victorian Women: Good, Bad, and Indifferent* (London: John Lane, the Bodley Head, 1923) pp. 81–2.

14. All quotations from the novel are taken from the serial version, *Cornhill Magazine*, XXIX–XXX (1874). References to chapter numbers are included in the text.

15. Arlene M. Jackson makes this point in *Illustration and the Novels of Thomas Hardy* (London: Macmillan Press, 1982), p. 79.

16. 'Dorset Art Ware', *Dorset County Chronicle*, 16 June 1910, p. 4.

17. Photographs of Paterson in her twenties are reproduced in Ina Taylor, *Helen Allingham's England: An Idyllic View of Rural Life* (Exeter: Webb & Bower, 1990) pp. 25, 32. The earlier of these photographs is also reproduced in the *Thomas Hardy Year Book, 3, 1972–1973*, p. 7.

18. Reproduced in Jackson, *Illustration and the Novels*, plate 24.

19. *Life and Work*, p. 103.

20. Reproduced in Jackson, *Illustration and the Novels*, plate 27.

21. 4 December 1873, *The Collected Letters of Thomas Hardy*, ed. Richard Little Purdy and Michael Millgate, 7 volumes (Oxford: Clarendon Press, 1978–88) vol. I, p. 25. Hereafter cited as *Collected Letters*.

22. See Pamela Dalziel, 'Anxieties of Representation: The Serial Illustrations to Hardy's *The Return of the Native*', *Nineteenth-Century Literature*, LI (1996) 89–90.

23. Reproduced in Jackson, *Illustration and the Novels*, plate 4.

24. Mrs S. M. Bentley collection; reproduced in Taylor, *Helen Allingham's England*, p. 27.

25. Ruskin described the painting as 'for ever lovely; a thing which I believe Gainsborough would have given one of his own pictures for, – old-fashioned as red-tipped daisies are – and more precious than rubies' (*Notes on Some of the Principal Pictures Exhibited in the Rooms of the Royal Academy: 1875, The Works of John Ruskin*, ed. E. T. Cook and Alexander Wedderburn, Library Edition, 39 volumes (London: George Allen, 1903–12) vol. XIV, p. 264.

26. Marcus B. Huish, *Happy England as Painted by Helen Allingham, R.W.S.* (London: Adam and Charles Black, 1903) pp. 50–5, 61–5, points out not only the connection between *A Flat Iron for a Farthing* and *The Young Customers* but also the sources for *The Convalescent* (1879) and *In the Hayloft* (1880), woodblock illustrations for, respectively, Mrs Oliphant's *Innocent* (*Graphic*, 19 April 1873) and Eleanor Grace O'Reilly's *Deborah's Drawer* (London: Bell & Daldy, 1871).

27. Reproduced in H. L. Mallalieu, *The Dictionary of British Watercolour Artists up to 1920, Volume II – The Plates* (Woodbridge: The Antique Collectors' Club, 1979) p. 279.

28. *The Milkmaid* was sold during the exhibition and its present location is unknown; see Huish, *Happy England*, p. 45.

29. Listed in Anthony Lester, *The Exhibited Works of Helen Allingham, R.W.S. 1848–1926* (Crowmarsh Gifford: The Lester Gallery, 1979) p. 48.

30. Laura Dyer, 'Mrs. Allingham', *Art Journal*, n.s. XXVII (1888) 199; see also Huish, *Happy England*, pp. 3–5.

31. Dyer, 'Mrs. Allingham', p. 198.
32. See, for example, Huish, *Happy England*, p. 149; A. L. Baldry, *The Practice of Water-Colour Painting* (London: Macmillan and The Fine Art Society, 1911) p. 39; Taylor, *Helen Allingham's England*, pp. 97–8.
33. Taylor, *Helen Allingham's England*, p. 68. Cf. Jackson, *Illustration and the Novels*, p. 34: 'Besides the charm and peace of her rural scenes, [Paterson] also brought to her treatment of the English cottage a fine accuracy of detail. … These details, in her later watercolors as well as in earlier magazine engravings, captured and conveyed a way of life through the medium of graphic art much the same way that Hardy caught and presented a special (and vanishing) way of life through his fiction.'
34. Some of the reviewers in fact drew the readers' attention to the illustrations: see, for example, the *Academy* and *The Times*.
35. The *Westminster Review*, January 1875, did insist that 'in *Far from the Madding Crowd* sensationalism is all in all', but most reviewers pointed out the sensational aspects only to emphasize either their incongruity or their secondary role; see, for example, the *Pictorial World*, 6 February 1875, and the *World*, 2 December 1874.
36. Reddick's visual interpretation does occasionally acknowledge the more disturbing aspects of Hardy's text – in the representation of Fanny on the Casterbridge highway or Troy beside the open coffin, for example (pp. 271, 305) – but, as with Paterson, the overall impression of idyll remains.
37. See, for example, John Goode, *Thomas Hardy: The Offensive Truth* (Oxford: Basil Blackwell, 1988), and Marjorie Garson, *Hardy's Fables of Integrity: Woman, Body, Text* (Oxford: Clarendon Press, 1991).
38. The drawing is usually regarded as the least effective of Paterson's *Far from the Madding Crowd* illustrations; ironically, it was the first to be signed 'H. Allingham', a signature which can now price a watercolour at several thousand pounds. There may indeed be a connection between the new signature and the inferiority of the illustration: the honeymoon trip following Paterson's marriage to William Allingham on 22 August would not have left her with much time in early September before she would have had to submit the drawing for the November instalment.
39. Reproduced in Jackson, *Illustration and the Novels*, plate 23.
40. Paterson's ineffective representations of the dramatic can also be found in her drawings for Anne Thackeray Ritchie's *Miss Angel* (1875), the novel she illustrated for the *Cornhill* immediately after *Far from the Madding Crowd*.
41. Rosemarie Morgan makes this point in *Cancelled Words: Rediscovering Thomas Hardy* (London: Routledge, 1992) p. 136.
42. Dorset County Museum. All eight are arranged in a single frame: the first row includes proofs for the woodblocks depicting Bathsheba loosening Gabriel's neckerchief, Gabriel asking Bathsheba if she wants a shepherd, the sword exercise, and the shearing-supper; the second row includes those depicting Fanny beneath the haystack, the coffin scene, Troy caught in the current, and Troy's return.

43. *Collected Letters*, vol. I, p. 181; see also Hardy's 25 July 1906 letter to Edmund Gosse, quoted below.

44. See Dalziel, 'Note on the Illustrations', *A Pair of Blue Eyes* (Harmondsworth: Penguin, 1998) pp. 381–3, and 'Anxieties of Representation', pp. 92–105.

45. *Collected Letters*, vol. I, p. 25.

46. Frederick B. Adams collection.

47. Paterson's correct identification of Hardy's original suggests that there may have been more correspondence between illustrator and author than has hitherto been assumed. Alternatively, Hardy could have discussed some of these details when he and Paterson met in London in the spring of 1874.

48. *Life and Work*, p. 102; see Morgan, *Cancelled Words, passim.*

49. 25 July 1906, *Collected Letters*, vol. III, p. 218. Hardy was responding to Gosse's letter of 23 July (Dorset County Museum), which asked 'how the illustrations came to be made. Some are signed "H. Paterson" others "H. Allingham". Was the lady married while the book was appearing? Did you know her and direct her pencil?' See also Hardy's poem 'The Opportunity', dedicated to 'H. P.', in *Late Lyrics and Earlier*.

50. *Life and Work*, p. 103; Huish, *Happy England*, p. 39.

51. *Collected Letters*, vol. I, p. 30.

52. 4 June 1880, *Collected Letters*, vol. I, pp. 73–4.

53. Letter of 5 June 1880, Dorset County Museum.

54. See *Collected Letters*, vol. I, pp. 74–5 and the letters to Hardy from Dicksee (7 June 1880), Du Maurier (9 June 1880), and Small (14 June 1880), Dorset County Museum. Hardy seems to have written to both Small and Du Maurier on 8 June; Du Maurier's reply suggests that Hardy may in fact have asked him to recommend available illustrators rather than to take on the project himself. Du Maurier offered his own services ('I should be very glad to illustrate your tale myself if it is of a kind my style of drawing is likely to suit, and the first instalments could be got ready for illustration soon') before Small's (delayed) acceptance of Hardy's invitation arrived.

55. See Dalziel, 'Anxieties of Representation', pp. 92–5.

2

Less than Faithfully Presented: Fictions in Modern Commentaries on Hardy's *Tess of the d'Urbervilles*

ROBERT SCHWEIK

> *Literary criticism consists of 'manhandling the text, interrupting it'.*
>
> Roland Barthes

Nearly twenty years ago I published a study titled 'Fictions in the Criticism of Hardy's Fiction' in which I detailed how, often by ignoring relevant textual and other evidence, critics transformed what Hardy had written into something more nearly like an independent fiction.[1] In the generation since, Hardy's novels have been dissected by nearly every instrument of analysis known to modern literary study, and, amid much fine and revealing scholarship, a new crop of remarkably independent critical fictions has appeared. Hence, I think it may once again be useful to call attention to some of the more creatively imaginative of them, and to consider what influences on contemporary critical practice brought them about. Given, however, the extraordinary amount of scholarship on Hardy's novels produced in the last twenty years, I will this time limit my illustrations to those drawn from writings on *Tess of the d'Urbervilles* published or reprinted between 1980 and 1995.

First, however, I want to explain briefly what I mean by the word *fictions* in my title. Of course, all human discourse is fictive in the sense that it selectively generalizes upon and so more or less distorts features of the world to which it refers. Similarly, all interpretations of human discourse may be said to be fictive in the sense that they are constructs which vary from one interpreter to another, and, in the case of complex literary works, multiple interpretations are the rule rather than the exception. But not all interpretations will be equally plausible, and whatever construction any given interpreter puts upon a literary work may be judged by others to be sensible or foolish, creditably consistent with or absurdly remote from existing textual and other evidences of its author's intentions.[2] Consider, for example, these concluding lines from Hardy's *Tess*:

> 'Justice' was done, and the President of the Immortals (in Aeschylean phrase) had ended his sport with Tess. And the d'Urberville knights and dames slept on in their tombs unknowing. The two speechless gazers bent themselves down to the earth, as if in prayer, and remained thus a long time, absolutely motionless: the flag continued to wave silently. As soon as they had strength they arose, joined hands again, and went on.[3]

Here, first, is Ian Gregor's exceptionally illuminating comment on those last four sentences of *Tess*:

> How often the opening sentence of that paragraph has been quoted in isolation and made to serve as 'the conclusion' to the novel, when in fact Hardy, true to his practice, makes his conclusion multiple in emphasis. The first sentence is a sombre acknowledgment of forces in the world over which we should seem to have little or no control. It is followed by a sentence which shifts from metaphysics to history, proclaiming the serene indifference of the past to the present. These two sentences are followed by two others which indicate contrary possibilities. We see an intimation of human resilience in the 'speechless gazers' who seek in the earth itself – in the conditions of man's terrestrial existence, notwithstanding his mutability – hope and not despair. In the last sentence, hope turns into strength, strength to affirm the human bond and to give direction to action: 'they … joined hands again, and went on'. It is a sentence which recalls, in its rhythm, the sadness – and the resolution – present in the final lines of *Paradise Lost*. … It would be as foolish to isolate Hardy's last sentence, and see the final emphasis of the novel lying there, as it would be to isolate the first. For him, it is the four sentences

taken together which constitute a human truth, by catching in varying lights our condition, flux followed by reflux, the fall by the rally; it is this sense of continuous movement which suggests that the fiction which records it should be described as 'a series of seemings'.[4]

To be sure, Gregor's remarks inevitably involve the kinds of 'fictive' elements I have described above: in this case, for example, he ignores the relationship of Hardy's final paragraph to the seven others preceding it in the concluding chapter, and, unlike many readers, he regards all four sentences in that paragraph as carrying equal rhetorical weight. But, in spite of the inevitable simplifications and individual peculiarities even his circumspect analysis involves, Gregor's comment provides more than ample compensation by alerting us to a relevant complexity in those last four sentences of *Tess* and to one kind of closer relationship they may have to Hardy's artistic practice in the novel as a whole.

By way of contrast, consider another recent critic's comment on the conclusion of *Tess*:

> [Tess] becomes a martyr to Hardy's ideal of womanhood, and her sacrificial death at the end of the novel is, I propose, a neat escape from the inevitable tainting this figure would suffer if she continued in a life of sin with Angel.[5]

There are obvious fictive elements in this comment too – but ones very different from those in Ian Gregor's: the assertions that Tess is 'a martyr to Hardy's ideal of womanhood' and that Tess's death is a 'neat escape' from what she 'would suffer if she continued in a life of sin with Angel' bear at best very remote and tangential relationships to the text of *Tess of the d'Urbervilles*. Such readings can be remarkably creative, ingenious, and original constructs in their own right, but rather than bringing to Hardy's *Tess* that 'generous imaginativeness' he hoped for in his readers,[6] they are so remote from Hardy's novel that they take on the status of independent fictions, which often obscure rather than illuminate his art. It is modern critical commentaries which tend toward fictions of this latter kind that concern me here.

Let me begin, then, with some examples that involve relationships between Hardy, his narrator, and his fictional characters. There are a host of evidences, both in the texts of *Tess* and outside them, that show that Hardy felt a deep sympathy for the heroine he created.[7] But the relationships between Thomas Hardy the author, his various narrative voices, his complex and sometimes inconsistent portrayals of the fictional characters he created, and the implied readers of the novel – these interconnections are anything but simple. David Lodge's seminal study of Hardy's narrative voices[8] and the subsequent development of relevant modern narratological theories[9] have led to sophisticated analyses of the extraordinary breadth and diversity of narrative modes and attitudes in *Tess*: we understand better now how these vary from extremes of intellectualized detachment to deep emotional involvement, and how they comprise a wide range of sometimes conflicting voices, shifting perspectives, and subtle changes in narrative strategy.[10] But even without the light of what such modern studies have revealed of the complex narrative structure of *Tess*, it might seem odd of a contemporary critic not only to speak of Tess as if she were a real person rather than a literary construct but also to imagine Hardy's narrator, or Hardy himself, to be hiding in the text or disguising himself as a character in order to derive sexual pleasure by secretly spying on Tess or taking sadistic delight in giving her pain. Yet some recent commentators have created just such fictions.

MAKING TESS AN INDEPENDENT PERSON AND HARDY'S NARRATOR A VOYEUR

One of the most remarkable fictive acts of some recent critics writing on *Tess* is to treat Hardy's character as if she were a person existing independently of her creator: they have imaginatively endowed her with a 'secret being' that 'the novel never attempts to penetrate', with a specific sexuality that Hardy is unable to construe correctly, and with a 'point of view' that Hardy cannot comprehend. Consider, for example, the following comments:

[W]e know almost nothing substantive about Tess's 'character', for the novel never attempts to penetrate her secret being.[11]

[T]he narrator's defence of Tess involves his recognition of her sexual nature and, as he sees it, its naturalness; but his reading of that aspect of her is an eccentric one, expressive of bewilderment.

Since she is not sexless he construes her as all sex, reaching a de-scription of generic 'woman' which is highly reductive.[12]

Hardy is unable to challenge Angel's refusal to see Tess' story from her point of view, to see the *meaning* of the events in The Chase as she sees them, that is, to see them as forgivable. Angel, like Hardy, persists in reading her flesh, even after her confession.[13]

Neither Angel nor 'Liza-Lu nor Hardy nor anyone else in the novel witnesses Tess's execution. She has turned her back on them all. ... Thus Hardy at last – and his reader with him – joins the others, his power to see indistinguishable from theirs.[14]

Closely allied to such fictions that Tess has an independent exist-ence (whose 'secret being', 'specific sexuality', and 'point of view' are beyond Hardy's ability to perceive or understand) are those that image him or his narrator as deriving sexual pleasure from se-cretly spying on her, or taking sadistic delight in giving her pain. Of course in many of his novels Hardy employed the commonplace literary device of having a hidden character see or overhear another,[15] and some of those instances can reasonably be construed to portray one character experiencing sexual stimulation from se-cretly looking at another. Nowhere in *Tess*, however, is Hardy's narrator dramatized as taking part in any such covert watching; yet this has not deterred some contemporary critics from imaginatively constructing that narrator as a voyeur. In many cases the impulse for creating this peculiar kind of critical fiction derives from the ideas of Jacques Lacan, for whom voyeurism is central to human sexuality and involves imaginary creations of images in order to satisfy sexual desire.[16] Unfortunately, by applying Lacan's ideas crudely to *Tess*, some critics have been led to portray Hardy's nar-rator and Hardy himself as sneaking about the text of the novel, hiding behind or disguising themselves as one or another character, in order to seek sexual gratification by obsessive 'looking' at the character Tess as if she existed independently. Consider the follow-ing examples of that kind of critical fictionalizing:

At the beginning of the novel the narrator hides behind a few passing 'strangers' who 'would look long at her in casually passing by, and grow momentarily fascinated by her freshness' to excuse the detail in which he describes Tess's physical charms.[17]

The narrator may parade under the fictional guises of tourist, landscape painter and ethnographer, but he betrays his true erotic colors as soon as he isolates Tess from the other May-Day celebrants on the basis of her 'mobile peony mouth' and 'large innocent eyes'.[18]

[T]he narrator seems to retreat from and close his eyes to the most explicit and direct manifestations of the sexuality which so fascinates him.[19]

[T]here is no male spy as such in *Tess of the d'Urbervilles* simply because the voyeur in that novel is Hardy himself in the guise of the male narrator.[20]

Some other recent critics have carried this fiction even further by portraying Hardy's narrator as involved in a sexual assault on Tess, and Hardy himself as a sadist:

Time and again the narrator seeks to enter Tess, through her eyes ... through her mouth ... and through her flesh. ... The phallic imagery of pricking, piercing and penetration ... serves ... to satisfy the narrator's fascination with the interiority of her sexuality, and his desire to take possession of her.[21]

The narrator attempts to establish his own moral distance from what happens to Tess by inveighing against providence. ... However, since the narrator himself is the only transcendental agency on the horizon when Alec violates Tess, this outcry constitutes a classic disavowal, implicating him in the very action he abominates.[22]

We are all of us Alecs, Angels, Hardys. ... We are all sadists, producing images or cadavers to induce sexually titillating pain.[23]

In short, by writing about Tess as if she were a person independent of Hardy and his narrator – and then by picturing Hardy or his narrator as experiencing sexual pleasure from 'looking' at that person, or seeking to 'take possession of her', or feeling sadistic pleasure in her pain – some recent commentators have created fictions that seem less revealing of Hardy's art in *Tess* than they do of the critics' own imaginative lives as those have been influenced by Lacan and other theorists.

PERSONIFYING 'THE TEXT' AND OTHER ABSTRACTIONS

Similarly unrevealing has been the practice of some critics who tend to minimize Hardy as the author of *Tess of the d'Urbervilles* by substituting for him some personified abstraction – such, for example, as did the commentator who compounded the fiction described above by speaking not of 'the narrator's' but of 'the *narrative's* obsessive voyeuristic gazing at Tess'.[24] Following the impact of the twenty-year-old 'death of the author' theories of Roland Barthes and Michel Foucault,[25] there remains a residual temptation for some critics to assume that evidences of Hardy's intentions are irrelevant or may be treated selectively, and that Hardy himself is a fiction which may be ignored or made to do whatever some commentator wishes. Thus, Peter Widdowson has described Hardy as 'a creature of post-modernism' who '*is made* to expose' the '(mis)representations by which the dominant ideology and culture sentence us all to lives of false being'.[26] What is striking about such critical practices is the elaborate fictions they create. In Widdowson's case, the abstraction '*post-modernism*' is not only reified but personified, and Hardy is imagined as its 'creature' who is 'made' to do its work.

One queer result of this kind of critical fictionalizing is that a real person, Thomas Hardy – for whom there exist manifold evidences of actions and intentions in creating literary texts – is imaginatively replaced by such abstract reifications as 'the text', 'the narrative', 'the epigraph' or the like, which a critic then endows with a fictional persona having supposed intentions of its own.[27] Peter Widdowson has frequently resorted to such personification, as he does, for example, in his assertions that 'the narrative deploys strikingly visual devices and motifs' or that 'the text produces phrase after defining phrase'.[28] Other contemporary critics have been even more creatively imaginative. Marjorie Garson, for instance, invests 'the text' of *Tess* with awareness and other personal attributes:

The text, aware that 'nature' is itself a cultural construct, nevertheless allows the figure of Tess to draw power from the Romantic illusion. ...[29]

Or, again, one recent critic created a dramatic personification of Hardy's epigraph to *Tess* and of his surrender to its desires:

[E]pigraphs want to usurp the authority of the narrative voice, not only by getting the first word in, but by attempting to familiarize for us the text that follows, by advancing a pattern for understanding, a fugal announcement to be completed and fulfilled in a different voice...

I want to let that epigraph do its job; I want to let it take control. ...[30]

In short, in the last fifteen years commentators on *Tess* have created a truly astonishing conglomeration of fictions: of a Hardy unable to 'penetrate' Tess's 'secret being'; of a Hardy unable to 'challenge' Angel Clare's view of her; of a narrator hiding in the text of the novel to spy on Tess for sexual stimulation or to sexually assault her; or – it being explicitly stated or tacitly assumed that there is no Hardy for the critic to reckon with – of various personified abstractions such as 'the text', 'the narrative', 'the epigraph', and 'post-modernism' that go about doing ... well, doing whatever some critics imagine their personifications might do. Individually, such highly fanciful critical constructs can, and often do, pass unnoticed. Hence, I have assembled the examples provided here by way of calling attention to how these imaginative but eccentric readings create – both by themselves and collectively – fictions having so remote and peripheral a relationship to the text of *Tess* that they do little to advance our understanding of Hardy's art, and may often positively obscure it.

IMPOSING THEORIES AND THESES ON HARDY'S TEXT

What is striking about the critical fictions I have so far adduced is that so many of them came about because the commentator, instead of both closely and circumspectly attending to Hardy's text, was led to impose some theory or thesis upon it. Consider two such critics' remarks on a scene from Chapter 30, where Angel and Tess

deliver milk to the local railway station, and Tess takes shelter from
the rain under a holly tree. Here is Hardy's rendering of that scene:

> Then there was the hissing of a train which drew up almost
> silently upon the wet rails, and the milk was rapidly swung can
> by can into the truck. The light of the engine flashed for a second
> upon Tess Durbeyfield's figure, motionless under the great holly-
> tree. No object could have looked more foreign to the gleaming
> cranks and wheels than this unsophisticated girl with the round
> bare arms, the rainy face and hair, the suspended attitude of a
> friendly leopard at pause, the print gown of no date or fashion,
> and the cotton bonnet drooping on her brow.   (Ch. 30)

Hardy's emphasis here is on how foreign are the locomotive's
mechanical 'gleaming cranks and wheels' to Tess's animate appearance revealed by the momentary flash of the engine's light. This
scene could well repay closer study than it has so far received –
particularly of the striking image of Tess in the attitude of a
'friendly leopard at pause' which Hardy injected into an otherwise
bleakly human picture of her as a rain-soaked, unsophisticated
country girl. But, in any case, no character or thing in this scene is
dramatized as 'gazing' at anything.

Nevertheless, one recent commentator, John Goode, in what he
described as a 'politically committed' Marxist reading of *Tess*,
approached this passage with the thesis that it exhibits what he
called the 'gaze of the social relations of production', which is a reciprocal gaze: 'the gaze in exchange'. Beguiled by this idea, Goode
created a fiction so very different from Hardy's that it is scarcely
recognizable – a scene in which the locomotive gazes at Tess and
Tess gazes back at it, while we readers outside the novel must
become passengers on the train in order to see Tess while we
'consume' her story. And – if our supposed seeing Tess as passengers on the train is, as Goode seems to insist, 'reciprocal' – he may
be implying that Tess also looks back at us who are 'outside the
novel'. Here, at any rate, is Goode's rather confused but highly
imaginative impression of Hardy's scene:

> the change in perspective is not merely from her [Tess] to an
> opposing gaze, but her visibility to the opposing gaze of some-
> thing outside the novel. ... Moreover it is not the eye of the painter
> who picks out a girl from a landscape, or of a god, but the eye of

the gleaming cranks and wheels of a locomotive. This estrangement of Tess involves therefore the construction of the reader's
eye in terms of a specific social and cultural medium. We have to
transpose ourselves to an unspecified passenger seeing Tess as an
image lit only by the form of transport in which we are carried.

*   *   *

But what is different here is that he [Hardy] is not artificially
selecting Tess but suppressing the real social relationship by
which she relates, and thinks of herself as relating, to the world
as a whole. More specifically, since the relationship is defined in
the reciprocal gaze (the train watching Tess watching the train), I
mean *our* world, the world of the consuming reader who will not
only drink milk without ever having seen a cow but consumes
Tess's story without having to undergo it.[31]

Compare this somewhat confusedly expressed but highly original fiction Goode created by following the *ignis fatuus* of a theory
about 'reciprocal gazes' with a very different one created by John
Humma, whose thesis was that Hardy secretly disguised his
imagery. Proceeding with dogged ingenuity to find what imagery
Hardy had concealed, Humma created from the same railway
station scene something imaginatively very different from Goode's.
Fixing upon Hardy's sentence, 'Then there was the hissing of a
train which drew up almost silently upon the wet rails', he elaborated a scenario in which the train – coming from what Humma
(not Hardy) called 'the frightening world of people and commerce'
– evokes, by disguised images, Alec d'Urberville as the serpent
Satan, hissing yet drawing silently up on Tess to violate her:

> The contrast here between the train, which comes out of the
> frightening world of people and commerce, and Tess is a striking
> one, made even more so by our recollection of a previous image.
> When Tess returns from Trantridge, where Alec had deflowered
> her, Hardy tells us that she 'had learnt that the serpent hisses
> where the sweet birds sing'. The way the image of the latter
> passage picks up that of the first typifies Hardy's method
> throughout the novel. We can especially admire the skill in the
> 'drew up almost silently', as Alec – the Satan – himself drew up
> silently (at least so far as Tess is aware) upon her as she slept in
> the Chase.[32]

Here, as in so many other cases, an eccentric fiction results from a critic's attempt to read Hardy's *Tess* in terms of some theory or thesis at the cost of paying judicious and circumspect attention to his text. Of course there is an enormous distance between the image of Tess and a locomotive exchanging gazes with one another and the image of Alec as a hissing Satanic locomotive drawing silently up to violate a sleeping Tess, but both are fictions so imaginatively remote from Hardy's novel that neither greatly helps to elucidate the art of the scene Hardy created.

As one other example of the consequences of this kind of critical behaviour, consider the case of a commentary on a dialogue between Tess and Angel from Chapter 19. Tess is peeling off the specialized outer leaf of jack-in-the-pulpit-like plants to reveal the inner spike-like bud, 'a lady' if it is pale, a 'lord' if it is purple.[33]

'Why do you look so woebegone all of a sudden?' he [Angel] asked [Tess].

'O – 'tis only – about my own self,' she said, with a frail laugh of sadness, fitfully beginning to peel 'a lady' meanwhile. 'Just a sense of what might have been with me! My life looks as if it had been wasted for want of chances! When I see what you know, what you have read, and seen, and thought, I feel what a nothing I am! I'm like the poor Queen of Sheba who lived in the Bible. There is no more spirit in me.'

'Bless my soul, don't go troubling about that! Why,' he said with some enthusiasm, 'I should be only too glad, my dear Tess, to help you to anything in the way of history, or any line of reading you would like to take up – '

'It is a lady again,' interrupted she, holding out the bud she had peeled.

'What?'

'I meant that there are always more ladies than lords when you come to peel them.'

'Never mind about the lords and ladies: would you like to take up any course of study – history for example?'

'Sometimes I feel I don't want to know anything more about it than I know already.'

'Why not?'

'Because what's the use of learning that I am one of a long row only – finding out that there is set down in some old book some-body just like me, and to know that I shall only act her part;

making me sad, that's all. The best is not to remember that your nature and your past doings have been just like thousands' and thousands', and that your coming life and doings 'll be like thousands' and thousands'.'

'What, really, then, you don't want to learn anything?'

'I shouldn't mind learning why – why the sun do shine on the just and the unjust alike,' she answered, with a slight quaver in her voice. 'But that's what books will not tell me.'   (Ch. 19)

'She went on', Hardy says, 'peeling the lords and ladies till Clare ... lingeringly went away.'

Certainly Hardy created here a remarkably subtle yet evocative scene: one in which Tess – dramatized as sadly contemplating the inequity and futility of life exhibited in matters so diverse as the game of 'lords and ladies' and the sweep of human history – displays a capacity for a profoundly tragic vision of life that makes Angel Clare's well-meaning offer to help her study history seem by comparison shallow and limited.

Compare Hardy's scene with that created by Jean Jacques Lecercle, who, writing under the influence of the semiotic theories of Gilles Deleuze, turned what Hardy wrote upside-down by describing it as portraying a 'violence of language' by which Angel dominates Tess:

My thesis is that the main object of [*Tess of the d'Urbervilles*] is ... 'becoming violent' of language, to use a Deleuzian phrase.

*   *   *

Let us turn to the pedagogic violence of Angel's teaching. ... Tess is peeling lords and ladies, an old custom in her culture, and ironically expresses the truth about the situation: 'I meant that there are always more ladies than lords when you come to peel them'. Angel replies: 'Never mind about the lords and ladies. Would you like to take up any course of study – history for instance?' In this scene, a pre-linguistic semiotic activity, a game which does not need elaborate language, is repressed by the articulate language of the dominant culture. Exactly as the unspoken past, which flows in Tess's veins, must be replaced by the spoken past, history as 'a course of study'. Angel's question, in spite of appearances, does not allow Tess any choice: it is preceded by an imperative, and takes on the force of an order (if she wants to reach Angel's elevated position, to be worthy of him, she *must* abandon her culture and her language, she must study). We are entering the world of Deleuze and Guattari's 'signifying semiotics'. ...[34]

Here, under the influence of a theory that led him to believe there is 'violence of language' in *Tess*, Lecercle ignored the numerous places in Hardy's text which dramatize how Tess's expressions of *her* views, and the choices *she* makes, dominate what happens in the scene: *it is Tess* who expresses her sense of deficiency in reading and other experience, and so prompts Angel's response; *it is Tess* who interrupts Angel in his proposal to help her in further reading; *it is Tess* who, in response to Angel's offer, asserts eloquently why she doesn't want to read history; *it is Tess* who insists that she does want to learn 'why the sun do shine on the just and the unjust alike'; *it is Tess* who proclaims that books will not give her that information; and, at the end of the scene, *it is Tess* who, far from being 'repressed', 'went on peeling the lords and ladies till Clare ... lingeringly went away'.

Lecercle ignored all this and instead created a fiction in which Clare did 'pedagogic violence' to Tess and 'repressed' her game of lords and ladies. We may be entering the fictive world of Deleuze and Guattari's 'signifying semiotics' here, but certainly we have left far behind the imaginative world of Hardy's *Tess*.

LETTING 'GENEROUS IMAGINATIVENESS' RUN WILD

So far, I have drawn the bulk of my illustrations from commentators who, influenced by some ready-made theory, have imaginatively constructed fictions which, although certainly not lacking in creativity, are remarkably independent of Hardy's text and, hence, shed relatively little light upon his art. But this is by no means the only generator of such interpretations; they sometimes appear in the writings of critics otherwise engaged in that 'exercise of a generous imaginativeness' which, Hardy wrote, might find in his fiction 'what was never inserted by him, never foreseen, never contemplated', but which 'by the intensive power of the reader's own imagination' can sometimes be 'the finest parts' of the novel.[35] To illustrate this, I want to return to the passage I have already quoted from Chapter 19, where Tess is 'fitfully beginning to peel "a lady"'.

In an often illuminating study of the question of whether or not Hardy wished to picture Tess as a passive victim, Rosemarie Morgan called attention to the ways Hardy portrayed her as having 'a fully developed sexual nature as sensitive to the needs of her impassioned lover as to her own auto-erotic powers and desires'. In doing so, Morgan pointed out how 'Hardy's poetic sensibility comes into play to embed within seemingly innocuous figures of speech a language of sexuality which is neither fastidious nor fey but, rather, earthy and physical.' And, with what I think Hardy would term a 'generous imaginativeness', she provided some telling examples to support her view. But even theses developed from close readings of Hardy's text can sometimes skew critics' perceptions and prompt them to create the kinds of fictions which concern me here. And so Morgan produced this fiction of her own about that 'lords and ladies' scene:

> at a loss to explain to Angel how she would love him ... Tess instinctively draws close to the physical world of nature and sensuously rubs down the skins of the 'Lords and Ladies'; which for some perverse reason rouses in Angel the desire to teach her *history*.[36]

Here, drawn on by her thesis that in 'seemingly innocuous figures of speech' Hardy embedded 'a language of sexuality', Morgan invented a scene that Hardy did not create either directly or by implication. Nothing in the Hardy passage I have quoted, nor anything preceding it, refers to Tess's beginning to peel 'lords and ladies' because she is 'at a loss to explain to Angel how she would love him'. Furthermore, Hardy's image of a 'woebegone' Tess 'fitfully peeling' a plant leaf 'with a frail laugh of sadness' is transformed by Morgan into an erotic scene in which Tess 'sensuously rubs down the skins' of the lords and ladies – though the emotional overtones in Hardy's words *woebegone, fitfully, making me sad* and *with a frail laugh of sadness* run counter to that interpretation. And then, caught up in her creation of a hidden eroticism in this passage, Morgan ignores the fact that Angel's offer to help Tess study history is a perfectly natural response to her complaint that she knows so much less than he; in the erotically charged episode Morgan has created, Angel's offer to teach Tess history is so out of place it must stem from 'some perverse reason'. In short, led on by her thesis, Morgan rewrote Hardy's scene so as to create a fiction remarkably independent of Hardy's text.

Or, again, consider these passages that involve some of Tess's experiences at Alec's estate and after:

> He conducted her. ... to the fruit-garden and green-houses, where he asked her if she liked strawberries.
> 'Yes,' said Tess. 'When they come.'
> 'They are already here.' D'Urberville began gathering speci-mens of the fruit for her. ...   (Ch. 5)

* * *

> One among her fellow travellers addressed her more pointedly than any had spoken before: 'Why – you be quite a posy! And such roses in early June!'   (Ch. 6)

Recently, Dale Kramer, exercising the kind of 'generous imagin-ativeness' Hardy spoke of, made the following comment on those passages:

> But there is care in his [Hardy's] presentation [of Alec], for instance in the imagery employed in his early actions that implies a good deal about his character and the society of modern com-merce turned 'genteel' that he at least partly represents. The straw-berries Alec makes Tess eat are *forced* – i.e., *made to ripen early* – as Alec makes Tess 'ripen' at sixteen or so. Likewise, the roses with which he decorates her are early for the season.[37]   [My italics]

There is little reason to suppose that Hardy was aware of what Kramer was to see in those passages: at least neither the words *forced* or *ripen early* appear in Hardy's text. But here, certainly, is an excellent example of what Hardy meant by a critic's seeing 'what was never inserted ... never contemplated', but which 'by the intensive power of the reader's own imagination' can sometimes be among 'the finest parts' of the novel: Kramer's observation not only was consistent with the whole of Hardy's text but enhanced what in many other ways it conveyed of a prominent feature of Alec's character.

But then, caught up in exercising this 'generous imaginativeness', Kramer proceeded to extend his association of the word *forcing*

with Alec to a sentence fully ten chapters later in which Hardy
conveyed something of Tess's humdrum work-a-day life during the
winter at Marlott after the death of Sorrow:

> She remained in her father's house during the winter months,
> plucking fowls, or cramming turkeys and geese, or making
> clothes for her sisters and brothers out of some finery
> d'Urberville had given her, and she had put by with contempt.
> (Ch. 15)

'Cramming turkeys and geese', Kramer reasoned, was just another
kind of 'forcing', and so, swept along by the idea he had developed
from two passages ten chapters earlier in *Tess*, he proceeded to
'force' this sentence of Hardy's into the procrustean bed of his own
thesis by this combination of rhetorical device and imaginative
transformation:

> Indeed, ironically, as a worker in the Stoke-d'Urberville house-
> hold she herself 'crams', or 'forces', turkeys and geese in order to
> make them fatter than they would in nature become.[38]

In this single sentence of Kramer's, one can find a number of the
ways critics go about creating the kinds of fictions I have been discussing. First, Kramer selectively presented the textual evidence by
mentioning only that Tess 'crams' turkeys and geese, while ignoring two other activities Hardy closely associated with it; at the
same time, he added his word *'forces'* in quotation marks along
with Hardy's *'crams'*, without clearly discriminating between the
(semi) quotation of Hardy's word and his own. Furthermore, he
attempted to minimize the fact that Hardy portrayed this 'cramming' as Tess's activity, not Alec's, by speaking of it as 'ironic' but
without explaining what artistic purpose might be served by ironically associating Alec's despicable character trait with only one of
three activities Tess does in her own home. And then, caught up in
his thesis, and anxious to link Tess's activity more closely with
Alec, Kramer (no doubt unconsciously) imaginatively transformed
the location where Tess does this work from her father's house
where Hardy had located it to the Stoke-d'Urberville household.
Here, in just one sentence, he created a fiction more the product of
his own thesis than of circumspect attention to Hardy's text.

CREATING REDUCTIVE SIMPLICITIES

Still one other common way that such critical fictions come about is by a commentator's ignoring the complexities of Hardy's text and substituting for them some simplistic summary which, though it may accord with some thesis the critic wishes to develop, greatly deviates from the substance, focus, and significance of Hardy's narrative. Consider, for example, these components of the complex narrative in which Hardy rendered Tess's killing of Alec:

> [Tess to Alec] 'Now he is gone, gone! A second time, and I have lost him now for ever …. and he will not love me the littlest bit ever any more – only hate me … O yes, I have lost him now – again because of – you!'
>
> […]
>
> 'And he is dying – he looks as if he is dying ….. and my sin will kill him and not kill me! … O you have torn my life all in pieces …. made me be what I prayed you in pity not to make me be again! … My own true husband will never never – O God – I can't bear this! I cannot!'
> There were more and sharper words from the man; then a sudden rustle; she had sprung to her feet. Mrs Brooks, thinking that the speaker was coming to rush out of the door, hastily retreated down the stairs.   (Ch. 56; ellipses are Hardy's except where in square brackets)

*   *   *

> 'Angel,' she said … 'do you know what I have been running after you for? To tell you that I have killed him!' A pitiful white smile lit her face as she spoke.
> 'What!' said he, thinking from the strangeness of her manner that she was in some delirium.
> 'I have done it – I don't know how,' she continued. 'Still, I owed it to you, and to myself, Angel. *I feared long ago, when I struck him on the mouth with my glove, that I might do it some day for the trap he set for me in my simple youth, and his wrong to you through me.* He has come between us and ruined us, and now he can never do it any more. I never loved him at all, Angel, as I loved you. You know it, don't you? You believe it? You didn't come

back to me, and I was obliged to go back to him. Why did you go away – *why* did you – when I loved you so? I can't think why you did it. But I don't blame you; only, *Angel, will you forgive me my sin against you, now I have killed him? I thought as I ran along that you would be sure to forgive me now I have done that. It came to me as a shining light that I should get you back that way.* I could not bear the loss of you any longer – you don't know how entirely I was unable to bear your not loving me. Say you do now, dear dear husband: say you do, now I have killed him!' ... 'He heard me *crying about you, and he bitterly taunted me; and called you by a foul name; and then I did it: my heart could not bear it: he had nagged me about you before – and then I dressed myself, and came away to find you.'*   (Ch. 57; italics and ellipses mine)

These passages – surely among some of the most poignant in the history of English literature – comprise by no means a simple narrative. Hardy's complex dramatization of Tess's various actions and states of mind is divided into two major parts. In the first extract, at the time of the killing, Tess's repeated use of such words as *never* and *for ever,* and her expressions of belief that Angel will 'not love me the littlest bit ever any more', dramatize her utter hopelessness and excruciating mental agony. In the second, the last five lines I have italicized continue the narrative Hardy broke off in the first extract in a way which conveys that her murder of Alec was an impulsive act finally triggered by his taunting and nagging her about Angel. In between these, are two other passages I have also italicized which pertain to states of mind not at the time of the killing but before and after. The first, beginning 'I feared long ago ...', recalls an earlier impulsive act that made Tess think she might at some future time kill Alec in revenge for the trap he set for her and the wrong he did to Angel. The second, beginning 'only, Angel, will you forgive me ...', conveys not only Tess's guilty sense that she has 'sinned' against Clare and wants his forgiveness but also that her distraught idea that she might get Angel back by having killed Alec was an afterthought which came to her 'as a shining light' while she was running to find him.

Such are some central elements in Hardy's account of Tess's killing of Alec; not only do they involve temporal shifts that convey different manifestations of her mental torment and emotional instability both before, during, and after the act, but they also reveal that Tess's killing of Alec was done impulsively in a moment of utter hopelessness and unbearable mental anguish. Although a sense of this complexity is certainly conveyed by some recent commentators on *Tess*,[39] others have all but completely ignored it and instead created highly simplistic fictions very different from Hardy's. Here are some typical examples:

To be able to have Angel's love, if only briefly, Tess kills Alec.
    She ... kills Alec ... in search of a few moments of self-realisation with Angel.[40]

Her healthy act of self-defense and self assertion is punished swiftly, while the logic of that event – the rationalization of its meaning and hence of her experience – remains for her community an unknown history and, except for the narrator's sympathetic memory, is lost with her.[41]

Tess is bound to him [Alec] by powerful ideological fetters. ... In this sense Tess really has nothing to lose but her chains and her slaughter of Alec could be read as a throwing off of shackles little short of revolutionary.[42]

Tess's acts of will represent the culmination of the whole sequence. The events involved figure the monstrousness of the only choice that is left to her, the only meaning she can express after the final shock of Angel's coming to claim her when she has already returned to Alec as his mistress. In stabbing Alec to release herself for Angel she feels free even from guilt.[43]

Note how the first two of these summaries – those stating that Tess's killing of Alec was motivated by a desire to 'be able to have Angel's love, if only briefly', and that she was in 'search of a few moments of self-realisation with Angel' – substitute for Hardy's persistent and emphatic dramatization of Tess's mental agony, emotional instability, and half-crazed impulsiveness a simplistic account in which Tess kills Alec not only with a purposeful goal in mind, but even with apparent foreknowledge of the brevity of her subsequent association with Angel. Similarly the commentator who characterized the killing as a 'healthy act of self-defense and self assertion', and the one who described it in terms that reflect Marx and Engels' language rather than Hardy's, both stripped his narrative of the complex emotional and mental stresses so central to it and substituted a tendentious and reductive narrative of their own. And, of course, the critic who described Tess's conduct as stemming from 'acts of will' and representing a 'choice' she makes in 'stabbing Alec to release herself for Angel' not only also eliminated that emotionally distraught impulsiveness which plays such a dominant role in Hardy's narrative but, in addition, by describing Tess as feeling 'free even from guilt', she ignored altogether the fact that Hardy had Tess say, 'Angel, will you forgive me my sin against you, now I have killed him?' What these critics' fictions have in common is that they all strip Hardy's narrative of those powerful emotional and impulsive elements that are at its very centre, while the differences they exhibit seem less a consequence of attention to Hardy's text than to what particular thesis the critic was advancing.

CONCLUSION

In this study I have considered some of the ways that contemporary critics of *Tess* have created fictions which so greatly deviate from Hardy's text that they are largely independent of it and tend to obscure rather than illuminate his art. The following account of Tess's arrest at Stonehenge – the product of a theory that there are 'hidden' elements in Hardy's novels – is characteristic of the kind of critical fictionalizing that has concerned me here:

> The sun rises and Tess is arrested. Christianity and post-christian modernism, personified by the guardian Angel sent to oversee Tess's life at the point where she is chosen as scapegoat, has failed to rescue her, conceivably because the angel can no longer believe in god. Since the orphan of Paulinism has failed her (and since, not coincidentally, she has killed an ex-Pauline preacher), she is abandoned to the cruder forces of paganism and sun-worship.[44]

There is certainly no single explanation that accounts for the production of such fictions. In the earlier study to which I referred at the beginning of this paper, one common feature that ran through the examples I cited was a failure to consider all the evidences available to the interpreter. Unquestionably that is also a contributing cause in many of the examples I have considered here. But in my earlier study 'theory' and 'thesis' played a relatively small role;

today they are the dominant influences in creating the kinds of critical fictions I have just examined, and I expect that influence to persist at least in the near future.

Given the diverse orientations represented by the critics from whom I have drawn illustrations, it should at least be clear that the creation of such fictions is not peculiar to any particular theory, thesis, or critical point of view – though the roughneck attitude that literary criticism entails 'manhandling the text' (in the language of my epigraph) can no doubt encourage especially dotty interpretations. Rather, if any common thread appears in the fictions I have examined it is that although the critics who created them repeatedly refer to *Tess*, in every instance they failed, in one way or another, to pay both close and circumspect attention to the text they were interpreting. It is to the text of *Tess* that this study has repeatedly appealed, and, in the last analysis, I can do no more than invite readers to compare for themselves Hardy's words with the examples of the highly creative critical fictions I have considered; they must judge whether, as I have maintained, those fictions are often more likely to obscure than to illuminate Hardy's art. But the temptation to claim to interpret a Hardy text while selectively ignoring its details in favour of constructing an independent fiction shaped by some theory or thesis is a particularly powerful one today, and I have, of course, no expectation that my exposition of the kinds of critical fictions which result will do more than slightly weaken a cultural pressure in academia just now so pervasive and powerful. Still, if this paper has the happy consequence not only of calling attention to a widespread problem in contemporary Hardy criticism but of encouraging one or more future commentators to pay closer and more judicious attention to Hardy's texts, then it will have served its purpose.

Notes

1. Robert Schweik, 'Fictions in the Criticism of Hardy's Fiction', *English Literature in Transition*, 20 (1977) 204–9.
2. On considerations of authorial intention in the interpretation of texts, see, for example, Alexander Nehamas, 'The Postulated Author: Critical Monism as a Regulative Ideal', *Critical Inquiry*, 8 (Autumn 1981) 133–49. For analyses of the social nature of literary texts and the function of readers in determining textual meanings see, among

others, Claire Badaracco, 'The Editor and the Question of Value: Proposal', *Text*, 1 (1984) 41–3; Colin Falck, *Myth, Truth and Literature* (Cambridge: Cambridge University Press, 1989); Josephine Guy and Ian Small, *Politics and Value in English Studies* (Cambridge: Cambridge University Press, 1993); David Novitz, 'The Integrity of Aesthetics', *Journal of Aesthetics and Art Criticism*, 48 (1990) 9–20; and Stein Haugom Olsen, *The End of Literary Theory* (Cambridge: Cambridge University Press, 1987).

3. Thomas Hardy, *Tess of the d'Urbervilles*, ed. Juliet Grindle and Simon Gatrell (Oxford: Clarendon Press, 1983) ch. 59. All further citations are to this edition, and chapter references are given parenthetically in the text.

4. Ian Gregor, 'Contrary Imaginings: Thomas Hardy and Religion', in *The Interpretation of Belief: Coleridge, Schleiermacher and Romanticism*, ed. David Jasper (London: Macmillan Press, 1986) p. 206.

5. Karen Scherzinger, 'The Problem of the Pure Woman: South African Pastoralism and Female Rites of Passage', *Unisa English Studies*, 29: 2 (September 1991) p. 30.

6. 'The Profitable Reading of Fiction', in *Thomas Hardy's Personal Writings*, ed. Harold Orel (Lawrence: University of Kansas Press, 1966; London: Macmillan, 1967) p. 112.

7. For summaries of these evidences, see Kristin Brady, 'Tess and Alec: Rape or Seduction?', in *Thomas Hardy Annual No. 4*, ed. Norman Page (London: Macmillan, 1986) pp. 127–47, and Marjorie Garson, *Hardy's Fables of Integrity: Woman, Body, Text* (Oxford: Clarendon Press, 1991) p. 138.

8. David Lodge, 'Tess, Nature, and the Voices of Hardy', in *The Language of Fiction* (London: Routledge, 1966) pp. 164–88.

9. Among the sources cited by modern commentators on *Tess* are Mikhaïl Bakhtin, *The Dialogic Imagination*, ed. Michael Holquist, trans. Michael Holquist and Caryl Emerson (Austin: University of Texas Press, 1981); Peter Brooks, *Reading for Plot: Design and Intention in Narrative* (New York: Alfred A. Knopf, 1984); Ross Chambers, '"Narrative" and "Textual" Functions (with an Example from La Fontaine)', in *Reading Narrative: Form, Ethics, Ideology*, ed. James Phelan (Columbus: Ohio State University Press, 1989) pp. 27–39; Seymour Chatman, *Story and Discourse: Narrative Structure in Fiction and Film* (Ithaca: Cornell University Press, 1978); Gérard Genette, *Narrative Discourse*, trans. Jane E. Lewin (Oxford: Basil Blackwell, 1980); Paul Ricoeur, 'Narrative Time', in *On Narrative*, ed. W. J. T. Mitchell (Chicago: University of Chicago Press, 1981); Franz K. Stanzel, *Theorie des Erzählens* (Göttingen: Vandenhoeck & Ruprecht, 1979); and Susan Sniader Lanser, *The Narrative Act: Point of View of Prose Fiction* (Princeton: Princeton University Press, 1981).

10. See, for example, Jakob Lothe, 'Hardy's Authorial Narrative Methods in *Tess of the d'Urbervilles*', in *The Nineteenth-Century British Novel*, ed. Jeremy Hawthorn (Baltimore: Arnold, 1986) pp. 157–70; Adena Rosmarin, 'The Narrativity of Interpretive History', in *Reading Narrative: Form, Ethics, Ideology*, ed. James Phelan (Columbus: Ohio

State University Press, 1989) pp. 12–26; and Margaret R. Higonnet, 'Tess and the Problem of Voice', in *The Sense of Sex: Feminist Perspectives on Hardy*, ed. Margaret R. Higonnet (Urbana: University of Illinois Press, 1993) pp. 14–31. For evidences of Hardy's diverse narrative attitudes revealed by the textual history of *Tess*, see Simon Gatrell's 'Introduction' to *Tess of the d'Urbervilles*, The World's Classics Edition (Oxford: Oxford University Press, 1988) pp. xvii–xxiv.

11. Peter Widdowson, '"Moments of Vision": Postmodernising *Tess of the d'Urbervilles*; or, *Tess of the d'Urbervilles* Faithfully Presented by Peter Widdowson', in *New Perspectives on Thomas Hardy*, ed. Charles P. C. Pettit (London: Macmillan Press, 1994) p. 96.

12. Patricia Ingham, *Thomas Hardy*, Feminist Readings (Hemel Hempstead: Harvester Wheatsheaf, 1989) p. 73.

13. Ellen Rooney, '"A Little More than Persuading": Tess and the Subject of Sexual Violence', in *Rape and Representation*, ed. Lynn A. Higgins and Brenda R. Silver (New York: Columbia University Press, 1991) p. 104.

14. Janet Freeman, 'Ways of Looking at Tess', *Studies in Philology*, 79:3 (Summer 1982) 322–3.

15. For citations of many examples, see Sheila Berger, *Thomas Hardy and Visual Structures: Framing, Disruption, Process* (New York: New York University Press, 1990).

16. See Robert Davis, *Lacan and Narration: The Psychoanalytic Difference in Narrative Theory* (Baltimore: Johns Hopkins University Press, 1983). Lacan's ideas, for example, are explicitly one of the bases of T. R. Wright's *Hardy and the Erotic* (Basingstoke: Macmillan Press; New York: St Martin's Press, 1989).

17. Wright, *Hardy and the Erotic*, p. 108.

18. Kaja Silverman, 'History, Figuration and Female Subjectivity in *Tess of the d'Urbervilles*', *Novel: A Forum on Fiction*, 18:1 (Fall 1984) p. 10.

19. Kristin Brady, 'Tess and Alec: Rape or Seduction?', *Thomas Hardy Annual No. 4*, ed. Norman Page (London: Macmillan, 1986) p. 129.

20. Judith Mitchell, 'Hardy's Female Reader', in *The Sense of Sex: Feminist Perspectives on Hardy*, ed. Margaret R. Higonnet (Urbana: University of Illinois Press, 1993) p. 178.

21. Penny Boumelha, *Thomas Hardy and Women: Sexual Ideology and Narrative Form* (Sussex: Harvester Press, 1982) p. 120.

22. Silverman, 'History, Figuration and Female Subjectivity', p. 11.

23. James Kincaid, '"You Did Not Come": Absence, Death and Eroticism in *Tess*', in *Sex and Death in Victorian Literature*, ed. Regina Barreca (Basingstoke: Macmillan Press; Bloomington: Indiana University Press, 1990) p. 14.

24. Widdowson, '"Moments of Vision": Postmodernising *Tess*', p. 80.

25. See Roland Barthes, 'The Death of the Author', in *Image–Music–Text*, trans. and ed. Stephen Heath (London: Fontana, 1977) pp. 142–8, and Michel Foucault, 'What Is an Author?', in *Textual Strategies: Perspectives in Post-structuralist Criticism*, trans. and ed. Josué Harari (Ithaca: Cornell University Press, 1979) pp. 141–60. For one of many

telling arguments to the contrary, see the Nehamas article cited in note 2 above.

26.   Widdowson, '"Moments of Vision": Postmodernising *Tess*', p. 88.
27.   For an analysis of this tendency in modern criticism, see Richard Levin, 'The Poetics and Politics of Bardicide', *PMLA*, 105 (1990) 491–504.
28.   Widdowson ' "Moments of Vision": Postmodernising *Tess*', pp. 81, 97.
29.   Garson, *Hardy's Fables of Integrity*, p. 142.
30.   Reuben J. Ellis, 'Joan Durbeyfield Writes to Margaret Saville: An Intermediary Reader in Thomas Hardy's *Tess of the d'Urbervilles*', *Colby Library Quarterly*, 24:1 (March 1988) 15.
31.   John Goode, 'The Offensive Truth: *Tess of the d'Urbervilles*', in *Tess of the d'Urbervilles / Thomas Hardy*, ed. Peter Widdowson, New Casebooks (Basingstoke: Macmillan Press; New York: St Martin's Press, 1993) pp. 199, 186–7.
32.   John B. Humma, 'Language and Disguise: The Imagery of Nature and Sex in *Tess*', *South Atlantic Review*, 54:4 (November 1989) 66.
33.   James Gibson (ed.), *Tess of the d'Urbervilles*, Everyman Library (London: J. M. Dent, 1984) p. 401.
34.   Jean Jacques Lecercle, 'The Violence of Style in *Tess of the d'Urbervilles*', in *Tess of the d'Urbervilles / Thomas Hardy*, ed. Peter Widdowson, New Casebooks (Basingstoke: Macmillan Press; New York: St Martin's Press, 1993) pp. 148–9. Lecercle's reference is to Gilles Deleuze and F. Guattari's *Mille Plateaux* (Paris, 1980).
35.   'The Profitable Reading of Fiction', in *Thomas Hardy's Personal Writings*, p. 112.
36.   Rosemarie Morgan, 'Passive Victim?: *Tess of the d'Urbervilles*', *The Thomas Hardy Journal*, 5:1 (January 1989) 32.
37.   Dale Kramer, *Thomas Hardy: Tess of the d'Urbervilles* (Cambridge: Cambridge University Press, 1991) p. 51.
38.   Ibid., p. 51.
39.   See, for example, Graham Handley, *Thomas Hardy: Tess of the d'Urbervilles*, Penguin Critical Studies (London: Penguin Books, 1991) pp. 43–4.
40.   Kramer, *Thomas Hardy: Tess of the d'Urbervilles*, pp. 4, 58.
41.   Elizabeth Ermarth, 'Fictional Consensus and Female Casualties', in *The Representation of Women in Fiction*, ed. Carolyn G. Heilbrun (Baltimore: Johns Hopkins University Press, 1983) p. 13.
42.   George Wotton, *Thomas Hardy: Towards a Materialist Criticism* (Totowa: Barnes & Noble; Goldenbridge: Gill and Macmillan, 1985) p. 91.
43.   Ingham, *Thomas Hardy*, p. 88.
44.   Joe Fisher, *The Hidden Hardy* (Basingstoke: Macmillan Academic and Professional, 1992) p. 164.

3

Characterization in Hardy's
Jude the Obscure:
The Function of Arabella

JOHN R. DOHENY

D. H. Lawrence insists in 'The Novel and the Feelings' that the conscious understanding of the dark and deep, unconscious passions is the only salvation for the human race and that great novels can bring us to this understanding. I agree with Lawrence's view, and I also agree with his assertion in that essay that characterization is the most important aspect in a novel.[1] On the initial and most obvious level, characterization tells us what kind of novel we are reading.

One need only compare, say, William Golding's *Lord of the Flies* with Hardy's *Jude the Obscure* to see the difference. Golding's characters are hardly developed at all and are moved about woodenly by the author as symbolic devices to illustrate Golding's view of 'human nature', which is the purpose of the novel. Hardy's characters are developed as complex and engaging, partial representations of doing and suffering human beings whose lives are the substance of the novel, and no abstract argument is possible. What we gain is illumination and insight not argument and conviction. Hardy's novel is about social, psychological, and sexual relationships between characters, just as most great novels are.

It also seems to me that Lawrence is right when he says, 'The novel is a perfect medium for revealing to us the changing rainbow of our living relationships. The novel can help us to live, as nothing else can. … If the novelist keeps his thumb out of the pan.' I would only add that this novel can also teach us how not to live, for 'to read a really new novel will *always* hurt, to some extent. There will always be resistance. … You may judge of [its] reality by the fact that [it does] arouse a certain resistance, and compel, at length, a certain acquiescence.'[2] I think this is another way of saying that

great novels lead readers to new and significant insight into immediate, living human experience in ways and in intensity which
no other kind of writing can do. The novelist creates from feelings
and experience the powerful felt life of the novel. The felt life
makes a commentary which is much more rich and varied, much
more moving and lasting, much more incisively critical of the
destructive qualities of human society than any straightforward
argument can be.[3]

I also wish to argue that by its very nature, the novel is too large
and contains too much life, to function effectively as polemic. In the
great novels the artist's intuitive creative imagination overwhelms
conscious intellectual efforts to sustain argument and develops
characters who are seen in the round. This makes it impossible to
create a character who functions as an effective mouthpiece for the
author. The difference between a Hardy novel and those written by
Mickey Spillane and Ian Fleming, for example, is that in Spillane
and Fleming, the hero's position is the novel's position while in
Hardy no such hero is possible. Jude exists in the round, not in one
dimension. Of course, he remains a fictional character and cannot
be supplied with human characteristics which his author hasn't
created for him, but at the same time, his ideas, his view of life, are
not the ideas or view of life which provide the values of the novel.

There is a good deal of confusion in the story of *Jude the Obscure*
itself which is never completely sorted out even in the revisions of
the many editions, but Hardy wasn't very much concerned about
these matters of probability. In a note from his notebooks included
in *The Life of Thomas Hardy*, Hardy writes, 'it is not improbabilities
of incident but improbabilities of character that matter. ... My art is
to intensify the expression of things ... so that the heart and inner
meaning is made vividly visible.'[4]

Therefore, what I wish to consider here is the question of characterization, the probabilities of character, and Hardy's attitudes
towards his creations. It is obvious that Hardy cannot 'keep his
thumb out of the pan' because he is so thoroughly engaged with his
characters as representations of people, but his characters overcome
his engagement, and they take on a life of their own. Because he is
writing a novel where so much of living experience is being represented, Hardy's intuitive creative imagination creates characters
and experience which are beyond his conscious knowledge.

It is usual (almost routine) for Hardy to create characters of
lower-class origin – labouring rural working class, artisans, and

small contractors. Usually the central characters of lower-class origin are striving to rise out of their class into middle-class professional status, and without consciously planning it, they also take on the more stringent ethical concepts of middle-class morality which come willy nilly with that struggle for higher status, and which seriously distort their ability to live anything near satisfying and fulfilling lives. Some of the supporting characters are quite articulate lower-class characters who retain their more open lower-class morality and comment on the values and behaviour of the central characters and the dilemmas which their attempts to cope with middle-class morality create for them. There are also those characters from the lower class who are hardly developed at all but who make occasional comments which add to the insight presented in the novel.

In *Jude the Obscure*, Jude and Sue (with the main emphasis on Jude) are the two who are striving upwards. Phillotson is already lower middle class, settled as a schoolmaster. Arabella, the widow Edlin, and Jude's great-aunt Drusilla Fawley, remain more easily in the lower class and retain its less stringent values more comfortably, i.e. they feel much less anxiety, less guilt, and they judge others much less harshly. It is my intention here to develop what I see as the very important and much neglected function of Arabella in this novel.[5]

Early on Jude begins to day-dream of rising to very high places and what it takes to get there. Though the structure and goal of his phantasy shifts and changes as he lives through the experience of his 30 years of life, he remains obsessively devoted to an ideal of some sort, and it leaves him unable to see clearly the reality of the situations he is in and the people with whom he associates. This seriously affects his ability to function in those situations.

Jude's insecure early life, his love of books along with his short experience (about one year) as a night student during Phillotson's teaching stint in Marygreen, and Phillotson's confession of his own ambition to be a university graduate, are enough to set Jude onto his day-dream to do the same in order to be influential, highly thought of, even rich and famous, a Christminster scholar, a divine, a Bishop. Having acquired Latin and Greek textbooks early on, Jude was getting quite advanced in Latin through hard study by his sixteenth year. In order to support himself financially for the long grind of preparing himself for what he hopes will be entry into one of the colleges of Christminster, he arranges an apprenticeship with a stonemason in Alfredston. Though he thought of the work as a means to an end, Hardy tells us that 'he yet was interested in his pursuit on its own account' and 'thus he reached and passed his nineteenth year'.[6]

Though it is difficult to believe, Jude apparently was so absorbed in his project that he passed through puberty and all its thrilling phantasies and physiological changes usual in young males without noticing it. When Arabella interrupts his dreams of fame and fortune, Hardy writes, 'It is scarcely an exaggeration to say that till this moment Jude had never looked at a woman to consider her as such.' Yet he is certainly not immune once Arabella has hit him with the pig's pizzle. Hardy presents the whole episode as if Jude were simply responding biologically to Arabella's charming and sensual being 'in commonplace obedience to conjunctive orders from headquarters, unconsciously received by unfortunate men when the last intention of their lives is to be occupied with the feminine' (Pt I, Ch. 6).

Some potential difficulties with characterization and presentation arise here in the use of 'unfortunate men' and so on. While it is clear from the way that matters work out between them that Jude eventually believes his love affair and marriage with Arabella is detrimental to his great plans and is, therefore, a mistake, the problems occur because Hardy seems to indicate that he, as author, also thinks so. He intrudes with his own commentary in various places. For example, as Jude leaves this first stage of the romantic and sexual seduction by Arabella with his own eager but naive participation, he tells himself that 'it's only a bit of fun', and Hardy helps him along by telling us that Jude is

> faintly conscious that to common-sense there was something lacking, and still more obviously something redundant, in the nature of this girl who had drawn him to her, which made it necessary that he should assert mere sportiveness on his part as his reason in seeking her – something in her quite antipathetic to that side of him which had been occupied with literary study and the magnificent Christminster dream.   (Pt I, Ch. 6)

In so far as this is Jude's own way of diverting his mind and conscience from the seriousness of his eager participation in the initial stages of a courtship, it is important character development because it is the beginning of his continuing efforts in this relationship with

Arabella to excuse his own part in it as mere fun, a brief diversion from his more serious purpose in life, which traps him into a marriage which does serious harm to his great expectations and, later, to his prospects with Sue. This is a pattern which he follows often in the novel. It allows him to see his own actions as a weakness in his otherwise strong character, a weakness which Arabella takes advantage of in the pursuit of her own less honourable ends. Thus is Jude able to avoid his own very strong guilty conscience and salvage his own vision of himself as a man above the ordinary run of his class.

Apparently not satisfied to let the situation and characters develop, Hardy again helps Jude along this path which will allow him to blame Arabella's coarse nature for his behaviour and his troubles.

It had been no vestal who chose *that* missile for opening her attack on him. He saw this with his intellectual eye, just for a short fleeting while, as by the light of a falling lamp one might momentarily see an inscription on a wall before being enshrouded in darkness. And then this passing discriminative power was withdrawn, and Jude was lost to all conditions of things in the advent of a fresh and wild pleasure, that of having found a new channel for emotional interest hitherto unsuspected, though it had lain close beside him. He was to meet this enkindling one of the other sex on the following Sunday.   (Pt I, Ch. 6)

Fortunately for the novel, Hardy is not very successful in his efforts to support Jude's own early tendency to load the situation against Arabella as a character. A few lines later when Anny asks her if she has caught Jude, Arabella replies, 'I don't know. I wish I had thrown something else than that!', and her character begins to develop independently of Jude's self-protective interpretation of her and the situation.

On the following Sunday, after pretending to himself that there was some question about whether or not he would keep his date with Arabella even though he was already dressed in his Sunday best, Jude arrives at her door. He is slightly unnerved by Arabella's father's reminder that he is courting, for the obvious reason that he has tried to convince himself that this is not the serious activity of courtship but merely a bit of fun, but Arabella puts a stop to doubt as she comes down the stairs, as Hardy writes, 'so handsome amid

her untidy surroundings that he felt glad he had come, and all the
misgivings vanished that had hitherto haunted him' (Pt I, Ch. 7).
Once more unwilling to let matters alone, Hardy interferes again
with what can only be seen as heavy-handed irony in a long paragraph from which I quote the last part:

> An indescribable lightness of heel served to lift him along; and
> Jude, the incipient scholar, prospective D.D., Professor, Bishop,
> or what not, felt himself honoured and glorified by the conde-
> scension of this handsome country wench in agreeing to take a
> walk with him in her Sunday frock and ribbons.   (Pt I, Ch. 7)

Within the dramatic context and content of the novel, as opposed
to deliberate authorial intervention, there is a sense in which this
irony is directed at what Hardy calls Jude's '*so-called* [my italics] elevated intentions', intentions which cannot be realized given his time
and circumstances. Hardy probably knew this. Certainly, his contemporary readers knew that there was no chance for Jude to realize
his 'elevated intentions'. The most he could expect for this movement out of his class was somewhat less. He could have become a
schoolmaster, as Phillotson was and as Sue later on expects to
become, or he could more easily have remained an artisan. A stonemason's income and expectations for the future would have allowed
Jude to carry on a life much like Hardy's father did. To aim so high
and to fail does, in the eyes of his author and of some of his readers,
give Jude a heroic quality which Sue later defines as the potential
tragedy which makes him attractive to her.

For the purposes of his plot and his conscious novelistic aims, it
is pretty clear that Hardy wishes to provide Jude with a conflict
between his biological, sexual drives and his intellectual intentions,
a conflict which results in an unsatisfactory marriage. He is so
determined to make this clear that he must tell us what it is rather
than let it develop through the dramatic content: he presents Jude
to us as one drawn to keep his date with Arabella against all his
better judgement and good sense,

> as if materially, a compelling arm of extraordinary muscular
> power seized hold of him – something which had nothing in
> common with the spirits and influence that had moved him hith-
> erto. This seemed to care little for his reason and his will, nothing
> for his so-called elevated intentions, and moved him along, as a

violent schoolmaster a schoolboy he has seized by the collar, in a direction which tended towards the embrace of a woman for whom he had no respect, and whose life had nothing in common with his own except locality.   (Pt I, Ch. 7)

It never occurs to Hardy and certainly not to Jude at this point that something so strong as to pull him away from his seven or eight years of study may be more important than the elevated intentions and could lead to something worthwhile. Yet, it seems, from commentary here that we, though not Jude, are expected to see that he is pulled along by a dangerous and unworthy biological need toward the destruction of all his worthy elevated intentions. I say 'seems', because Hardy creates ambivalence with the phrase 'so-called elevated intentions'. He also allows Arabella, the character, her full development just as he allows her relationship with Jude to develop to its full state so that all the divergence of their characters comes fully into play. In other words, Hardy's creative imagination overcomes his impulse to write the sort of novel William Golding successfully wrote in *Lord of the Flies*. Hardy, unlike Golding, succeeds in creating important insight, and he does this through the interaction of complex and revealing characters. In many of Hardy's novels sexuality interferes in troublesome or, as in this novel, disastrous ways, but here, when Jude feels, thinks, speaks, and acts for himself, something beyond his creator's deliberate and conscious intentions emerges. Hardy allows for this himself in the last sentence of his 1912 'Postscript' to his original Preface: 'no doubt there can be more in a book than the author consciously puts there'.

To begin with, it is clear that Jude's wish to follow Phillotson to Christminster is part of his childhood wish to be taken seriously as an important person, one who is far above the general run of people. In spite of his occasional pronouncements about elevated humanitarian aims, it is clearly a desire to rise far above his class which drives him on. Jude's growth into biological sexual maturity conflicts with his idea of rising out of his class to such high status. In order to maintain his ideal, Jude judges those natural activities of his life which interfere with the ideal as unworthy of noble and ethical human conduct, thus creating a dilemma for himself which he is never able to resolve. Long before Sue announces the position after her collapse at the end of the novel, Jude already believes that passionate human nature needs to learn 'self-mastery' (Pt 6, Ch. 3).

Jude is also a desperate snob who insists that Arabella is beneath him in sensitivity, intelligence, and sophistication, while remaining attractive and desirable sexually for a time. In other words there is much of Angel Clare in him, and perhaps some of those aristocratic ancestors of Tess whom Hardy castigates for seducing or raping village girls who were vulnerable to them because of their inferior positions. However, Arabella is not inferior to Jude – whatever he tells himself – and she is not dependent upon him in any way except in passionate love, and she can handle that well enough. In spite of Jude, even sometimes in spite of his own comments, Hardy creates a character in Arabella who reaches full development. Instead of functioning as a novelistic device, an obstacle in Jude's way, Arabella introduces a different and contrasting view of life.

In part because Arabella's character is fully developed, Jude becomes a fully rounded character himself in the novel rather than an extension of the author. We see him and his ideas all around; his ideas are tested against the reality of living, where they have less chance of standing unquestioned, and they don't survive the test very well. We see them in relation to Arabella's values, ideas, and general position (and at other times to those of other characters), and this allows Jude's character to develop in ways which he doesn't recognize himself. The process makes him a more complex, more human character however less heroic he appears.

Had Jude been seeking a decently healthy, financially secure, and satisfying life, even one in which he could indulge his pleasures in books and in learning ancient languages for their own sake, his marriage to Arabella had prospects which were promising. She was so overwhelmed by Jude that she was determined that he should have her, that he should marry her. She responds to Anny's early congratulations for the beginnings of her success with Jude in what Hardy describes as 'a curiously low, hungry tone of latent sensuousness,'

> I've got him to care for me: yes! But I want him to more than care for me; I want him to have me – to marry me! I must have him. I can't do without him. He's the sort of man I long for. I shall go mad if I can't give myself to him altogether! I felt I should when I first saw him!   (Pt I, Ch. 7)

She is a fully sensual, sexual woman, as no other woman in the novel is, perhaps as no woman except Eustacia Vye is in any Hardy novel. She is a good manager, realistic about the requirements for a decent life, and accomplished in many tasks including raising pigs, tending a bar, and managing finances when they are scarce. Most of all, she is prepared to get on with the life they have committed themselves to. The absurdity of the marriage vows never bothers her because she recognizes the marriage as a living, sexual partnership just as Widow Edlin does and did in her own marriage. It is a commitment to live together for mutual pleasure, support, and gain, and what she expects from Jude is the same commitment and the ability to stick to his trade. She is also independent enough and strong enough to leave Jude when she has decided that the marriage is not a good one. And since she is able to do this so easily and with no dire consequences, she introduces into the novel, both here and continuously whenever she reappears, not only a different set of values from those of Jude and Sue but a commentary on theirs which changes our view of the various manifestations of their dilemma.

Arabella's practicality versus Jude's squeamishness and sentimentality, which he justifies as a version of being kind, a sort of merciful high mindedness, can be seen quite clearly in the scene where they must butcher their own pig because the weather has prevented the butcher from reaching them in time (Pt I, Ch. 10). Apparently without consulting Arabella, Jude had decided that they should live in the country where Arabella could use her experience from home by raising a pig for slaughter to supplement their income as well as keeping a vegetable garden, she being, as Jude erroneously thinks, 'absolutely useless in a town-lodging' (Pt I, Ch. 9). The butchering can't be put off, the pig has eaten the last of his food 24 hours earlier in the time honoured pattern of saving 'bother with the innerds'. Jude's response to this news of the business is typically contradictory: he feels sorry for the pig because the pig has had no food, forgetting that he is about to be butchered, and then saying that he will do the sticking 'since it must be done'.

Once the pig is bound, his tone changes from hunger to something else which Jude sentimentally hears as despair. 'Upon my soul I would sooner have gone without the pig than have had this to do. ... A creature I have fed with my own hands.' Though Jude is content to have bacon, chops, and roast on his table, he is not so easy about taking the action necessary to get it there, and he panics. He refuses to follow Arabella's instructions for making the pig die slowly in order for the meat to be well bled since they 'shall lose a shilling a score' if it is red and bloody: 'Just touch the vein, that's all. I was brought up to it, and I know. Every good butcher keeps un bleeding long. He ought to be eight or ten minutes dying, at least.' Jude plunges the knife in with all his might, and in response to Arabella's cry of criticism, he replies, 'Do be quiet, Arabella, and have a little pity on the creature!' Hardy himself adds the revealing contradiction when he writes, 'However unworkmanlike the deed, it had been mercifully done', apparently assuming that some kindness can be preserved in the killing if it is done quickly (Pt I, Ch. 10).

Arabella reminds Jude of their purpose in having the pig in the first place, 'Pigs must be killed', she says in response to Jude's comment that it is a hateful business. She does not remind him again of the serious loss of income, a shilling for every 20 pounds of meat, and the loss of blood for blackpot brought about by his panic. Hardy, in his own voice, continues Jude's sentimental evasion of the nature of the business by seeing the stain of the two-thirds of the bucket of blood which Jude spilled on the snow when he kicked it over in his panic as 'a dismal, sordid, ugly spectacle – to those who saw it as other than an ordinary obtaining of meat' (Pt I, Ch. 10). Since the experience causes neither Jude nor his creator to give up eating meat, the protestation rings hollow. The spectacle must be somehow less dismal, sordid, and ugly when it is done out of sight and the meat arrives ready for cooking. Neither Arabella nor Jude in particular gets the last word in the situation: she is practical, he is idealistic. He says, 'Thank God! ... He's dead' and feels

> dissatisfied with himself as a man at what he had done, though aware of his lack of common sense, and that the deed would have amounted to the same thing if carried out by deputy. The white snow, stained with the blood of his fellow-mortal, wore an illogical look to him as a lover of justice, not to say a Christian; but he could not see how the matter was to be mended. No doubt he was, as his wife had called him, a tender-hearted fool.
>
> (Pt I, Ch. 10)

Again Hardy is revealing Jude in ways which are the product of his creative imagination and probably opposed to his own sympathy, for this is Jude's typical manner of disguising his contradictions from himself, reducing his own part in the situation to a helpless but humane participation and pushing a blame somewhere else, this time merely into the nature of things since he can't find a person at fault who is not himself. The thought is parallel to his earlier behaviour with Arabella and will occur again and again in both thought and deed.

Arabella's response is, 'What's God got to do with such a messy job as a pig-killing, I should like to know! ... Poor folks must live' (Pt I, Ch. 10). Because Arabella's directly practical attitude is given equal weight to Jude's idealistic self-protection here, we gain more knowledge of both characters of course, but, more important, it also makes it impossible for a careful reader to identify with Jude's high-mindedness and to follow him in his conclusion that killing his 'fellow-mortal' quickly instead of slowly because he must be killed can partially satisfy his love of justice and his Christian conscience.

That Arabella has had adequate experience in raising pigs, while demeaning for Jude, is a great practical advantage, as we see. That she also has had some experience tending a bar and has the personality for it, while this also is demeaning and immoral for Jude, is again of great practical advantage. Had Jude been able and willing to accept her possible earnings, they could have lived in the town while Jude finished his apprenticeship and it would not have been necessary for him to travel such a long distance, which would have left him less exhausted at the end of his long day, which could have given them both time for more life together or even have given Jude more time to carry on with his reading and learning for its own sake.

Of course, it is obvious that Jude was not seeking this kind of life. His aims were much higher and, in fact, more monkish. Therefore, he sees his marriage to Arabella as a disaster born of his irresistible sexual instincts and his high principles which won't allow him to abandon her. In his own view, succumbing to pleasure in this relationship becomes his downfall, and Hardy presents him so convincingly, even apart from his own authorial commentary, that nearly every critic has accepted it as such. Some even go so far as to accept Jude's need to fix a blame on Arabella, to make her responsible for his situation, by accepting Jude's assertion that Arabella has lied about her pregnancy when the novel itself quite explicitly disproves this belief.[7] Significantly enough, throughout the novel Jude persists in his belief that 'Arabella's word was absolutely untrustworthy' (Pt III, Ch. 8) even though she never does tell him lies as Sue does, and he sees Sue as always sure and trustworthy even when she isn't. Her evasions and contradictions he merely describes as 'one lovely conundrum' (Pt III, Ch. 2). Therefore, it is easy to see that Jude's judgement is more nearly a matter of what he wants to believe than it is an understanding of reality while we, as careful readers, are provided with more understanding than any of the characters can have.

Arabella clearly desires Jude for more than the bit of fun which Jude tells himself he is after, as both her comments to her friends and her efforts to get pregnant indicate. She is also more innocent of the means for attaining her desire than some readers assume because they identify too fully with Jude's position and his acts of self-justification. Arabella doesn't know what Anny and Sarah mean by the right way to catch Jude. She only knows, she says, about 'plain courting, and taking care he don't go too far'. To her surprise, their advice is to make sure that he does go too far; that is, she should get pregnant. While it is sometimes risky because the man might let her face it alone, 'Nothing venture nothing have', they tell her. They also assure her that she 'would be safe enough' with Jude. They tell her that 'Lots of girls do it; or do you think they'd get married at all?' (Pt I, Ch. 7). The history of the times tells us not only that lots of girls do it, especially in the working class, but that the marriage ceremony was never the large issue in the working class that it was in the middle class where the tie that binds was taken as a moral as well as a legal trap, and Jude is nearer to that set of values than Arabella is.

Once she has managed the difficulty of getting Jude into her bed, the ice is broken, and two months later, meeting the patent medicine man Vilbert who passes for the medical expert in these parts, Arabella tells him of her experience in order to discover whether she is pregnant or not. Arabella's knowledge of the signs of pregnancy are apparently inadequate, and she must be informed. The news is what she wanted to hear. Hardy writes, 'before [Vilbert] left her she had grown brighter' (Pt I, Ch. 9). She tells Jude the news that very night.

A few weeks after the marriage she tells her friend Anny that she was mistaken, she is not pregnant. Anny immediately assumes that Arabella has gone one clever step further than she or Sarah could imagine, but Arabella, who has no reason to lie, insists that she was convinced that she was pregnant. She owns up to the first trick – to get herself pregnant – but not to the second – to pretend to be pregnant (Pt I, Ch. 9). To Jude, who has accused her of double trickery because he has overheard one of Arabella's friends say it, she says, 'I'll declare afore Heaven that I thought what I told you was true. Doctor Vilbert thought so' (Pt I, Ch. 10).

However, Jude still has another moral arrow in his quiver. He can blame her for seducing him into her bed in the first place in an effort to get pregnant. At this point it is clear why it was so important for Jude to believe that he was not in control of his own actions; since Arabella was manipulating him through what he calls his 'weakness' into her bed, the whole episode, pregnant or not, is, in his view, Arabella's doing from start to finish. His own early assertion that he was in it himself for fun is forgotten. When Arabella tells him that 'Every woman has a right to do such as that. The risk is hers', she also allows him to make her culpable even though Jude enjoyed the experience for two months himself and felt that for the first time he was really living. Jude's moral high ground produces a lecture:

> I quite deny it, Bella. She might if no life-long penalty attached to it for the man, or, in his default, for herself; if the weakness of the moment could end with the moment, or even with the year. But when effects stretch so far she should not go and do that which entraps a man if he is honest, or herself if he is otherwise.
>
> (Pt I, Ch. 10)

He feels safe in his own defensive position as the honourable man trapped by the scheming woman. We should compare his response to the other woman's confession of her scheme to trap him into loving her without loving him herself in order to see how thoroughly Jude's idea of the woman affects his response to her (see Pt VI, Ch. 3).

When Arabella asks, 'What ought I to have done?', Jude answers, 'Given me time.' This comment, intended as it is to leave his own conscience clear by seeing himself as victim of a clever woman, ought to remind us of Jude's intention to give up the affair at the end of two months. Arabella's anger doesn't boil over until the next day. They have their battle during which Jude feels that all is over between them, that their life together is intolerable. He blames the union which binds them; she blames him as one of those abusive Fawleys and feels no guilt herself for what she has done. Jude walks off to consult Drusilla, then to try suicide on the icy pond. When he returns, Arabella has gone.

Arabella is a developed but comparatively uncomplicated character. Jude is a different matter altogether. He is developed, but he is also a complicated character whose nature is contradictory. Once he is awakened to Arabella as a sensual woman, 'he felt as a snake must feel who has sloughed off its winter skin, and cannot understand the brightness and sensitiveness of its new one' (Pt I, Ch. 7). And though he was a bit unnerved by Arabella's father referring to his arrival as courting, her presence destroyed the misgivings.

During the long afternoon and evening of courting during which Arabella must lead the unpractised Jude into intimate behaviour (kissing, holding hands, and walking arm in arm), Jude was an eager participant. For a moment when they returned to Arabella's home where her parents and some neighbours took him seriously as 'Arabella's intended partner', Jude felt 'out of place and embarrassed', and reached the bizarre conclusion that they 'did not belong to his set or circle', and he was glad to get away.

> But that sense was only temporary: Arabella soon reasserted her sway in his soul. He walked as if he felt himself to be another man from the Jude of yesterday. What were his books to him? what were his intentions, hitherto adhered to so strictly, as to not wasting a single minute of time day by day? 'Wasting!' It depended on your point of view to define that: he was just living for the first time: not wasting life. It was better to love a woman than to be a graduate, or a parson; ay, or a pope!   (Pt I, Ch. 7)

The next day on his way back to Alfredston, he stops to gaze at the footprints on the ground where he had given her the first kiss, where they had stood 'locked in each other's arms', and realizes that 'a void was in his heart which nothing could fill' except Arabella. And a few lines later we learn that Arabella feels the same way, she wants him to marry her because she 'can't do without him' (Pt I, Ch. 7). Obviously, in anybody's terms this can only be called falling in love. Jude's passion is in full play, as is Arabella's, and she eventually gets him into her bed to fulfil her desire for him as well as to reach toward the marriage she will go mad without. However, Jude is trapped by his ambition to rise in the world. The passion, the love, carries him for 'some two months' until, finally satiated, he begins to wish himself out of the relationship, which he sees as a guilty surrender to his sexual passion, and he announces to Arabella that he thinks he ought to go away: 'I think it will be better both for you and for me. I wish some things had never begun! I was much to blame, I know. But it is never too late to mend' (Pt I, Ch. 9).

This prudish stand is part of the impedimenta which Jude carries as a handicap throughout his short life, but here it also functions as a ruse of sorts, of which he is probably not conscious himself because it occurs so automatically. Presuming to speak for Arabella's good as well as his own desire is one of those attempts to disarm which the righteous often use. It is clear, given Arabella's feelings and desires, that breaking off the relationship is not only the opposite of what she desires, it would drive her mad, as she announced to Anny. However, as we and Arabella and Vilbert know, events have progressed too far for Jude to run away with the clear conscience which he must have for his peace of mind. Jude can neither follow his impulse to run away, because his strict, middle-class morality would force him to see himself as a cad, nor can he accept what the promise of a life with Arabella would bring, because he has his 'so-called elevated intentions'. Therefore, he follows a pattern which will be consistent for him throughout the novel: he arranges to marry Arabella while, 'in the secret centre of his brain', he believes that 'Arabella was not worth a great deal as a specimen of womankind. ... His idea of her was the thing of most consequence, not Arabella herself' (Pt I, Ch. 9).

If we consider it, this thought is absurd in general and even more inappropriate for Arabella. His idea of Arabella is a negative one. It is his sensual response which has been positive. His idea is permanently an erroneous one just as later on the novel proves that his idea of Sue is erroneous, and his idea of Christminster is erroneous. Arabella is, as a character, a fine specimen of womankind in the novel, especially for an artisan like Jude whose sexual and social and financial needs would do very well in partnership with her. But Jude sees himself as an artisan only by default. He has higher ambitions, and his sexuality, sexual love in general, is seen by Jude, and often by Hardy, as a serious hindrance to ambition rather than as human fulfilment and expansion of life. Had it been any different, there would have been no tragedy, no novel. The ideal which Hardy presents with Giles Winterborne and Marty South in *The Woodlanders* is not a position which Jude can reach, but it is the position clearly behind the destructive forces of this novel. Sue is drawn to the ideal and Jude is trapped by it in the quest for higher social status. That this ideal is also part of the middle-class society of the novel's time (as well as ours) is clear. The importance of this novel is that it demonstrates the destructive nature of middle-class ideals, and Arabella is an important figure in that demonstration.

Hardy, as commentator, is also sometimes seriously caught up in the idealism, and when he interjects commentary, as he does by his insertion of a paragraph about the absurdity of the marriage vows, or forces issues in the action or thought of the characters, as he does occasionally throughout the novel, he is usually distorting and weakening the results of his intuitive creative imagination. The class from which both Hardy and his character, Jude, emerged – the class to which both Arabella and the Widow Edlin belong – was never troubled by such matters. The history of the working class, Hardy's own ancestors, and the novel itself demonstrate this effectively. The novel exposes the tragedy of the middle-class commitments to the ideals including the rule of law, purity, nobility, sobriety, sex-less love, and the duties inherent in the idea of marriage, which lead Sue, and Jude with her, to disaster if only because, in their attempts to reject the social forms, they invest them with a power which the lower-class Arabella, for example, does not. Almost as if by magic, those same forms have no affective power for Arabella and no effect on her.

Jude's objection to Arabella's false hair illustrates clearly his narrow morality as well as his 'idea' of what Arabella should be in his eyes. He wished for – and because he has an 'idea' of her, he expects her to be – one of those 'unsophisticated girls [who] would and did go to towns and remain there for years without losing their simplicity of life and embellishments'. A bit later when Jude is critical of her when she is practising making dimples and is shocked to hear that she spent some time serving in the tap-room in a public house instead of always living at home as he had assumed, characteristically without asking, Arabella puts Jude's idealism and his narrow morality into clear focus. She tells him that he ought to have seen that she 'was a little more finished than I could have been by staying where I was born', seeing her three months' work in the pub as her finishing school (Pt I, Ch. 9).

Jude's enthusiastic response to the sensual, fully sexual Arabella has had little effect on his perceptive abilities; he married an 'idea' of country innocence which never existed in the country. There are certainly shades of Angel Clare here. Faced with the reality of his situation, Jude judges the marriage a mistake born of his innocence, an entrapment born of Arabella's cunning, and with Hardy's apparent blessing, he turns to condemnation of 'social ritual', and this allows him to continue to practise self-deception and practically ensures that he will learn nothing from experience:

> There seemed to him, vaguely and dimly, something wrong in a social ritual which made necessary a cancelling of well-formed schemes involving years of thought and labour, of foregoing a man's one opportunity of showing himself superior to the lower animals, and of contributing his units of work to the general progress of his generation, because of a momentary surprise by a new and transitory instinct which had nothing in it of the nature of vice, and could be only at the most called weakness. He was inclined to inquire what he had done, or she lost, for that matter, that he deserved to be caught in a gin which would cripple him, if not her also, for the rest of a lifetime? There was perhaps something fortunate in the fact that the immediate reason of his marriage had proved to be non-existent. But the marriage remained.
>
> (Pt I, Ch. 9)

There is much of importance to the understanding of Jude's attitude and to the novel as a whole in this passage. Of course, there is something wrong with the 'social ritual', and the criticism is apt, but Jude forgets that he was also passionately in love with Arabella. Furthermore, there is nothing except his own idealistic commitment to it which keeps Jude in the situation, as Arabella easily demonstrates when she simply walks out of the marriage without penalty or guilt, even to marry again before Jude did her the favour, when she asked for it, of divorcing her so that she could get the truly legal status of wife again for mainly practical reasons which she explains later on to Sue while advising her to do the same with Jude (see Pt IV, Ch. 5 and Pt V, Ch. 2).

When Arabella quits the marriage, Jude can only expiate his own guilt and regain his sense of self-worth by sending Arabella all his money and the furniture they have accumulated. Even then, he doesn't feel satisfied with himself until he discovers that Arabella has also thrown his framed photograph into the auction pile. Then he feels free to take up his plan where he had left it when he met Arabella, with the difference that now, having been sexually awakened, he begins to dream of Sue, his cousin, who also lives in Christminster. Apparently because he has recognized his own need for female contact, companionship, and sex, Jude sets off for the disastrous destruction which awaits him.

Neither Jude, nor Hardy for him, offers this explanation for his changed plans. Jude is only pleased that he can return to his idealized academic project unimpeded by his marriage. His own sexuality is, as he sees it, merely a temporary weakness, coarse and below his great concerns. It becomes more and more obvious as time passes that though Jude has been very good at applying himself to the drudgery of the study of Latin and Greek, he is not an intellectual in the sense that he actually learns about life from experience and from reading. In the space between the end of his marriage and the beginning of the next chapter of the book – about a page and a half – Jude has undergone a slight but significant change, a change which solidifies him as a complex character in conflict with himself and his values. Not incidentally, the change also makes him more prone to the disasters which Hardy has in mind for him.

Three years after his separation from Arabella, or what he describes to himself as 'the disruption of his coarse conjugal life with' Arabella, he is on his way to Christminster to ply his trade, but, as Hardy shows, he is not so devoted to his day-dream as he himself thinks: 'The ultimate impulse to come had had a curious origin – one more nearly related to the emotional side of him than to the intellectual' (Pt II, Ch. 1). Arabella had aroused his sexual instincts to action, and we find that they are not so easily put back where they were before her. He has seen a photograph of Sue which his great-aunt Drusilla has, and she has told him that Sue lives in Christminster.

Every novel is a story which has its progression, and characters develop and change as they experience the progression of events. Every assertion, therefore, has a context which must be taken into account because that context helps to determine the nature and sometimes the purpose of the assertions, and it is important in any discussion of a scene to keep this in mind.

Between three and four years after he set out for Christminster, Jude meets Arabella again. He has just gone through the ordeal preceding and following Sue's marriage to Phillotson. Having received a letter telling him that his great-aunt Drusilla is dangerously ill and another letter inviting him to return to work in Christminster, he capitalizes on these events to invite Sue to meet him on his return journey from Christminster and to continue on with him to Marygreen for a last visit to Drusilla. He has been moping about

Melchester depressed at the loss of Sue, and the same depression exists for him at Christminster. Meeting Tinker Taylor, his crony from Christminster days, they decide to go drinking together. Tinker is put off by the upgrading of their old pub and leaves. Jude stays on to wait for his return train and is surprised to find that Arabella has returned from Australia and is working in a part of the pub where she can't see him though he can observe her in a mirror. After Arabella's remark to a customer about her estranged husband, Jude decides that he must speak to her and come to some arrangement.

Arabella is surprised to see him, and though she is not interested in his proposal to arrange something, she is not displeased to see him: 'their glances met. She started; till a humorous impudence sparkled in her eyes, and she spoke' (Pt III, Ch. 8). She thought he must have died, she tells him, since she had heard nothing of him, and she notices by his clothes that he has not reached the heights he was aiming for and which was the prime cause of the failure of their marriage. Jude also notices a good deal about her, especially her clothes, her looks, and her 'amplitudes', all of which are quite attractive to his eye. When Arabella had said that her husband was in Australia, Jude assumed that she referred to him but disguised the circumstances. However, Arabella tells him that she did it for other reasons which she doesn't care to go into. 'I make a very good living,' she says, 'and I don't know that I want your company.' Apart from Jude's careful cataloguing of Arabella's attire and her looks and his persistence in arranging to talk matters over with her, to 'arrange something', there is no obvious indication that at least one possible intention could be functioning in Jude's mind. Having lost Sue to marriage, Jude might see or feel the possibility of consoling himself with his own still legal wife, but the only reference to that idea suggests the opposite. Before he enters the compartment of the pub where Arabella is working to speak to her, piqued by her flirtatious behaviour with a customer and her reference to her husband, Jude thought he 'could not realize their nominal closeness' and 'he was indifferent to the fact that Arabella was his wife indeed' (Pt III, Ch. 8). This attitude makes what happens very strange.

Since it is too busy for them to talk in the bar, Arabella invites him to wait for her to get off work. She can arrange to leave early, at nine. Jude agrees saying they should arrange something, but Arabella replies, 'O bother arranging! I'm not going to arrange anything'; then Jude changes to a need to 'know a thing or two'. While he is waiting, Jude works up his honourable reasons for a strict adherence to rule, and he thinks to himself:

> Here was a rude flounce into the pellucid sentimentality of his sad attachment to Sue. Though Arabella's word was absolutely untrustworthy, he thought there might be some truth in her implication that she had not wished to disturb him, and had really supposed him dead. However, there was only one thing now to be done, and that was to play a straightforward part, the law being the law, and the woman between whom and himself there was no more unity than between east and west being in the eye of the Church one person with him.   (Pt III, Ch. 8)

This is a magnificent passage of convoluted self-deception and rationalization for waiting around for Arabella, and a typical example of the way Jude's mind works. First, had he genuinely wanted to avoid Arabella, he needn't have approached her. Even after speaking to her, he could quite simply have wished her well and agreed to continue to go their separate ways. Arabella gives every indication that this is her own wish, though Jude's persistence seems to have perked her interest. Jude insists upon a meeting and discussion, first for one purpose and then for another. And when Arabella agrees, he must also work himself up to the righteous key and present himself as bound, even trapped, by the law and the eye of the Church, neither of which has any interest in him at all as has been obvious from the first and will also be obvious when he obtains his divorce from Arabella. The reason why Jude must convince himself of this honourable, straight, and honest procedure becomes immediately clear: 'Having to meet Arabella here, it was impossible to meet Sue at Alfredston as he had promised. At every thought of this a pang had gone through him; but the conjuncture could not be helped.' He thinks this to himself and goes on to speculate that 'perhaps' Arabella was an 'intervention to punish him for his unauthorized love' (Pt III, Ch. 8). Jude's capacity for self-justification through self-deception is indeed heroically large!

The only plausible explanation for Jude's persistence here is that he does want to spend time with Arabella to provide some compensation for the loss of Sue, but he can't bring himself to know it since it would tarnish his own idea of himself. What follows when they do meet can only be explained in these terms. When Arabella meets him at nine, she takes his arm and asks him what arrangements he wants to come to; he answers, 'none in particular' and begins to think of Sue again, and suggests that he should have gone back to Marygreen because his aunt is ill. In spite of what seems an effort to back off, when Arabella proposes they take the train to Aldbrickham and spend the night together, Jude readily agrees but in such a way as to put the responsibility for it onto Arabella: he says, 'As you like.' He is successful then in spending a night of conjugal pleasure with Arabella without being responsible for it himself.[8]

Returning the next morning to Christminster, Jude asks Arabella again what she meant when she told him as they were getting out of bed that morning that she had something to tell him but didn't because he wouldn't promise to keep it a secret. When he does promise not to tell it around, she informs him of her marriage in Australia, and Jude grows angry because she didn't tell him of what he sees as her 'crime' before they spent the night together. Is this a suggestion that he would not have spent the night in sexual pleasure with her had she told him this? Of course, he has no answer because the question is a means of keeping the active responsibility shifted away from himself toward Arabella to avoid feeling guilty about it and about missing the appointment with Sue. In other words, it allows him later to say to Sue that he couldn't help it, a favourite phrase for them both. Arabella is less bound by conscience and is a match for Jude. 'Crime! Pooh. They don't think much of such as that over there! Lots of 'em do it. … Well, if you take it like that I shall go back to him! He was very fond of me, and we lived honourable enough, and as respectable as any married couple in the Colony!' (Pt III, Ch. 9). The whole scene deserves careful reading, for it reveals a great deal about Jude.

Having tested out the possibility of some sort of return to Jude, Arabella decides that it isn't a good idea and makes it clear to Jude that she wants nothing more than the night of pleasure from him. Jude, on the other hand, feels tremendous guilt for his night of pleasure. Since he cannot feel 'resentment towards her' he can only expiate for his great sin by patronizingly pitying Arabella 'while he contemned her', hence the emphasis on her 'crime'. Sue also makes much of the crime later on (Pt III, Ch. 9).

Without his full conscious knowledge Arabella did bring his sexual feelings into full play, and in spite of his feelings of degradation, or perhaps because of them, he sits beside Sue in the train comparing the 'small, tight, apple-like convexities of her bodice' with 'Arabella's amplitudes'. Sue, whom Jude now finds more attractive in her nervous evasions than he did Arabella's straightforward directness, has come up from Marygreen to find him and to indirectly scold him for not meeting her the night before. She is described as 'bodeful', 'anxious', 'her little mouth nervous, and her strained eyes speaking reproachful inquiry ... not far from a sob' because, she says, ever so indirectly, that she fears that Jude might have forgotten his promise to her never to get drunk again and, suffering because she was not there anymore, he might have gone on a binge again.

Jude is, as usual, thrilled by her attention and concern, seeing her as 'a good angel' come 'to hunt [him] up, and deliver [him]' (Pt III, Ch. 9). So far as I know, no one has taken up this need on Jude's part to re-enact the care of a lost mother. In spite of the fact that she made him deeply miserable by marrying Phillotson (as she will soon make Phillotson deeply miserable by leaving him for Jude), Jude looks upon her as his loved one, 'in his tender thought the sweetest and most disinterested comrade that he had ever had, living largely in vivid imaginings, so ethereal a creature that her spirit could be seen trembling through her limbs', and this makes him feel 'heartily ashamed of his earthliness in spending the hours he had spent in Arabella's company'. And, we can add for him, in bed with her (Pt III, Ch. 9).

The only possible relationship with a woman on an equal footing and in full adult relation for Jude would be with Arabella, but that is clearly not what he wants. He prefers the nervous, anxious, neurotic relationship he can and does establish with Sue.

In a monograph called *The Panzaic Principle*, Wayne Burns argues that in nineteenth-century novels, with few exceptions, there are two oppositional factors at work: the 'crystalline orb of the ideal' in the form of the highest ideals of the noblest characters is opposed by the sensual reality of life, usually in the form of a character descended from Sancho Panza in Cervantes's *Don Quixote*. In a novel, the Panzaic character succeeds in giving the lie to the ideals of the idealistic characters by demonstrating the physical reality of life, by living from the senses and thereby bringing the ideals down to earth. Panzaic characters are, of course, never noble or idealistic. They are coarse, and unless there are idealistic noble characters in the novel, there are no Panzaic characters. Burns insists that in great novels the senses are always right.[9]

Arabella is such a character. Each time she appears in the novel, she brings this conflict into sharp focus. When she comes to Aldbrickham, mainly to ask Jude to take on their child, she stirs Jude into some sort of sexual response which he has kept suppressed for nearly a year while living with Sue on her non-sexual, non-physical terms. Sue is thrown into panic at the arrival of, in her words, 'a fleshy, coarse woman'. Jude remarks that Arabella was 'rather handsome' when he knew her, and Sue must agree that she still is, but '[s]he is such a low-passioned woman', she says, 'I can see it in her shape, and hear it in her voice' (Pt V, Ch. 2). Sue is the opposite of all this easy sensuality of Arabella, and her panic at Jude's own coarseness, which he laments is probably natural to him, leads her to fall from her idealistic, immaculate heights into a sexual relationship which she later explains to Jude as the greatest mistake of her life (Pt VI, Ch. 3).

On her side, Arabella sees the development as a good thing, good humouredly taking credit for bringing it about, and giving Sue what she herself sees as practical advice on the advantages of marriage. All this is too coarse for Sue, and it only makes her more anxious. The chapter ends on a wonderfully emphatic note. When Sue 'hastily' prepares to end her visit, Arabella, also wishing to prepare to leave, springs out of bed, as Hardy writes, 'so suddenly that the soft parts of her person shook. Sue jumped aside in trepidation', and Arabella assures her, 'Lord, I am only a woman – not a six-foot sojer!' (Pt V, Ch. 2). Sue, who is not afraid of Jude because she can twist him into submission to her plan, is frightened by the 'soft parts' of the stronger, comfortably sexual female who caused her fall into sexual experience. Arabella does the same sort of exposure in the scene at the Great Wessex Agricultural Show (Pt V, Ch. 5) and later at the spring fair at Kennetbridge (Pt V, Chs 7 and 8).

In a book called *Darwin and the Naked Lady*, Alex Comfort discusses a long history of fiction in which characters find their lover's chains (both literally and figuratively) more attractive than their bodies, and romantically heroic death becomes the climactic fulfilment of love instead of sexual orgasm.[10] Hardy's Jude and Sue are variants of this. In one of those typical intimate encounters with a window-sill between them, Sue expresses directly her fascination for Jude as the tragic and heroic sufferer: 'You are Joseph the dreamer of dreams, dear Jude. And a tragic Don Quixote. And sometimes you are St Stephen, who, while they were stoning him, could see Heaven opened. O my poor friend and comrade, you'll suffer yet!' (Pt IV, Ch. 1).

Arabella persistently and consistently reminds us of life outside and beyond the scope of those rigidly narrow and deeply destructive patterns followed by Jude and Sue who, in their efforts to rise above what they see as common life, never recognize that the idealistic code of values and behaviour which they tenaciously cling to is part of that system which drives them to mutual self-destruction. And because their struggles strike a chord in us as readers, we also need Arabella and those like her to remind us of that other, more sensually based and satisfying reality.[11]

Arabella gets the last word in the novel, observing to Widow Edlin that Sue won't find peace until she is where Jude is now; that is, dead. Thus she confirms that Jude and Sue fit into Alex Comfort's analysis. However, her most telling and Panzaic commentary occurs earlier. When Jude returns from his last encounter with Sue weak and soaked with rain and announces that he meant to kill himself with this one last gesture, Arabella says in shocked surprise, 'Well, I'm blest! Kill yourself for a woman.' After Jude's Quixotic explanation (his wish to see Sue once more then to die) Arabella can only marvel at the absurdity of it. 'Lord – you do talk lofty!' she replies, and she suggests that Jude have something warm to drink as a practical measure to avoid the chills (Pt VI, Ch. 9).

In this way, throughout the novel, Arabella brings into blinding relief the sheer horror of what Jude and Sue do to themselves and to each other, and thereby she helps to destroy the 'crystalline orb of the ideal'. This, in turn, indicates the great importance of this novel for the present since we, as a society, have refined the processes even beyond those of Jude and Sue. According to Lawrence's evaluative terms, *Jude the Obscure* must be a great novel because it hurts. It certainly shows us how not to live, and it makes us see what we are up against more clearly than we could see it without Arabella.

Notes

1. D. H. Lawrence, *Phoenix: The Posthumous Papers of D. H. Lawrence*, ed. Edward D. McDonald (London: William Heinemann, 1936) pp. 759–60.
2. D. H. Lawrence, 'Morality and the Novel', in *Phoenix: The Posthumous Papers of D. H. Lawrence*, pp. 532, 531.
3. See my '"The race for money and good things": *Far from the Madding Crowd'*, *The Thomas Hardy Year Book*, 21 (1995) 8–30, where I develop this position.
4. Florence Emily Hardy, *The Life of Thomas Hardy: 1840–1928* (London: Macmillan, 1962) pp. 176–7. Hardy is defending *The Mayor of Casterbridge* even before it is criticised.
5. Wayne Burns, 'Flesh and Spirit in *Jude the Obscure'*, *Recovering Literature*, vol. 1, no. 3 (1972) 5–21, and Rosemarie Morgan, *Women and Sexuality in the Novels of Thomas Hardy* (London: Routledge, 1988) both give extended treatment to Arabella and arrive at very different conclusions about her function in the novel. Other critics pass over her with brief comment or none at all. She gets only brief mention, mostly in dependent clauses, in *The Thomas Hardy Journal*, vol. XI, no. 3 (1995), which 'celebrat[es] the publication of' the novel 'a hundred years ago' (p. 8).
6. Thomas Hardy, *Jude the Obscure* (London: Macmillan, 1974) Pt I, Ch. 5. Future references will appear in parentheses as Pt and Ch. after quotations or groups of quotations.
7. Mary Jacobus, 'Sue the Obscure', *Essays in Criticism*, XXV (1975) 304–28, simply asserts that it is a 'fake pregnancy' (p. 308). Penny Boumelha, *Thomas Hardy and Women: Sexual Ideology and Narrative Form* (Brighton: Harvester, 1982) offers two possibilities: either Vilbert advises her to 'pretend to be pregnant' or he gives her some 'female pills', which she writes, without providing a source, was 'a widely-understood euphemism for abortifacients' (p. 152). And in her World's Classics edition of the novel (Oxford: Oxford University Press, 1985) Patricia Ingham also offers this latter solution: 'possibly meaning she had obtained abortifacient "female pills", and so doubly deceives Jude' (p. 436). This seems to me to be an unwillingness to allow Arabella her full human dimension as a character, as a young working-class girl without extensive knowledge of human reproduction. In fact, I suspect that even middle-class girls were less worldly wise than these assertions imply.
8. As an indication of Jude's eagerness to get Arabella into bed, he ignores the danger of Arabella's offer to go to Marygreen with him to visit his Aunt Drusilla who is ill, especially when we remember that Sue is also likely to be visiting Drusilla.
9. Wayne Burns, *The Panzaic Principle* (Vancouver, 1965), reprinted in *Recovering Literature* (Spring, 1976), reprinted in William K. Buckley, *Sense Tender: Recovering the Novel for the Reader* (New York: Peter Lang, 1989).

10.   Alex Comfort, 'The Rape of Andromeda', in *Darwin and the Naked Lady: Discursive Essays on Biology and Art* (London: Routledge & Kegan Paul, 1961) pp. 74–99.
11.   Widow Edlin in a smaller role adds to this Panzaic function, reminding us of other less disastrous lives and values. Her comments on marriage are particularly pertinent. See Pt V, Ch. 4 and Pt VI, Ch. 9.

4

HARDY Promises: *The Dynasts* and the Epic of Imperialism

CHARLES LOCK

But old Laws operate yet; and phase and phase
Of men's dynastic and imperial moils
Shape on accustomed lines.[1]

Some eight years of concentrated composition (*c.*1900–1908),[2] by a writer at the height of his power and ambition, formed the culmination to a fascination with the Napoleonic Wars which Hardy had lived with, tended and nurtured his entire life. Reading in typescript the first volume of Florence Hardy's biography, *The Early Life of Thomas Hardy*, Sir James Barrie commented: '*the* most striking thing in the book is that all his life he was preparing, getting ready, for his *Dynasts*, chopping his way through time to the great event'.[3] *The Dynasts* was evidently intended by Hardy to set a crown upon his lifetime's effort, and it has no less evidently failed.

Proper evaluation might begin with the assumption, the act of faith, even, that *The Dynasts* is and ought to be Hardy's greatest work. That it is not generally recognized as such may have something to do with its similarities to other great and ambitious works of the early twentieth century, works such as Pound's *Cantos* (1925–69), David Jones's *In Parenthesis* (1937), Joyce's *Finnegans Wake* (1939) or the six-volume poem by Hardy's near-contemporary C. M. Doughty (1843–1926), *The Dawn in Britain*, published in 1906, the same year as the second volume of *The Dynasts*. Such works as these may share more than bulk, density and difficulty of access.[4] *The Dynasts* has sometimes been invoked along with *The Cantos* as virtual proof that modern epic is an impossibility, that the most one can hope for is a noble or splendid failure. Thus the perceived failure of *The Dynasts* as a formal structure can be justified by reference to Pound's confession 'I cannot make it cohere' (Canto CXVI), itself an echo of Donne's "Tis all in pieces, all coherence gone.' If one finds oneself making a fresh attempt to vindicate the project of *The Dynasts*, as a modernist text that measures itself against classical precedent, and is not entirely dwarfed thereby, such a move is not unrelated to a recent event in literary history: the publication in 1990 of Derek Walcott's *Omeros*, controlled, ordered, shaped, polished, not unworthy of the most august comparison. Walcott's epic has exposed one of the great alibis of modernism, the necessity of incoherence, fragmentation – 'These fragments I have shored against my ruins' – the inevitability of falling short.

In considering *The Dynasts* in terms of imperial epic, I do not propose any form of allegorical reading, by which one might show how the epic of the Napoleonic Wars can be interpreted in terms of the Edwardian sense of the power and imminent decline of the British Empire. Such an allegorical reading is certainly possible – and would be no more far-fetched than Christopher Hill's reading of *Paradise Lost* as an allegory of the English Civil War. Indeed, such allegorization is constitutive of the reception, tradition and prestige of the epic. We cannot read the *Aeneid* innocent of the fact that Virgil's task, in telling the story of the founding of Rome, was to glorify the modern emperor, Augustus.

Every epic invents or retells a past which both justifies and lends glory to the present. That much was understood by Harley Granville-Barker in his dramatization of scenes from *The Dynasts* during the First World War, and by John Maynard Keynes's invocation of *The Dynasts* as apposite to the Paris Peace Conference:

> The proceedings of Paris all had this air of extraordinary importance and unimportance at the same time. The decisions seemed charged with consequences to the future of human society; yet ... one felt most strongly the impression, described by Tolstoy in *War and Peace* or by Hardy in *The Dynasts*, of events marching on to their fated conclusion uninfluenced and unaffected by the cerebrations of Statesmen in Council.[5]

Remarkably among epics, and characteristic of a dependence on historical records rather than on myth, legend and oral report, *The Dynasts* is so steeped in the documents of the age it represents that it contains hardly one anachronism to remind the reader of the twenti-

eth century. (As a work of historical literature, its documentary
saturation creates an exceptional sense of lexical homogeneity.)

One hint, however, is dropped with the force of an invitation, in
Part Second, when, after the division of Europe has been settled
with Tsar Alexander I on a raft in the middle of the river Niemen,
at Tilsit, Napoleon flirts with Queen Louisa of Prussia, whose
nation has just been signed into non-existence:

QUEEN:	I had no zeal to meet you, sire, alas!
NAPOLÉON	(after a silence):
	And how at Memel do you sport with time?
QUEEN:	Sport? I! I pore on musty chronicles,
	And muse on usurpations long forgot,
	And other historied dramas of high wrong!
NAPOLÉON:	Why con not annals of your own rich age?
	They treasure acts well fit for pondering.
QUEEN:	I am reminded too much of my age
	By having had to live in it.

> (Part Second, I, viii, 130–8;
> Hynes, IV, 229)

It was of course Hardy, rather than any historic personage of
Napoleonic or Edwardian times, who had been poring on musty
chronicles in the British Museum, and was devoting his life's work
to events that took place before his life began. Another, rather more
subtle hint of a bridge to the present is to be found earlier in the
same Act, when the Chorus of Ironic Spirits contemplates the plight
of Napoleon after the defeat of Trafalgar:

> This, O this is the cramp that grips!
> And freezes the Emperor's finger-tips
> From signing a peace with the Land of Ships.
>
> The Universal-empire plot
> Demands the rule of that wave-walled spot;
> And peace with England cometh not!
> > (Part Second, I, vi, 63–8;
> > Hynes, IV, 216–17)

The first two lines of the latter tercet manage to allude both to
the literariness of Empire and to the present Edwardian age. The

'Universal-empire plot' is the plot of epic: imperialism, by the definition of all its exemplars and by the logic of all its ideologues and poet-praisers, must aspire to the global, the universal. That is the plot of its narrative, which is also the plot of epic. Alexander the Great understood both poles of the tension: the logic of Empire, that 'Heaven cannot brook two suns, nor earth two masters'; and the logic of plot: his dread of lacking new worlds to conquer is a dread of narrative foreclosure.

The limits of Empire are set by ignorance, and imperialism has always found justification by its expansion into the unknown, which is an expansion of the known – the opening up, in typical phrase, of the dark continent. And even England is unknown to the French, in that an enemy, 'known' or identified, evades the only sort of knowledge recognized by Empire – knowledge from the centre, by internal assimilation. Napoleon's need to conquer England – rather than merely to make peace – is not a matter of strategy or geopolitics: a peace-settlement might have been the wiser strategy. What drives Napoleon is the plot of Universal Empire, a plot which has already been scripted, by Homer, Virgil, Milton. And the most remarkable part of this Chorus is the ambiguity of the 'Hebrew genitive' – 'the rule of that wave-walled spot' – which, through translations of the Old Testament in the sixteenth century, gives to modern English phrases of the form, 'the age of reason' or 'the rule of law'. If one sets 'the rule of law' alongside 'the rule of that wave-walled spot' one sees the radical, polarizing ambiguity: either rule over England, or rule by England. In the one hundred years between 1807 and 1906 the Universal-empire plot had unfolded itself, and unfolded the ambiguities of that phrase, from Napoleon as frustrated Emperor to the unchallenged rule of the British Empire.

One outstanding task for Hardy scholarship is to consider what sort of political and imperial nexus is constituted by the names of those with whom Hardy was pleased to be invited to various gatherings and soirées, names that he found worthy of assiduous recording. How much must Hardy have been reminded of his own age at such parties as these:

[A]lso attending a most amusing masked ball at his friends Mr and Mrs Montagu Crackanthorpe's, where he and Henry James were the only two not in dominos, and were recklessly flirted with by the women in consequence; meeting at dinner here and there Mr and Mrs J. Chamberlain [Colonial Secretary, 1895–1903], Mr and Mrs Goschen [Chancellor of the Exchequer], the Speaker and Mrs Gully, the Russian Ambassador and Mme de Staal, Mr and Mrs Barrie, Lady Henry Somerset, Mr Astor, the Poet-Laureate, and others. ...[6]

Hardy appears to have met almost all the leading figures of British imperial policy, and of course enjoyed a close friendship with Rudyard Kipling.[7] Hardy's profoundly sympathetic relationship with T. E. Lawrence might be illuminated by detailed consideration of their views on imperialism.[8] Two important figures in late Victorian and Edwardian imperialism are, however, absent, neither mentioned in Hardy's correspondence nor listed among the guests at any function attended by Hardy: Cecil Rhodes and Lord Milner. While Rhodes is entirely absent, Milner enjoys a curious shadow-life as the name of the dog belonging to Florence Henniker, daughter of Baron Houghton. We have recently learned that in 1914 Florence Henniker wished to present to her namesake, the new Mrs Hardy, a puppy, 'the daughter of her two dogs – Milner & Empire – named Britannia. I must confess,' writes Florence Hardy, 'I was weak enough to feel that I wanted to have little Britannia, as a playmate for Wessex.' Wessex would have been much larger than little Britannia, and far more aggressive, indeed a threat to her very existence: even among pets a game of imperial allusion is being played and enjoyed. Florence Hardy adds: 'But my husband objected – quite wisely I am sure.[9] We shall return shortly to Lady Henniker's non-canine connections.

Hardy's *Life* is long on guest-lists and, to the frustration of every reader, very short on topics of discussion. What might Hardy and Henry James have said to one another in their undominoed distinction? And what interesting subjects might have been raised and broached at those house-parties? Topics, we can safely assume, quite as pertinent to public affairs as those discussions at the various balls and soirées in *The Dynasts*. There is, in everything written by Hardy, a devious artistry. Listen to this catalogue of guests:

From letters it can be gathered that at a dinner his historic sense was keenly appealed to by the Duchess of St. Albans taking a diamond pin from her neck and casually telling him it had been worn by Nell Gwynne; and that in May or June he paid a few

days' visit to Lord Curzon at Hackwood Park, where many of the
house-party, which included Lady Elcho, Mr and Mrs Charteris,
Sir J. and Lady Poynder, Lord Robert Cecil, Mr Haldane, Alfred
and Mrs Alfred Lyttleton, Mr and Mrs Rochfort Maguire, Lord
and Lady Cromer, Arthur Balfour, and Professor Walter Raleigh,
went into the wood by moonlight to listen to the nightingale, but
made such a babble of conversation that no nightingale ventured
to open his bill.[10]

With far less embarrassment and unease even than attends critical
neglect of *The Dynasts*, readers of Hardy freely dismiss or even
presume to apologize for such passages, amidst dark murmurings
of snobbery and the inferiority complex of a rustic autodidact.

Yet our neglect of these catalogues, and of their cunning artistry,
is, I would propose, intrinsically bound up with our inability to
appreciate *The Dynasts*. There is, first, Nell Gwynne's pin, worn naturally enough by the wife of Nell Gwynne's direct descendant: too
obvious, surely, to point out that Hardy's sense of history was
equally appealed to by the fact that Lord Curzon and his guests
were among those chiefly responsible for the Nation's destiny, subjects of the Universal-empire plot, filling some of the very same
political offices as Pitt and Fox and Sheridan a hundred years
before. At one level we can point to our continuing condescension
to the good little Thomas Hardy, whose fascination with local and
regional details and continuities – including his childhood memories of meeting veterans of Waterloo and the Peninsular Wars – we
are pleased to approve; by contrast, we look with disdain and
unease on Hardy's equal fascination with national and international patterns and intrigues, preferring that they be addressed by
educated and metropolitan writers – Byron, Carlyle, or Thackeray.
There survives even now a regrettable consensus that Hardy is at
his best and most authentic when writing about and speaking for
shepherds and rustics, as an early reviewer protested when Hardy
first dared to stray outside that 'Wessex' which remains both his
kingdom and his prison.

There is another level at which we fail to read Hardy to the
measure of his artistry. Let us treat the description of Lord
Curzon's house-party as a literary text. The guests – all those
famous names held in a subordinate clause – went into the wood
by moonlight to listen to the nightingale. 'The' nightingale is the
conventional, hackneyed phrase (we are at Hackwood): we do not

listen to nightingales, nor wonder whether we might be fortunate enough to hear *a* nightingale. The conventional phrase of the guests is met in response by the poet assuming knowledge of the nightingale's intention, through pathetic fallacy: 'such a babble ... that no nightingale ventured to open his bill'. The poet thus assumes an intimacy with the bird which he does not claim at all with his fellow-guests; an intimacy, and a preference, for he would, it seems, rather hear the bird's song than listen to their 'babble'.

We might recall the last sentence of *Under the Greenwood Tree*: '"O, 'tis the nightingale," murmured she, and thought of a secret she would never tell.' Nightingales traditionally go with secrets, or sing in their stead. Ovid's Philomel declares a secret, that Procne's tongue has been cut out so that she cannot speak of her rape by Tereus. When Fancy Day, on hearing the nightingale, decides not to tell her secret, she might be said to have 'bitten her tongue': the nightingale was renowned in antiquity for lacking the tip of its tongue.[11]

If we think of the rooting-out of the tongue – as in *Titus Andronicus* and *Cymbeline*, both with specific reference to Philomel – we will understand why Hardy's apparently pedestrian paragraph opened not at Lord Curzon's party but at another, a party at which a duchess removed a diamond pin from her neck. In our frustration at what is not disclosed by Hardy's narrative, we might realize that the nightingale who would not sing because of the babble of the guests is not singing in order to keep a secret, but rather because from such guests no secrets could be kept. In the narrative of the moonlight walk our poet observes (in both senses) the silence of the nightingale: he will not divulge to the babbling mass of readers the topic of conversation, affairs of state, presumably, even state secrets. The poet merely twitters, and distracts us with lists of names. The nightingale has of course been a figure of the poet since Homer and Callimachus – as celebrated in Cory's version of 1858: 'They told me, Heraclitus, they told me you were dead. ... Still are thy pleasant voices, thy nightingales, awake, / For Death he taketh all away, but them he cannot take.' The nightingale is a figure of the poet both in his songs and in his secrets: a secret she would never tell: he resolves to say no more.

To put such weight, such allusive literary implication on the account of Lord Curzon's house-party is not, I trust, a strain. What is far-fetched is our refusal to consider what function in a writer's life, in the *Life* of a writer, those parties and guest-lists might serve. Our lack of interest in, or actual discomfort at, Hardy's self-presentation of the poet among aristocrats and statesmen is matched by our reading and slighting of *The Dynasts*, in which we celebrate 'the Wessex scenes' and the 'lyrics' (often celebrating them by anthologizing, which is akin to cutting out the tongue of the work from its unmusical body); we may look in *The Dynasts* for signs of our author's philosophy, but we ignore the explicit theme, international politics, military strategy, European history, all that fascinated Hardy about the Napoleonic era, and all that surely made conversation at those house-parties so engaging and resonant to Hardy: in the silence of Max Gate he was, after all, not short of opportunities to listen to the nightingale.[12]

The central theme of *The Dynasts* is of course power: *dynast* is a word cognate with *dynamic*. *Dynamo* had entered English in 1882 as a short form of the 'dynamo-electric machine' invented by Siemens in 1867, the same year in which the Swedish physicist Alfred Nobel chose to name his new explosive *dynamite*. The *Oxford English Dictionary* records the first figurative or transferred sense of *dynamo* in 1892, when Meredith writes of 'his whirring dynamo of a brain'. These new words and usages form part of the lexical context of Hardy's title. It is worth also pointing out the contemporaneous significance of *dynamo* to Henry Adams (1838–1918) in whose speculative scheme history is played out between the Virgin and the Dynamo: *Mont-Saint-Michel and Chartres* was privately issued in 1904, published in 1907; *The Education of Henry Adams* was privately issued in 1907, and published posthumously in 1918.[13]

Hardy claimed that he had taken his title from quite another source, far removed from the neologisms of technology, the *Magnificat*: 'he hath put down the mighty from their seats, and exalted them of low degree' (Luke 1:52). This allusion is first made explicit by Hardy in a letter to Reginald Bosworth Smith (son of the rector of West Stafford), a classical scholar who had asked Hardy, after reading the first two parts of *The Dynasts*, whether his title had been taken from the opening speech of Aeschylus' *Agamemnon*:

> This year-long watch … I keep,
> Marking the confluence of nightly stars;
> And those bright potentates [δυναστται] who bring to men
> Winter and summer, signal in the sky,
> Both in their wane I view and when they rise.[14]

Hardy's reply to Bosworth Smith, of 20 February 1906, is character-istically oblique:

> I do not quite remember what first suggested the title (which, by the way, Lord Rosebery writes to day to tell me is the only part of the book that he does not like.) [Lord Rosebery, by the way, had been Foreign Secretary and Prime Minister in the 1890s; he was an ardent imperialist, and a historical writer whose books included *Pitt* (1891) and *Napoleon: The Last Phase* (1900). Rosebery's daughter was married to Florence Henniker's brother, Lord Crewe.]¹⁵ I imagine that the passage you refer to in the *Agamemnon* about the stars to be the watchman's speech in the opening lines. I was not thinking of that, however, but rather of where the word δυναστασ occurs in the *Magnificat* – "He hath cast down the dynasts from their thrones", or as we have it in our translation, "the mighty from their seat [*sic*]" (I used to read the Gk. Testt in my younger & theological days.)¹⁶

Hardy's title, despite this explanation, remains problematic, for in English *dynasty* denotes a succession of kings or rulers, and in any one dynasty there can be, at one time, only one dynast. Usage does not permit successive rulers of a dynasty to be known collec-tively as 'dynasts'. It may have been the plural of Hardy's title which, not being in accord with usage, displeased Lord Rosebery; usage may itself have followed the decision of the earliest English translators of the New Testament (including Wycliffe and Tyndale) to render δυνασται by 'the mighty' – and of the early translators of the *Agamemnon* by 'potentates'¹⁷ – rather than by the anglicized form, *dynasts*.

There is of course a dynastic theme to *The Dynasts*, but it is restricted to the one dynast and his desire for an heir through whom to establish a dynasty.¹⁸ As we shall see, that desire provides an opportunity for unheroic behaviour not unmatched among the heroes of epic. Napoleon must divorce his beloved Josephine, 'to null this sterile marriage' and then 'solve the question of my dynasty'. When in 1814 Napoleon entrusts his new wife Marie-Louise and their son the King of Rome to the protection of his sol-diers, the officers respond: 'We promise. May the dynasty live forever!' (Part Third, IV, ii, 44; Hynes V, 101). This is one of the few occurrences of *dynasty*, *dynast* or *dynastic* in the entire text of *The Dynasts*. In each instance *dynast* or *dynasty* bears the conventional sense. Only in the After Scene to Part Third is the exact title-word found within the text, when the Semi-Chorus of the Pities sings a sort of metrical paraphrase of the *Magnificat*:

> To Thee whose eye all Nature owns,
> Who hurlest Dynasts from their thrones,
> And liftest those of low estate
> We sing, with Her men consecrate!

The published text (though not Hynes's edition, V, 252) gives at this point Hardy's footnote, the citation of Luke 1:52 in Greek. Part Third was published in February 1908, but in that first edition there was no footnote, nor is one to be found in either the reprint of 1910 or in the one-volume edition of that same year. The footnote first appears in the reprint of the one-volume edition, dated 1915 but actually of 1914.[19] Thus we learn that it was only in 1914 that Hardy decided to make public the source of his title, which he had divulged to Bosworth Smith almost ten years earlier.

As from 1914, then, the Chorus of the Pities alludes to the *Magnificat* and prays that all dynasts will be overthrown: this was a suitable hope for 1914, and we have numerous expressions of pious patriotism on Hardy's part after the outbreak of the War. Hardy later remarked that he would not have ended *The Dynasts* on such a cheerful note if he had foreseen the outbreak of the Great War. Instead of rewriting the final chorus, or tampering with the text in any way, Hardy inserted a mirror beneath the text, subjoining a glimmer of hope by way of a footnote. The footnote should perplex the alert reader, who might be sent by reaction to the *Agamemnon*. For if there is no conscious Will, let alone God, who is responsible for overthrowing the dynasts? 'Thee' is the only apostrophized figure in all the discourse of the Spirits, for the Will, as 'It', cannot be addressed in the second person. This 'Thee', whose eye owns all nature, is the benevolent conscious God whom only the Pities can invoke. However, if the Pities truly believed in this 'Thee', they would hardly care whether or not the Will were conscious.

If we turn for guidance not to the *Magnificat* but to Aeschylus, we see the dynasts not as the great and powerful men of the day, but as 'Spirits' themselves, those 'bright potentates' of the sky, 'the Overworld'. We have already noted the mechanistic associations of dynamo circa 1900, and we need only link those to the *deus ex machina* of classical stagecraft to understand Fate, Destiny, the Will and the Spirits in terms of a machine, a dynamo, dynasts. The Will, in so far as its consciousness is still unfolding – so the Chorus of the Pities prays: 'Nay; – shall not Its blindness break? / Yea, must not Its heart awake' (After Scene, 95–6; Hynes, V, 255) – is a machine: the possibility of a machine acquiring consciousness has long been a theme of intellectual and scientific speculation.

If we pursue this mechanistic sense of *Dynasts* – the one most plausibly plural – we need no longer be concerned with Napoleon's establishing of a dynasty, nor with Lord Rosebery need we be troubled by the title. We should instead attend to the functioning of celestial machinery, and to the shift from *dynamo* to *dynast*. These two words, from one root, neatly divide over the phenomenon of consciousness. A dynamo is unconscious; a dynast is conscious: two forms of power, and two figures of power. We must now look more closely at the last line of the already-cited quatrain:

> To Thee whose eye all Nature owns,
> Who hurlest Dynasts from their thrones,
> And liftest those of low estate
> We sing, with Her men consecrate!

Who is this 'Her' – whom we have consecrated – who sings with us 'to Thee'? Not, surely, the Virgin Mary, though in this context, and with the footnote of 1914, her shadow at least is near. One of the muses, or Nature? Or the female principle which can oppose or resist the masculine or neutral machinery of the Will? We are close to Henry Adams's tension between the Virgin and the Dynamo. Like Goethe, Adams draws on the tradition of the Virgin Mary as a version or manifestation of Athene, and the revision of that tradition at the end of Goethe's *Faust*: *das ewige Weiblichheit zieht uns hinan* (the eternal feminine draws us on). Adams writes of the tradition of the virgin goddess: 'She was Goddess because of her force; she was the animated dynamo.'[20]

Without exception, the Spirits of the Overworld are without gender, while the Will is always referred to by the uppercase neutral 'It'. The phrase 'with Her men consecrate' is (apart from the apostrophized 'Thee') the only other uppercase personification in the entire text, and the single feminine personification. 'Her', then, is the invisible, intangible, immaterial, perhaps non-existent tendency that, if it must be named at all, might be named consciousness – that which is in itself no thing but which might one day inform the Will:

> Consciousness the Will informing, till It fashion all things fair!
> (After Scene, 110;
> Hynes, V, 255)

The 'It' here cannot be consciousness – which would be 'She' – but the Will. Only the Will can act or fashion; She merely 'informs'. The Virgin is thus to be reconciled with the Dynamo, and the machine is one day to become conscious. It has often been remarked that there are no heroes in *The Dynasts*: it may be that there are no dynasts either, but only dynamos.

Hardy is recorded as having met Henry Adams just once, at another house-party, in 1895, just before the publication of *Jude the Obscure*.[21] We do not, of course, know what they talked about: it was the nightingale, again. But their host was Lord Curzon, who had leased Reigate Priory from Lady Henry Somerset. Again, we are among potentates: Lord Curzon was then Under-Secretary for Foreign Affairs and would shortly be appointed Viceroy of India. At such gatherings, of writers and politicians, intellectuals and statesmen, there was every opportunity for Consciousness to meditate on Will.

Imperialism is not only the common theme of epic; it is its very constitution. As the *Aeneid* tells of the founding of the Roman Empire, so *The Dynasts* tells of those quite recent events which have led – in the words of Napoleon to Queen Louisa – to 'our own rich age'. Epic usually narrates events at a considerable distance in time – historic, heroic or mythological time – and the temporal gap between the events narrated and the time of narration is bridged in and by the very act of telling the story. Most famously in the *Aeneid*, this is achieved through the prophecy of Book VI in which the far-distant consequences of Aeneas' deed of founding are made manifest, with the purpose of encouraging the hero:

> Now fix your sight, and stand intent, to see
> Your Roman race, and Julian progeny.
> The mighty Caesar waits his vital hour. ...
> Augustus promised long and long foretold,
> Sent to the realm that Saturn ruled of old,
> Born to restore a better age of gold.[22]

It is appropriate to cite Virgil in Dryden's English, 'that translation which Hardy's remarkable mother gave to her son when he was eight years old', in the words of Donald Davie.[23]

Davie's argument in 'Hardy's Virgilian Purples' is for a reading of Hardy's poetry on the assumption that it was shaped by a profound love and knowledge of classical poetry:

> We must stop thinking of [Hardy's] classicism as no more than skin-deep, or as (worse still) the pathetic pretentiousness of the self-educated. ... we are determined to condescend to Hardy ... [yet] biographers have exploded all notions of sturdy simplicity. What they have shown ... is that Hardy ... was a remarkably devious and tortuous man – just the sort of man who would at once convey and cloak his meanings with allusive deviousness. (pp. 142, 151)

Davie goes on to make his claim for the 'Virgilianism' of Hardy through a reading of the 'Poems of 1912–13' and their epigraph *Veteris vestigiae flammae*, from *Aeneid* IV, 23. Yet in his broader argument Davie fails to adduce a most singular and compelling piece of evidence. The epigraph to *The Dynasts* reads: *Desine fata Deûm flecti sperare precando*, from *Aeneid* VI, 376: 'cease to hope that fate and the Gods are moved by prayers' or, in Dryden's words (VI, 572), 'Fate and the dooming gods are deaf to tears.'

This epigraph is a most extraordinary afterthought, pulling in the opposite direction to the late-thought footnote of 1914. In no printing of *The Dynasts* until 1927 does the epigraph appear, and then in a special limited edition of 500 copies signed by the author. It is just one of many touches in Hardy's preparation of his image for posterity and immortality.[24] On 8 May 1927 Hardy wrote to Sir Frederick Macmillan:

> If they have not yet printed the titlepage I think I should like to insert an additional short quotation to improve its appearance. Perhaps you can send me a proof of the page, that I may write in the quotation. If however they have done with it, the matter is not important.[25]

For *Magnificat*, read *Agamemnon*. For 'not important', read 'of the utmost significance'.

The Virgilian epigraph points us, first, to the unworthiness, the helplessness, of the main characters. Even if none of them is shown to be a dynast, a true potentate, we might still expect to see the representation of a hero, or of heroic deeds. Napoleon, though obviously the protagonist, is far from heroic, and even Nelson's heroism is muted in this presentation.[26] In 1921 Hardy received a letter from the well-known eccentric, classicist, historian and Eton master, Oscar Browning, who protested that *The Dynasts*

> does not give to the man who must be the central character in that period the position which in my opinion he ought to have. ... To me Napoleon is the greatest man who ever lived in the world except, or shall we say, after Julius Caesar and the best man that ever lived in the world after Jesus Christ. He was sent by God into the world to set it in order. ... the Waterloo campaign was a crime.[27]

Had Oscar Browning written *The Dynasts*, we should have had in Napoleon a hero of some stature. Instead we find a protagonist who comes to discover only his own powerlessness, whose culminating anagnorisis is the recognition that he had never been a true protagonist, but had had only the appearance, filled the role, served the function of a hero. Napoleon regrets that he had not died young, at the height of his power and prestige, yet this regret only increases the reader's sense of how understated in *The Dynasts* is the heroism of Nelson, whose death is surely the best-timed in all English history.

Napoleon catches the words of the Spirit of the Years, whom he cannot see:

> Thus, to this last,
> The Will in thee has moved thee, Bonaparte,
> As we say now.

NAPOLÉON:

> Whose frigid tones are those,
> Breaking upon my lurid loneliness
> So brusquely? ... Yet, 'tis true, I have ever known
> That such a Will I passively obeyed!
>   (Part Third, VII, ix, 7–12;
>   Hynes, V, 247–8)

The ambivalence that has always attended evaluations of Aeneas – especially for his treatment of Dido – is the model for the representation of Napoleon. Each is clearly the protagonist; each treats his wife with less than heroic dignity; and both excuse their behaviour with the recognition that they are destined to fulfil the commands of the gods, even at the expense of their virtue, of the very quality of heroism. Aeneas tells Dido that he must be moving on:

> This, only let me speak in my Defence ...
> For if indulgent Heav'n would leave me free,
> And not submit my Life to Fate's Decree,
> My Choice would lead me to the *Trojan* Shore. ...
> But now the *Delphian Oracle* Commands,
> And Fate invites me to the *Latian* Lands.
> That is the promis'd Place to which I steer,
> And all my Vows are terminated there.[28]

Let us listen now to Napoleon explaining himself to his wife:

> And selfish 'tis in my good Joséphine
> To blind her vision to the weal of France,
> And this great Empire's solidarity. ...
>
>   Nay, nay!
> You know, my comrade, how I love you still. ...
>
> Come, dwell not gloomily on this cold need
> Of waiving private joy for policy.
> We are but thistle-globes on Heaven's high gales,
> And whither blown, or when, or how, or why,
> Can choose us not at all!
>   (Part Second, II, vi, 59–61, 67–8, 146–50;
>   Hynes, IV, 260–3)

One could cite many more parallels, including those between Hardy's Spirits and Virgil's gods, who share their frustration at their impotence to bring about their desires on earth, or to realize their vision of human society.

Mortals show themselves in both epics to be as deaf to the pleas of the gods as the gods are to mortals' prayers. One's sense that Hardy's chosen epigraph should be thus reversed is endorsed by the fact that an expression of such a reversal was on Hardy's mind just a few months later:

> As it grew dusk, after a long musing silence, he asked his wife to repeat to him a verse from the *Rubáiyát of Omar Khayyám*, beginning
>
> > Oh, Thou, who Man of baser Earth –
>
> She took his copy of this work from his bedside and read to him:
>
> > Oh, Thou, who Man of baser Earth didst make,
> > And ev'n with Paradise devise the Snake:
> >   For all the Sin wherewith the Face of Man
> > Is blacken'd – Man's forgiveness give – and take!
>
> He indicated that he wished no more to be read. ... Shortly after nine he died.[29]

One cannot resist citing here a note penned by Hardy and preserved in the *Life*: 'January (1899) – No man's poetry can be truly judged till its last line is written. What is the last line? The death of the poet.'[30]

The Virgilian presence in *The Dynasts* can be traced far back in Hardy's life, to that moment when a mother made a gift to her son. This is how that deed was recalled and acknowledged some seventy years later in Hardy's drafting of *Life and Work*:

> 1848. First School. ... Here [at the village school in Lower Bockhampton] he worked at Walkingame's *Arithmetic* and at geography, in both of which he excelled, though his handwriting was indifferent. About this time his mother gave him Dryden's *Virgil*, Johnson's *Rasselas*, and *Paul and Virginia*. He also found in a closet *A History of the Wars* – a periodical in loose numbers of the war with Napoleon, which his grandfather had subscribed to at the time, having been himself a volunteer. The torn pages of these contemporary numbers with their melodramatic prints of serried ranks, crossed bayonets, huge knapsacks, and dead bodies, were the first to set him on the train of ideas that led to *The Trumpet-Major* and *The Dynasts*.[31]

Again, we must admire the artistry, a deviousness without which we might gasp at the presumption implied. Young Tom is given the Classics, imposed from above by the authority of a parent. By contrast, found in a closet, loose numbers, torn pages, ragged things but one's own – local, personal, intimate – that which will serve as resistance to and modification of the Classic. Even the grandfather becomes the object of riddling, for a subscriber and a volunteer invoke most pressingly a third term, conscription. Is Hardy a volunteer or a conscript in the Virgilian ranks? And the paragraph concludes with a statement of the obvious – that his early interest in the Napoleonic Wars led him to write two books on the theme – which leaves unstated the irrefutable: that it was the *Aeneid* that gave Hardy the idea of writing an epic, and that the war with Napoleon was any old theme, found in a closet.

The Virgilian epigraph has been incorporated into the main title-page of every edition of *The Dynasts* since 1927, with the exception of Harold Orel's New Wessex edition of 1978. On sound editorial principles, this edition is based on the text of the Mellstock edition of 1919–20, the last version of *The Dynasts* which Hardy had seen through the press in its entirely. As if to make up for almost twenty years of suppression, in the Oxford edition (1995) the epigraph is placed – without any precedent – on the title-page of each of the three parts: thus it insists on our notice.[32]

One of the very few notebooks which Hardy did not destroy dates from 1867, some sixty years before Hardy's last amendment to the text of *The Dynasts*. We find as note 88 of the '1867 Notebook' a series of phrases from Dryden's *Aeneis*; 88e reads: 'The *dooming* gods: the *inhuman* coast:' two phrases separated in Book VI (ll. 512–15) by two lines:

> Fate, and the dooming Gods, are deaf to Tears.
> This Comfort of thy dire Misfortune take;
> The Wrath of Heav'n, inflicted for thy sake,
> With Vengeance shall pursue th' inhumane Coast.

Björk helpfully adds: 'The first line only is marked in Hardy's copy.'[33]

That which Hardy had first read as a schoolboy, from which he copied extracts in his twenties – and used in his own early poetry, for the 'dooming Gods' cited in 1867 are not far from the 'purblind

Doomsters' of 'Hap' (1866) – a book which he kept throughout his life and which now forms part of the Memorial Collection in the Dorset County Museum: from this volume Hardy wished to take one line, in its Latin original, to add as a second epigraph to the title-page of *The Dynasts* – 'an additional short quotation to improve its appearance'.

How are we to receive such an explanation? To improve the appearance of the title-page in terms of its layout? To add, with some words in Latin, the appearance of learning to a text that might otherwise seem frivolous? No: this epigraph is the close and cap of his life's work, the very last editorial amendment to be published in Hardy's lifetime, for the 1927 edition of *The Dynasts* was the last of his publications that he would see and hold. On 30 November 1927, six weeks before his death, Hardy wrote to Sir Frederick:

> My dear Macmillan:
>   I am delighted to receive the two copies of The Dynasts. There was great excitement here when they came, & they are all that I expected. ... I notice that you have embodied all the latest corrections.[34]

And the latest of all those corrections is a supplementary text, a quotation of such density that we can trace it back through eighty years, a Virgilian signature.

Hardy's life as a writer begins and ends with Virgil: his mother determined its beginning, and Hardy's Virgilian quotation adds the final touch, closes the circle, improves the appearance of a career, lending to a life that might be mistaken for that of a provincial writer, inspired only by locality and family, a classical sense of symmetry, purpose, destiny. Lawrence Lipking has studied the ways in which poets shape their careers:

> The idea that poets share a peculiar destiny was not invented ... by Virgil. But no other poet has ever done more to define it. Right from the start Virgil has been famous for knowing above all others how to cultivate his gifts. ... What he created, at last, was something larger than poems. ... His master-creation was the sense of an inevitable destiny: his life as a poet.
>   The poet who lives with such a responsibility has only one way to meet it: planning ahead. To husband a destiny ... one must be able to think in terms of decades, perhaps generations. The plot,

structure, characters, themes of an epic project will precede its concrete realization by a span of years. Virgil spent his life preparing the *Aeneid*.[35]

Such words recall J. M. Barrie's response: 'all his life he was preparing, getting ready, for his *Dynasts*'.

We should also note the cunning in Hardy's modest disclaimers about how he composed poetry, devising 'skeleton stanzas' into which he would, like a brick-maker, insert words or syllables. Not that this is not how Hardy composed: the evidence remains in the extant drafts of Part Third of *The Dynasts*, of Hardy's compositional technique which he named 'blocking-in'. He would write out the words in prose of a parliamentary speech, or of a general's address to his commanding officers, and would then arrange those same words, with minimal changes, as blank verse. The surviving pages (consisting of the first four acts of Part Third) bear annotations on the process itself, in Hardy's own hand: 'Rough draft (written as "blocking in")' or 'Rough Draft (jotted on "Blocking in")'.[36] This method has attracted a predictable share of critical disdain, and has sometimes been invoked to explain the tired and wooden effect of much of the verse in *The Dynasts*.[37]

As a rustic, Hardy was a most consummate performer. His method of 'blocking-in' is not the desperate resort of a provincial autodidact, but a precise and laborious tribute to Virgil's own method as reported by Suetonius:

> After first preparing the draft of a prose *Aeneid* and dividing it into twelve books, he commenced to compose it bit by bit, just as he pleased, taking nothing in order. And lest he should retard an impulse, he left some parts unfinished, and propped up others with very light words, as it were, which he said in jest were inserted as scaffolding to sustain the work until solid columns should arrive.[38]

That Hardy's career had been modelled on that of Virgil was signalled by Hardy himself, in hints picked up by critics such as Davie. All that we have done here is to fill in certain details, and specifically to show how Hardy organized his life and work (and his *Life and Work*) so that Virgil's were the first words that he read, and the last words that he wrote for publication in his lifetime.

Such a pious *imitatio* in itself tells us little of Hardy's own project, but it may provide us with a key to understanding Hardy's distinctiveness, and specifically that of *The Dynasts*. Clearly, Hardy's elaborate negotiations with Virgil and the Virgilian inheritance in English poetry had other aims than to replicate the *Aeneid* in modern dress. Because Virgil defines the classical, he is the enduring model for those who would redefine and renegotiate classicism: Dante and T. S. Eliot come at once to mind. Hardy's distinctive approach to Virgil – what might by an optical figure be termed his angle of refraction – is, I shall argue, derived from that which Hardy most articulately disdained: his earlier practice as a novelist.[39]

The novel has been the most controversial of literary genres in modernity, championed by moderns as the new genre, the only one that has come into being since the classical age, the only genre to have escaped definition and prescription by Aristotle – and deplored by 'the Ancients' for the very same reasons. A great novelist does not give up novel-writing simply in order to go back to the classics, to revert to the Aristotelian genres. If he goes back to the classics, he goes armed with a weapon of which they know nothing. And so it is with *The Dynasts: An Epic-Drama ...*,[40] an epic which is not an epic, a drama which is not a drama, a text whose greatest imaginative vitality is (by every reader's account) in its stage-directions and 'dumb shows'.

The generic problem of *The Dynasts* was apparent to the earliest reviewers, if only because in the Preface to Part First, Hardy had gone out of his way to deny that there was a problem:

> Readers will read[il]y discern, too, that *The Dynasts* is intended simply for mental performance, and not for the stage. Some critics have averred that to declare a drama as being not for the stage is an announcement whose subject and predicate cancel each other. The question seems to be an unimportant matter of terminology.   (Hynes, IV, 8)[41]

Denying the offence before a suspicion has been voiced is the surest way to draw an accusation, and Hardy got what he wanted from the drama critic of *The Times*, A. B. Walkley (1855–1926), who understood immediately that Hardy was challenging Aristotle's foundational distinction between drama and narrative, dialogue and diegesis. Walkley was properly scandalized, and offered, through the columns of *The Times Literary Supplement*, to salvage *The Dynasts* as theatre by suggesting that it be performed as 'a puppet-show – or rather (for the perspective of vast crowds is best managed that way) a series of shadow pictures'.[42] To this suggestion, Hardy took the predicted exception, carefully ignoring Walkley's high praise of Hardy's dramatic method, praise articulated in terms of the absence of novelistic features and devices:

> he allows himself no passages of analysis, reverie, mere description, or other expedients of the novelist which are non-transferable to space of three dimensions.   (Hynes, V, 388)

Walkley has here paraphrased diegesis, the telling of what happens, which, as Aristotle affirmed, is characteristic of epic but must be absent from drama. Drama consists only of dialogue. Criticism of the novel has tended simply to extend the Aristotelian distinction, and to assume that the novel, like the epic, is a narrative mode in which dialogue may be present, but in which it will be contained within diegesis.

The Russian theorist Mikhaïl Bakhtin has, by contrast, argued that the novel is truly a new genre, and that it is composed of neither diegesis nor dialogue as they are found in epic or drama. The novel provides a radically new form of discourse, as exemplified, for Bakhtin, by Dostoevsky. Hardy had not the confidence in the novel as a literary genre, fit to rival drama or poetry, which has been generally acquired only in the twentieth century. Yet for all the lack of confidence which prompted Hardy to abandon fiction for poetry and *The Dynasts*, and despite all his published denigrations of fiction, notably his own, Hardy displays in *The Dynasts* a most astonishing freedom from Aristotelian constraints. His 'return' to poetry is not a surrender to the traditional genres, nor a renunciation of what the novel has made possible.[43]

Hardy's answer to Walkley is of a sharpness that has a life's thinking behind it. Taking the phrase from his own Preface – 'an unimportant matter of terminology' – which Walkley had disputed, Hardy arranges for Aristotle to be arraigned instead:

> The methods of a book and the methods of a play, which he [Walkley? Aristotle?] says are so different, are fundamentally similar. It must be remembered that the printed story is not a representation, but, like the printed play, a means of producing

a representation, which is done in the one case by sheer imaginativeness, in the other by imaginativeness pieced out with
material helps.   (Hynes, V, 390–1)

This is a radical contribution to the debate about literary genre that
has continued since Aristotle. To the latter, diegesis is telling, dialogue is showing; and that distinction between telling and showing,
between narration and representation, has been commonly invoked
by novelists such as James, Conrad and Lawrence. The two modes
are distinct, and irreducibly so: there would seem to be no possibility of a text that can be classified neither as dialogue nor as diegesis.
Nor can we posit the function of a text that neither shows nor tells.

Yet in a mere letter to *The Times Literary Supplement*, Hardy dis-
agrees with Aristotle, and everybody since, to declare that there is
little difference between the story and the play because each is only
'a means of producing a representation'. Dialogue represents the
words that people speak by those very words. Diegesis narrates
speeches and actions in words that need not be those spoken by the
characters. Hardy discards the idea of narration itself: narration is
nothing in itself but only a means to create a representation. The
play affords us material for a representation on the stage: the story
affords us material for a representation in the imagination, a mental
representation.[44]

The implications of this are enclosed in an even more scandalous
phrase from the same Preface: 'The Spectacle here presented to the
mind's eye in the likeness of a Drama.' Not a drama but a likeness
of a drama: not a likeness of life (as might be suggested by the echo
of the title of Bunyan's *The Pilgrim's Progress … under the Similitude
of a Dream*) but a likeness of a text.[45] Not a literary form but a likeness of a literary form; not itself, then, a literary form at all, but a
likeness thereof. Not even literature but only (nothing less than) a
likeness of literature. Aristotle has been overturned. It has been
widely assumed in Western theories of representation that literature provides an imitation, mimesis, of life or reality or whatever is
outside literature. Literature might sometimes find itself imitated
by life, but Hardy proposes that literature itself will be imitated and
represented, by a text that is itself not literature but in the likeness
of literature.

Nowhere is *The Dynasts* less like literature, nor more like 'a likeness of literature', than in its stage-directions. Stage-directions in
drama are generally taken to be valid when they provide instruc-

tions for actors and directors, or, for the reader of the dramatic text, when they describe the stage and the movements of the actors as an audience would see them. But stage-directions that cannot be translated into visual and dramatic elements are unjustifiable. There are two kinds of illegitimate stage-direction, the one that informs us about a character's inward mental state – that which cannot be visualized or dramatized; the other, that details a visual element too minute or obscure to be visible to the audience, or to have any dramatic effect. Both are evidence of a novelist at work, or at any rate of the influence of the novel.

Examples of each kind abound in *The Dynasts*, as numerous critics have observed, and complained. Simultaneously, however, it has been widely agreed that the stage-directions are the best parts of *The Dynasts*. This is not a paradox, but merely a discounting of *The Dynasts* as drama, and as a challenge to generic norms. This is indicated in Garrison's summary of the view of various critics that 'the prose-passages [stage-directions and dumb shows], of all the elements of the drama, contribute the most to its poetic vision'.[46] Without wishing to discredit the celebrated dumb shows and lyrical sections – often anthologized and in other ways excerpted from the whole – I wish to take a closer look at Hardy's stage-directions, and to see in how calculated a manner they offend against generic conventions.

The death of Nelson at Trafalgar (Part First, Act V, scene iv) is a gift to the dramatist, yet within a few lines we have an instance of each kind of unwarranted stage-direction. Nelson lies dying in the presence of Captain Hardy, and before Nelson makes his last speech, the stage-direction informs us '(symptoms of death beginning to change his face)' (Hynes, IV, 135). The direction is explicitly visual, but not usefully so in terms of dramatic effect. Shortly before this we witness a stage-direction of the diegetic kind. Nelson instructs Hardy to look after Emma:

> Let her have
> My hair, and the small treasured things I owned,
> And take care of her, as you care for me!
> HARDY promises.
>
> (Hynes, IV, 135)

The point, the defining quality of a promise, is that it must involve an outward act or sign, made by words spoken or written, confirmed by a nod, a handshake or an embrace. It is worthless to make a promise in pure interiority: even a promise to oneself ought to have a written testimony. A promise must be manifest; it must therefore be subject to representation, because a promise is a representation of itself as intention: the spoken promise is also a representation of the potential fulfilment of that promise. The discourse of a promise represents the intention, and stands for its fulfilment, for that which will be delivered. A promise is fulfilled or discharged by another sign, another representation, which itself cancels the prior representation.

'HARDY promises' is the raw material of a representation, that is to say, the promise that a promise will be made, dramatized, enacted. What sort of promise is that? The reader can determine how the promise will be made: does Hardy say 'Yes'? If so, such a word, or any sequence of words, would surely be given in the form of dialogue. Does Hardy, in silence, nod his head, or reassure Nelson with a touch? If so, such a gesture could be specified by a stage-direction. There is, the reader realizes, no way in which the promise could be outwardly made that would not demand its own simple stage-direction. 'HARDY promises' is truly a *mise-en-abyme*, so cunning, so punning, the raw material of a representation in the likeness of a stage-direction: Aristotelian stringencies are resisted, the order of representation trembles.

No less remarkable than the stage-directions, nor any less threatening of the securities of representation, are the dumb shows. Take, for example, that in Part Third, Act IV, scene ii, 46. 1–6, when Napoleon leaves Paris on his last campaign in 1814:

Amid repeated protestations and farewells NAPOLÉON, the EMPRESS, the KING OF ROME, MADAME DE MONTESQUIOU, etc., go out in one direction, and the officers of the National Guard in another.

The curtain falls for an interval.

When it rises again the apartment is in darkness, and its atmosphere chilly.

(Hynes, V, 102)

It is impossible to 'translate' this into dramatic or visual terms because the apartment and the curtain seem to be on the same level of representation. What we usually find in the Dumb Show is the description of a play that is already taking place in the mind – the 'mental performance' recommended by Hardy in his Preface – not instructions or directions for a potential actualization. But here, even the idea of a mental representation breaks down, is rendered anomalous.

It is impossible to imagine a curtain falling without imagining a theatrical space, but that theatrical space is precisely what we do not need in a mental representation: do not need, and must do without. We cannot hold in one mental representation both Napoleon and the curtain. Unless all the world's a stage, which is a fine metaphor inside the theatre, but one that renders both superfluous and absurd a distinct space of theatrical representation. Hardy's response to Walkley had challenged the Aristotelian distinction between dialogue and diegesis, and argued that the written text precedes either form of representation, on stage, 'pieced out with material helps', or in the mind, by 'sheer imaginativeness'. The problem, the challenge of *The Dynasts*, is that in the sorts of conundrum afforded by some of the stage-directions and dumb shows, even sheer imaginativeness is baffled: for imaginativeness itself has its place, is accorded its status, in the Aristotelian scheme of representation that is under threat.

Walkley was responding to Part First of *The Dynasts*, whose subtitle in 1904 was simply 'A Drama'. This was the subtitle of each of the subsequent parts. Only in 1910, on the title-page of the first one-volume edition, did Hardy reinforce his challenge with the hybrid term that has graced and defined all subsequent printings: 'An Epic-Drama'.[47] It is strange that the word 'epic', so central to the critical reception of *The Dynasts*, should not have been found on the title-page or anywhere in the text as first published. The 1910 subtitle announces clearly that *The Dynasts* is a generically hybridized text, one whose purpose is to challenge, even to overthrow the literary inheritance, the dynasty of classicism.

A century later, we can appreciate how that challenge had already been inaugurated by the novel. Hardy and Henry James had both contributed greatly to the prestige of the genre in the 1870s and 1880s, but both abandoned novel-writing, James temporarily from 1890 to 1895, Hardy permanently from 1896. Apparently each had some doubts about the value of fiction. Hardy invested his energies successfully in a new career as a poet. James attempted to write plays, and was humiliated by failure. He returned to fiction, to write his greatest novels, and the prefaces to the volumes of the New York Edition that have become canonical and constitutive statements of the legitimacy and potential of fiction as literature. By contrast, Hardy's successful remaking of himself as a poet led him to disparage his own fiction, and fiction in general, for the remainder of his life. James, not Hardy, is credited with the establishment of the novel as a literary genre.[48]

Yet whatever Hardy is doing in *The Dynasts* is done with the experience of novel-writing behind him. Walkley notes, approvingly, that Hardy avoids the specifically internalized discourse of fiction, he 'sees solid', and so he asks: 'why, if you are writing a narrative to be read, forgo all the privileges of narrative art and hamper yourself by the restrictions proper to a spectacle?'[49] The point is that *The Dynasts* is neither one thing nor the other, neither a narrative nor a spectacle. It is a text that refuses either of the Aristotelian options of representation. As such it opposes, through the pacifism sanctioned by the 'Magnificat', the dynasty of literature, the Aristotelian empire of representation.

Representation is power: in so far as the subject is represented, the subject forfeits autonomy. Thus the literary representation of armies which, by distance and perspective, transforms a multitude of human subjects into a single slow-worm, a caterpillar or a column of ants. The view from above is the imperial view: imperialism takes its viewpoint, positions itself at that point at which subjects appear only as representations, and at which individuals can be subordinated to the group, the class, the mass. The reverse also occurs, whereby the undifferentiated is made distinct, as most famously in the Chorus before the Battle of Waterloo, and it is these reversals, the world seen through the microscope rather than the telescope, that expose the horror of the elevated, distant view.[50] The greatest act of magnification concerns the treaty of the Triple Alliance (1813), represented as a document the size of a cloud, drifting across Europe:

SPIRIT OF THE PITIES

Something broad-faced,
Flat-folded, parchment-pale, and in its shape
Rectangular; but moving like a cloud
The Dresden way.

...

The object takes a letter's lineaments

Though swollen to mainsail measure. ...
(Part Third, II, iv, 80–5;
Hynes, V, 71)

To sheer imaginativeness such a swollen conceit as this – 'each feature bulks / In measure with its value humanly', 'The document, / Sized to its big importance' – is incongruent, incoherent, an affront to the conventions of representation. Such distortions and incongruities are not exceptional features of an otherwise proportional and performable drama: they exemplify the text's constitutive resistance to any form of representation. Indeed, representation – mimesis, dialogue, diegesis – is itself to be identified as the instrument of dynasts and imperialists, those who have the capacity to 'size' subjects according to their importance, and thus to reduce, negate, destroy.

How are we to reconcile this sense of *The Dynasts* as a text no less ambitious in its radicalism than *The Cantos*, 'The Waste Land' or *Ulysses*, with our insistence on the significance of the Virgilian signature? Joyce's *Ulysses* suggests a relatively straightforward explanation, in terms of parody. *The Dynasts* goes much further than that. Throughout Western civilization there has been a tendency to favour the spoken over the written word. The literary text, lyric or epic or drama, is a representation of voice which is to be properly realized through speech. Poems ought, we still assume, to be read aloud; a drama ought to be performed. Hardy was himself not interested in the theatre (with the conspicuous exception of local and amateur dramatizations of his own novels), and preferred Shakespeare to be left on the page. That preference was also, notoriously, Charles Lamb's, and it attracts a certain disapproval, a suspicion of an anti-social attitude. Our frustration with *The Dynasts* issues not only from our conventional and educated wish to turn every text into a spoken representation, into a representation of speech: it is grounded also in an ethical principle, of a common culture, of a society united by speech.

The resistance to *The Dynasts* – that text which resists voicing – is not unlike the resistance to Jacques Derrida's 'grammatology', the philosophical claim for the self-sufficiency, the autonomy, even the priority of writing over speech. Grammatology is opposed to the traditional or classical 'logocentrism' which holds the spoken word to be the source and measure of all meaning. Throughout Western culture, texts which resist voicing have been judged

inferior to those texts which afford pure mediation for the representation of voices, just as phonetic alphabets have been judged
superior to pictographic or hieroglyphic scripts.[51]

Here, in the value of mute, unspeakable words, words bound to
the page, may be our clue to the importance, for Hardy, of Virgil.
For Virgil has often, almost by tradition, been deemed inferior to
Homer on precisely this point. Homer is the bard who sings –
whose very blindness speaks for his independence from the text, for
his authentic distance from the silence and civility of texts; Virgil is
the bookish scribe, the poet as courtier, whose studied composition
everywhere betrays the act of writing, the pen in hand, the silence of
the study. No less studious and study-bound a poet than Alexander
Pope could thus preface his translation of the *Iliad* with the conventional comparison, inevitably to the advantage of Homer:

> We oftner think of the Author himself when we read Virgil, than
> when we are engaged with Homer. All which are the effects of a
> colder invention, that interests us less in the action described:
> Homer makes us Hearers, and Virgil leaves us Readers.[52]

Virgil leaves us readers. That, for Hardy, is not his deficiency but
his distinction. The poet-servant of Augustus knew how best to
compromise his art, to keep it in the text, to make the reader aware
of Virgil the scribe at the expense of Aeneas the hero – and at the
expense of Aeneas' heir, Augustus. *The Dynasts*, by the cold invention of its crafty design, also leaves us readers. In our resistance to
mere reading, reading that stays mute, that resists its elevation to
representation, we have been poor readers, selective of our texts.
In collusion with those who would insist that we make representations out of words, who would not respect the unrepresenting
word, who ever coerce text into voice, we have read in the manner
of imperialists. The critical tradition concerning *The Dynasts* has
held that, since the text is unperformable and even unutterable, it is
therefore unreadable, not worth reading. Hardy knew well his
readership: as intimate as Virgil with the Roman Emperor, so was
Hardy with those who governed the British Empire, some of the
most powerful men in all European history, to whose chattering he
attended, men and women who would not cease from talk even to
listen to the nightingale.

Text has been classically figured as a promise, a piece of paper to
be redeemed, discharged, fulfilled and cancelled by speech. A text

is a promise of a representation. But what Hardy promises, his text fails to deliver. That is the distinctive achievement of *The Dynasts*, from an author so celebrated for his power to deliver worlds from texts, to conjure Wessex from mere words. *The Dynasts* frustrates its readers so deeply that we must question and challenge the very act and activity of reading: I know of no other text that makes one feel so inadequate, not to say dumb, in the reading of it. The text's stubborn refusal to be fulfilled – 'to come alive' as might be said – its resistance to the function of representation, ensures that we can only study it, study it as a text only. And wonder about the procedures and legitimacies of promises, textual and otherwise.

In *The Dynasts*, HARDY promises; and Hardy promises to disclose a secret in the very silence of the text – a secret about promises, about texts, about the old Aristotelian lies of representation, of the classical imperialism of voices, and sounds of insult, shame, and wrong, and trumpets blown for wars: voices and trumpets all silenced forever on this great battle-field of a text. And in that silence,

...

O, 'tis the nightingale... .

[53]

Notes

1. Thomas Hardy, *The Dynasts*, ed. Samuel Hynes [vols IV and V of *The Complete Poetical Works of Thomas Hardy* (Oxford: Clarendon Press, 1995)], Part First, Fore Scene, lines 76–8 (vol. IV, p. 17). All quotations from *The Dynasts* are cited from this edition, abbreviated as 'Hynes'.
2. It might be supposed that the rapid and regular publication of the three volumes in 1904, 1906 and 1908 would indicate that *The Dynasts* was largely prepared before publication commenced. That this was not the case is clear from the endpapers of both the first and second printings of Volume One, in which (i–v) are outlined the 'Contents of Second and Third Parts (subject to revision)'; to this a note is subjoined: 'Note. – The Second and Third Parts are in hand, but their publication is not guaranteed' (v). The differences between the advertised outline and the published text are clearly presented in Richard Little Purdy, *Thomas Hardy: A Bibliographical Study* (Oxford: Clarendon Press, 1954) pp. 126–34; see also Hynes, *Complete Poetical Works*, vol. V, Appendix C.
3. *Letters of J. M. Barrie*, ed. Viola Meynell (London: Peter Davies, 1942) p. 152, cited in Chester A. Garrison, *The Vast Venture: Hardy's*

Epic-Drama 'The Dynasts' (Salzburg: Institut für Englische Sprache und Literatur, 1973) p. 4.

4. *The Dynasts* is placed in the context of the vast enterprises of modernism in the following recent essays: Samuel Hynes, 'Mr. Hardy's Monster: Reflections on *The Dynasts'*, *Sewanee Review*, vol. 102, no. 2 (1994) 213–32; review by Jerome McGann of *Porius* by John Cowper Powys, *Times Literary Supplement*, 1 December 1995, 4–5; George Steiner, 'Do-it-Yourself' [review of Franco Moretti's *The Modern Epic*], *London Review of Books*, 18 (10), 23 May 1996, 14.

5. J. M. Keynes, *The Economic Consequences of the Peace* (London: Macmillan, 1919) pp. 4–5, cited by Hynes, *Complete Poetical Works*, vol. IV, p. xxii.

6. Thomas Hardy, *The Life and Work of Thomas Hardy*, ed. Michael Millgate (London: Macmillan Press, 1984) p. 292. Subsequently cited as *Life and Work*.

7. See Harold Orel, 'Hardy, Kipling, Haggard', *English Literature in Transition*, vol. 24, no. 4 (1982) 232–48.

8. See Ronald D. Knight, *T. E. Lawrence and the Max Gate Circle* (Weymouth: Bat and Ball Press, 1995).

9. *The Collected Letters of Thomas Hardy*, ed. Richard Little Purdy and Michael Millgate, 7 volumes (Oxford: Clarendon Press, 1978–88) vol. V, p. 340; vol. VI, pp. 9, 10, 44, 63 (subsequently cited as *Collected Letters* followed by volume and page number); *Letters of Emma and Florence Hardy*, ed. Michael Millgate (Oxford: Clarendon Press, 1996) p. 102.

10. *Life and Work*, p. 368.

11. See Gregory Nagy, *Poetry as Performance: Homer and Beyond* (Cambridge: Cambridge University Press, 1996) p. 65, n. 25: 'It may be pertinent to the mythical detail about the cutting-out of Philomela's tongue that the nightingale is described in ['Aristotle's'] *Historia animalium* as bereft of a tongue-tip.'

12. Walter de la Mare records a visit to Max Gate, in which Hardy met him at the station in Dorchester and drove with him back to Max Gate. The young de la Mare attempted what he thought was appropriate conversation, about the bird-songs to be heard *en route*. Hardy displayed indifference ('Meeting Thomas Hardy', *The Listener*, 28 April 1955).

13. The chapter of *The Education* concerned with 1900 is entitled 'The Dynamo and the Virgin', that on 1904, 'A Dynamic Theory of History'.

14. This is the translation of Anna Swanwick, first published in 1865. The meaning of the Greek text is not entirely clear: both dynasts and stars are to be watched in their falling and rising. According to William R. Rutland, *Thomas Hardy: A Study of his Writings and their Background* (Oxford: Basil Blackwell, 1938) p. 34, Hardy had marked precisely these lines in his Greek text of Aeschylus.

15. *Collected Letters*, vol. II, p. 216; *One Rare Fair Woman*, ed. Evelyn Hardy and F. B. Pinion (London: Macmillan Press, 1972) p. 77; *Letters of Emma and Florence Hardy*, pp. 196–7.

16.   *Collected Letters*, vol. III, p. 197. The printers and proof-readers at the Clarendon Press today are entirely innocent of Greek: the word is hopelessly mangled in both the *Collected Letters* and *The Complete Poetical Works*, through no fault of the respective editors.

17.   See Liddell and Scott: δῠνᾰστεύω is 'to hold power or lordship, be powerful'; δῠνάστησ is 'a lord, master, ruler'; οἱ δῠνάσται, 'the chief men'.

18.   Hardy's letter to Edmund Gosse, 31 January 1904, is an evasive answer to a most pertinent question: 'As for the title, it was the best & shortest inclusive one I could think of to express the rulers of Europe in their desperate struggle to maintain their dynasties rather than to benefit their peoples.' *Collected Letters*, vol. III, p. 102.

19.   Simon Gatrell, 'An Examination of some Revisions to Printed Versions of *The Dynasts*', *The Library* (6th series), I, 3 (September 1979) 266–7.

20.   Henry Adams, *The Education of Henry Adams* (New York: Library of America, 1983) p. 356.

21.   *Collected Letters*, vol. II, p. 89. One of Adams's closest friends was John Hay, the American Ambassador in London; when Hardy met Hay in 1897, the Ambassador 'reminded [him] that they were not strangers as he seemed to suppose, but had met at the Rabelais Club years ago' (see *Life and Work*, p. 315). The common friend of Hardy, Hay and Adams in the Rabelais Club was, no doubt, the father of Florence Henniker, Richard Monckton Milnes, 1st Baron Houghton (see *Life and Work*, p. 140; *The Education of Henry Adams*, pp. 118–19: 'Milnes was the goodnature of London: the Gargantuan type of its refinement and coarseness').

22.   *Virgil's Aeneis*, trans. John Dryden, VI, ll. 1073ff.

23.   Donald Davie, 'Hardy's Virgilian Purples', *Agenda*, vol. 10, nos 2–3 (Spring–Summer 1972) 143. See also Edmund Blunden on Hardy's conversation as reported in Ronald Knight, *T. E. Lawrence and the Max Gate Circle*, p. 51: 'a mixture of the trifles with which old age amuses itself, and details of real importance in reading his life – e.g. his first reading book (Dryden's Vergil)...'.

24.   So copious were Hardy's preparations for posterity that this detail is not mentioned by Michael Millgate in his pioneering study in 'literary thanatography', *Testamentary Acts: Browning, Tennyson, James, Hardy* (Oxford: Clarendon Press, 1992).

25.   *Collected Letters*, vol. VII, p. 66; 'an additional short quotation' because *The Dynasts* has always had one epigraph, printed in all editions, from Tennyson's 'A Dream of Fair Women':

          And I heard sounds of insult, shame, and wrong,
               And trumpets blown for wars.

26.   A point made by Hynes in 'Mr. Hardy's Monster: Reflections on *The Dynasts*', p. 224: '[Napoleon aside] in Nelson and Wellington he had two potential epic heroes. ... Yet as Hardy tells the story neither man achieves epic stature.'

27. Oscar Browning, letter to Thomas Hardy, 24 November 1921 (Dorset County Museum); in his wonderfully humorous response Hardy disqualifies himself from getting involved in an argument about Napoleon 'whom I have considered only vaguely since I had occasion to look into his history 25 years ago or so, when I touched on it in a book I wrote just after called The Dynasts ...' (*Collected Letters*, vol. VI, p. 105).

28. *Virgil's Aeneis*, trans. John Dryden, IV, ll. 487–99.

29. *Life and Work*, pp. 480–1. The editor of the 1914 edition of Palgrave's *Golden Treasury* annotates the last line and gives due credit to Fitzgerald: 'This tremendous line, with its last two words flinging on God's shoulders the responsibility for man's sins, is not in the original.'

30. *Life and Work*, p. 325.

31. *Life and Work*, p. 21.

32. Hynes's Oxford edition is the very first to ascribe and identify the source of the epigraph; to my knowledge, the earliest published annotation of the source is in Garrison, *The Vast Venture*, p. 3, n. 6. The epigraph is not cited under Virgil in the lists of Hardy's literary sources and allusions compiled by Rutland, *Thomas Hardy: A Study of his Writings*, pp. 24–5; F. B. Pinion, *A Hardy Companion* (London: Macmillan Press, 1968) p. 209; or Lennart A. Björk (ed.), *The Literary Notebooks of Thomas Hardy* (London: Macmillan Press, 1985) vol. 1, pp. 276–7 (263–8 nn.).

33. Björk (ed.), *Literary Notebooks*, vol. 2, pp. 463, 562 (88e, 88e n.); Hardy records that in 1868 he re-read 'Virgil's *Aeneid* (of which he never wearied)', *Life and Work*, p. 61.

34. *Collected Letters*, vol. VII, p. 86.

35. Lawrence Lipking, *The Life of the Poet: Beginning and Ending Poetic Careers* (Chicago and London: University of Chicago Press, 1981) pp. 76–7, 79; so devious was Hardy in his presentation of himself as inspired only by local life, loose numbers and torn pages in closets that he is one of the very few major poets to receive not a single mention in Lipking's book. Only a fellow-poet could see through the cunning: Ezra Pound wrote of Hardy: 'No man ever had so much Latin and so eschewed the least appearance of being a classicist', *Confucius to Cummings: An Anthology of Poetry* (New York: New Directions, 1964) p. 325.

36. The draft is in the Lock and Mann Collection in the Dorset County Museum: see Hynes, vol. V, p. 380; Purdy, *Thomas Hardy: A Bibliographical Study*, pp. 130–1; and Charles Lock, 'Obscurest Leaves: History and Hardy's Pages' (forthcoming).

37. Even Dennis Taylor, the most metrically astute and sensitive of all Hardy's critics, can write: 'Nothing in *The Dynasts* is as [metrically] interesting as "The Souls of the Slain"', *Hardy's Metres and Victorian Prosody* (Oxford: Clarendon Press, 1988) p. 155.

38. Suetonius, 'Life of Virgil', cited by Lipking, *The Life of the Poet*, pp. 79–80.

39. On Hardy's systematic devaluation of his novels in favour of his poetry and *The Dynasts*, see Charles Lock, *Thomas Hardy: Criticism in Focus* (London: Bristol Classical Press, 1992) pp. 49–54.

40. The conflict of genres in Hardy's subtitle may be compared to Fielding's play with genres in *Tom Jones*, 'prosai-comi-epic writing' (Book V, Ch. 1).

41. Hynes's edition gives 'ready' instead of 'readily': one of 20 substantive misprints so far identified in his text of *The Dynasts*. These are detailed in Charles Lock, 'Though *Dynasts* pass', *Essays in Criticism*, vol. XLVII, no. 3 (July 1997) 270–81.

42. Hynes, vol. V, p. 389; both sides of the debate between Hardy and Walkley are usefully reprinted by Hynes as Appendix E, in vol. V, pp. 385–96. Some years later, T. E. Lawrence suggested that *The Dynasts* might be performed, cinematically, 'if it could be produced on similar lines to the Walt Disney cartoons' (Knight, *T. E. Lawrence and the Max Gate Circle*, p. 55).

43. See Garrison, *The Vast Venture*, p. 128: 'Aristotle carefully distinguishes epic from drama: Hardy discounts the difference between them.' See also Susan M. Dean, *Hardy's Poetic Vision in 'The Dynasts': The Diorama of a Dream* (Princeton, NJ: Princeton University Press, 1977) p. 11, on Hardy's Preface: 'These remarks do not describe a work whose genre we can even identify.'

44. The subtitle of *The Queen of Cornwall* reads: 'Arranged as a play for mummers in one act requiring no theatre or scenery.' A prefatory paragraph then describes the stage, an archway, doorways, benches, even 'a gallery (which may be represented by any elevated piece of furniture on which two actors can stand…)'. These elaborate instructions are followed by a note: 'Should the performance take place in an ordinary theatre, the aforesaid imaginary surroundings may be supplied by imitative scenery.'

45. Hardy's letter to Henry Newbolt, 16 January 1909, makes even more explicit the allusion to Bunyan when he proposes a subtitle for the one-volume edition:

> I want to put on the titlepage … something more explicit than the words 'A Drama', which mislead the public into thinking that it is not for reading. I have thought of
> A mental drama
> A vision-drama
> A closet-drama
> An epical drama, &c.
> or 'A chronicle poem of the Nap[oleoni]c wars, under the similitude of a drama', but I cannot decide.

Collected Letters, vol. IV, p. 5; first printed in *My World as in My Time: Memoirs of Sir Henry Newbolt 1862–1932* (London: Faber & Faber, 1932) p. 283.

46. Garrison, *The Vast Venture*, p. 207, n. 6.

47. See Hynes, vol. IV, pp. 409–10, and Hardy's letter to Newbolt cited in n. 45, above. The point is stressed by Hardy through the use of a footnote to his Preface: 'It is now called an Epic-drama (1909).'

48. On the parallels between James and Hardy, see Michael Millgate, *Thomas Hardy: His Career as a Novelist* (London: Bodley Head, 1971) pp. 353–8; Lock, *Thomas Hardy: Criticism in Focus*, pp. 10–17.

49. Hynes, vol. V, pp. 393–4.

50. See the finest of the early critics of *The Dynasts*, Lascelles Abercrombie, *Thomas Hardy: A Critical Study* (London: Martin Secker, 1919 [1st edn 1912]) pp. 149–50. The satirical and subversive implications of microscopic and telescopic views can be traced back via Lewis Carroll to *Gulliver's Travels*.

51. See Charles Lock, 'Petroglyphs, Pictograms, Alphabets, and the Fallacy of Scriptorial Evolution', *The Semiotic Review of Books* (forthcoming).

52. *The Iliad of Homer, translated by Alexander Pope*, ed. Susan Shankman, Penguin Classics (Harmondsworth: Penguin Books, 1996) p. 8.

53. In a lecture the problem is inescapable. In the muteness of the text the question has not been raised: how do you *pronounce The Dynasts*? Hardy himself pasted on to the front fly-leaf of his own 1910 one-volume text these words, reprinted from Tract No. IV of the Society for Pure English, John Sargeaunt's *The Pronunciation of English Words derived from the Latin* (Oxford, 1920): 'I do not know what Mr. Hardy calls his poem, but I hope he follows the old use and calls it "The Dynasts". It might be thought that "dynasts" was safe, but it is not. Some modern words like "dynamite" have been misused from their birth.'

5

From Fascination to Listlessness: Hardy's Depiction of Love

MICHAEL IRWIN

I

The love which dominates Hardy's fiction is romantic or sexual. Other kinds of affection are featured, of course, but only in bit parts. The nature of his interest in this habitual theme is unusual – and perhaps unexpected in a writer famous for the creation of individualized characters. In relation to love, as to other aspects of human life, Hardy is concerned to generalize, to diagnose. He's constantly saying: 'This is what the thing called love is like. This is how it happens. Is it not strange? Why does it work like this? Why do these delights lead to these miseries?'

When Hardy is observing in this diagnostic spirit, his 'idiosyncrasy of regard', his tendency to see what other people don't, or to see familiar things from a different point of view, leads him to resort to a specialized personal vocabulary of key terms that come up again and again. Here is a selection of disparate examples: 'pulsation', 'organism', 'convergence', 'aspect', 'comer', 'flexuous', 'nerves', 'scan', 'indifference', 'morbid', 'vision', 'juxtaposition', 'irradiation'. A great deal can be learned about Hardy by an examination of his use of such terms, and by considering what it is in his view of life that makes him resort to them so *often*. 'Listlessness' and 'fascination' are words of this kind. In what follows I hope to use them as conceptual skeleton-keys to open up Hardy's ideas about love. I'll also be invoking, though less systematically, two or three of the other terms I've mentioned.

Let me first, however, develop the point about Hardy's taste for asserting general positions. The habit is in evidence from the very start of his novelistic career:[1]

It has been said that men love with their eyes; women with their ears.   (*Desperate Remedies*, Ch. 3.1)

It is an almost universal habit with people, when leaving a bank, to be carefully adjusting their pockets if they have been receiving money; if they have been paying it in, their hands swing laxly. (Ibid., Ch. 19.2)

... to have an unsexed judgment is as precious as to be an unsexed being is deplorable.   (*The Hand of Ethelberta*, Ch. 8)

... in obedience to the usual law by which the emotion that takes the form of humour in country workmen becomes transmuted to irony among the same order in town.   (Ibid., Ch. 26)

Not the lovers who part in passion, but the lovers who part in friendship, are those who most frequently part for ever.   (Ibid., Ch. 37)

... darkness makes people truthful...   (*The Mayor of Casterbridge*, Ch. XVII)

Generalization being out of fashion I'd like to offer a paragraph or two in its defence. It is a mode that has suffered at the hands of the politically correct and has often been misrepresented in the process. Repeatedly it is pointed out that this or that general statement is a simplification. Well, yes, it would be: such is the nature of generalizations. They must be taken for what they are. In many workaday areas this doesn't seem to be too much of a problem. We may curse the BBC's meteorologists when it rains after they have said that it won't, but we don't stop listening to them. We accept the generalized status of the weather forecast. In this case, as in many others, the fallibility of the statement in question doesn't make it deceitful or pointless. Like all generalizations it should be judged in the light of context, scope and tone. Pope's warning that 'A little learning is a dangerous thing' is intended for potential critics: it isn't an argument against mass education. When Hardy says 'darkness makes people truthful' we know that he doesn't mean that it's impossible to lie at night. Typical responses to such statements should be: 'Is this broadly true?' or 'Is there something in it?' Often, as in this latter case, the claim is designed primarily to be suggestive. At a further stage the seeming generalization can be aphoristically provocative, as in Shaw's 'He who can, does. He who cannot, teaches.'

Hardy does on occasion deal specifically in this kind of aphorism, especially in passages of deliberately formalized comedy featured in *The Hand of Ethelberta*.[2] More basically he clearly assumes that there are observable common denominators in human psychology and conduct – as in the examples about darkness or one's deportment when leaving a bank. The assumption is intrinsic to his descriptive method, which regularly invites the reader to draw inferences: a man stands or moves in a particular way and is therefore (for example) unhappy or rebellious. Hardy likes to share with his readers his ability to observe, and the further ability to diagnose on the basis of the observation.

But he is aware of the limits of such diagnosis. A passage near the beginning of *Desperate Remedies* puts the case very fairly. Cytherea and Owen Graye have been left orphaned and destitute:

> There is in us an unquenchable expectation, which at the gloomiest time persists in inferring that because we are *ourselves*, there must be a special future in store for us, though our nature and antecedents to the remotest particular have been common to thousands. Thus to Cytherea and Owen Graye the question how their lives would end seemed the deepest of possible enigmas. To others who knew their position equally well with themselves the question was the easiest that could be asked – 'Like those of other people similarly circumstanced.'   (Ch. 1.5)

The tone is boldly confident, but in fact, in defiance of the prediction, the Grayes' future proves to be anything but typical. In no time at all they're involved in a maze of mystery, conspiracy and manslaughter. But equally Hardy knows, as he hints here and shows in comparable cases, that even the most orthodox life cannot seem merely 'typical' to the individual who leads it. We may inhabit generalizations, but we feel unique. Hardy's diagnosis of human behaviour typically acknowledges its own externality and allows for exceptions.

To return to my key-words: 'listlessness' and 'fascination' both figure in Hardy's first novel, *Desperate Remedies*, the former term

frequently. A glance at some of the contexts in which it appears
may suggest the coloration it has for Hardy:

> ... tracing listlessly with his eyes the red stripes upon her scarf ...
> (Ch. 3.2)

> Here she sat down by the open window ... and listlessly
> looked down upon the brilliant pattern of colours formed by the
> flower-beds on the lawn ...   (Ch. 5.2)

> ... he listlessly observed the movements of a woman wearing a
> long grey cloak ...   (Ch. 9.3)

> ... his eyes listlessly tracing the pattern of the carpet.   (Ch. 11.1)

> ... their eyes listlessly tracing some crack in the old walls, or
> following the movement of a distant bough or bird ...   (Ch. 12.8)

> He listlessly regarded the illuminated blackness overhead ...
> (Ch. 15.2)

What this pattern of usage suggests is that, for Hardy, the word
'listless' denotes an emptiness of mind, an absence of internal stimulus. The eyes automatically seek an external one, but bring no
inner resources to bear upon it. In this frame of mind you 'idly
trace', you see passively.

This mental inertia is a matter of common experience. But Hardy
also uses the word 'listless' in contexts in which feeling has been
violently numbed or confused. I'll give examples here, from *Far from
the Madding Crowd*, which may serve to suggest how conscious, and
consciously expressed, is Hardy's interest in this extreme and peculiar state of mind. He presents three parallel vignettes in which his
main characters, Oak, Boldwood and Bathsheba, are shown in the
heightened state of listlessness that derives from shock. Each of the
scenes takes place at dawn or daybreak, and in the vicinity of a gate
or broken fence, these factors hinting that the life of the character
concerned is about to enter a new phase – that this is a turning
point. In each case the scene which confronts him or her is in some
sense unnatural and forbidding, a metaphorical expression of the
observer's confused state of mind.

The first shows Gabriel Oak immediately after the discovery that his whole flock of sheep has been destroyed:

> Oak ... listlessly surveyed the scene. By the outer margin of the pit was an oval pond, and over it hung the attenuated skeleton of a chrome-yellow moon, which had only a few days to last – the morning star dogging her on the left hand. The pool glittered like a dead man's eye ...   (Ch. V)

The second passage concerns Boldwood, in mental turmoil after receiving Bathsheba's valentine. Having risen early he leans over a gate and looks around:

> ... over the snowy down ... the only half of the sun yet visible burnt rayless, like a red and flameless fire shining over a white hearthstone. The whole effect resembled a sunset as childhood resembles age.
> ... Over the west hung the wasting moon, now dull and greenish-yellow, like tarnished brass.
> Boldwood was listlessly noting how the frost had hardened and glazed the surface of the snow till it shone in the red eastern light with the polish of marble ...   (Ch. XIV)

After opening Fanny's coffin and being spurned by Troy, Bathsheba rushes blindly out into the night. At random she goes through a gate into a spot apparently reminiscent of the hollow in which Troy dazzled her with his sword-play. At daybreak, when she comes to herself and looks about her, the place seems very different:

> ... the general aspect of the swamp was malignant. From its moist and poisonous coat seemed to be exhaled the essences of evil things in the earth and in the waters under the earth. The fungi grew in all manner of positions from rotting leaves and tree stumps, some exhibiting to her listless gaze their clammy tops, others their oozing gills.   (Ch. XLIV)

In each of these cases there might seem to be a contradiction between the distortion and ugliness of what is seen and the reported listlessness, or unresponsiveness, of the seer. But all three natural settings might have looked quite different, even quite peaceful, to an untroubled observer. As I implied earlier, the distortion is in effect a projection of appalled intensities of feeling, and these intensities are so diverse as to cancel each other out and produce the listless state. Hardy makes the point in describing Troy's motionless stance over Fanny's coffin:

> So still he remained that he could be imagined to have left in him no motive power whatever. The clashes of feeling in all directions confounded one another, produced a neutrality, and there was motion in none.   (Ch. XLIII)

Thus for Hardy listlessness is likely to be found both before the beginning and after the end of a cycle of emotion. In the former phase it characteristically involves an appetite, a hunger, for the feeling which is absent. Eustacia and Mrs Charmond are chronically listless in consequence of an unfulfilled desire for passionate love. Another such character is Viviette in *Two on a Tower*, described by Tabitha Lark as 'eaten out with listlessness'. Hardy glosses the term a few pages later:

> The soft dark eyes ... were the natural indices of a warm and affectionate – perhaps slightly voluptuous – temperament, languishing for want of something to do, cherish, or suffer for. (Ch. III)

Each of the three women is roused from her languor by just the kind of romantic passion she has been craving. In each case the feeling experienced is described as 'fascination'.

Once again *Desperate Remedies* offers a convenient introduction to the term concerned. Its young heroine, Cytherea, has had a taste of the relevant emotion by the beginning of Chapter Three: 'A responsive love for Edward Springrove had made its appearance in Cytherea's bosom with all the fascinating attributes of a first experience ... (Ch. 3.1). But she encounters it in more melodramatic fullness when meeting the daemonic Aeneas Manston for the first time. As she leaves him she thinks: 'O, how is it that man has so fascinated me?' (Ch. 8.4).

The episode that produces this reaction is suggestive of some of the factors that might be involved in 'fascination' as opposed to, say, 'interest' or 'attraction'. Not only is Manston physically handsome, he has a touch of diabolism about him, and has been playing the organ to her in an isolated and decaying Elizabethan manor house in the middle of a ferocious storm:

> The thunder, lightning, and rain had now increased to a terrific force. The clouds, from which darts, forks, zigzags, and balls of fire continually sprang, did not appear to be more than a hundred yards above their heads ...
> ... Cytherea, in spite of herself, was frightened, not only at the weather, but at the general unearthly weirdness which seemed to surround her there. (Ch. 8.4)

Perhaps it's hardly surprising that she sits 'spell-bound before him' and finds herself 'shrinking up beside him, and looking with parted lips at his face'. What seems to be involved is sexual attraction exaggerated by an element of shock to produce total imaginative absorption. The scene is typical of other episodes of 'fascination' in Hardy in that the effect produced is sudden, involuntary, and is achieved despite near-total ignorance of the individual found fascinating. It differs from many others in that elsewhere the dramatic external context, 'the general unearthly weirdness', can be absent, so that the fascination derives almost solely from the impassioned imaginings of the person who is fascinated.

That situation is at its diagrammatically clearest in the short story 'An Imaginative Woman', a case-study of fascination, in which the heroine, Ella Marchmill, never so much as meets the object of her adoration. She has to make do with his poems, his photograph and a few of his clothes – but her 'passionate curiosity' and 'subtle luxuriousness of fancy' do the rest. As nearly as may be she is made pregnant by the photograph. The feeling she unilaterally generates is strong enough to be the indirect cause of her eventual death.

Ella self-confessedly gets into 'a morbid state'. Her story is one of several in which Hardy suggests that passionate love, or something that seems very much akin to it, is a quasi-neurological phenomenon. In 'The Fiddler of the Reels' Car'line Aspent's 'fragile and responsive organization' makes her hypersensitive to the 'fascination' exercised by the music of Mop Ollamoor. At the climax of the story his playing reduces her to 'hysteric emotion' and convulsions. A similar vulnerability in Barbara, of the House of Grebe, is exploited by her sadistic second husband. Nightly, in bed, he invites her to stare at the statue of his predecessor, scrupulously mutilated to reproduce the terrible injuries he had suffered in a fire:

'... such was the strange fascination of the grisly exhibition that a morbid curiosity took possession of the Countess'. Against her will she does keep glancing at the hideous object until she is reduced to an epileptic fit. Each of the three stories is a caricature of the workings of love as displayed elsewhere in Hardy. Imaginative excitement preys upon a hypersensitive nervous system.

Various of the apparently more substantial relationships in Hardy's fiction start from reactions almost as hyperbolic. Dick Dewy has only to get a glimpse of Fancy Day's boot, and later of Fancy herself, with her hair down, illuminated in a window, to become a 'lost man'. De Stancy, in *A Laodicean*, is persuaded to spy on Paula Power taking exercise in her private gymnasium. The 'sportive fascination of her appearance' not only wins his heart forthwith, but causes him to abandon that same day his long-kept vow of teetotalism.

The paradigmatic case is probably that of Eustacia's infatuation with Clym in *The Return of the Native*. Though it is Book Third of the novel which is actually entitled 'The Fascination', the process has started well back in Book Second. Eustacia's attention is first attracted when she overhears a conversation about the new-comer by means of a chimney which functions as a sort of giant ear-trumpet:

> That five minutes of overhearing furnished Eustacia with visions enough to fill the whole blank afternoon. Such sudden alterations from mental vacuity do sometimes occur thus quietly. She could never have believed in the morning that her colourless inner world would before night become as animated as water under a microscope, and that without the arrival of a single visitor.   (Book Second, Ch. I)

After spending 'the greater part of the afternoon ... imagining the fascination which must attend a man come direct from beautiful Paris', she goes out at dusk to look at the house where he is to stay. She passes him in the darkness and, though she cannot see him, hears him say good-night. 'No event could have been more exciting':

> On such occasions as this a thousand ideas pass through a highly charged woman's head; and they indicate themselves on her face; but the changes, though actual, are minute. Eustacia's features went through a rhythmical succession of them. She glowed; remembering the mendacity of the imagination, she

flagged; then she freshened; then she fired; then she cooled again. It was a cycle of aspects, produced by a cycle of visions.   (Book Second, Ch. III)

That night she dreams of Clym, and the charm grows stronger. Hardy sums up her condition in a description to which I'll return – a description in which he again uses the word 'vision':

> The perfervid woman was by this time half in love with a vision. The fantastic nature of her passion, which lowered her as an intellect, raised her as a soul.   (Book Second, Ch. III)

Truly a case of 'fascination': all these intensities are directed towards a man she has yet to set eyes on. When she does eventually come to see him, through pertinacious scheming, it is in unusual and heightened circumstances. As a newly slain Turkish soldier in the mummers' play, she has time and opportunity to study his face in detail through the ribbons that do duty for her visor. Later that night he does speak two casual sentences to her, but, as Hardy proceeds to explain, she scarcely needs this additional stimulus:

> She had undoubtedly begun to love him. She loved him partly because he was exceptional in this scene, partly because she had from the first instinctively determined to love him, chiefly because she was in desperate need of loving somebody. Believing that she must love him in spite of herself, she had been influenced after the fashion of the second Lord Lyttleton and other persons, who have dreamed that they were to die on a certain day, and by stress of a morbid imagination have actually brought about that event. Once let a maiden admit the possibility of her being stricken with love for some one at some hour or place, and the thing is as good as done.   (Book Second, Ch. VI)

If *The Return of the Native* were the only Hardy novel you'd read you might linger on such a passage as this and think that, as in the short stories I've mentioned, he was exploring what he takes to be an aberrant emotional condition. The emphasis on Eustacia's lack of rational motive and the reference to 'morbid imagination' would certainly seem to convey such a suggestion. But comparison with other works shows that for Hardy this is what romantic love, in general, is *like*. This, he is claiming, is how 'fascination' works.

Regrettable as it might well appear, Hardy's views seem to be fairly
summed up by the dubious Fitzpiers:

> Human love is a subjective thing ... it is joy accompanied by an
> idea which we project against any suitable object in the line of
> our vision ...
>   ... I am in love with something in my own head, and no thing-
> in-itself outside it at all.   (*The Woodlanders*, Ch. XVI)

Hardy displays this phenomenon again and again. 'Falling in love',
the great antidote to listlessness, is shown to be a delusive process
based on a subjective dream, a 'vision'. When the fascination gives
way to reality, as eventually it must, listlessness sets in once more.
Bathsheba is already talking 'listlessly' when she returns from Bath
after her marriage. Angel Clare is listless on his wedding night.

The subjectivity of love is emphasized nowhere more strongly
than in Hardy's later novels. Angel's emotional processes are
sufficiently close to those of Fitzpiers for him to be able to say,
truthfully, to Tess: 'the woman I have been loving is not you'. *The
Well-Beloved* is exclusively a meditation on this very theme.
Pierston, the main character, falls passionately in love with a series
of women, over a period of forty years, including Avice Caro, her
daughter and her grand-daughter. These fits of infatuation begin
and end randomly. Nothing the unfortunate woman concerned
says or does would seem to have any significant influence on the
arousal, the prolongation or the termination of the feeling. The
status of this parable is left uncertain, in the sense that it isn't clear
how representative a figure Pierston is supposed to be. Although
Hardy calls his novel 'a fanciful exhibition of the artistic nature' he
also suggests in his Preface that the 'delicate dream' concerned 'is
more or less common to all men'.

Two parenthetical comments may be made about *The Well-
Beloved* by way of emphasizing the singularity of Hardy's views on
love. Despite scattered references to Shelley, to Plato, to the Ideal or
ethereal, Hardy never implies that the infatuated one might be
content with worshipping from afar. Courtly love is never felt to
be an option: the vision must be pursued in physical terms. If you
are smitten you should go in and try to win. On the other hand
there is no suggestion that the feeling concerned is appeased or
extinguished by sexual conquest: Pierston is no Don Juan. The love
Hardy writes about certainly involves sexual desire, but it is never

simply a transcription of that desire. Fascination isn't lust in a fanciful package. The balance of needs is clearly displayed again in *Jude the Obscure*. For Jude, Sue is at first 'more or less an ideal character, about whose form he began to weave curious and fantastic daydreams'. In time, however, he also needs to make love with her in physical terms. Yet the fact that he eventually succeeds in this aim does nothing to diminish his devotion to her.

If I might risk a generalization of my own: I suppose most of us hope that the solipsistic aspect of 'falling in love' can be interfused with, and actually strengthened by, a growing sense of the 'objective' individuality of the loved one. What can seem unnerving in Hardy is the exclusivity of his concentration on the subjective element or phase. Noticeably absent from his work is that substantial aspect of real-life love-affairs which consists of *getting to know* the other person. Hardy's tendency is bluntly to disregard it. In *The Return of the Native* eleven chapters span the time between the conversation Eustacia hears down the chimney and what seems to be the possible beginning of Clym's courtship. The two are still on surname terms. The next chapter describes a lovers' rendezvous:

> 'My Eustacia.'
> 'Clym dearest.'
> Such a situation had less than three months brought forth.
> (Book Third, Ch. IV)

With one bound Clym has been trapped. The getting-to-know phase is similarly elided in *The Woodlanders* after Grace and Fitzpiers have become acquainted: 'There never was a particular moment at which it could be said they became friends; yet a delicate understanding now existed between two who in the winter had been strangers' (Ch. XIX). The social aspect of the relationship is left unimaginable. Perhaps Giles actually errs in trying to provide a social context for his courtship by holding a party for Grace. The project would probably have been doomed even with a less disastrous guest-list. Love, in Hardy's fiction, tends to stay hermetically sealed, a private and obsessive involvement between two individuals who scarcely know one another in the normal sense.

When I ask students to write about Hardy's view of love many of them notice the tendencies I've been sketching, and react uneasily. At twenty you don't want to believe that love might be no more than the passionate infatuations which Hardy describes. They look for an escape route, and almost always find the same one – an account of the eventual relationship between Oak and Bathsheba:

> Theirs was that substantial affection which arises ... when the two who are thrown together begin first by knowing the rougher sides of each other's character, and not the best till further on, the romance growing up in the interstices of a mass of hard prosaic reality. This good-fellowship ... is unfortunately seldom super-added to love between the sexes. ... Where however happy circumstance permits its development the compounded feeling proves itself to be the only love which is strong as death – that love ... beside which the passion usually called by the name is evanescent as steam.   (*Far from the Madding Crowd*, Ch. LVI)

This, my students conclude, is the mature kind of love which Hardy 'really' espouses, the substantial love of a Gabriel Oak rather than the evanescent love of a Troy. It may be a consoling conclusion, but it overlooks some significant factors. One is an incidental comment in the penultimate paragraph of the novel: '... Bathsheba smiled, for she never laughed readily now'. Another consideration is that *Far from the Madding Crowd* is an early work. It isn't easy to find comparable accounts of a seasoned relationship in Hardy's later novels. The love he is to portray again and again has much more to do with passion than with camaraderie.

But those seeking the escape route have good reason to do so. Here is a major author apparently arguing that romantic love is mere fantasy, self-defeating and short-lived. There would seem to be a depressing logic in Hardy's position: intensity of feeling is an index of the furious imaginative energy that has gone into the creation of a 'vision'. The exposure of its unreality will bring an equivalent intensity of listless disappointment.

Hardy exaggerates the painful aspects of this process by isolating it from what, in real life, are usually considered mollifying consequences of fading passion. Child-rearing is typically the emotional or psychological parachute that permits a sufficiently gentle descent from the giddy heights of romantic love. Childless himself, Hardy denies his characters children. The birth-rate in his Wessex is generally pitiful. Some of his heroines perish too soon, some remain single, some die in childbirth. Little Time's Malthusian measures are almost predictable: he is rectifying an anomaly. The Fawley children are in danger of outnumbering those produced by the protagonists of all the other Wessex novels put together.

A prior point is that even weddings feature only irregularly and glumly. Several are aborted at the last minute, through misunder-standings or changes of heart. Those of Viviette, Cytherea and Ethelberta are desperate and loveless proceedings. Pierston eventu-ally marries in his sixties, his rheumatic wife being brought to the church in a wheelchair. Hardy's habitual topic is the rising of the rocket of love: marriage is the stick hitting the ground.

II

At this point the argument forks. One of the alternative roads has been clearly sign-posted by a number of recent critics of Hardy. Progress along it would involve making points of approximately the following kind. Hardy's exclusive absorption in the excitements of romantic and sexual liaison is symptomatic of his essential immaturity – an immaturity he himself acknowledges in the *Life*.[3] He shows a morbid over-sensitivity to the symptoms of physical ageing, especially in the case of women. His novels are full of unhealthy sexual manifestations – voyeurism, fetishism, masochism masquerading as stoicism. This obsessiveness is all of a piece with the adolescent sexual susceptibility he retained to an embarrass-ingly late age and to his notorious estrangement from his first wife. He returns again and again to the shallow drama of flirtation and titillation, being incapable of portraying the kind of controlled, reciprocal love that he never experienced.

And so it would be possible to go on. This is a comfortable road, smooth-surfaced and much travelled – but I don't care to take it because I think it leads away from Hardy's actual writings and arrives nowhere very interesting. There is a further consideration: it would seem that many literary commentators are at home on that route for reasons of personal moral taste. They feel able to assume that a controlled, balanced view of romantic passion is available to all right-thinking and intelligent people. A comment such as 'she was in desperate need of loving somebody' would seem to mean little to them. It thus becomes a matter of easy confidence to award any author marks out of ten for maturity of sexual outlook, whether in art or life. I don't share this frame of mind. In fact one of the things I most value in Hardy is the way he grapples with the problems posed by the elusiveness, capriciousness and uncontrolla-bility of love and desire. So I will take the other fork in the argu-ment, which requires an attempt to empathize with Hardy's views.

Certainly his presentation of love poses difficult questions. If the account I've given is fair he would seem to allow virtually no middle ground between the listlessness or disengagement which leaves one less than fully alive, and the nervous excitability of deluded infatuation. Is he implying that it is actually impossible to 'fall in love' reasonably and justifiably? Intermittently he seems to suggest that there could be such a phenomenon as the right person, the right 'comer'. Could there? If Angel Clare had danced with Tess the first time he set eyes on her, if Bathsheba had accepted Gabriel Oak's initial proposal, if Farfrae had married Elizabeth-Jane before Lucetta appeared on the scene ... Certainly things might still have gone wrong, but they would have gone wrong *differently*. Why does Hardy never tell that kind of story?

Then, for so convinced a Darwinian, he seems oddly oblivious to the evolutionary implications of his views on love. Repeatedly, and in the very grain of his descriptions, he shows that human beings are subject to the energies that dominate the animal and vegetable world. It might have been expected, then, that simple sexual appetite would loom large as a motive in his fiction. Fitzpiers does a little in this line, and Alec d'Urberville does more, but they are atypical. The love Hardy depicts is controlled by ideas, and even derives from them. Fascination, not lust, is the great driving force. What evolutionary hope can there be for a species spurred to breed by baseless fantasies and agitation of the nerves?

But I want to leave these queries suspended and attempt a defence, even a celebration, of Hardy's views on love. It entails looking at them from a vantage-point rather different from any adopted so far in this essay. My key terms, 'fascination' and 'list-lessness', offer a possible starting point. Though Hardy uses them so often in relation to love they relate to a deeper dialectic in his work – a dialectic much analysed and discussed by critics. On the one hand he repeatedly refers to the unimaginable scale and antiq-uity of the universe we inhabit, in comparison with which the indi-vidual human being is an unnoticeable speck. On the other hand he regularly reminds us that each of these specks has an intelligence – perhaps the only intelligence – that apprehends the universe, and a passionate and unique inner life. When the emphasis is on the former consideration the human figure is reduced, as are Cytherea and Tess, to a depressed sense of being negligible – 'one of a long row only' – a sense that conduces to listlessness. When the emphasis is on the latter there is a sudden surge of vitality, a revived feeling of uniqueness – very much the reactions associated with 'fascination'.

One of Hardy's recurring images offers both alternatives, both views of life, simultaneously. It is the image of a living creature suddenly illuminated in darkness:

> As Eustacia crossed the fire-beams she appeared for an instant as distinct as a figure in a phantasmagoria – a creature of light surrounded by an area of darkness: the moment passed, and she was absorbed in night again. (*The Return of the Native*, Book Fifth, Ch. VII)

> Gnats, knowing nothing of their brief glorification, wandered across the shimmer of this pathway, irradiated as if they bore fire within them; then passed out of its line, and were quite extinct. (*Tess of the d'Urbervilles*, Ch. XXXII)

In Hardyesque terms an unhappy man seeing these sights or reading these descriptions would feel the oppressive force of darkness, brevity, extinction. A happy man would respond to the irradiation, the glorification that serves as a metaphor for the vividness of the individual existence.

In these instances, as in countless others, the light is a literal one. But frequently it is figurative – the light of love. Pierston watches the second Avice, 'for the moment an irradiated being ...: by the beams of his own infatuation

> '... robed in such exceeding glory
> That he beheld her not"' (*The Well-Beloved*, Part Second, Ch. 9).

Tess feels despair when, after her confession, she realizes that Clare now sees her 'without irradiation ... in all her bareness'.

Admittedly 'irradiation', or something very like it, can be achieved by more mundane means, such as conviviality and drink. Mrs Durbeyfield finds that, at Rolliver's, 'A sort of halo, an occidental glow' comes over life. Hardy says something rather similar, in the succeeding chapter, about Mr Durbeyfield and his fellow-drinkers:

The stage of mental comfort to which they had arrived at this hour was one wherein their souls expanded beyond their skins, and spread their personalities warmly through the room. In this process the chamber and its furniture grew more and more dignified and luxurious, the shawl hanging at the window took upon itself the richness of tapestry, the brass handles of the chest of drawers were as golden knockers, and the carved bedposts seemed to have some kinship with the magnificent pillars of Solomon's temple.　(Ch. IV)

The irony in the passage modifies the transformations described, but doesn't annul them; '… their souls expanded beyond their skins …': the experience falls well short of the 'exaltation' that Tess achieves through love, or through gazing at a star, but it's a step in that direction. Hardy pursues the theme with greater intensity when describing the tipsy dancers walking home from Chaseborough:

… however terrestrial and lumpy their appearance just now to the mean unglamoured eye, to themselves the case was different. They followed the road with a sensation that they were soaring along in a supporting medium, possessed of original and profound thoughts; themselves and surrounding nature forming an organism of which all the parts harmoniously and joyously interpenetrated each other. They were as sublime as the moon and stars above them; and the moon and stars were as ardent as they.　(Ch. X)

'Terrestrial and lumpy' / 'sublime as the moon and stars': the polarities are those of listlessness and fascination. The ambivalence in the description of these revellers is structural, not incidental. Hardy is further developing a theme central to *Tess of the d'Urbervilles*: the process of falling in love will be shown to be similarly transformative. Angel Clare sees Tess as Artemis or Demeter; Tess is spiritually transformed by the sound of a second-hand harp only passably well played. Love resembles drunkenness in that it makes one see and hear things differently, feel more richly alive.

As a novelist Hardy can easily be misread because he modulates so effortlessly and unpredictably between realism and modernism. The critics least responsive to him are those unable to go beyond the literal reading. A little earlier I described Eustacia's early contacts with Clym in roughly such terms: an overheard conversation, a muttered good-night, a first sight of his face and she was already 'in love'. From a common-sense perspective, how absurdly precipitate. But Hardy isn't simply telling a particular story – he is showing what falling in love is *like*. We snatch glimpses, hear voices, make guesses, over-interpret, see things in dreams. The relevant section of *The Return of the Native* isn't simply a narrative that shows Eustacia succumbing to infatuation: it's an *expression* of that infatuation. To read it for the story alone is to extract a skeleton.

There's a comparison here with Shakespeare's comedies, which clearly had great influence on Hardy. In those plays the extravagances of plot become a means of suggesting the extravagances of romantic feeling. The suggestion is that love, at least among the young, produces behaviour so confused that it's *as though* they'd swallowed a magic potion, or come to question their own gender, or had fallen in love with identical twins. The same 'as though' is constantly operative in Hardy's fiction, making narrative simultaneously metaphor. The effect can be anywhere along the spectrum from comic to melodramatic. It's a commonplace that when one is infatuated one sees reminders of the beloved one everywhere. Hardy burlesques the idea in *Desperate Remedies* when Cytherea becomes aware that her lover's initials are branded on the buttocks of all the sheep in the vicinity of Knapwater House. An energetic lover may break through the reserve of a reluctant girl. *The Trumpet-Major* images such an irruption when Bob Loveday literally cuts through the partition-wall that separates him from Anne Garland. More grandiosely, in *A Pair of Blue Eyes* Hardy proposes an answer to the question 'What does it feel like to fall unexpectedly in love for the first time in your mid-thirties?' It feels something like hanging from the face of a high cliff in a powerful wind with a huge drop below your feet, with heavy rain falling upwards and a dark sea waiting to swallow you if you lose your grip.

In scenes which work something like that one – and Hardy's fiction is full of them – the effect could be described as operatic. The peculiar beauty of opera is that it can make two things happen at once. A story is told in words and actions but emotion can be projected into a fourth dimension of music. The story tells you who the heroine falls in love with, and why. Her aria tells you what that love feels like, and makes you share the feeling. The duplicity of effect is so easily understood by audiences for anything from *Evita* to *La Traviata* that it tends to be taken for granted, and its complexity overlooked. One justification of the mode could be stated in the following terms: 'If this lonely courtesan could project the love in her heart, it would be with this kind of beauty and passion.' Another might be expressed something like this: 'All of us would wish to capture, or to re-capture, the intensities of love. This aria, in its context, will enable you to do so.' Violetta sings for all of us.

With regard to opera I'm talking (in general) about the transcription of feeling into melody. In Hardy's work, of course, the transcription is into metaphor. I think most lovers of Hardy read him, and re-read him, whether they know it or not, primarily for the 'arias', those potent, memorable scenes – subjective correlatives – which in many cases may seem extraneous to the narrative proper, but are means of projecting the emotions which that narrative has unleashed.

To recapitulate: I am saying that Hardy's presentation of love is wonderfully adept at making us experience, or remember, the transforming power of passion; and I am arguing that he values this sensation as a type of the joy that can transform, 'irradiate', a dulled life of diurnal habituation and make us feel to the full the singularity of our separate existences. But in asserting this position I may seem to have drifted a fair way from my comments on Hardy's desire to anatomize, to diagnose. After all, he does again and again attribute the exalted sensations I'm talking about to self-delusion or 'morbid imagination', and in so doing he might well be said to be importing the literal view for which I've expressed a distaste. Is not the romantic love he brings to poetic life delusive or immature, however good it makes the lover feel? Isn't it – as he might be thought to imply in *Tess* – akin to mere drunkenness?

I conclude by offering two possible answers to these questions. The first is a summary 'yes' – but it's followed by (colon) 'but so what?' If you read the 'Digression on Madness' in Swift's *A Tale of a Tub*, you find that you are dialectically manoeuvred towards a conclusion that proffers alternative attitudes to life: you can be a Knave among Fools or a Fool among Knaves. The former is smarter than his fellows in being constantly aware, unlike the complacent Fools, of the essential animality of human existence. The price paid is cynicism and self-loathing. The Fool among Knaves, blind to this truth, is content with surfaces, happy because 'well-deceived'. Swift clearly presents these alternatives as a deliberate Hobson's Choice: heads you lose, tails you also lose.

At the risk of further simplifying what has already had to be a simplified summary I suggest that Hardy's position on love functions rather similarly. Fired with love you can be, at least for a short time, an optimist among pessimists, living in an irradiated world. Alternatively your head may point out that this transfiguration is merely the product of emotional need compounded with self-deception and over-heated imaginings. You can become a pessimist among optimists. But Hardy, I feel, differs from Swift in NOT making the alternatives a Hobson's Choice. His bleak honesty may repeatedly record his awareness that romantic love is largely, perhaps wholly, a matter of delusion. But always his heart, his imagination, his prose are saying 'Go for it, anyway: follow the instinct for joy.' He's in good company. Shakespeare continually describes love in terms of madness. Specifically he likens the lover to a lunatic in terms of capacity for delusion. But none of his comedies recommends that we take the cure.

My second answer is more complicated, and goes back to one of Hardy's comments on Eustacia, quoted earlier: 'her passion, which lowered her as an intellect, raised her as a soul'. What does he mean? How can something both lower you as an intellect and raise you as a soul? What 'lowers' is obvious: it's the fantastical, irrational nature of the feeling concerned. But how does the 'raising' come about?

I think, in the following way – which, incidentally, differentiates its 'irradiations' from those produced by drink. Love may be delusory for the reason given by Fitzpiers, in that it springs not from the character of the loved one, who is only uncertainly perceived, but from the character of the lover. But nevertheless there can be a richness in that love, derived not from its object but from its sources. What is quickened in the lover goes far beyond petty egotism: diverse perceptions and imaginings are fired and fused into transcendent feeling. This is the process which may be said to 'raise' the soul: your *being* is brought to life.

I haven't scope here to develop the point: I have space only for a single illustration of it, which happens to consist of one of my favourite passages in Hardy's fiction, the account of Avice Caro's funeral, as seen by Jocelyn Pierston:

> The level line of the sea horizon rose above the surface of the isle, a ruffled patch in mid-distance as usual marking the Race. ... Against the stretch of water, where a school of mackerel

twinkled in the afternoon light, was defined, in addition to the distant lighthouse, a church with its tower, standing about a quarter of a mile off, near the edge of the cliff. The churchyard gravestones could be seen in profile against the same vast spread of watery babble and unrest.

Among the graves moved the form of a man clothed in a white sheet, which the wind blew and flapped coldly every now and then. Near him moved six men bearing a long box, and two or three persons in black followed. The coffin, with its twelve legs, crawled across the isle, while around and beneath it the flashing lights from the sea and the school of mackerel were reflected; a fishing-boat, far out in the Channel, being momentarily discernible under the coffin also.   (*The Well-Beloved*, Part Second, Ch. 3)

It might seem reasonable to put questions such as: Why doesn't Hardy let Pierston arrive at the funeral on time and mourn properly? What has this overcrowded, hyperactive landscape-description to do with Pierston's love for Avice? The answer to the latter question, and the indirect answer to the former, is 'everything'. Pierston has never adequately recognized the individuality of Avice – he would be the first to admit to that charge – but his feeling for her has none the less been powerful: a concatenation of his responses to the rocks, the sea, the movement, the light, the life of the island that had shaped both of them. The complex poetic vitality of the passage is an index to the complex nature of an emotion which may have been irrational and subjective but was remote from empty fancy or casual sexual desire.

If I had to summarize the Hardyesque views that I have been trying to analyse, it would be in something like the following terms. However confused and deceiving its origins, however uncertain its subsequent course, love can irradiate, can quicken and heighten and poetically cross-relate our responses to everything around us. In illustrating the process so feelingly in his work Hardy enforces his point by conveying the very tang of enhanced vitality. To read his accounts of love literally and censoriously, with a 'mean unglamoured eye', is scarcely to read them at all.

Notes

1. Quotations from *Desperate Remedies*, *The Hand of Ethelberta* and *A Group of Noble Dames* are taken from Macmillan's New Wessex Edition (London: Macmillan, 1974–7). Quotations from Hardy's other novels and short stories come from The World's Classics Edition (Oxford: Oxford University Press, 1985–93). Chapter references for quotations are given in parentheses in the text.
2. See, for example, Chapter Six.
3. 'I was a child till I was 16; a youth till I was 25; a young man till I was 40 or 50.' Thomas Hardy, *The Life and Work of Thomas Hardy*, ed. Michael Millgate (London: Macmillan Press, 1984) p. 408.

6

'The Worthy Encompassed by the Inevitable': Hardy and a New Perception of Tragedy

RAYMOND CHAPMAN

Hardy was still smarting from the general execration of *Jude the Obscure* when he wrote a 'Postscript' to his original Preface, for the novel's 1912 edition. His apologia explained that the marriage theme had 'seemed a good foundation for the fable of a tragedy' and that he was 'not without a hope that certain cathartic, Aristotelian qualities might be found therein'. His gentle boast may be seen not only as a defiance of the reviewers but also as a pleased acceptance of those admirers who were beginning to hail him as a great tragic novelist.

The phrase has since become inseparable from Hardy's reputation, and if greatness or tragedy are meaningful words, the ascription may be regarded as well justified. Critics were able to find analogues with Greek tragedy, encouraged by some of Hardy's many classical references such as Clym Yeobright's mouth in 'the phase more or less imaginatively rendered in studies of Oedipus'; 'dramas of a grandeur and unity truly Sophoclean'; Sue's fear that 'a tragic doom overhung our family, as it did the house of Atreus'; and the too-familiar 'President of the Immortals, in Aeschylean phrase' (*The Return of the Native*, Bk 5, Ch. 2; *The Woodlanders*, Ch. 1; *Jude the Obscure*, Pt 5, Ch. 4; *Tess of the d'Urbervilles*, Ch. 59). Such comparisons, though apparently flattering, do little justice to Hardy's originality as a tragic writer. He cannot be dismissed as an imitator of past writers, or assigned to a particular school or clear definition of tragedy.

Yet it is clear that he saw himself as learning from the masters of the past, and drawing on some of their criteria for tragedy. No one perhaps can have a concept of literary tragedy which does not take some account of practice and theory in the periods of high tragic achievement. It may be as unprofitable to seek a definitive model for literary tragedy as it is to seek one for literary greatness. In both attempts, we may find qualities which recur and which assist criticism without constraining it, if they are found in sufficient number in any given text. Each tragic work, each literary text in any genre, is unique and poses its own questions for the reader's response. There is no final litmus test, but the tragic sense seems to be part of the mature human consciousness. It is a dimension of life which rejects complete answers but invites continual examination. That is why tragedy is written, and why it is so much discussed. Hardy follows some of the tragic criteria and also departs from them; his innovations are more compelling because they develop from a shared centrality. The points of contact are worth attention, as making us more fully aware of his true originality when he breaks new ground and accommodates in the tragic mode the realities of his own time.

The greatest periods of literary tragedy, in classical Greece and Renaissance England, pre-dated the novel. They used the dramatic mode, in societies where power was exercised by right of birth or by force of conquest. The hierarchy of unelected power seemed to stand apart from the expectations of ordinary life. Remoteness brought a charisma which election could not match, and the figures of the hierarchy could embody the diverse and more limited concerns of the many. The fall of the great was a wound to society that needed instant repair, and a warning to the ambitions and follies of lesser persons. These social realities were the ground on which the theory and practice of tragedy were built.

Such societies declined, in western Europe at least, from the seventeenth century, and tragedy of the classical type declined with them. The great ones who had been the heroes and also the victims of tragedy gradually faded away.[1] Napoleon Bonaparte was perhaps the last to possess the old charisma, an attraction for Hardy throughout his life and one which he turned to final account when he wrote *The Dynasts*. The rise of the novel, a bourgeois genre resting more on the uncertainties of a mobile society than on the rigidities of a fixed order, may not have destroyed the tragic sense but certainly accompanied its movement into a different perspective.

It has been claimed that tragedy is no longer a possible literary form. Humanity now seems not to stand at the centre of a universe governed by meaningful laws. There can be no true heroism if there is no superior force which is at least aware of human struggles. As one writer suggests, 'individualism has become either unrestricted or all but totally repressed.'[2] The fear of meaninglessness, which Paul Tillich saw as the specific ontological fear of this age, may indeed seem to disenable tragedy in its long-understood sense. I hope to show that Hardy confronted these problems directly and in so doing brought the tragic spirit into a new mode which did not lose contact with its past. Whatever may be true from the late nineteenth century onwards, the decline of classical tragic possibilities certainly begins much earlier. The general absence of tragedy in the developing novel is not a proof of Aristotle's denial of tragedy to the narrative form.[3] A novelist like Hardy creates characters who, once we accept a new vision of tragedy, can grow in our own image and reflect our real condition more convincingly than the visual representations of the stage.

Fielding's claim to write 'a comic epic in prose' pointed one way for the novel. Richardson's overriding moral sense pointed another, and the one which novelists would essentially follow for the rest of the eighteenth century and most of the nineteenth. The moral sense, however worthy as an ideal for life, inhibited the novel as a tragic form. It even ante-dated the mature novel, as Addison noted when he wrote:

> The English writers of tragedy are possessed with a notion, that when they represent a virtuous or innocent person in distress, they ought not to leave him till they have delivered him out of his troubles or made him triumph over his enemies.[4]

That could be said to summarize the conclusion of a large proportion of Victorian novels. Hardy would have no such simplistic conclusions. He was particularly troubled by the suppression of sexuality in the novel, which brought him much hostile criticism when he tried to break the mould. His regret for the disappearance of literary tragedy centred on this, but touched on the whole condition of the contemporary novel. His exasperation and his own defiance of fashion were firmly expressed:

[I]n representations of the world, the passions ought to be proportioned as in the world itself. This is the interest which was
excited in the minds of the Athenians by their immortal
tragedies, and in the minds of Londoners at the first performance
of the finer plays of three hundred years ago. They reflected life,
revealed life, criticised life. Life being a physiological fact, its
honest portrayal must be largely concerned with, for one thing,
the relations of the sexes, and the substitution for such catastrophes as favour the false colouring best expressed by the regula-
tion finish that 'they married and were happy ever after', of
catastrophes based upon sexual relationship as it is.[5]

The authors and readers of Victorian fiction did not lack a conception of heroism, as strong as in any period, but they had suffered a dislocation, a loss of shared role models. The cult of the
Superman, led by Carlyle, did nothing to restore the tragic hero as a
meaningful representative of society. His quest was robustly articulated but ultimately artificial, seeking models from a variety of past
cultures. Despite brief hopes of Robert Peel, Carlyle never found a
satisfactory contemporary hero. The words 'hero' and 'heroine' are
constantly used by Victorian novelists and critics. The hero has all
the 'manly' virtues. He is brave, honest and faithful, qualities which
the heroine shares with the addition of 'womanly' virtues of tenderness and sympathy. The hero is allowed a few slight moral
flaws, to be corrected by the end of the story; absolute purity is required of the heroine. The dramatists created characters in the same
mould, thinly veiled by the Shakespearean language of poetic plays
or made explicit in the melodramatic dialogue shared with prose
fiction.

Now Hardy of course creates neither supermen nor conventional
heroes and heroines. He worked with the insight that superior dis-
missal of the rustic 'Hodge' failed to discern 'men of many minds,
infinite in difference; some happy, many serene, a few depressed;
some clever, even to genius, some stupid, some wanton, some
austere; some mutely Miltonic, some Cromwellian'.[6] He opened a
new dimension of tragic fiction by making Henchard and Jude the
central figures of novels, by demanding sympathy rather than condemnation for Eustacia and Tess. He accepted a flawed, essentially
tragic, state of the world to an extent which very few of his contemporaries equalled. Now this at first sight may seem a dubious claim
to uniqueness in a singularly moralistic age, and one in which we

can now discern more disquiet than the complacent optimism attributed to it by the anti-Victorian reaction earlier in the twentieth century. The Victorians certainly had no doubt about Original Sin and the disposition of uncorrected human nature to go astray, but they seldom envisioned a generality of conflict and alienation. Such is the vision of minor writers like James Thomson, and the occasional nightmare of major ones like Tennyson, but it found no leading voice before Hardy. At least, this was true of Britain; elsewhere the later *angst* was anticipated by philosophers like Nietzsche and Kierkegaard, writers like Büchner and Kleist, and later by Ibsen and Strindberg.

One of the essentials of tragedy is surely that it embodies the strong enforcement of values, whether they be religious, judicial or social. Judgement is given, consequences are enforced; the traditional 'happy ending' of comedy means not just the 'happy ever after' which Hardy denigrated in the contemporary novel, but rather that, before our eyes, people escape the penalties that would be imposed in a tragic world. The Victorian mind had no difficulty about rewards and penalties; public morality was based largely on the assumption that they were the inevitable results of conduct. Where they missed the tragic sense was in a rigid categorizing of good and bad behaviour, and a desire to see the consequences of each proportioned to its quality. The literary result was the tidy ending of many novels, with potted biographies of the principal characters after the end of the story. The final chapters of *David Copperfield* are a prime example. Even those like Samuel Butler who chafed against the convention liked to bring their sympathetic characters through to a happy future. The ending of *The Way of All Flesh* is a gift to those who still like to speak of Victorian complacency. Many even of the finest Victorian novels justify the comment of Wilde's Miss Prism, 'The good ended happily, and the bad unhappily. That is what Fiction means.' This does not make for a tragic world, as some contemporary Continental writers saw it. Tragic consequences may be predictable, within the given assumptions of the writer, but they are not neatly proportioned.

To say all this is not to depreciate the achievement of undoubtedly great writers, some of whom had qualities which Hardy lacked. None shared his capacity to carry through the consequences of choice without reserve or flinching. George Eliot has much to say about consequences, and she alone approaches Hardy in this respect. But she does not avoid the sense of just punishment in climaxes like the deaths of Tito Melema and Grandcourt. It is unwise to make too much of single instances, but one cannot help comparing the last-minute reprieve of Hetty Sorrel with the unrelenting fate of Tess. Hetty serves her punishment and dies offstage, and we are spared the sense of cruelty and waste to which Hardy leads us.[7] Here and elsewhere Eliot can be seen as still partly constrained by the Evangelical background which she had overtly repudiated.

For Eliot, and for most of her contemporaries, there is a clear source of tragic judgement, a set of identifiable values. Circumstances often operate to make characters act against their better knowledge, but there is a general supposition that the will is free and that choices are activated by the proportions of goodness and badness in the individual. High tragedy acknowledges the variableness of human beings but does not assume complete freedom of the will. The conflict between free will and some kind of external control is fundamental to the tragic catastrophe in the dramas of ancient Greece and in those of Elizabethan and Jacobean England.

What control operates on Hardy's characters, in a universe where neither classical philosophy nor Christian conviction offers an ultimate canon, though both have left their mark? Certainly they are afflicted by the frustration of their best desires, the escalation of momentary weakness into inescapable disaster. What makes his universe tragic is partly the sense that humanity is somehow an alien within it and that the individual, in the discerning words of one critic, 'gains no special attention from the forces that are unconscious and therefore supremely indifferent to his hopes and efforts'.[8] This sense of being alien and consequently insignificant in the totality of things is powerfully expressed in pictorial imagery. Clym Yeobright walks on Egdon Heath like one who has strayed into a pre-human world: 'The scene seemed to belong to the ancient world of the carboniferous period, when the forms of plants were few, and of the fern kind; when there was neither bud nor blossom, nothing but a monotonous extent of leafage, amid which no bird sang' (*The Return of the Native*, Bk 3, Ch. 5). In the same novel there is the flippant description of Charley appearing on the dark heath 'like a fly on a negro' (Bk 2, Ch. 4), which is later developed into something much more foreboding. When Tess is going to Talbothays, she 'stood still upon the hemmed expanse of verdant flatness, like a fly on a billiard-table of indefinite length, and of no more consequence to the surroundings than that fly' (*Tess of the d'Urbervilles*, Ch. 16). The same sense of insignificance in the face of the cosmos appears in the vivid account of Knight confronting a fossil trilobite on the cliff edge. The fly on the billiard-table suggests a more positive alienation, a creature that has no business in something it cannot comprehend, to be swept aside or destroyed as an intruder. So too in *The Woodlanders* human misery seems part of the perpetual struggle for natural survival, the condition of a starkly Darwinian world. Lyell, Spencer and Huxley, as well as Darwin, overshadowed the years of Hardy's maturing with ideas that tended to diminish human significance and free will.

To write under the influence of such ideas must mean facing ultimate indifference rather than benevolence, however remote. If Hardy restores a Shakespearean dimension to the depiction of a tragic world, it is not that of the divinity that shapes our ends but rather of the gods to whom we are as flies to wanton boys. The force that drives the minor failures of life to complete disaster is not clearly conceived or consistently named. It may be malignant, amused, indifferent, or even forgetful of its own creation.[9] In his Preface to the 'Wessex' edition of 1912, Hardy emphasized that 'Positive views on the Whence and the Wherefore of things have never been advanced by this pen as a consistent philosophy.' He did not set out to explain the universe, or polemically to support or refute any systematic creed. What he did was to give imaginative expression to a belief that there is something which seems frequently to work against human endeavour. In 1892 he wrote in his notebook, 'The best tragedy – highest tragedy in short – is that of the WORTHY encompassed by the INEVITABLE. The tragedies of immoral and worthless people are not of the best.'[10]

What is this encompassing Inevitable? Perhaps it is not important whether it is called Fate, Destiny, Doom, the gods, the Spinner of the Years, the Immanent Will or the Supreme Power. Hardy does not offer a philosophical system or a pantheon in which these forces are precisely differentiated. He, and his characters, invoke these and other names so indiscriminately that any attempt to assign a distinct identity to each must end not in clarification but in confusion. It is enough that he frequently asserts that sense of a controlling power which has always been deemed to be as basic to tragedy as the assertion of individual will. Without freewill the protagonists are puppets, and there is no conflict; without some greater influence, we are moved by a sad story of human frailty but miss the tragic grandeur.

Hardy's Inevitable does not actively punish transgression of its laws as in classical and Renaissance tragedy. No Furies are sent to pursue offenders, there is no concession to the morality which believes that, 'The gods are just, and of our pleasant vices / Make instruments to plague us' (*King Lear*, V, iii). If there is an order of things, it remains as background, as the billiard-table on which the fly must wander. Retribution may be exacted by human law, or there may be only Clym Yeobright's regret 'that for what I have done no man or law can punish me' (*The Return of the Native*, Bk 5, Ch. 9).

Yet punishment is often awarded, by the judicial system which takes the life of Tess or by the cumulative rejection of Henchard and Jude. In several of the novels there is an unresolved tension between unseen, overarching power and the anger of a violated social order. It is a tension which could be regarded as dodging the problem of where ultimate tragic sanction lies, but I would argue that it is a step forward in the fashioning of tragedy in a world from which the old certainties have gone. Henchard seems for much of his story to be a character subject to fate, but he ends as an outcast from the human society to whose morality he would not conform. Jude Fawley might be a more classically heroic figure if the epic scale which the novel partly suggests were developed to the end, but the human faithlessness with an accompaniment of communal jubilation which leaves him on his deathbed is tragedy of a different kind, more ironic, perhaps more distressing. The killing of the children is artistically disturbing not so much for its shock of horror as for the sense that Hardy is trying to make the boy Time into a tragic icon when the plot is growing more intense in human terms. The real tragedy of Jude is foreshown in his childish despair when 'nobody did come, because nobody does' (*Jude the Obscure*, Pt 1, Ch. 4). That is a succinct and significant statement of Hardy's view of tragedy.

There is, however, another element besides the unresolved idea of external fate and the unaccommodating rules of human life. The misfortunes which sway the plot at some critical moment have aroused much mirth in Hardy's detractors, and some discomfort in his admirers. The point has been somewhat exaggerated and laboured, over episodes like the undiscovered confession by Tess, and Fanny's mistaking of the church for her wedding. Hardy does sometimes cut a naturalistic corner in this respect, but seldom to the detriment of his art. There is more to be said, which can put the chance encounters, the misdirected messages and the overheard conversations into a different perspective.

More consideration must be given to Hardy's idea of Chance. It is to be separated from the set of words like Fate and Doom, because it introduces a rather different element into the tension between human endeavour and the perversity of things as they are. It is well known that Hardy often uses the word *chance*, and also one of his favourite Saxon words, *hap*. The usage is sometimes regarded as an excuse for coincidence, but in fact it is much more; it can refer to a positive factor in the tragic course of life. What happens to the worthy may indeed sometimes seem to be directed by a malignant force, but there is also the power of the random element in events. In periods of doubt and transition, the belief in Fortune as a directing force has often been strong. Fortune appears as a kind of minor deity in the Roman Empire, was rediscovered in the late Middle Ages and was further developed when the English Renaissance was passing from Tudor expansion to the threatening shadows of the seventeenth century. Fortune is an important element in Elizabethan drama, with a specific iconography and set of attributes based on earlier presentations. She is blind and distributes good or bad without regard to merit. She stands upon a sphere that represents the world, and her power is often shown by a wheel on which people rise to the top and as suddenly fall to be crushed beneath it. The pattern of rising and falling is particularly marked in Shakespeare's historical plays.[11]

Hardy does not personify Chance in this way, but he makes more than casual use of the force which distributes favours and disasters without apparent reason. He had good precedent in earlier dramatic tragedy for suggesting that a random element sometimes seems to prevail and frustrate human endeavour. It is perhaps not enough for a whole theory of tragedy, but the pity and the terror may well be evoked when it works together with human weakness and a malignant or indifferent destiny. In *The Mayor of Casterbridge* we follow a course like the turning of Fortune's Wheel as Henchard rises from shameful obscurity to the mayoralty. Farfrae slowly approaches him, the wheel turns and the new mayor sits on top while the old one falls back to poverty and loneliness. Henchard speaks as one of those whom Chaucer's Monk describes as fallen 'out of heigh degree / Into miserie' in his lament, 'the bitter thing is, that when I was rich I didn't need what I could have, and now I be poor I can't have what I need!' (*The Mayor of Casterbridge*, Ch. 33). It should be added that in his later years Hardy was prepared to give less credibility to Chance, but by then he had made good use of it as a tragic device.[12]

If these are the forces of the Inevitable, who are the Worthy that are thus encompassed? Hardy never suggests that tragedy comes only as either chance or inescapable fate. His characters are often tormented by powers that push them beyond the limit, but they never seem to be mere puppets. Nor does he portray extreme human wickedness as the source of evil. He sometimes lapses into melodramatic language – in which the majority of Victorian novelists also indulged – but he does not let tragedy disappear into the simplistic world of melodrama which pits the bad against the good and, in the words of one theatre historian, 'saw the triumph of virtue everywhere'.[13] He has few real villains; there is no Iago or Edmund, not even Uriah Heep or Dolge Orlick. Manston and Dare might qualify, but in the major novels characters are flawed rather than evil. Troy and Wildeve are scoundrels but scarcely villains. Henchard is no villain, unless quick temper and family injustice are villainy, in which case King Lear, with whom he has been compared, is a villain. He is a flawed character certainly, but then so is his rival and supplanter Farfrae. Alec d'Urberville is weak and self-indulgent rather than calculatingly bad. Meredith's comment that 'in tragic life … No villain need be! / Passions spin the plot: / We are betrayed by what is false within' is apposite (*Modern Love*, xliii).

There is neither heroism nor villainy in the clear-cut sense in which the Victorians understood these things, and their vision disenabled the highest tragedy. There are ordinary people who are both flawed and afflicted. Even George Eliot, who comes nearest to Hardy in tragic achievement, tends to give too much positive virtue to her sympathetic characters, particularly the men. Adam Bede and Felix Holt are just a little too good to be true, powerful creations though they are, and Ladislaw has found few admirers. I would agree with the judgement that Tess is not just a milkmaid who is, in the Victorian sense, 'ruined' and Jude is not just a bright country boy who failed to get into a university:

> [W]e have to see that they belong to a different dimension from that of Hetty Sorrel and Felix Holt; that they have rather the epic quality …[14]

This is important, indeed it goes to the heart of Hardy's position as a tragic writer. His tragic characters are ordinary in status, people of an age from which the demigods have departed and the kings are in decline. They are not ordinary in conception; we are compelled by the force of Hardy's own compassion to care for them, so that their distress feels like our own. They do not fulfil the classical criterion of being, in simplistic terms, 'better than we are'. They touch not only our basic humanity but also our individual humanity. We do not see them as creatures of rank and experience beyond our reach, suffering in a way that we cannot fully comprehend although it may fill us with pity and terror. They are close enough to us to touch our existential condition, greatly conceived enough to be images that point to things beyond themselves. They can be the victims, the scapegoats who seem to suffer for us, to carry the penalty of what we fear could easily be our lot. They take this role in a different way from the vicarious suffering which we feel in Oedipus and Lear. It is not society, not the commonwealth, which is purified because misjudgement and unbalance have been set right. It is rather that the reader, individual and solitary as a member of a theatre audience can never be, feels their distress as coming near to his or her reality.

It was Hardy's great and perhaps unique achievement in the creation of a new tragic form, to make his characters representatives on a heroic scale, without betraying his basic presentation of the simple and commonplace. It may be urged that his characters are not conceived grandly enough for the epic roles implied for them through the frequent echoes of Sophocles and Shakespeare. I would argue that they can match their conception not by heroic virtue or courage, but by their remarkable degree of self-awareness. They commit faults, make mistakes, but seldom offer false justification or withdraw into negative insensitivity in face of the forces they cannot comprehend. Ordinary people though they are, they rise to tragic dignity at the moment when self-knowledge illuminates the catastrophe. It is the classical *anagnorisis*, the revelation of identity or of the truth of the situation, which has been described as 'the essence of tragedy'.[15] Henchard shows a late-won nobility characteristic of the tragic hero when he accepts the loss of Elizabeth-Jane:

> If I had only got her with me – if I only had! ... Hard work would be nothing to me then! But that was not to be. I – Cain – go alone

as I deserve – an outcast and a vagabond. But my punishment is *not* greater than I can bear! (*The Mayor of Casterbridge*, Ch. 43)

Tess gains heroic stature when she confronts the police at Stonehenge:

It is as it should be. ... I am almost glad – yes, glad! This happiness could not have lasted. It was too much. I have had enough; and now I shall not live for you to despise me! (*Tess of the d'Urbervilles*, Ch. 58)

So too is Jude's self-recognition: 'My God, how selfish I was! Perhaps – perhaps I spoilt one of the highest and purest loves that ever existed between man and woman!' (*Jude the Obscure*, Pt 6, Ch. 3). For their effect in context, these declarations are not inferior to Lear's 'I am a very foolish fond old man.'

The essential greatness of these characters is heightened by the way in which they have the seeds of this self-knowledge long before the catastrophe which brings to fulfilment what they have partly known and come fully to comprehend through suffering. Henchard goes to death with the same sullen defiance that has marked all his life since his wife warns him not to try her too far before she goes with Newson. Tess learns the personal reality of her sad acceptance of living in a blighted world, Jude dies confirming his boyish discovery that 'Events did not rhyme quite as he had thought' (ibid., Pt 1, Ch. 2). The more shallow characters fail to understand the course of events until it is too late. Angel Clare is dismissive when Tess talks of suicide: 'It is nonsense to have such thoughts in this kind of case, which is rather one for satirical laughter than for tragedy' (*Tess of the d'Urbervilles*, Ch. 35). Farfrae wishes to give up the search for Henchard because a night away from home 'will make a hole in a sovereign' and responds to news of his death with 'Dear me – is that so!' (*The Mayor of Casterbridge*, Ch. 45).

If the major characters gain such iconic stature, it is mainly through the seriousness with which Hardy presents them as individuals. It is also because the environments of the novels are so much more than mere background or 'local colour'. Many have commented on Hardy's power of investing places with significance, creating in his Wessex a country of the mind which is rooted in actuality. The ancient history, the background of generations, makes the power of place very potent. Hintock House, afflicted with damp in a situation 'prejudicial to humanity', is an image of the corrupting, destructive nature of Mrs Charmond and of the exposure which kills Giles Winterborne. The derelict background of the wife-sale – 'pulling down is more the nater of Weydon' – prepares for Henchard's course of self-destruction. The garden at Talbothays, 'rank with juicy grass which sent up mists of pollen at a touch', suggests the pressure of latent sexuality in which the tragedy of Tess and Angel develops, and the harsh chill of Flintcomb-Ash figures her suffering after their separation. The stones of Christminster set up an impassable barrier to Jude's hopes in the college façades and offer him succour only as a labourer on their unshaped blocks. Hardy's reflection on a possible dramatization of *Jude the Obscure* in 1926 is highly significant. Would Arabella be the real villain, or Jude's personal constitution? 'Christminster is of course the tragic influence of Jude's drama in one sense, but innocently so, and merely as crass obstruction.'[16]

These are not just settings for action; they are silent but strangely dynamic witnesses to the mysterious Inevitable that encompasses the Worthy. They increase the sense of tragic doom which hangs over the characters from the beginning of their stories and is asserted as they move towards their catastrophes. Not only the wider town and country settings, but the small spots of place can carry the same force. Tess stops at the sinister monolith – an episode similar to that described in the poem 'Near Lanivet, 1872'. Jude chalks on the gate of Biblioll a verse from the Book of Job, a book which he will quote in his last delirium. These preceding shadows of doom match the forebodings of dramatic tragedy: the cold midnight battlements at the opening of *Hamlet*, the stormy sea through which Othello and Desdemona come to Cyprus, the rain which falls outside the claustrophobic house in the first scene of *Ghosts*. Few novelists show such power: Emily Brontë certainly, in her one novel; later Conrad, Faulkner and perhaps Greene. Dickens is of course a master of the sinister and threatening environment, but he carries it to conclusions different from those of high tragedy.

Individual suffering is compounded by the mysterious nature of inimical forces and by the influence of natural or man-made settings. It is made harsher also by the fact, which writers of tragedy have always recognized, that no individual lives quite alone. The Greek dramatists ended with a Chorus reflecting on the nature of human affairs and offering hope that the world will continue, even if the tragic course is to be for ever repeated. Shakespeare and his contemporaries frequently closed a play with similar reflections and the assurance that at least the business of ordered government would be carried on. Societies change their structures and their hopes, but no man is an island and every catastrophe shakes what Hardy called the 'great web of human doings' (*The Woodlanders*, Ch. 3).[17]

Yet in Hardy's world this sense of coinherence is troubled by his conviction that the mutual support of dwellers in the same community was being steadily eroded all through the nineteenth century. The conflict of old and new is emphasized in *A Laodicean* by that between church and chapel and between the claims of birth and money to the de Stancy heritage. It is stated in a wryly humorous regret for the disappearance of the reddleman as a means of frightening children, who 'has in his turn followed Buonaparte to the land of worn-out bogeys, and his place is filled by modern inventions' (*The Return of the Native*, Bk 1, Ch. 9). Society seems to become increasingly the enemy of the individual, not so much in active hostility as in the deprivation of sympathy that could arrest the tragic course or mitigate its catastrophe. The indifference of the mysterious Inevitable seems to be replicated in the world of men and women. The shared concern shown in *Under the Greenwood Tree*, and still in *Far from the Madding Crowd*, declines until Tess and Jude are destroyed with scarcely a ripple beyond their immediate circle. Society no longer needs the traditional assurance of renewal and continuity; it simply closes its ranks to conceal the gap which a doomed individual has left, a temporary blemish rather than a wound. The tragic sufferer has become important only to the self and not to the community, and this marks a significant change in the conception of tragedy. By the time of the last novels, it seems that the great web can be touched at one point without visibly shaking the whole.

The finality of death, the ultimate catastrophe for some at least of the protagonists in tragedy, also becomes a private matter. It is not that society destroys the individual in any positive way, but that there is an indifference amounting sometimes to hostility, which makes death solitary and unfriended. Eustacia and Wildeve die in flight from a society that would condemn them, torn apart by the wildness of natural forces. Giles Winterborne loses consciousness of other people before he is found dying. Henchard and Jude die alone, Tess in the sad irony of strange and hostile company, isolated from those she has loved. The great deathbed scenes of Victorian fiction were social and moralistic. In Hardy's novels, those who have struggled in life against increasing rejection go out in a final loneliness. They cannot even recognize or nominate their successors: no Fortinbras, no Edgar, neither a fresh champion nor another potential victim. The world will go on but the whole does not seem reassured or purified by the cathartic loss of a part. The heroic age is over; capacity to shake society by a tragic death proves as unattainable as the ideal of love pursued, from the gentle cynicism which ends *Under the Greenwood Tree* to the final sardonic laugh of *The Well-Beloved*.

The next century brought the final destruction of conditions and presumptions which had informed classical tragedy. The Great War gave a new and unliterary meaning to words like 'tragedy' and 'catastrophe', associations which the next war strengthened and which they have never lost in popular usage. At the time of the Boer War, Hardy recognized the coming of a conflict which destroyed the obscure individual who never intended to be a hero. Drummer Hodge, and the gunners' wives who speak in 'The Going of the Battery', respond to war in a different way from the noble six hundred, different even from the earlier hero whose trumpet was 'silenced for ever upon one of the bloody battle-fields of Spain' (*The Trumpet-Major*, Ch. 41).

Hardy writes in the tragic mode for and about a world which has lost or abandoned the old conditions of tragedy. He must assert the worth of the individual, the shared suffering, the remorseless enforcement of judgement and consequences, where there seem to be none of the ancient powers which make for righteousness to make these things acceptable. The individual must make his or her own significance, not depending on social or divine validation. This is the new world of writers in the Modernist era and beyond, of Conrad and O'Casey, of William Faulkner, Eugene O'Neill, Arthur Miller and Tennessee Williams. Tragedy becomes psychological rather than social. It depicts personal inadequacies and uncertainties, the shadow side to be shared by the reader or spectator, with society as a source of sullen indifference rather than inexorable values. This is the line which begins with Hardy's great tragic novels, and it runs on to Camus, Bellow and Murdoch, who depict the tragic enforcement of values in a world that seems to have no rational principle, which is, in the philosophical sense, absurd.

We find, as he was at pains to make clear, no holistic system of philosophy or belief in Hardy's work. He offers a tragic vision which contains the terror and pity, but not the assurance of a continuing restored stability, or an explanation of why things are as they are. Classical and Renaissance tragedies rest in the security of an ordered society, though the threat of mutability was heavy as the sixteenth century moved into the seventeenth, but they do not answer the great question 'Why?' Seeking explanations and finding answers is a habit of the Victorians, and yet another reason why they did not produce memorable literary tragedy. The conflicts in a tragic situation must remain in ambiguity and tension if the ever-present danger of melodrama is to be avoided. Hardy never falls into the error of passing judgement too confidently on the facts and so falsifying the conclusion. His meliorism does, as he wrote, exact a full look at the worst.

Yet he never fails in compassion, and this is what sets him apart from many writers who have pursued the tragic line in the twentieth century. He cares about his people, and even in depicting their sorrow he has the zest for all aspects of life which is typical of the Victorian age. There may be no other carers, or at least none who have power to help. His greatest novels could be viewed by a mingling of the Spirits in *The Dynasts*, a work which has been criticized in many details but perhaps undervalued for its overall view of an inexplicably tragic world. The Spirit Ironic may seem to dominate in the tragic endings, but the Spirit of the Pities is equally present, and prevails when we recollect the whole. He gently touches the reader's personal shadow and strengthens endurance. Life is to some extent for all, and preponderantly for some, a matter of damage limitation.

Hardy moved the tragic perspective some way from the traditional modes of which critics have rightly found echoes in his work. The question is not whether Michael Henchard is a Victorian King Lear, or whether classical analogues are found on Egdon Heath. Like all great writers, Hardy built partly on the achievements of the past, but set his own seal on his creation. His tragic novels are like a building set beside a noble ruin still retaining its majesty; perhaps like the new Coventry Cathedral built within the remains of the old, which visually perpetuates its own tragic story. The comparison might have pleased him, for although he took a cool view of contemporary Christian institutions, he never lost his love for small churches and great cathedrals, and for the traditional liturgy that comforted the victims of true human tragedy.

Notes

Quotations from Hardy's novels are taken from Macmillan's New Wessex Edition (London: Macmillan, 1974–6). Quotations from his poems are taken from *The Complete Poems of Thomas Hardy*, ed. James Gibson (London: Macmillan, 1976).

1. I am not ignoring the considerable achievements of Renaissance 'domestic tragedy' at its best. Heywood's *A Woman Killed with Kindness* and the anonymous *Arden of Feversham* are among several which claim respect, and the eighteenth-century plays of George Lillo have perhaps been underestimated. However, these are few and exceptional; dramatic tragedy has generally dealt with the great.

2. William Van O'Connor, *Climates of Tragedy* (Baton Rouge: Louisiana State University Press, 1943) p. 3. See also J. W. Krutch, 'The Tragic Fallacy', in *The Modern Temper* (New York: Harcourt Brace, 1929) pp. 115–43.

3. Murray Krieger argues that in an age which comes after thinkers like Kierkegaard and Nietzsche there is room only for a 'formless' tragedy, which can best be accommodated in the novel: *The Tragic Vision: Variations on a Theme in Literary Interpretation* (Chicago and London: University of Chicago Press, 1960).

4. Joseph Addison, *The Spectator*, 16 April 1711.

5. 'Candour in English Fiction', in *The New Review*, January 1890, pp. 16–17. [Note that there is no awkwardness in this passage as it appeared in *The New Review*. A printing error in Harold Orel's transcription of Hardy's article in *Thomas Hardy's Personal Writings* (see note 6 below) results in the awkward reading 'based upon sexual relations as it is'. This has been frequently quoted, with some bewilderment at Hardy's apparent grammatical lapse. The correct reading of 'based upon sexual relationship as it is' reads much more happily. My thanks to Michael Millgate who pointed me in the direction of the original printing in *The New Review* – Ed.]

6. 'The Dorsetshire Labourer', in *Longman's Magazine*, July 1883; quoted from Harold Orel (ed.), *Thomas Hardy's Personal Writings* (Lawrence: University of Kansas Press, 1966; London: Macmillan, 1967) pp. 170–1.

7. It is true that Boldwood is saved from execution by a last-minute reprieve, but the whole affair is in a much lower key. Troy and Boldwood cease to be important to the novel after the murder, and there is no strong moral judgement about either man getting what he deserved.

8.   Dale Kramer, *Thomas Hardy: The Forms of Tragedy* (London: Macmillan Press, 1975) p. 35.

9.   As in Hardy's poem 'God-Forgotten':

     – 'The Earth, sayest thou? The Human race?
     By Me created? Sad its lot?
     Nay: I have no remembrance of such place:
     Such world I fashioned not.' –

10. 24 October 1892. In Thomas Hardy, *The Life and Work of Thomas Hardy*, ed. Michael Millgate (London: Macmillan, 1984) p. 265. Hereafter cited as *Life and Work*.

11. See Raymond Chapman, 'Fortune in Elizabethan Drama' (unpublished MA thesis, University of London); F. Kiefer, *Fortune and Elizabethan Tragedy* (San Marino, CA: Huntingdon, 1983); H. R. Patch, *The Goddess Fortuna in Medieval Literature* (Cambridge, MA: Harvard University Press, 1927).

12. '[N]either chance nor purpose governs the universe, but necessity' (*Life and Work*, p. 364).

13. 'What began at the beginning of the eighteenth century as a modish cult became an intellectual bias which saw the triumph of virtue everywhere, not only in all human affairs, political as well as domestic, but in the firmament; not only as the fulfilling of personal destinies, but as the law of cosmos besides. Nature's partiality to the good was generally credited.' Maurice Willson Disher, *Blood and Thunder: Mid-Victorian Melodrama and its Origins* (London: Muller, 1949) pp. 12–13. This of course reads as the polar opposite of what Hardy believed.

14. R. J. White, *Thomas Hardy and History* (London: Macmillan, 1974) p. 19.

15. 'This [*anagnorisis*] – not *catharsis* as an ultimate effect, not *hamartia* – comes as near as we can get to the ultimate essence of tragedy' (C. Leech, *Tragedy* (London: Methuen, 1969) p. 84).

16. *Life and Work*, p. 467.

17. As Marty and Giles walk together 'their lonely courses formed no detached design at all, but were part of the pattern in the great web of human doings then weaving in both hemispheres from the White Sea to Cape Horn'. Hardy had earlier, on 4 March 1886, made a note of the great web 'which quivers in every part when one point is shaken, like a spider's web if touched' (*Life and Work*, p. 183).

7

Hardy and Time

PHILLIP MALLETT

In 1876 Hardy copied two sentences from an address by John Morley into his *Literary Notebooks*:

Life. 'The stuff of which life is made is Time.'

The unknown Great 'You never know what child in rags that meets you in the street may have in him the germ of gifts that might add new treasures to the storehouse of beautiful things or noble acts'[1]

One wonders why Hardy troubled to copy the first sentence, since Time, with or without the initial capital, is the subject of so much of his work. Few writers can have had less need to remind themselves of how much human life is shaped by the sense either of time past, of memories pushing into or pulling against the present, or more often of time as passing, the present undermined even as it is experienced by the anticipation of its loss. The second is more teasing. Was it taken down as the starting point for a story about wasted potential and the careless cruelty of social judgements, or perhaps for a poem about the gradual disclosure of the beauty hidden in the commonplace and everyday? Either of these might be a 'typical' Hardy subject. The sense of ambiguity in the sentence, and the idea of the 'germ', are among the topics I want to explore further in the course of this paper.

   The most familiar of a number of passages in which Hardy explores man's confrontation with Time with a capital T is in *A Pair of Blue Eyes*, when Henry Knight finds himself stranded on the 'Cliff without a name', gazing at the fossil of a trilobite embedded in the rock face:

Time closed up like a fan before him. He saw himself at one extremity of the years, face to face with the beginning and all the intermediate centuries simultaneously. Fierce men, clothed in the hides of beasts, and carrying, for defence and attack, huge clubs and pointed spears, rose from the rock. ... Behind them stood an earlier band. No man was there. Huge elephantine forms, the mastodon, the hippopotamus, the tapir, antelopes of monstrous size, the megatherium, and the mylodon – all, for the moment, in juxtaposition. Further back, and overlapped by these, were perched huge-billed birds and swinish creatures as large as horses. Still more shadowy were the sinister crocodilian outlines – alligators and other uncouth shapes, culminating in the colossal lizard, the iguanodon. Folded behind were dragon forms and clouds of flying reptiles: still underneath were fishy beings of lower development; and so on, till the lifetime scenes of the fossil confronting him were a present and modern condition of things ...[2]

The passage pulls us in various directions. Knight's fall is literally down the cliff in space, but it also takes him back in time to the meeting with the trilobite, and metaphorically down as well as back through the evolutionary scale, from the plant life at the top of the cliff to the fossil on its face, with the inorganic rock and primordial sea below. The experimenter seems about to become the subject of Nature's 'experiment in killing', the observer one with the observed: 'He was to be with the small in his death.' Everything that has happened has been in accord with scientific laws, yet Knight finds himself sharing the rural notions that Nature operates not predictably but by 'lawless caprice', with a sense of 'feline fun' in her tricks (the personification seems inevitable). The law he wanted to demonstrate, that air currents run up the cliff face, is confirmed, but with effects he had not foreseen: when it rains, it rains upwards, and only his shoulders and the crown of his head remain dry. This too is scientifically coherent, but it makes Knight's position absurd as well as terrifying. Understandably, the force of subjective impression threatens to overwhelm his powers of rational observation, and the sea which would in normal circumstances have seemed azure now seems black, the rain seems preternaturally cold, Elfride's absence longer than it is. Knight's role as conscious observer of nature isn't entirely undermined; his courage, and Elfride's ingenuity, enable them both to escape death. Yet for all his self-possession, and his clever reviews for *The Present*, he finds himself hanging face to face with a fossil, wet, cold and afraid.

Humanity stands at the top of the evolutionary scale, but it remains trapped in the temporal world whose laws Knight professes to understand.

Hardy's passage can be compared with another key Victorian image, William Dyce's picture of *Pegwell Bay: a Recollection of October 5th, 1858*, exhibited at the Royal Academy in 1860. The tide is out, the sky is calm but grey, the cliffs loom over the figures in the foreground – the artist's son, his wife and her two sisters – strung out in apparent isolation from each other, fishing in the rock pools along the beach. Contemporary viewers recognized in the chalk cliffs and shell-strewn beach a reference to alarming conclusions about the great age of the earth, made ever more certain as what Ruskin called the 'dreadful Hammers' of the geologists chipped away at the rocks (in 1851 he complained that he heard their clink at the end of every Biblical verse).[3] Most mid-Victorian geologists accepted the theory of uniformitarianism, which held that the world's surface had been shaped by the same forces as those now operating, and not by such catastrophes as the Mosaic flood. The difficulty with this argument was that it required the conclusion that the world was millions of years older than anyone had imagined before the nineteenth century. According to the chronology established by Archbishop Ussher, the world began in 4004 BC; by his reckoning, the 6,000th birthday of humanity was due to be celebrated on 23 October 1996. It is still possible to find Bibles with the date 4004 BC printed alongside the first chapter of Genesis. Henry Knight, a competent geologist, would have understood that Dyce's picture contained the evidence that pushed out Ussher's dating.

There is another key feature in Dyce's picture. In the sky, unnoticed by those below, is Donati's comet, first observed in June 1858 and at its brightest on the date in the title. The comet evokes the immensities of time and space, and the growing awareness that the universe was not fixed but unstable, and that the sun and the earth might one day perish together. We have no record of whether Hardy observed it, though we know he made use of the big brass telescope handed down in the family; he records in the *Life* that in this very summer of 1858 he rushed out between his morning study of the classics and his breakfast, in time to observe the hanging of James Seale in Dorchester – his figure dropping just as Hardy raised his telescope.[4] But he certainly understood the impact discoveries in astronomy were making on his contemporaries. In *Two on a Tower*, the young astronomer Swithin St. Cleeve comments on the way the phenomena revealed by his telescope seem to reduce human life to insignificance, and dismays Viviette by showing her that 'the actual sky is a horror', its beauty masking the evidence of destructive forces on a monstrous scale.[5]

Nor would the figures on the beach at Pegwell Bay have found much comfort if they had taken with them Charles Kingsley's *Glaucus; or, The Wonders of the Shore*, published in 1855, as they might well have done, for this was the age of the terrarium and in particular of the aquarium. Knight is among those many Victorians who practised in the drawing room or study the habits of collection and classification which were taking place on a far larger scale at Kew Gardens and the London Zoological Gardens. Kingsley intended his readers to discover evidence of the creative energy of the Christian God in the many different life forms along the beach, but his own confidence falters when he comes to describe Nemertes Borlasii, 'a worm of very "low" organization, though well fitted enough for its own work'. Coiled up, it is 'a black, shiny, knotted lump among the gravel, small enough to be taken up in a dessert spoon'; stretched out, it looks like a strip of dead seaweed, but then the little fish who plays over it 'touches at last what is too surely a head':

> In an instant a bell-shaped sucker mouth has fastened to his side. In another instant, from one lip, a concave double proboscis … has clasped him like a finger; and now begins the struggle: but in vain. … The victim is tired now; and slowly, and yet dexterously, his blind assailant is feeling and shifting along his side, till he reaches one end of him; and then the black lips expand, and slowly and surely the curved finger begins packing him end-foremost down into the gullet …[6]

This is nature red in tooth and claw, yet small enough to be held in a spoon: with the corollary, of course, that lying in the dessert spoon or the family aquarium might be a black-lipped, blind assailant waiting for its prey. This is not far from Knight's sudden sense that he belongs with the 'mean' form of the trilobite. Kingsley's passage, like Hardy's, pulls in different directions; its last words describe the now well-fed Nemertes Borlasii as 'motionless and blest', identifying it as part of a Divine scheme. The contemporary reader is likely to suspect that the final word owes more to will than to belief.

Astronomical space, and the time scale that implies; the time scale of geology; and the time scale suggested by evolutionary development: all of these seem to threaten or diminish mankind. In a book published in 1902, the art historian D. S. MacColl described *Pegwell Bay* as 'the truest of Dyce's histories': 'It is as if a man had come to the ugly end of the world, and felt bound to tell.'[7]

MacColl's comment is more than a piece of eloquence. Other writers had thought about the end of the world: H. G. Wells in *The Time Machine*, for example, in 1895. In the second half of the century, the geologists' views about the age of the earth had been disputed by those physicists who studied the sun, in particular by William Thomson, later Lord Kelvin. Thomson believed that the sun's heat came from combustion of oxygen and hydrogen. The sun expended energy, but had no means of renewing it once spent. By Thomson's calculations, the rate at which its energy was used up meant that it was necessary to reject the time scale proposed by geologists like Charles Lyell in his *Principles of Geology* (1830–3), and by evolutionists like Darwin who accepted Lyell's views, since the sun simply could not be that old. More disturbingly, it also meant that the sun would itself burn out within a time scale that might be very long – estimates ranged from decades to several million years – but would at some point be measurable and definite. Solar physics, in other words, really did feel bound to tell the public about the ugly end of the world. If the sun is cooling down, 'the time must come', wrote Thomas Huxley in 1891, 'when evolution will mean adaptation to an universal winter, and all forms of life will die out, except such low and simple organisms as the Diatom of the arctic and antarctic ice'.[8] Had Henry Knight been a better scientist, he might have compared his life not just with that of the 'mean' trilobite of the past, but also with the 'low' organisms which would outlive him.

The point at issue here can be put like this. Evolutionary theory caused anxiety enough, but it could be understood as progressive. In the penultimate paragraph of the *Origin of Species*, Darwin had written that 'as natural selection works solely by and for the good of each being, all corporeal and mental endowments will tend to progress towards perfection'.[9] Evolution had worked and was still working from the low and mean towards the more complex and (it seemed) the higher. But the argument from solar physics drove back in the other direction, towards the exhaustion of the sun, the coming of universal winter and, eventually, the dissipation of all energy. Thomson's arguments were not to be rebutted until 1904, when Ernest Rutherford described the sun's energy in terms of radioactivity. That theory, of course, was later to lead to other reasons to fear the end of the world. Which way, in Hardy's novels, is Time pointing? Is it progressive, towards perfection, or is it regressive, towards the exhaustion of life energy?

Scientific ideas, even when part of the intellectual life of a generation, are rarely transferred lock, stock and barrel from one context to another. We know that Hardy was interested in 'the origin of things, the constitution of matter, the unreality of time' – these were the topics he recollected discussing with Leslie Stephen when Stephen asked him to witness his renunciation of holy orders – but the wider question, of progression or regression, appears in his work in less immediate forms.[10] In *Jude the Obscure*, for example, it is suggested both that Jude and Sue were pioneers of a new way of life, and their failure the consequence of their being fifty years before their time, and that they are the symptoms of a general mood of unrest and discontent. Late in the novel, Jude describes himself as simply 'a paltry victim to the spirit of mental and social restlessness', but while admitting that he lives in 'a chaos of principles' he refuses to give up the possibility that some man or woman with greater insight will one day uncover what is wrong with existing social formulas: 'who can tell a man what shall be after him under the sun?'[11]

Victorian readers had to hand the term for the victims of unrest: they were degenerate. The word itself acquired a special currency in 1895 when Max Nordau's book *Entartung* appeared under the title *Degeneration*, but the idea was already current. Those reviewers who seized on Sue as an example of neurasthenia, as sexless, perverted, and so on, were classing her among a range of degenerates – the homosexual, the insane, the criminal, the slum-dweller – all of whom could be and were seen as signs of failure in the development of the race, to be controlled, and if need be suppressed (some eugenicists were already calling for compulsory sterilization). Edmund Gosse used the word 'degenerate' of Sue, putting it in quotation marks as if to signal that it was a technical medical term, but he thought that Jude too showed signs of 'hereditary degeneracy', in what Gosse called his 'megalomania'.[12] The evidence for this seems to be only that Jude struggles for the right to education at Christminster, but we need not be surprised that those who enjoyed the benefits of the status quo were quick to use the term of anyone who seemed to challenge their position. Yet Jude himself wonders if he hasn't got 'the *germs* of every human infirmity' in his nature.[13]

The idea that there was something bad in the Fawley inheritance, that his was a family sinking into degeneracy, could be supported by looking at the medical literature, in particular that dealing with insanity. In the 1880s Hardy made extensive notes on Henry Maudsley's *Natural Causes and Supernatural Seemings* (1886).[14] Maudsley, himself a difficult and gloomy man, was increasingly persuaded that heredity was the most powerful influence on character, and that much of our mental life was beyond the control of the will. His position was thus opposed to that of most mid-century practitioners, who preferred to stress the need to develop 'moral force' in those threatened by insanity. One of the passages Hardy copied argues that despite our instinctive belief in our moral and intellectual freedom, in fact 'everybody, in the main lines of his thoughts, feelings & conduct, really recalls the experiences of his forefathers'. It is true that consciousness tells us that we have 'infinite potentialities of freewill'; but it also tells us that the sun goes round the earth. Maudsley was determined that we should be undeceived: 'No one can escape the tyranny of his organization; no one can elude the destiny that is innate in him.'[15] Moreover, Nature was ruthless in disposing of the mentally unfit; when the 'hereditary predisposition' reached the beginning of degeneracy, it would lead inexorably on to the production of idiocy, unless checked by 'impotence and sterility'. This sense of weakness deepening into insanity and leading finally into a dead end can be compared with Jude's family history: his mother's suicide, his own attempt, the death of Little Father Time. ....The doctor's fashionable interpretation of Time's death as a sign of the 'coming universal wish not to live' associates individual pathology with the growing sickness – degeneracy – of a generation.

How does this relate to ideas about the anticipated death of the sun? I mentioned that one of the topics debated between Hardy and Leslie Stephen in March 1875 was 'the constitution of matter'. A few months earlier, in August 1874, John Tyndall had given his 'Belfast Address' to the British Association, a much-discussed lecture in which he staked out the claim of science 'to unrestricted right of search'. It was central to Tyndall's conception of science that there was no sharp discontinuity between inorganic and organic matter, or between matter and consciousness. This was not an attempt to downgrade the mind, so much as to elevate matter. Nor was Tyndall an eccentric; Thomas Huxley, whom Hardy admired, argued in similar fashion in his lecture 'On the Physical Basis of Life'. All the universe was made of the same basic stuff: in Tyndall's words, 'all our philosophy, all our poetry, all our science, all our art – Plato, Shakespeare, Newton, Raphael – are potential in the fires of the sun'.[16] The heat of the sun was the source of human achievement; with its cooling would come the falling off of that achievement. Or, as Bertrand Russell would put it later, 'the noonday brightness of human genius' was destined to extinction in 'the vast death of the solar system'.[17] The moral and physical degeneracy Maudsley and others detected in the *fin-de-siècle* was a foreshadowing of this greater decline. In effect, evolution would begin to run backwards; in place of Shakespeare, there would be Huxley's Diatom in the ice of the Antarctic. The cause of degeneration was partly social, the result of what Jude calls the spirit of unrest, and partly psychological, the end result of the unstoppable downward spiralling of a poor genetic inheritance – what Jude speaks of as 'the germs of every human infirmity', or Aunt Drusilla less technically but no less graphically calls 'sommat in our blood' – but it was also built into the structure of our cosmos, driven on by the death of the sun. *Fin-de-siècle*, fin du globe, with a vengeance.

Gosse was right to recognize Hardy's interest in ideas of degeneracy in *Jude the Obscure*, but that is not to say that Hardy endorses them. In the Preface to *Two on a Tower* Hardy said he wanted to set 'the emotional history of two infinitesimal lives against the stupendous background of the stellar universe', and to show that the smaller of these two might be the more interesting. In the same manner, I want now to shift my ground, towards the emotional history of Tess. Of all Hardy's novels, *Tess of the d'Urbervilles* is the most deeply saturated in the sense of time. Its division into Phases suggests as much. Even more than the *Mayor of Casterbridge*, it deals with an event which in one sense cannot be undone – Tess rubs her cheek to ensure that Alec's kiss is 'undone' so far as physically possible, but she can't staunch the flow of blood from Prince, and she can't rub away the night in the Chase and the birth and death of Sorrow.[18] But is it simply the case that what's done is done? One of the questions asked in the novel is, what is the nature of the past, and what room is there for manoeuvre?

We get a sense of this saturation if we look at the parallels set up in the novel between Tess and Jack Durbeyfield. In Chapter 1 Jack asks Parson Tringham why, 'when I be plain Jack Durbeyfield the haggler', the parson calls him Sir John. Within minutes, plain Jack is content to assume a new identity: "Tis recorded in history all about me.' He is not the only person in the story who easily assumes a new name and history: Alec's family have done the same, to become Stoke-d'Urberville. Tess of course resists such a change. She does not wish to claim kin, and when Angel addresses her fancifully as Artemis or Demeter she looks 'askance' with 'Call me Tess' (Ch. 20). Nor is she pleased that 'all about her' has been recorded in history: 'what's the use of learning that I am one of a long row only ...?', she asks Angel bitterly. 'The best is not to remember that your nature and your past doings have been just like thousands' and thousands', and that your coming life and doings 'll be like thousands' and thousands'.' (Ch. 19)

But it is not only Jack Durbeyfield's past that is uncovered; so too is his future, when Mrs Durbeyfield shapes her forefinger like a letter C to show how the fat is enclosing his heart, and tells Tess that he might die at any time, as the C closes into a circle. The fact is certain, if not yet the date. Tess reflects at one point that we can celebrate our birthdays, but don't know which day of the year will become the anniversary of our dying; for her, of course, in one of the most poignant ironies of the book, the date of her death will be foreknown.

Between our past history and our certain death there is a small space, as the C closes, in which to negotiate with our identity and our own story. In the early stages of the novel, Tess seems to contract this space, as she accuses herself of the murder of Prince. Like Henchard, she has an instinct of self-punishment as part of her nature. Guilt, for example, makes her submit to her mother's ambitions in sending her to work at Trantridge, and she offers no protest when Joan dresses her to look older than her years. Such deception comes easily to Joan. In the evenings at Rolliver's inn, a little ale renders impalpable the troubles which might otherwise chafe body and soul; they become 'mere mental phenomena' without the power to threaten (Ch. 3). There is no problem for Joan in referring to Tess's past as a 'bygone Trouble' (Ch. 31); she simply wishes it gone by, and it is. The women with whom Tess works in the fields after the birth of Sorrow are less careless than this, but more willing than Tess to trust to the future: 'Lord, 'tis wonderful what a body can get used to o' that sort in time!' (Ch. 14).

'In time': in time, through time, it is possible to 'rally', and Tess herself begins to wonder if 'the recuperative power' which pervades all of organic nature is denied only to virginity (Ch. 15). She tries to stamp out the past, as if it is a smouldering coal, or to annihilate it by escaping from the scenes associated with her unhappiness. And gradually the 'invincible instinct towards self-delight' which pervades all nature thrills through her too, as it does the other dairymaids at Talbothays (Ch. 15). But Tess cannot set her 'trouble' aside. It becomes a kind of absolute once she falls in love with Angel. To lie to him would be to violate herself, by closing within her Alec's violation of her. She can neither forget her past, as Joan suggests, nor rewrite it as simply as her father rewrites himself as Sir John.

Hardy comments in Chapter 16 that Tess was still so young that 'it was impossible that any event should have left upon her an impression that was not in time capable of transmutation'. The question arises, how far can our sense of an event, the way we shape it or tell it to ourselves, transmute the event itself? What are the limits which distinguish healthy 'transmutation' from mere submission to the past on the one hand, and on the other a morally dishonest refusal of it? The answer to Tess's longing can only come from Angel. There are times when her love for him in the early days at Talbothays 'irradiate[s] her into forgetfulness' of her past unhappiness (Ch. 31). Her confession is made in the sudden hope that he will still see the loved Tess in the woman in front of him, and hold her past and present selves together as one reality. It is precisely this that Angel is unable to do: 'the woman I have been loving is not you' (Ch. 35). Angel has rejected his father's 'untenable redemptive theolatry' (Ch. 18); and he has no redemption for Tess. Her present self is denied by the 'hard logical deposit' in his character, and she is thrust back alone into the burden of her past (Ch. 36). He meets her guilt, not her love, and forces her to define herself by that.

Angel's blame is as absolute as Tess's self-reproach, and both are felt to be excessive. When Prince dies, Tess takes all the responsibility for what has happened ('''Tis all my doing – all mine!' (Ch. 4)), and Angel takes effectively the same view of her relations with Alec. It is not until Chapter 49 and his time in Brazil that he comes to the recognition that the 'true history [of a character] lay not among things done, but among things willed', and can then make the distinction between what is inherent in Tess's character, and what belongs to the accidents of the life which she has suffered as well as acted. The ambiguity with which Hardy renders events in the Chase in Chapter 11 serves to underline how we both choose our life and find it happening to us. Our ethical judgement is clear-cut: Alec overwhelms Tess, and in doing so violates her – violates her sense of herself, as well as takes her virginity – but it is difficult to construct an account of what took place that would hold up in a courtroom. The narrator recalls rapes by the earlier d'Urbervilles, and we learn later that others heard Tess sobbing, but as she leaves she admits to Alec that for a time he had managed to make her believe she loved him, and we also hear of her as having been 'stirred to confused surrender awhile' (Ch. 12). The phrase is poised between response and submission. It suggests something more than the thing done, but less than the thing willed.

Events, then, the nature of what is past, may not be absolute in the way Angel wishes to make them. And we do have some choice about how to regard them. Angel is guilty of bad faith when he tells Tess they should part 'till I can better see the shape that things have taken'; the crucial question concerns the shape he has given them (Ch. 36). Tess tells him, 'It is in your own mind, what you are angry at, Angel; it is not in me' (Ch. 35). In the very act of making his judgement against Tess, Angel is abdicating from judgement, pretending that the shape of events is unalterably given. By the time he decides to go to Brazil, his manner has changed from 'self-control' to 'indifference', and he has come to assume 'the passive interest of an outsider' in his own existence (Chs 35, 39). In the moment of crisis, he takes towards his own moral stance the same fatalistic view the people of Marlott take towards events: 'It was to be.'

The later sections of the novel show Tess's attempt to rally from, or to get used to, her second violation. Unlike her father, who can move from plain Jack to Sir John, taking on a new history at ease, she is now without a name of her own. She is no longer Tess Durbeyfield, but nor is she Mrs Angel Clare. Everything seems to work against her recovery – Farmer Groby, the wind and rain of Flintcomb-Ash, the exhausting work on the threshing machine. In her letter to Angel, she writes 'I am the same woman, Angel, as you fell in love with; yes, the very same!' (Ch. 48). But as the external pressures on her young life become yet heavier, she is compelled to take up the identity his judgement had fixed on for her: that of the woman who surrenders herself to Alec for the sake of her family. The past Angel leaves her to deal with alone returns as her present. When he does return, it is, as she tells him, 'Too late'. The only way forward for her now is to 'undo' the past by killing Alec, or, more precisely, as Hardy noted, by killing the situation, destroying the past to prepare for a future that cannot now come into being. Her act is both an assertion of herself and her love for Angel, and the abandonment of her life: 'What must come will come.' As she flees with Angel, she tells him that she doesn't want to think of 'outside of now' (Ch. 58). Her life story is reduced to the present tense, a brief curve of happiness in the closing circle of her life.

Before Angel realizes that Tess has in fact done what she says, he thinks she is hallucinating, dreaming of the d'Urberville legend of the coach and murder; he wonders 'what obscure strain in the d'Urberville blood' has led her to this 'aberration' (Ch. 57). The question of Tess's d'Urberville past is among those he wrestles with in Brazil. In recalling her face, he recalls too the portraits of earlier d'Urbervilles, and is touched by the 'historic interest of her family'. Previously he has thought of old families in political terms, as 'a spent force'; now he begins to think instead about the 'imaginative value' of her aristocratic descent to 'the moralizer on declines and falls'. Hardy too was given to moralizing on declines and falls, including that of his own family ('So we go down, down, down'), and he explored his own pedigree eagerly.[19]

Tess has varying responses to her ancestry. At times she takes a robust and dismissive view; it is a common story, easily matched by other local girls – the Debbyhouses are now carters, but were once the De Bayeux family, and so on. But she is also oppressed by the idea that her thoughts and feelings may have been forestalled by her ancestors, and that what appears to her as her own life may be merely an image or echo of the past. 'Forestalled' is the word Hardy uses in his poem 'The Pedigree', to explain his sense that 'every heave and coil and move I made / Within my brain, and in my mood and speech' had been anticipated by ancestors now lost in the mists of time:

> Said I then, sunk in tone,
> 'I am merest mimicker and counterfeit! –
> Though thinking, *I am I,*
> *And what I do I do myself alone.*'

Hardy's poem takes us back to the world of Victorian scientific debate, and in particular towards the work of August Weismann on heredity, which Hardy was reading soon after its publication in 1882.[20] Weismann moved forward (if forward is the right word in this context) the discussion of the mechanisms of inheritance, by proposing the continuity from one generation to the next of what he called the 'germ plasm' – in contemporary language, the genotype. This germ plasm was passed intact down the generations, and it was not possible for the individual to alter it. No skill or grace developed in the one life could be transmitted to the next, no error made less likely. The individual life seems secondary or accidental; the germ plasm seems the essential reality. As Samuel Butler put it, the hen is just an egg's way of creating another egg. More brutally, our genetic history operates (as Tess fears) automatically, below our conscious, choosing self. We are all mimickers and counterfeits of those who came before us. Worse than that: like any system of energy closed in itself, unable to be refreshed or renewed from without, this germ plasm would weaken, run down, as it passed through the generations.

Angel's objection to old families as a 'spent force' apparently derives from political restlessness, but it accords with late Victorian biology. He applies the idea in its scientific sense when he terms Tess 'the belated seedling of an effete aristocracy', ascribing her 'want of firmness' to her lateness in the family line, much as Parson Tringham sees the d'Urberville features 'a little debased' in Jack Durbeyfield (Ch. 35). When in Chapter 55 Angel returns to Tess at Sandbourne, he is reduced to silence by his sense that she 'had spiritually ceased to recognize the body before him as hers – allowing it to drift, like a corpse upon the current, in a direction dissociated from its living will'. This comes close to the biological determinism advanced by Maudsley and Weismann. In Brazil, Angel has learned to distinguish the thing done from the thing willed, and to regard the latter as the true test of worth; now it seems to him that Tess has no will. Perhaps it would be too much to argue that the Tess who lies asleep at Stonehenge merely counterfeits the vibrant, sun-drenched Tess of Talbothays; but in the last chapter of the novel, as Angel and Liza-Lu gaze towards a horizon 'lost in the radiance of the sun', their faces seeming to have 'shrunk to half their natural size', it is hard not to feel that Hardy treats them as the counterfeit image of what Angel and Tess might have been at that earlier time.

Tess of the d'Urbervilles is not a novel about Victorian science, or even about the way that science led contemporaries to think about their experience of time – whether time was progressive, as the evolutionists were tempted to argue, or running out, as solar physics seemed to suggest, or whether the past governed our every mood and thought through the mechanisms of inheritance. None the less these ideas do inform the work, and where they are felt most strongly they suggest how sensitive Hardy was to what was threatening in them. But for every movement in this novel there is a counter-movement, and *Tess* remains the richest of Hardy's prose fictions. Tess lies down exhausted at Stonehenge, on the stone where it was supposed victims were sacrificed in order to ensure the return of the dying sun, yet she also says 'I am ready', and her words express more than the defeat of her will to live (Ch. 58).[21] If the potential of her life is squandered, the rich profusion of the garden at Talbothays suggests nature's endless capacity for renewal. Even the ironies surrounding Angel and Liza-Lu are modified by our recognition that Tess's desire for them to marry can be seen as one more attempt to transmute the conditions of her life after her seduction by Alec. Hardy's imagination seized on the idea that we carry our destiny within us, in the form of that 'sommat in our blood' that Victorian science was beginning to define more closely, and no English novel before *Tess of the d'Urbervilles* had brooded so deeply on the precariousness of individual identity; but it is named after the most compelling, and memorable, of his heroines.

Notes

Quotations from Hardy's novels are taken from The World's Classics Edition (Oxford: Oxford University Press, 1985–93). Quotations from his poems are taken from *The Complete Poems of Thomas Hardy*, ed. James Gibson (London: Macmillan, 1976).

1. Entries 841 and 842 in *The Literary Notebooks of Thomas Hardy*, ed. Lennart A. Björk, 2 volumes (London: Macmillan Press, 1985) vol. 1, p. 84 (subsequently cited as *Literary Notebooks*).

2. Thomas Hardy, *A Pair of Blue Eyes*, Ch. 22. Quotations in the following paragraph are from the same chapter. The episode is discussed by Tess Cosslett in her *The 'Scientific Movement' and Victorian Literature* (Brighton: Harvester, 1982).

3. John Ruskin, letter to Henry Acland, in *The Works of John Ruskin*, ed. E. T. Cook and Alexander Wedderburn, Library Edition, 39 volumes (London: George Allen, 1903–12) vol. 36, p. 115.

4. Thomas Hardy, *The Life and Work of Thomas Hardy*, ed. Michael Millgate (London: Macmillan Press, 1984) pp. 32–3 (subsequently cited as *Life and Work*). In June 1881 Hardy and Emma observed Tebutt's comet, which was soon to feature in *Two on a Tower*, from their house in Wimborne; see *Life and Work*, p. 154.

5. Thomas Hardy, *Two on a Tower*, Ch. 4.

6. Charles Kingsley, *Glaucus; or, The Wonders of the Shore*, 5th edition (London: Macmillan, 1890) pp. 136–8.

7. See D. S. MacColl, *Nineteenth Century Art* (Glasgow: J. Maclehose, 1902) p. 115. Marcia Pointon provides a valuable discussion of *Pegwell Bay* in her 'The Representation of Time in Painting', *Art History*, I (March 1978) 99–103. The painting is now in the Tate Gallery in London.

8. Thomas Huxley, 'The Struggle for Existence in Human Society', in *Evolution & Ethics, and Other Essays* (London: Macmillan, 1895) p. 199.

9. See *Darwin: A Norton Critical Edition*, ed. Philip Appleman (New York: Norton, 1979) p. 131. E. Ray Lankester, with whom Hardy sometimes dined at the Savile Club, was among those who pointed out that the existence of parasites proved that the less complex form could arrive after the higher: for example, the parasitic organisms living in the intestines of the higher animals.

10. *Life and Work*, p. 109.

11. Thomas Hardy, *Jude the Obscure*, Bk VI, Ch. 1. Jude is quoting from Ecclesiastes 6:12.

12. Gosse's review, which Hardy valued, appeared in *Cosmopolis* in January 1896, and is reprinted in the Norton Critical Edition of the novel, edited by Norman Page (New York: Norton, 1978) pp. 386–91. The fullest account of the degeneration debate is by William Greenslade in his *Degeneration, Culture and the Novel, 1880–1940* (Cambridge: Cambridge University Press, 1994); for its relevance to Hardy, see especially chapter 8.

13. *Jude the Obscure*, Bk V, Ch. 2 (italics added).

14. See entries 1495–8 and 1501–20 in *Literary Notebooks*, vol. 1, pp. 195–201.

15. Henry Maudsley, *Body and Mind*, enlarged and revised edition (London: Macmillan, 1873) pp. 75–6; quoted from Vieda Skultans, *Madness and Morals: Ideas on Insanity in the Nineteenth Century* (London: Routledge, 1975) pp. 206–7. Other quotations from Maudsley in this paragraph are from his *Responsibility in Mental*

Disease (London: H. S. King, 1874); see Skultans, *Madness and Morals*, pp. 208–9. There is a valuable account of Maudsley's work in Elaine Showalter, *The Female Malady: Women, Madness and English Culture, 1830–1980* (London: Virago, 1987); see especially pp. 112–20.

16. John Tyndall, 'On the Scientific Use of the Imagination', in *Fragments of Science for Unscientific People* (London: Longmans, 1871) pp. 163–4. The passage is quoted by Hardy's friend Edward Clodd in his biography for the Modern English Writers series, *Thomas Henry Huxley* (Edinburgh and London: Blackwood, 1911) p. 134, in a discussion of Huxley's views on the relation of matter and spirit.

17. Bertrand Russell, *Mysticism and Logic and Other Essays* (London: Longmans, 1918) p. 47.

18. Thomas Hardy, *Tess of the d'Urbervilles*, Ch. 8. Subsequent chapter references to the novel are given in parentheses in the text.

19. *Life and Work*, p. 224.

20. See *Literary Notebooks*, vol. 1, p. 148. Hardy read Weismann's *Essay on Heredity* (1889) in 1890.

21. See J. B. Bullen, 'The Gods in Wessex Exile: Thomas Hardy and Mythology', in J. B. Bullen (ed.), *The Sun is God: Painting, Literature and Mythology in the Nineteenth Century* (Oxford: Oxford University Press, 1989), for an account of the sun and sun worship in *Tess of the d'Urbervilles*.

8

How to be an Old Poet: The Examples of Hardy and Yeats

SAMUEL HYNES

Ten or twelve years ago I wrote an introduction to a volume of Hardy's poems in which I considered the consequences for the poetry of the fact that most of it was written in the last decades of a long life.[1] I want to return to that subject here, but in a different way, expanding it to include another great modern poet, and shifting it upward to the level of theory: The Theory of Old Poets. That's how our thinking about art works, isn't it? We have an idea, time passes, the idea grows, spreads, changes, until particulars begin to look like principles, and we have a *theory*. I'm a decade and more older than I was when I first wrote about Hardy and old age. And so, I might add, are you. A decade nearer our own old age: high time we thought about it.

When in my theorizing I use the term Old Poets – with those capital letters – I mean, obviously, poets who lived a long time. But not all poets who live past middle age become Old Poets. Some fall silent at the end, as Eliot and Larkin did. Some go on in their poems being their younger selves: Robert Graves, for example. Graves was ninety when he died, and was still writing poems in his eighties, but his bargain with the White Goddess seems to have been that she would continue to inspire him on the condition that he continued to write the kind of poems he had always written. Some poets abandon poetry altogether for another medium: like Kingsley Amis, who turned to fiction – I suppose because it was a better form in which to be bilious about the world.

But most poets go on being poets, and in time become old poets (note the lower case here), just as old painters, old gardeners, old carpenters, old literary critics go on practising their crafts long past the age at which you might think they should retire. The reason is obvious: it's what they *do*, what they have always done; it fills their days, and more than that, it defines them to themselves. To the question: Who am I? our work provides us with an immediate and irrefutable answer.

But longevity isn't the sole defining condition of being an Old Poet: as I conceive the category, Old Poets are those who in their old age make poetry out of that state – make age not simply their subject, but the condition of consciousness in their poems, and so make the perceived world of age real to other minds.

Let me describe that world, as I find it in the work of Old Poets. It is a world of *less*, *fewer*, and *last*: there is less activity there than in our world, and less possibility of action; in the grammar of that world words like *act* and *love* are past-tense verbs. Things happen there for the last time, and that affects the poetic tone; for as Dr Johnson said, 'No man does anything consciously for the last time, without a feeling of sadness.' (The titles of eleven poems in Hardy's *Complete Poems* begin with the word *last*.)

So old age is a *tone*. It also has a spatial dimension. Age is a reduced space, the horizons closed in, the interiors confining and disfurnished, like an old, unoccupied house. Age is a place in which the present is less present than it is in the world of ordinary being; there are fewer people there, fewer friends. But if it is unpopulated by the living, it is crowded with the dead: age is ghost-haunted.

If space is different in the world of old age, so is time. Time there stretches backward like a long road taken, into the distant past; forward it has almost no length at all, only a little span, like a short corridor, with a closed door at the end.

This world of age is difficult to talk about. We mustn't be too easily sad or sentimental about what is, after all, only ordinary human reality; and we mustn't let ourselves become mortality-bores. The best of the Old Poets avoid those traps: they are neither sentimental nor boring; they simply confront the world time has given them, and compel it to be poetry.

It's an exclusive world, this poetic world of old age. Younger poets may visit it, in the poems of their elders, but they can't practise there. There is no place in Old Poet Theory for poems by younger poets in which they *imagine* age: 'Here I am, an old man in a dry month' won't do; nor 'Grow old along with me! / The best is yet to be'; nor 'Do not go gentle into that good night.'[2] Those poems have permanent places in our English-language canon, but they don't tell us what age is *like*. They can't. For age clearly is one of those human experiences – like love, sex, war, and religion – that aren't anything like what you imagine they will be, before you've had them. (Auden said fame is like that, too.)

When I think about old age as a separate and distinct human condition I think of the Seven Ages of Man speech in *As You Like It*. Jaques's Seventh Age is pretty grim:

> Last scene of all,
> That ends this strange eventful history,
> Is second childishness and mere oblivion,
> Sans teeth, sans eyes, sans taste, sans everything.[3]

You must recognize, as I do, that those lines do not accurately describe old Hardy, or old Yeats, or any other Old Poet. And yet ... I am caught by Shakespeare's sense of age as diminishment and loss – *sans*, *sans*, *sans*, what Hardy called time's 'takings away' – and of oblivion. And so, even though it isn't quite fair, I think of this poetry as Seventh Age poetry: poetry that is about the reality of loss-in-time, and how to live with it, and make poetry out of it.

Hardy and Yeats are Seventh Age poets, in this sense. But not in the same way. Indeed, I think they can be seen as two distinct subtypes, which we might identify with Shakespeare's two greatest old men: Prospero and Lear. Pause for a moment to think of those two figures of Age. Prospero, in the last act of *The Tempest*: calm, accepting, beyond action, having resigned his place in the public world of power to return to Milan and think about death. An old man who has accepted diminishment and has given it dignity: Hardy at Max Gate, voluntarily withdrawn from the literary marketplace of London, retired from the novel-writing that had made him famous, living the diminished life of age, and writing the poetry of that condition; the old poet as sage, the truth-teller, no longer an agent in his life, but an observer.

Then think of Lear: Lear on the heath, passionate and raging, without court or courtiers, without comforts, exposing himself to suffering – an old man who would rather be a mad diminished king than no king at all, tragic, and consciously so, playing the role of Old Man as Tragic Hero. Yeats in his late years, not withdrawn, still *in* the world but raging against it, a passionate public man, the old poetic self re-made once more as Seventh Age Hero, the old man who remains an agent in his life by an act of will.

So: two Old Poets, both role-playing, but in different roles, which yet have this in common, that they make Old Poetry possible.

Just when the Seventh Age begins in a poet's life is unpredictable. No door slams on the earlier life, not at three-score-and-ten or any other age. But in individual cases one can usually locate the point of change quite precisely in the poetry, and if one knows the life one can conjecture reasons. It happened in Hardy's poetic career between the publication of *Time's Laughingstocks* in 1909 and *Satires of Circumstance* in 1914 – between his seventieth and seventy-fifth year. The cause is perfectly clear: it was of course the death of Emma Hardy in 1912. It was Hardy's greatest loss, his greatest personal diminishment; Emma's death emptied his life of his strongest link with his own past, with youth, hope and happiness, and shifted her presence and all that she meant to him into the ghost-world of memory.

There is another thing to be said about the effect of Emma's death. She was Hardy's exact contemporary, and when someone our own age dies, we feel a tremor in our life: our own death takes on a felt certainty then that is quite different from the untroubling proposition that all men are mortal. That's why old people read obituary pages, starting with the death-dates; they hope they'll find that the dead are all older than *they* are, and that death can therefore be postponed into the uncertain future, and thought about another day. The death of a contemporary has a different message: it says death is *here*, in the present.

You can see this change to Seventh Age poetry in the 'Poems of 1912–13' that Hardy wrote immediately after his wife's death, most explicitly in the first poem, 'The Going':

> Well, well! All's past amend,
> Unchangeable. It must go.
> I seem but a dead man held on end
> To sink down soon. ... O you could not know
> That such swift fleeing
> No soul foreseeing –
> Not even I – would undo me so!

But it is everywhere in his later poems, in poems about his coffin, his grave, his ghost – a curious line of posthumous poems by a living Old Poet.

For Yeats the point of change occurred somewhere in the 1920s, between *Michael Robartes and the Dancer* (1921) and *The Tower* (1928) –

earlier in his life than in Hardy's (Yeats was only fifty-six in 1921). The cause seems of a different kind: the Troubles, the Irish Civil War, and the settlement that was a defeat for his dreams of a romantic Ireland made him an Old (and a bitter) Poet before his time. The great poems that came out of those last years, the final two decades of his life, are full of age and loss.

Two great poets become Old Poets, then, for different reasons that reflect their different relationships to the world. Hardy, the private man, suffers a private loss that leaves him memory-haunted; Yeats, the public man, suffers a public loss that leaves him haunted by his country's history, and by the impotence of poetry in the public world. In both cases the book that follows the loss is the poet's greatest single volume. What shall we make of that? That loss is gain, for a poet? That great art may come out of the diminishments of the Seventh Age of Man? The history of Western culture offers us considerable evidence that this may be true: old Michelangelo, deaf Beethoven, ageing Degas (who only became Degas, Renoir said, as his health and sight began to fail), Renoir himself, old and crippled, a brush strapped to his arthritic hand, still painting Renoirs.

When Seventh Age poets speak in their own voices they often do so in images of their diminishment. Here is a stanza from Hardy's most poignant poem of age, 'An Ancient to Ancients':

> Where once we danced, where once we sang,
>   Gentlemen,
> The floors are sunken, cobwebs hang,
> And cracks creep; worms have fed upon
> The doors. Yea, sprightlier times were then
> Than now, with harps and tabrets gone,
>   Gentlemen!

And here are some lines from Yeats's poem of age, 'An Acre of Grass':

> Picture and book remain,
> An acre of green grass
> For air and exercise,
> Now strength of body goes;
> Midnight, an old house
> Where nothing stirs but a mouse.

You see the similarities: two passages of confinement, decay and loss, two imaged spaces emptied of human company – and of human energy, too, for Old Age's reality also has its kinetic aspect, life runs down at the end.

And yet, in these poems there are presences, not living but imagined, a company of the Old to be invoked against age. Hardy calls up classical authors who wrote into their old age: Sophocles, Plato, Socrates, Pythagoras, Thucydides, Herodotus, Homer, Clement, Augustin, Origen. And Yeats names old artists and their old creations, as images of how the mind's energy can defy age: Shakespeare's Timon and Lear, William Blake, Michael Angelo. By naming these aged heroes, Old Hardy and Old Yeats claim places in their company.

But not in the same way, not in the same tone. I suggested that Hardy and Yeats are two distinct types of Old Poet, one Prospero, the other Lear. Hardy, Prospero-like, ends his poem in a calm diminuendo, addressed to the young generation that will succeed him:

> And ye, red-lipped and smooth-browed; list,
>   Gentlemen;
> Much is there waits you we have missed;
> Much lore we leave you worth the knowing,
> Much, much has lain outside our ken:
> Nay, rush not: time serves: we are going,
>   Gentlemen.

A curious, energyless ending, like the soft speech of an old man short of breath, uttering one line at a time, and finally one phrase at a time:

> Much is there waits you we have missed; (breath)
> Much lore we leave you worth the knowing, (breath)
> Much, much has lain outside our ken: (breath)
> Nay, (breath) rush not: (breath) time serves: (breath)
>   we are going, (breath)
>   Gentlemen. (long breath)

Yeats is very different; he roars into his last stanza on a crescendo that only settles into calm at the end – one clause, without a single mark of punctuation to locate a pause in it, one continuous burst of energy, one breath. And then the final stanza, ending in a two-line closing diminuendo, its own vision of diminishment:

> Forgotten else by mankind,
> An old man's eagle mind.

Forgotten: as a poet, that is: a condition to fear and resist, if you're Yeats, because *poet* was for him an essential, self-defining term. Do you remember his little poem 'To Be Carved on a Stone at Thoor Ballylee'? In it Yeats refers to himself as 'the poet William Yeats', and prays that the characters of the inscription he has had carved on a stone at his tower-home in the West of Ireland will survive, when all is ruin again. These characters do remain on the tower, and a visitor can see them there. But *characters* means more in the poem than the carved words on that stone: it means the characters of the poem we are reading, and of all Yeats's other poems. Yeats isn't saying that they will certainly remain: what is certain is that ruin will return, in the cycle of changing things. Those last lines are more a prayer than an affirmation of the permanence of poetry: *may* they remain; *may* the words of a poet defeat forgetfulness.

Hardy is different, in many ways. First, in the absence from his poems of himself as a poet. You can't imagine him writing: 'I, the poet Thomas Hardy', because that isn't the role he plays in his poems. He isn't the artist, or the self-created hero; he doesn't remake himself to play the poet's role on the world's stage. He is simply what he is, an old man who used to notice things, a country walker, a rememberer. It is extraordinary how completely Hardy controls the scale of himself in his world, keeping it all small, human-scaled, *un*-poetic.

Another difference concerns forgottenness. Yeats feared it; Hardy didn't. To be forgotten is a natural and inevitable fate in Hardy's world: the past fades, memory grows dim, the dead survive for a time in the minds of the living, and then cease to exist even there. We all know many poems on that general theme: 'His Immortality', 'The To-Be-Forgotten', 'The Ghost of the Past', 'Ah, Are You Digging on My Grave?' Annihilation is a principle that Hardy accepted calmly and without resistance: everything changes, dies, falls; nothing that exists is exempt from Time – not a man, not a star. Hardyans will catch my reference there: it is to 'Waiting Both', a poem from *Human Shows*, published when Hardy was eighty-five:

> A star looks down at me,
> And says: 'Here I and you
> Stand, each in his degree:
> What do you mean to do, –
>   Mean to do?'
>
> I say: 'For all I know,
> Wait, and let Time go by,
> Till my change come' – 'Just so,'
> The star says: 'So mean I: –
>   So mean I.'

It is a poem of complete, motionless passivity: man stands on the earth, star stands in the sky. Both wait. There is nothing else to do.

Yeats was no less aware of the power of Time and Change than Hardy was, but he played the theme differently. In his old poems the will to create confronts the inevitable destruction of Time in a tragic opposition. Yeats celebrates that confrontation: don't stand, he says; don't wait: act; resist Time. You'll lose, but it is mankind's glory to oppose destruction with creation. The late poems are full of statements of that theme: 'Lapis Lazuli', for example, and the last stanza of 'Two Songs from a Play':

> Everything that man esteems
> Endures a moment or a day.
> Love's pleasure drives his love away,
> The painter's brush consumes his dreams;
> The herald's cry, the soldier's tread
> Exhaust his glory and his might:
> Whatever flames upon the night
> Man's own resinous heart has fed.

Such energetic images of defeat, such strenuous verbs: *drives, consumes, flames*. The end is the same as in Hardy: everything passes, nothing escapes the force of Time. But the energy makes a difference. That energy animates all those Yeatsian heroes in 'An Acre of Grass' – Timon and Lear and William Blake and Michael Angelo. I find no such energy in Hardy's Ancients. They are quiet, past-tense heroes; they 'Burnt brightlier towards their setting-day', Hardy says; but that day came. There is no resistance there, no energy extravagantly spent in the war against Time: they are simply dead old thinkers, fixed and motionless, like portraits on a wall.

Old age is a time of necessary loss. It's also an embarrassment: anyone past middle age knows that; Hardy knew it, and so did Yeats. 'I look into my glass, / And view my wasting skin' – that's Hardy; 'What shall I do with this absurdity – /O heart, O troubled heart – this caricature, / Decrepit age that has been tied to me / As to a dog's tail?'[4] – that's Yeats. If we look further into these two poems we will see that they express more than the decay of the flesh; they also reveal the separation between the outer and the inner self that all old people feel. Listen again to Hardy:

> I look into my glass,
> And view my wasting skin,
> And say, 'Would God it came to pass
> My heart had shrunk as thin!'
>
> For then, I, undistrest
> By hearts grown cold to me,
> Could lonely wait my endless rest
> With equanimity.
>
> But Time, to make me grieve,
> Part steals, lets part abide;
> And shakes this fragile frame at eve
> With throbbings of noontide.

This is the last poem in *Wessex Poems*: Hardy at about sixty. Wasting skin, fragile frame: the *exterior* is old. But inside is a heart that has not shrunk, but throbs as it did in the noontide of youth. That's the problem.

Now Yeats, at about the same age:

> What shall I do with this absurdity –
> O heart, O troubled heart – this caricature,
> Decrepit age that has been tied to me
> As to a dog's tail?
>   Never had I more
> Excited, passionate, fantastical
> Imagination, nor an ear and eye
> That more expected the impossible ...

Again, on the outside there is the caricature Age, and inside, the passionate heart. In both poets the same self-contradictory old/ young self.

How should an Old Poet deal with the dissonant reality of diminished flesh and undiminished heart? Hardy went one way – Prospero's way; Yeats went the other – the way of Lear.

Consider first Yeats/Lear. The Lear way with old age is to defy it, to deny diminishment, to proclaim the old heart's vigour. Be passionate, be furious, be insane if you have to; be physical, be sexual – frankly and grossly so. (Do I need to argue that these terms describe Lear? Surely not. Read the sixth scene of Act IV, one of Lear's mad scenes: 'Adultery? / Thou shalt not die: die for adultery! No: / The wren goes to't, and the small gilded fly / Does lecher in my sight. / Let copulation thrive ...'. There's a full and passionate old heart here, undiminished, full-throttle.)

Old Yeats adopted Lear's way, not in his life (which was seemly enough – most of the time) but in his old poems. One way he did so was by inventing Learish characters as masks of himself, a gallery of old, half-crazy (or entirely crazy) surrogates: the Wild Old Wicked Man, Crazy Jane, Tom the Lunatic, an unnamed Old Man and Old Woman. Through these masks Yeats could speak passionately, directly, coarsely about age, sex and physical change; he could utter truths that would not have come properly from the mouth of an Irish senator and Nobel Prize winner – lines like 'Love has pitched his mansion in / The place of excrement'.[5]

Yeats's poems of age are often fiercely sexual, yet in most of them sex is not really the subject; it is, rather, the energy that drives the poems, a way of affirming the undiminished heart and the undiminished imagination, against the evidence of the diminished body. It is a strategy for an Old Poet. Yeats explained that strategy in a little poem called 'The Spur'. It's a poem about the themes of lust and rage in his later poems. But the poem isn't really about sexuality or anger; it's about how to be an Old Poet. Cherish the furious passions for their energy, it says; better to lust and rage in your poems than to be silent and forgotten.

And what about Hardy? What is Prospero's way with diminishment? It is the opposite of Lear's: acceptance; forgiveness; resignation; calm. By the end of *The Tempest* we know that for Prospero sex is a disturbance of youth – of people like Ferdinand and Miranda; that lust belongs to Caliban's world; and that rage is inappropriate to age. Prospero has reached the calm seas beyond those storms. Old Hardy was like that; or so it seems, from his poems. For there the passionate acts and issues of human existence have been transposed from the first-person lyric voice (such as Yeats used in his mask-poems) into sexual dramas from other, imagined lives: mismarriages, adulteries, betrayals, suicides and other satires of circumstance, sometimes witnessed by the speaker of the poem ('The Harbour Bridge'), sometimes told as local history ('The Mock Wife'), or folk-memory ('A Set of Country Songs'), but always distanced – passionate situations that happened to somebody else. And in the rare poems where the desire is first-person personal, it is in the past tense, remote in time, remembered as one might remember an accident or a sickness that one suffered long ago. I am thinking here specifically of poems like 'Louie' and 'Thoughts of Phena', but the distancing of the erotic is also true of the 'Poems of 1912–13'. Look at those poems again: love is present, and very movingly so; but desire is far back, in Cornwall, when Hardy and Emma were young. Sex is only history, in the *now* of those poems.

You can see the difference in present-tense sexuality between Hardy and Yeats in two small poems in which the poets regard young women. Do you remember Yeats's 'Politics'? It comes near the end of his posthumous book, *Last Poems*. In the poem, Yeats stands in the midst of a political conversation, but can't fix his attention on it, because there is a young girl present. The poem ends: 'But O that I were young again / And held her in my arms!' This is the Irish Senator being the decorous old Public Man in public, but privately feeling intense, present-tense desire.

And Hardy? The poem that comes to mind is 'The High-School Lawn'. Hardy (so often the old voyeur in his poems) peeps through a hedge at a whirl of pretty schoolgirls; but what he feels is not desire, but their common mortality:

> A bell: they flee:
> Silence then: –
> So it will be
> Some day again
> With them, – with me.

How old must a man be, to see pretty girls and think of death?

Hardy, I conclude, was an old poet who was content to be entirely old, who was at ease with diminishment, and even with the prospect of approaching death, accepting silence, accepting

forgottenness. A philosophical old man – like Prospero; the opposite of Yeats and Lear, and to me a more disturbing model.

I wonder if posterity, or the lack of posterity, had something to
do with it. Yeats had a son and a daughter, and prayed for their
future in poems; Hardy had none. Perhaps because Yeats had children, he thought also of other, non-genetic heirs, and named their
inheritance in poems, most movingly in the third part of 'The
Tower', which begins:

> It is time that I wrote my will;
> I choose upstanding men
> That climb the streams until
> The fountain leap, and at dawn
> Drop their cast at the side
> Of dripping stone; I declare
> They shall inherit my pride,
> The pride of people that were
> Bound neither to Cause nor to State …

A will is an old man's utterance, a voice that is first heard from the
grave. You have to believe in posterity to write one. Yeats's posterity here is what he called 'the indomitable Irishry', his own defiant
and opposing people. In them he survives.

There is another sense of inheritance in Yeats. In 'Under Ben
Bulben', his last lyric poem in the edition of *Collected Poems* that I
prefer, he speaks to Irish poets who will come after him, as an aged
parent might speak to his children:

> Irish poets, learn your trade,
> Sing whatever is well made,
> Scorn the sort now growing up
> All out of shape from toe to top,
> Their unremembering hearts and heads
> Base-born products of base beds.

You can hear the old man's anger building there against the ugly,
artless, unremembering modern world – Yeats playing Lear to the
end. But you can also hear the pride of continuance, Irish poet to
Irish poet.

There is none of that in Hardy: no descendants, no choosing of
heirs, no address to poets to come. The end, in his mind and in his

work, was terminal and unconditional, and he accepted it with resignation. You hear none of Yeats's anger in Hardy's old poems, and
no pride. He said to his wife Florence, just before his death, that he
had done all that he meant to do, but did not know whether it had
been worth doing.[6] Was that diminished pride the source of his
calm at the end? The feeling, as he put it in a poem, that 'Nothing
Matters Much'? Is that why, in the final poem of his *Collected Poems*,
he resolved to say no more? Life and poetry ran down together, it
seemed, and ended in silence – without continuance, and without
regret.

Two old poets, at the close of life, regard their lives and their
work, and think about worth. These are old thoughts, but they are
not exclusively *poets'* thoughts: all old people must look back that
way, in reflective self-assessment. Some readers must have noticed
that that last point has hovered over this entire essay, that I
haven't really been talking about Old Poets – or not only about
Old Poets: I've been talking about Old Age. An unargued assumption all the way has been that poems chart life, or compose models
of life lived, that poets can embody truth though they cannot know
it (as Yeats said at the end). And that the poems of Old Poets
(those capital letters again) may embody truths about old age,
which we can learn. They say that age is a diminishment; that life
empties then, as memory fills; that age is a time of loss (of friends,
of powers, of hopes and expectations); and of self-judgement; and
that death becomes a presence, like another person in the room.
There is not much comfort in those truths; but then, we don't
desire truth for its comfortableness, do we? We desire truth
because that desire makes us human. We must know, and learn to
live with what we know.

How to Be an Old Poet, then, is simply How to Be Old. Hardy
and Yeats offer two possible ways, one modest, the other flamboy-
ant, one accepting, the other opposing. Hardy put on old age like
an old coat, and lived in it; it fitted him. Yeats made old age a set of
gawdy theatrical costumes to *act* in. Two ways, nearly antithetical,
of responding to and enduring what is both an unavoidable physiological fact and a state of mind. Is one way preferable to the other?
I can see no objective way of answering that question: your own
nature will answer it. But, the reader may say, surely I have leaned
toward Yeats, and made him the hero of my essay; surely it is better
to be a Wild Old Wicked Man than a Dead Man Held on End. If
you think that, it may be because you have been seduced by Yeats's

Old Man's Romanticism. For Yeats's old poems do have a high romantic style – 'High Talk', he called it – and high romantic heroes, and grand settings and stage properties – the Sistine Chapel, the cathedral of Saint Sophia, the art of the Quattrocento. And great, defiant gestures: that, surely, is the way to be old.

Hardy's old poems have none of that: the talk is not high but plain, and there are no heroes and no works of art. Only life (and, occasionally, Life with a capital L), seen clearly through old eyes, as it is, as it has been. And spoken – not sung, not ranted – in a quiet, unclamorous voice. I want to end this essay with the sound of that old voice, as we hear it in an interesting sequence of Hardy's poems: 'For Life I Had Never Cared Greatly', from *Moments of Vision*; 'Epitaph', from *Late Lyrics*; and 'He Never Expected Much' and 'A Placid Man's Epitaph', both from the posthumous *Winter Words*. These are all poems of self-assessment that are also assessments of life itself: the old man not so much judging as defining his own existence in the world. Listen to them – both what they say, and the tone they say it in:

> For Life I had never cared greatly,
> As worth a man's while;
> Peradventures unsought,
> Peradventures that finished in nought,
> Had kept me from youth and through manhood till lately
> Unwon by its style.
>
> I never cared for Life: Life cared for me,
> And hence I owed it some fidelity.
> It now says, 'Cease; at length thou hast learnt to grind
> Sufficient toll for an unwilling mind,
> And I dismiss thee …
>
> > ('Epitaph')

And a stanza in which World addresses Hardy as a child:

> 'I do not promise overmuch,
> Child; overmuch;
> Just neutral-tinted haps and such,'
> You said to minds like mine.
> Wise warning for your credit's sake!
> Which I for one failed not to take,

> And hence could stem such strain and ache
>   As each year might assign.
>   ('He Never Expected Much')

And the last of his epitaphs:

> As for my life, I've led it
> With fair content and credit:
> It said: 'Take this.' I took it:
> Said: 'Leave.' And I forsook it.
> If I had done without it
> None would have cared about it,
> Or said: 'One has refused it
> Who might have meetly used it.'
>   ('A Placid Man's Epitaph')

These are all poems written in the last decade of a very old poet's life: if any poems are Seventh Age poems, these are. Consider what they express: the Old Poet themes of loss, diminishment and limitation. But not as an experience peculiar to the winding down of age; *all* existence is neutral-tinted, *any* action may come to nothing, any time. Yet there is no pain or bitterness in the poems; they share a calm serenity. They are solitary poems – one voice in emptiness, speaking to nobody; and yet three of them take the form of direct address – to Life, to World – as though in extreme old age, when loss has emptied his world, the Old Poet still has company, the company of All Existence, which speaks to him as honestly as he speaks to us. And speaks in imperatives, says: Take this. Leave that. Cease.

These poems are as consistent in their untroubled acceptance as Yeats's poems of crazy old people are in their wild defiance. Perhaps, like Yeats's, they are also mask-poems – a face to wear and a voice to speak with, in order that an old poet near his death might go on making poems, as Hardy did to the very end, to his death-bed. A way to face the Seventh Age of life as a poet, and as yourself.

How to be an Old Poet? – which, I have admitted, is really How to Be Old? Yeats and Hardy offer distinct responses to that question, but with some common factors. 'How to' suggests a set of instructions, like a recipe. It isn't, of course, that simple, but I think I can abstract a few general principles from their cases:

1. Confront reality honestly: look into your glass.
2. Don't turn away either from the past, which is long and full of failures, nor from the future, which will surely be brief.
3. Seek no consolations. To be honest, in old age, is to be unconsoled.

There is one more principle, and it is the most important.

4. Preserve the life of the imagination: feed it with memories and inventions; because imagination *is* life.

Which turns my proposition of a minute ago around: the answer to How to Be Old? is: Be an Old Poet.

Notes

Quotations from Hardy's poems are taken from *The Complete Poetical Works of Thomas Hardy*, ed. Samuel Hynes (Oxford: Clarendon Press, 1982–95) 5 volumes. Quotations from Yeats's poems are taken from *The Collected Poems of W. B. Yeats* (London: Macmillan, 1950).

1. Introduction to *Thomas Hardy*, ed. Samuel Hynes (Oxford: Oxford University Press, 1984). The Oxford Authors series.
2. T. S. Eliot, 'Gerontion'; Robert Browning, 'Rabbi Ben Ezra'; Dylan Thomas, 'Do Not Go Gentle into that Good Night'.
3. Shakespeare, *As You Like It*, Act II, Sc. vii.
4. W. B. Yeats, 'The Tower'.
5. W. B. Yeats, 'Crazy Jane Talks with the Bishop'.
6. Thomas Hardy, *The Life and Work of Thomas Hardy*, ed. Michael Millgate (London: Macmillan, 1984) p. 478.

9

Variations on Two Enigmas:
Hardy, Elgar and the Muses

JOANNA CULLEN BROWN

We must begin with a familiar story. On 2 June, about in the middle of the nineteenth century, in a small cottage just off the heath, a baby boy was born. His father – something of a charmer, a dreamer, we are told – was in trade, his mother a woman of strong character who greatly influenced her children, imbuing at least this son with a love of reading and literature. He soon learnt to play the violin, for his family was much involved with music-making; his childhood memories, and the experience of the English country-side, were to be a lifelong inspiration to him in his art. So, increasingly, was an overwhelming nostalgia for the past. He was a sensitive man who needed constant reassurance; a man who loved life, but who also felt a pervasive melancholy. Thomas Hardy? Yes; but equally, in every detail, Edward Elgar, who was born at Broadheath, Worcestershire, on Hardy's seventeenth birthday, and whose life, in its external circumstances, bears an uncanny resemblance to the poet's.

Thus, like Hardy's 'Domicilium', Elgar's earliest dated composition was 'Humoreske, a tune from Broadheath', written during a return visit when he was ten. Like Hardy, as a child he often sat silently listening in a corner, studied in churchyards, and was frightened in Worcester Cathedral by a gruesome winged skull. Both as boys had fragile health and later found they were better living in the country than in London; leaving school in their teens, both were apprenticed, Elgar in a lawyer's office, Hardy to an architect. Hardy senior could not afford to send his son to Cambridge, nor Elgar senior his to Leipzig.

So both artists were self-taught: both set themselves an apprenticeship of rigorous exercises; both enjoyed great discussions with fellow-pupils, and habitually read at four or five in the morning to make up their educational deficiencies. And both had to struggle against the stifling Victorian class-system. They both married, technically, 'above' them, both brides' families reacting with horror; both wives had literary pretensions, Alice Elgar having before her marriage already published a novel and some verse; both, though Emma only for a time, considerably helped their husbands in the chores of writing – Alice, indeed, supporting Elgar in incalculable and sacrificial ways all her life. Both men needed relationships of some kind with other women (and largely unfounded rumours circulated about illegitimate children for both); both men were smitten, creatively and personally, by their wife's death.

When it came to honours, Elgar caught up his elder. Awarded a knighthood before Hardy refused one, and an O.M. only a year after Hardy, he was only 43 to Hardy's 73 when Cambridge gave them doctorates. Elgar reacted like A. A. Milne's Eeyore: 'I shan't accept it. ... It's too late. ... For Everything.' He accepted. As usual, a flurry of fans accompanied him, sketched with typical panache in a delightful letter. 'I feel Gibbonsy, Croftish, Byrdlich & foolish all over. ... Yours gownily, E. E.' Hardy, by contrast, barely mentioned the occasion: 'I feel no worse for my dissipations.'[1] As always, Elgar and he resembled the whirlwind and the still small voice.

What about their attitudes? Both loathed modern war, but had loved its past romance. Both were fascinated by technology. Both loved birds and animals. Elgar sent as a Christmas card Walt Whitman's litany of dogs' virtues, which included 'They do not lie awake in the dark and weep for their sins; / They do not make me sick discussing their duty to God'. Hardy's Dorset blackbird that cried 'Pret-ty de-urr!' was echoed by Elgar's diary note of 'chaffinches (many) singing "Three cheers!"'[2] (Incidentally, they both reminded people of hawks.)

All sorts of other little things seem to link them. Elgar, writing from America: 'My mind is a blank on which these people scrawl,' reminds us of Hardy's mind 'scored with necrologic scrawls'.[3] They both disliked what they meant by the words 'smart' and 'mechanic(al)'. Both chose to paint a sword scene: Bathsheba dazzled by light and sharp hisses (in *Far from the Madding Crowd*), Elgar's 'Sword Song' in *Caractacus, vivace e con molto fuoco*, 'with brilliant regular flashes through upper strings and woodwind'. And how Hardy would have loved Elgar's story, remembered after thirty years, of the time when, twice blocked on his chosen cycle route by hay-carts, he ended up near the grave of his old legal employer. At the churchyard he enquired of the sexton's wife. She looked dumbly aghast. Then, writes Basil Maine, who had this from Elgar himself, she said: '"Funny you should be askin'. Why, the stone o' that grave fell down and broke this very mornin'."'[4]

Why am I telling you all this, when it is the work, the art, that is of first importance? For two reasons: one, because it is of our humanity to be interested in people. Two, because it is from the life and the character that the work springs. In Hardy's own words, 'writers ... have held that anything, however imperfect, which affords an idea of a human personage in his actual form and flesh, is of value in respect of him'.[5] So before we move to their works, and how such creation happens, let us now look at the immense differences between these two great men.

Hardy is uniformly described as gentle and modest, 'high thinking and plain-living', subtle, sensitive, reserved. In company he usually appeared quietly cheerful and conversational, whatever his inner turmoil or need for reassurance. In contrast Elgar, possibly even more nervous and highly strung, apparently exercised little self-control over his words, feelings or wide fluctuations of mood. He frequently wrote so extravagantly as to contradict himself and the known facts; so, despite heartfelt tributes to his mother, to his saintly wife and to lifelong friends, he could write to Sidney Colvin: 'as a child and as a young man and as a mature man no single person was ever kind to me'.[6] He was difficult and often rude; but he could be, and often was, charming, generous, affectionate and full of fun. 'Japes' was one of his favourite words; he loved puzzles of all kinds, making puns in music (as Hardy did in poetry) and spelling words absurdly – such as 'score', which mutated into 'skourrghe' and even 'ssczowough*oh*r'.

Perhaps the chief difference from Hardy was Elgar's unrestrained exuberance. His letters bubble with life, and despite their predominating self-centredness, endear him to the reader and reveal the charisma which brought him the devotion of so many friends. From Italy: 'Bought some figs today – did not know the name, so asked for *"Frutti, per habilmenti d'Adam e Eva"'* ['Fruit, used to clothe Adam and Eve'].[7] Hardy's letters by comparison are in a minor key, and *pianissimo*; in no surviving letter does he express anything approaching the enthusiasm and the affection Elgar openly showed, for example to 'my very dear Jaeger'. His energy made him much more 'hands-on' than Hardy, who seems to have enjoyed few manipulative hobbies. Elgar, mercurial always, went through beagling ('no music like the baying of hounds after all'),[8] billiards, bug-hunting, buying cars (shades of Toad), chemistry (inventing the Elgar Sulphuretted Hydrogen Apparatus), fishing, kite-flying, peashooting, printing, woodwork, and rural pursuits like taking wasps' nests and, according to one friend, playing 'about the pond like a boy'. He nearly stood for Parliament; and when in 1926 a consultant enquiring about his lifestyle learnt that after breakfast he 'address[ed] the serious business of the day' – '... Composing?' 'No,' replied Elgar, 'making up my betting slips'.[9] But he and Hardy deliberately concealed their inner fires.

And so we come to their art. It is no surprise that their artistic styles should differ. Hardy valued 'the force of reserve, and the emphasis of understatement',[10] qualities which permeate his poetry as they did his demeanour. By contrast Elgar is famous for the tonal and harmonic colour of his music, and its exuberance. Yet valuable connections can be made in their work.

First, both were men who felt deeply, for whom emotion was paramount. For all Hardy's championing of reason, he averred in a letter of 1920 that 'human actions are not ruled by reason at all in the last resort'. 'Poetry is emotion put into measure,' he noted, 'The emotion must come by nature, but the measure can be acquired by art.' 'The Poet takes note of nothing that he cannot feel emotively.' 'My opinion is that a poet should express the emotion of all the ages.'[11] It was Hardy's emotion that created poems like 'Julie-Jane' and 'The Blinded Bird'; it was the deep feeling in *The Dream of Gerontius* which left one critic 'throbbing with emotions that no English work has raised in me heretofore'. Another wrote: 'It is music of the heart, and appeals to the heart, and yet the head that worked it is no scamper of workmanship.' When the Violin Concerto and the First Symphony appeared, the fine critic Ernest Newman wrote: 'Human feeling so nervous and subtle as this had never before spoken in English orchestral or choral music ... speaking eloquently ... of matters that concern the emotional life of each one of us.'[12] This could be said of Hardy too.

Secondly, these two artists both shared preoccupations with certain themes in their work. One was that of the outsider – derived from their common experience of social background and their non-academic training; and for Elgar, being also a Roman Catholic. Both remained personally sensitive in these areas. Many of Hardy's fictional characters are outsiders, from Egbert Mayne to Jude. Elgar too chose outsiders for most of his early settings, culminating in the arch-outsider Judas Iscariot, for whom he had an intelligent under-standing and wrote some of *The Apostles'* best music.

By the time Elgar composed his greatest orchestral works he had in a sense become the insider, for he was their subject and in them, he said, 'I have written out my soul.' Hardy said that there was more autobiography in a hundred lines of his poetry than in all the novels.[13] For both, more than anything else, what enriched their work was the time which had passed in their life's pilgrimage, and their distillation of it.

Time remembered – recapitulation – the return to a previous theme or vision to look at it again – is of course of the essence of music in its Western classical form. It is also a preoccupation of Hardy. Conscious of how 'our imperfect memories insensibly for-malize the fresh originality of living fact – from whose shape they slowly depart',[14] he believed in, and practised in his poetry, a con-stant revisitation of experience in order to stay in touch with reality. Recapitulation depends upon being conscious of the past; both men were particularly aware of it. Technically, Hardy would express this by, for example, a judicious use of archaisms, or by the circling rhythms of regret; Elgar by the use of the diatonic, the basic seven-note scale of old Western music – the past – set against the chromatic, twelve-note scale of the new. Both had a marked historical sense and loved the romance of the bygone: Elgar said he wrote *Cockaigne* because 'one dark day in the Guildhall: looking at the memorials of the city's great past ... I seemed to hear far away in the dim roof a theme, an echo of some noble melody'.[15] Hardy viewed Southampton as the place where Vespasian had landed; Elgar, feeling after the Overture he wrote near Alassio, wrote: 'In a flash it all came to me – the conflict of the armies on that very spot long ago, where now I stood ... and then, all of a sudden, I came back to reality. In that time I had composed the overture.'[16] Hardy, even in his twenties, could write a poem like 'Amabel', looking backwards to his youth; and countless buried emotions were exhumed for poems half a lifetime later. Elgar often retrieved early sketches and turned them into maturer meaning.

Both men shared a particularly retrospective view. Hardy shows what things or people (like Amabel) have become: the elegant sun-shade now 'a naked sheaf of wires'. The slow movement of Elgar's String Quartet was described by his wife as 'captured sunshine'; but the primary theme's negated, broken return was rather the capture, as J. N. Moore writes in his authoritative *Creative Life*, of 'the sunshine's evanescence'.

Both men tended to idealize the past. Elgar longed to leave Malvern – until he had left it: 'I envy you ... all the memories of the old loveliness remain[s]';[17] similarly when he left Worcester for London. In this love of the unattainable, how alike he and Hardy were.

But of all the attitudes to the past which they shared, the most significant was their nostalgia, their 'memoried passion', their yearning for what once was, or for what might have been. Nostalgia, writes Anthony Storr in his book *The Dynamics of Creation*, has inspired innumerable artists. Hardy dreamed 'In the Small Hours': 'It seemed a thing for weeping / To find, at slumber's wane / And morning's sly increeping, / That Now, not Then, held reign.' Elgar, thanking friends for their gift of Beethoven scores – 'some of the old dear things I played when a boy' – wrote: 'Nothing in later life can be even a shadow of those "learning" days: ... the old mysterious glamour is gone & the feeling of *entering* – shy, but welcomed – into the world of the immortals & wandering in those vast woods – (so it seemed to me) with their clear pasture spaces & sunlight ... is a holy feeling & a sensation never to come again.'[18]

Elgar's vision of loss can clearly be demonstrated in his music. Some claim that his subdominant tendency is nostalgic; but this is a technical point which cannot take space here. One of the most obvious elements is his characteristic downward movement, towards darker tones and flats. 'It had a dying fall.' Even that first, ten-year-old tune had gone ever down, and this repetition of downward sequences was to continue all his life. Probably the best known examples are the opening bars and first subject of the 'Cello Concerto, or the climax in the Second Symphony Finale.

In an indefinable way, most of us recognize in Elgar's music this nostalgia, this 'sunset quality', as Newman called it. But analysis of his work shows it to be of the essence. One section of the symphonic study *Falstaff* portrays the old man's happy dreams of his lost childhood, and his awakening to present harsh realities. 'It suggests', says Elgar, '"what might have been"'. The First Symphony begins in diatonic serenity with what Alice Elgar noted as a 'great beautiful tune'.[19] But it is subjected to all kinds of opposition – chromatic attacks and unpleasant strutting little marches, crude blaring appropriations of what he called a 'sad & delicate' moment, insistent rhythms which try to destroy that serenity. In the diatonic struggle against the chromatic, the slow movement, the Adagio, writes Moore, 'was finding the very definition of nostalgia: a vision of the past brought to focus by the implied contrast of what came after'.[20]

Another slow movement, that of the 'Cello Concerto, not only sounds nostalgic: it is all reminiscent melody. Some of it echoes particularly significant themes from the Violin Concerto; and its most tender theme returns poignantly in the last movement, which ends with the same chords that began the work. It is as if even in one work he is reliving a remembered emotion, needing the passage of time to look back and understand the past. Is not this in some way like what Hardy was doing in poems like 'At Castle Boterel' – superimposing today upon yesterday, and emerging with a new understanding? Elgar was explicit about his retrospection. Setting as epigraph to his Second Symphony Shelley's line 'Rarely, rarely, comest thou, Spirit of Delight,' he wrote that it 'was an attempt to give the reticent Spirit a hint (with sad enough retrospections) as to what we should like to have!'[21]

Elgar's sadness, his deep nostalgia, was not the only important element that fired him, as it fired Hardy, to create. For both, their childhood was a potent resource. Hardy's memories and his continuing proximity to his birthplace inspired numerous poems and, for example, the child's-eye view of the heath in *The Return of the Native*. For Elgar, perhaps because he left it when he was only two, there remained an aura about the Broadheath cottage all his life. As a new baronet he chose the title 'of Broadheath', and when Lady Stuart visited it in 1920 he wrote: 'So you have been to B[roadheath]. I fear you did not find the cottage – it is nearer the clump of Scotch firs – I can smell them now – in the hot sun. Oh! how cruel that I was not there – there's *nothing between* that infancy & now and I *want* to see it.'[22] But it was not just the aura that inspired him. He could actually plunder his childhood and youth for usable musical material: his early compositions. It was while he was working on these that, one day, the 'great beautiful tune' of his First Symphony came to him – just as Hardy was inspired to write new poems by re-reading his earlier works. Even in 1915 Elgar was so fired by his childhood that, for a fantasy play *The Starlight Express*, he wrote three hundred pages of score in one month. At another barren time his *Nursery Suite* also got rave reviews.

What the reviewers did not know was that a difficult problem in this work had been resolved by a novel method. While being given an injection, Elgar had jumped violently; and 'When you gave me that damned prod, it came to me!'[23] By such unforeseen spurs has human creativity been activated. What was it that impelled these two to create some of the finest art in Europe?

'The motive power of much creative activity is emotional tension.' '[S]ome split between the inner world and the outer world is common to all human beings; and the need to bridge the gap is the source of creative endeavour,' writes Dr Storr. That both men suffered from many tensions is clear. Hardy was greatly exercised by the discrepancies between the human mind and the world it lives in, the divergences between mind and reality. The tricks of time and memory, the 'inexplicable relations'[24] between cohabiting mind and body, the cruel fate of the sentient human being set in a world of alien laws: all caused him anguish. For a man with his erotic imagination and capacity for deep feeling, the failure of his marriage and any other desired relationship was suffering enough; and other sexual tensions show in his work. He was caught, too, in the pull between rationalism and belief, reason and emotion, the excitement of Darwin, intellectual discovery and growing scepticism against the poetic mysteries of his self-acknowledged 'churchy' tendency. He felt tension between town and country, his own rural and oral traditions and the written sophistication of Academe.

Elgar shared some of these tensions, and had others too. He needed solitude for creation, yet needed companionship and esteem; he felt acutely the composer's neglect in Britain, which at first accorded him neither enough money nor honour. His *'Enigma'* *Variations*, he told Jaeger, had earned him in five years just £8; worse, hack work paid but creative work didn't. He spent money freely, with first-class travel, hotels, bespoke suits, and beautiful artistic paper from Italy. If Hardy felt such temptations, he did not succumb. But adequate fees, for Elgar, denoted that appreciation which was his lifeline. He seems to have had the manic-depressive's lack of self-confidence and constant need for approval. He also clearly exhibited that greater polarity of temperament which Storr ascribes to creative artists: so that he could appear two different people, the one who constantly complained 'Such is life & I hate, loathe & detest it' – or the one of Fred Gaisberg's diary who 'seemed to have a word and a smile for everyone ... and all responded happily to his sunshine.'[25]

Creativity was certainly for both men a defence against the world and against their inner conflicts. Art bridges our inner and outer worlds, and fulfils our basic human desire to order our experience, to create some wholeness out of life's chaos. *How* did they make this whole, impose this order? Let us instance just three elements creatively used by Hardy and Elgar: rhythm, patterns and time.

Suzanne Langer claims that music helps us to order our fragmented emotions into a whole, a 'subjective unity of experience'. And it does it through rhythm – which is 'the principle that organizes physical existence into a biological design'. Hardy would have approved this, I think, as one important account of poetry too. Rhythm was a vital element in his reaching that 'subjective unity of experience'. It was part of what he called the 'rational content inside their artistic form' which both poetry and architecture must carry. As in that art, 'cunning irregularity' and spontaneity, learnt from Gothic principles, were vital in poetic metre and stress.[26] Hardy's reasoning and sensitivity about rhythm created all those wonderful lines where the rhythms image the rhythms of life – our inner rhythms against 'the conflicting rhythms of the universe ... the straitjacket of fate, time and circumstance against which the human heart bursts in its own rhythms of longing' and pain. 'The Ruined Maid' is thus written, tongue in cheek, to something like hymnal long metre, and agnostic poems to common hymnal metre – for tension and paradox are central to life. Rhythm highlights character; or in its awkward stumbling expresses inner disarray, much as Elgar used chromatic passages. On Hardy's page the shape of a certain metre often tells tales; Elgar too 'liked to see how it shaped, how it presented itself to the eye as well as to the ear.' He used rhythm in complex ways, and apparently his eyes would 'shine with excitement' in the discussion of finer points.[27]

If rhythm helps us toward that 'subjective unity of experience', so does pattern-making, 'the function of the mind which underlies aesthetic activity.' We know how Hardy saw and used patterns – lines and dapple and shadow – to dramatize and symbolize the growth of awareness and developing experiences. Musical phrases are patterns; and a score has vertical as well as horizontal patterns. Elgar's typical repeated sequences in both rhythm and melody have their pattern; and his works are full of thematic interconnections converging into a final design. W. H. Reed the violinist, who perhaps knew Elgar and his music more intimately than anyone except Alice, described his musical thinking in a way that reminds us of Hardy: 'Like Beethoven,' he wrote, '[Elgar] allowed an idea, which may have occurred to him as a short phrase, to germinate and transform and throw out branches.'[28]

Germination, and time, is our third element and plays a crucial part in the work of these two artists. In Hardy's poetry, time is a recognizable character who performs many functions, usually injurious to human beings – except when it clarifies our understanding. 'Hardy's central lyric', writes Dennis Taylor, 'recapitulates the life ... [He] achieves a wonderful parallel of a moment's sensation and a lifetime's experience.' Recapitulating a lifetime's experience is also part of Elgar's engagement with time. 'I have recorded last year in the first movement,' he wrote of his Second Symphony to Alice Stuart Wortley. We need time, of course, to objectify our experience; it can then, through memory, be transmuted into art. Hardy called his 'Poems of 1912–13' 'an expiation':[29] an expiation caused by his own sudden experiencing, with surprise and shock, how far his mind and imagination had lagged behind reality; how far that reality had moved from the early happy days of his courtship. His poem 'At Castle Boterel', as I have hinted, shows how time helped him to understand, so that he could begin to lay the experience to rest. After Emma's death, his poems evolved into 'recapitulations of the life', in which he seems to master time, combining past and present experience into an organic whole.

Many artists can dramatize our own experience of time behaving in different ways. In Racine's tragedies we are aware of time rushing headlong towards ruin, or, as we say, temporizing, holding us in agonized suspense. Stravinsky distinguished what he called 'psychological time' from 'ontological time': a time that varies with our inner feelings, from official, unemotional, clock time. Storr quotes a composer, Norman Kay: '[M]usical delight is bound up (for me) with the feeling that a great composer has mastered time. Not only that: he has reconciled two kinds of time. ... By drawing these two together, the great composer enhances my sense of well-being; he shares his mastery with me.'[30] Hardy had already anticipated Stravinsky and Kay in his similar understanding – in poems such as 'The Clock-Winder' and 'A Commonplace Day' – of the appalling drab 'psychological time' in which so many are imprisoned in hurtful lives on the treadmill. Yet people escape from 'the cell of Time', by love and death and memory – Hardy's sister Mary, 'Laughing, her young brown hand awave', the hidden son of 'The

Whitewashed Wall', and the one whom 'Time touches ... not' as she still 'Draws rein and sings to the swing of the tide'.[31]

Elgar makes us feel he has mastered time when in his Second Symphony he surveys and relives his conflicting life experiences, reconciling them all 'nobilmente' in the last bars. 'It resumes our human life,' wrote Lady Elgar in her diary, 'delight, regret, farewell, the saddest word & then the strong man's triumph.'[32]

We have seen that the need to resolve emotional tension, and to bridge the inner/outer world gap, is a prime impetus to creative activity. We have noted that for inspiration Hardy and Elgar both drew on their feeling for the past, including their childhood. What else inspired them?

Art, inevitably. Elgar loved literature, as Hardy loved music: where Elgar put a poetic epigraph above a work, Hardy wrote 'Song'. But asked by a physician what set his music off, Elgar replied: 'It is infinitely various. It may be the cry of a child: then I *see* a bar of music, and can write it down. It may be pain. Or it may be the sound of wind and waves, or the murmuring of a stream.'[33]

There is no doubt that both Hardy and Elgar found the solitude and beauty of the country a general inspiration to create. Both would make notes out of doors; and just as Hardy in 1868 was 'taking down the exact sound of the nightingale' at his birthplace, so, aged about nine, Elgar used, in his own words, to sit 'in the reeds by Severn side with a sheet of paper trying to fix the sounds & longing for something very great'.[34] 'I want something badly to encourage me,' he wrote to Jaeger while composing *The Apostles*, 'the weather is too cold for me to go and sit in the marsh with my beloved wild creatures to get heartened up and general inspiration.' He told W. H. Reed 'he had to go there more than once to think out those climaxes in the Ascension'.[35] Much of his finest music was written in solitary country cottages. 'I think of the holy peace at Brinkwells in the early morn.' There, amid general creative inspiration, one specific natural feature inspired a specific piece of music: a strange group of eerie, twisted dead trees nearby. They fascinated Elgar, as did the legend that the trees were impious Spanish monks, struck dead. Hence his wife's diary: 'E. wrote more of the wonderful Quintet – Flexham Park – sad "dispossessed" trees & their dance & unstilled regret for their evil fate...'.[36]

As everyone knows, Hardy also wrote about trees – about the wind 'shrieking and blaspheming ... [in] the devilry of a gusty night in a wood'; about 'Summer-time, / With the hay, and bees achime'; about the glory of Orion 'as it soared forth above the rim of the landscape'. Yet his attitude to the country seems to me different from Elgar's. Elgar had lost it from his childhood when at two he moved to the city, and it had become a nostalgic, possessive focus as well as an essential for refreshment. Hardy had never lost it, and could say to William Archer: 'The town-bred boy will ... rush to pick a flower which the country boy does not seem to notice. But it is part of the country boy's life. It grows in his soul – he does not want it in his buttonhole.'[37] Hardy's instinctive observation of nature was by his gifts transmuted into great art; but I think he could do this as well in the study as he could in the open. As a person he interiorized so much more than Elgar, who poured out everything. Yet it is interesting that Elgar's classic dictum that 'there is music in the air, music all round us, the world is full of it – and you simply ... take as much as you require', is matched in a note Hardy made from Matthew Arnold: 'the best ideas attainable in or about your time ... are, so to speak, in the air – to be seized by the finest spirits'.[38]

What always appealed to Hardy about the country was its human associations. His imagery is full of them. The heath, he writes, 'at all times ... appeals rather to the sentiment than to the eye'. Over thirty years earlier he had noted: 'An object or mark raised or made by man on a scene is worth ten times any such formed by unconscious Nature. Hence clouds, mists, and mountains are unimportant beside the wear on a threshold, or the print of a hand.' So places move him if they are linked with people – 'The names creeping out everywhere.'[39]

People, together with the past and the fruits of memory, seem to be Hardy's chief inspiration – for people of course mean love: not only erotic love, but the love of his much-quoted chapter from Corinthians. Compassion burns through his writing – for Tess and her family, for the Unborn Pauper Child, for Patty Beech; and a passion for social justice, a cry against cruelty and the apparent indifference of the First Cause. These always inspired him. But Emma's death, and her image as and where he had first known her, with her 'nut-coloured hair, / And gray eyes, and rose-flush coming and going'[40] – this was his special muse, leading him to a new realization of life and art. Elgar's muse, by contrast, was very much alive.

What is a muse? We have too briefly looked at some aspects of creativity. We have not touched on the unity of all the arts – the sort of thing that made the painter Ivon Hitchens speak of 'the instruments in a painter's orchestra'. This was the message Hardy received in the Hall of the Muses in Rome.[41] But here we must concentrate, not on the Nine Muses (whose mother, of course, was Memory), but on the muse which is defined, 'chiefly with the possessive', as the inspiring goddess of a creative artist. Why do male artists have, or need, muses; and do women artists also want a goddess?

Emily Dickinson needed no personal muse to inspire her; but she needed someone approaching a mentor, a lifeline, who knew her poetry even though he had judged it unpublishable. In the past many women painters, denied education, mobility or social approval, had to get these from established painters – their mentors, not their muse. Susan Hill's interest in Britten's music inspired her early novels; now just hearing his music triggers her desire to write. But many male creative artists from Dante and Petrarch seem to need a female muse to inspire them. Goethe had several in turn, potent inspirers of his poetry, including decorous married women and one he married. Samuel Beckett seems not to have needed, but to have found a muse in the actress Billie Whitelaw. She understood his plays 'intuitively'. Beckett rehearsed her in *Play*, and she writes: 'For the first time I felt part of the creative process. ... I knew I had something to offer.' She had. When he came to write *Not I*, years later, it was her voice that he heard in his head.

T. S. Eliot's beautiful, intelligent, creative muse Emily Hale for years 'provided a perfect impetus for his art', writes Lyndall Gordon, 'an ethereal love ... so long as she remain[ed] physically unobtainable'.

Lastly, Robert Graves developed the need for a muse possessed by the White, or Moon, Goddess, a muse 'to torment and inspire him'[42] – to provide him with the emotional tension crucial to his love poetry?

Many of the women who inspired Hardy's poems were dead when he wrote them. His future wife Florence was also 'unobtainable' when he wrote hers. So was Mrs Henniker. In the *Life* he wrote: 'Some of his best short poems were inspired by her,' but his wife excised that. Though we may not know just how far he had hoped to go with Mrs Henniker, he certainly longed for a soulmate; at least 'a friend', he wrote transparently to her, 'with whom mutual confessions can be made of weaknesses without fear of reproach or contempt. ... I wonder if I shall ever find one.' It was the 'ethereal intangible' features of her character that he loved, associating Shelleyan idealism with her as with Sue Bridehead, whose character Mrs Henniker influenced. For that, and for poignant poems like 'A Broken Appointment', she was his muse – though perhaps his 'love for her in its fulness she herself even did not know'.[43]

In contrast to Hardy, Elgar's lack of reserve ensured that every musical friend close to the Elgars knew that Alice Stuart Wortley was his muse. His wife's self-abnegation and devotion to his genius – and, I think, a basic confidence both in his love for her, and in her friends the Stuart Wortleys – allowed it full rein.

Nothing is simple about Elgar's relationship to the two Alices – but only a few words about his wife will have to suffice. Alice Elgar, nearly nine years older than Edward, perceived his potential before anyone else. Her effect on his music was astonishing. She gave him the confidence, and the adoration, that he needed: his first important work, *Froissart*, was written in the first year of their marriage. 'She had unerring judgement and aesthetic sense,' wrote W. H. Reed; Elgar altered music at her uplifted eyebrow, and it was she who first identified and commended the 'Enigma' theme from a tissue of idle improvization. She did everything, from preparing his scoring paper to housemoving. She saw to it that Elgar was surrounded by vivacious young women. Some, wrote a visiting niece, could *'make* him work as well as amuse him. My little aunt and Dora could run with him, bicycle, climb hills, fly kites ... their part was to get him ready for work. Mrs Elgar was a wonderful woman. ... I believe she *made* these friendships with younger women – all young and attractive – who could do the parts she couldn't always manage.'[44] When Alice died he was devastated: 'All I have done was owing to her'; 'thro' it all shines the radiant mind & soul of my dearest departed one. ... You ... must thank *her* for all of it.' Orchestrating a Bach fugue, he said: 'Now that my poor wife has gone I can't be original, and so I depend on people like John Sebastian for a source of inspiration.'[45] Alice had inspired, *inter alia*, the early *Salut d'Amour*, and a song called *Love* on his fiftieth birthday; she had even written poems for him to set in a crisis. In the widest sense she was his muse.

But with Alice Stuart Wortley, wife of a Sheffield MP (later Lord Stuart of Wortley), it was different. Like Mrs Henniker she was sympathetic and intuitive; as a daughter of the painter Millais she understood artists, and she was a fine pianist. The two couples met in 1902 but Elgar's special friendship with her only developed years later, at about the time when the noble Jaeger resigned from Novello's through ill-health. There may well be a connection. In May 1909 he died after years of tubercular suffering. His love and admiration for Elgar, constantly expressed, had surpassed all but Lady Elgar's; he had also pressed Elgar to improve the end of the *'Enigma' Variations* and part of *The Dream of Gerontius* – a mentor, with a muse's effect. Now he was gone. In June Elgar wrote asking Mrs Stuart Wortley's permission 'to put your belovèd name on' a part-song, *Angelus*, 'if you both allow it'.

Suddenly more letters are kept. They are not unlike Hardy's early Henniker letters, including teasing allusions to other lady friends. (One irony is that Hardy actually teased Mrs Henniker that if *she* was ungrateful for the opportunity he might teach architecture to Mrs Stuart Wortley.) One letter, on Florentine paper, said: '[T]his is what Petrarch and the rest wrote on! I would write a sonnet to you but it would not rhyme & if it did, would not be good enough for you otherwise. Anyhow I can *think* sonnets to you ... which probably had better not be scanned.' He sent her the sketches for some passionate songs – to his own words, but attributed to 'my confidant & adviser, Pietro d'Alba'.[46] (This Pietro was none other than his daughter's white rabbit.) They recall Hardy poems like 'Come Not; Yet Come!' He told an old friend that he was very unhappy.

Meanwhile he had resumed work on a Violin Concerto, begun five years earlier. Hearing part of it, Charles Stuart Wortley was impressed enough to ask for a copy. But Elgar, depressed, angled for approval by threatening to put it aside. He received a resounding endorsement: he *must* go on with it. So, alone in London, he sent it to Mrs Stuart Wortley.

A few hours after writing to her, Elgar was inspired with another theme for the concerto – a theme, he said, 'written in dejection as Shelley says', which he thought important enough to mark 'Feb. 7 1910 6.30 p.m.' It went on to produce a vital climax, which linked the first and second subjects – a bridge passage he had long been seeking. Opposite it in the sketch he wrote: 'This is going to be good! / "When Love and Faith meet / There will be Light" / Feby 1910 Queen Anne's Mansions.'[47]

February 7th was always kept afterwards as an anniversary between them. (It may remind us of that March 7th to which Hardy turned his calendar, commemorating his first meeting with Emma.) And so the first music directly attributable to his feeling for this Alice came and was attested. He called this theme, and the second subject to which it led (which he had sketched several years earlier), 'Windflower' themes; and he called Alice his Windflower. He was to send her windflowers in spring almost to the end of his life.

Until he had completed the Violin Concerto he needed her to be near. 'I have been working hard at the Windflower themes but all stands still until you come & approve!' And the next day, asking her to meet him: 'It is so dreary to-day & the tunes stick & are not Windflowerish – at present. Your E.' A month later, off to stay with their mutual friend Frank Schuster (a wealthy and ardent patron to artists), Elgar wrote to him in advance: 'I want to *end* that Concerto but do not see my way very clearly to the end – so you had best invite its stepmother ... too.'[48]

Much more can be said, but not here – about masculine and feminine themes, for example – to show how intimate a revelation of their relationship is the Concerto. His epigraph is a Spanish inscription from a poet's tomb – 'In here is enshrined the soul of .....' (with five dots). Shortly before the Concerto's première Elgar wrote to the Windflower: 'What a wonderful year this has been ... the radiance in a poor, little private man's soul has been wonderful & new & the Concerto has come!' ('Radiance' was a word Hardy used for his love in some highly-charged poems.)[49]

There was, indeed, an overflow of radiance which was immediately channelled into beginning the next symphony – 'your Symphony', as he later wrote. '[I] am ... weaving strange & wonderful memories into very poor music I fear.' And still, seven years later, in 1918: 'The music is yours as always.' Another echo of Hardeian scenes came when he suggested one passage 'might be a love scene in a garden at night when the ghost of some memories comes *through it*'; and early in April 'May not [cue] 87 be like a woman dropping a flower on the man's grave?' The Windflower had sent him roses at the end of March.[50]

There was, finally, another Hardy connection with this symphony. Shortly after Elgar first used the Windflower name, he and Frank Schuster visited the Stuart Wortleys – at Tintagel. Elgar's diary included these comments: '*Awfully* dreary village. Coast ... not so fine as Llangranog. ... [A]fter lunch by car to church beyond Boscastle – we four walked thro' lovely valley to B[oscastle]. – there

Tea ... by car back to Tintagel.' The map suggests that the church beyond Boscastle, and the lovely valley, could only be St Juliot: but we can never know. The next day the travellers slept at Falmouth. 'A very nice place,' says Elgar's diary, 'and the first on this car tour which I really feel I want to see again.' So much for Tintagel! Yet within a year he would inscribe the Second Symphony's full score 'Venice – Tintagel'. It was a perfect example of romantic fantasy winning over factual reality; and gives another clue as to the nature of creation and the inspiration of the muse. 'The poetry of a scene', wrote Hardy when Elgar was eight, 'varies with the minds of the perceivers,' and later: 'the beauty of association is entirely superior to the beauty of aspect'.

One postscript about Tintagel. In 1916 Hardy and Florence went to St Juliot, to check the new tablet erected to Emma. 'At Tintagel,' he wrote in the *Life*, 'they met quite by accident Hardy's friends the Stuart-Wortleys, which made their sojourn at that romantic spot a very pleasant one.'[51] Tintagel was still exercising its old spell.

We may never understand the complexities of Elgar's love for both Alices. It seems that an artist may focus on a sympathetic person as a support during the agonizing processes of creation. He (as it usually is) may attach a considerable degree of fantasy, of romance, of idealization, to the vision in his mind, his inner world. It seems, with many artists, including Hardy and Elgar, not to need sexual consummation. When they were both free Hardy did not marry Mrs Henniker, nor Elgar the Windflower. 'I have put it all in my music,' he wrote to her, '& also much more that has never happened.'[52]

There is still one question about Elgar. After his wife's death in 1920, he fell silent. '[M]usic I loathe – I did get out some paper – but its [*sic*] all dead.' He produced no original orchestral music until 1930. Enter George Bernard Shaw, who in the autumn of 1932 at last persuaded the BBC to commission a new symphony, with a fee of £1000.

Elgar's Third Symphony was cut short by his cancer and death early in 1934. But there are over one hundred pages extant and it has been reconstructed by Anthony Payne and the BBC. Most of the themes are drawn from old music; but at the centre is a sketch marked 'V.H's own theme.' Vera Hockman was a young violinist Elgar had taken up with who loved his music. Until he died she was frequently with him, and he gave her a precious book of his mother's, saying 'I want you to have it because you are my mother, my child, my lover and my friend.'[53]

The question is whether it was the love and admiration expressed by Vera Hockman, or that implied in the call for a new work, actually backed by money – or both? – which caused the first spark of Elgar's creative energy to glitter briefly again. The symphony sounds full of promise; would it have overturned the sad wry irony that while Hardy could only write his greatest body of poetry after his wife died, Elgar could only compose *his* when Lady Elgar was alive?

Notes

Quotations from Hardy's poems are taken from *The Complete Poems of Thomas Hardy*, ed. James Gibson (London: Macmillan, 1976). Quotations from his novels are taken from Macmillan's New Wessex Edition (London: Macmillan, 1974–6).

1. Percy M. Young (ed.), *Letters to Nimrod: Edward Elgar to August Jaeger 1897–1908* (London: Dobson, 1965) pp. 111, 114 (subsequently cited as *Nimrod*); Hardy to S. Cockerell, 15 June 1913, in R. L. Purdy and M. Millgate (eds), *Collected Letters of Thomas Hardy* (Oxford: Clarendon Press, 1978–88) vol. IV, p. 280 (subsequently cited as *Collected Letters*).
2. Walt Whitman, quoted in Jerrold Northrop Moore, *Edward Elgar: A Creative Life* (Oxford: Oxford University Press, 1987 pbk) p. 783 (subsequently cited as Moore, *Edward Elgar*); Thomas Hardy (subsequently cited as TH), 'The Spring Call'; Moore, *Edward Elgar*, p. 718.
3. Elgar to Mrs Alice Stuart Wortley, 26 April 1911 (subsequently cited as EE and ASW), in Jerrold Northrop Moore (ed.), *Edward Elgar: The Windflower Letters: Correspondence with Alice Caroline Stuart Wortley and Her Family* (Oxford: Clarendon Press, 1989) p. 84 (subsequently cited as *Windflower Letters*); TH, 'In a Former Resort after Many Years'.
4. Moore, *Edward Elgar*, p. 234; B. Maine, *Elgar: His Life and Works* (London: Chivers Press, 1973) vol. I, p. 116.
5. F. E. Hardy, *The Life of Thomas Hardy 1840–1928* (London: Macmillan, 1962) p. 330 (subsequently cited as *Life*).
6. EE to S. Colvin, 13 December 1921, quoted in Michael Kennedy, *Portrait of Elgar*, 3rd edn (Oxford: Oxford University Press, 1987 pbk) p. 15.
7. EE to A. J. Jaeger, 8 December 1903, in Percy M. Young (ed.), *Letters of Edward Elgar, and Other Writings* (London: Bles, 1956) p. 128.
8. EE to A. J. Jaeger, 21 February 1899, in *Nimrod*, p. 39.
9. M. de Navarro, quoted in Moore *Edward Elgar*, p. 588; Dr A. Thomson, quoted in ibid., p. 773.
10. *Life*, p. 363.

11.   Letter to J. McCabe, 18 February 1920, in *Life*, p. 403; *Life*, pp. 300, 342, 386.
12.   *London Musical Courier*, 12 October 1900; *Morning Leader*, 4 October 1900, both quoted in Moore, *Edward Elgar*, p. 333; *The Nation*, 16 November 1910, quoted in ibid., p. 593.
13.   EE to ASW, 29 August 1912, in *Windflower Letters*, p. 107; *Life*, p. 392.
14.   TH, Preface to *Wessex Tales*, dated April 1896–May 1912.
15.   EE, 'The Question of Programme Music' (undated), quoted in Moore, *Edward Elgar*, p. 342.
16.   TH, 'Embarcation'; EE interview, *Chicago Sunday Examiner*, 7 April 1907, quoted in Moore, *Edward Elgar*, p. 428.
17.   TH, 'The Sunshade'; Alice Elgar, diary 7 January 1919, quoted in Moore, *Edward Elgar*, p. 735; ibid., p. 731; EE to Rosa Burley, July 1913, quoted in Kennedy, *Portrait of Elgar*, p. 255.
18.   Anthony Storr, *The Dynamics of Creation* (London: Secker & Warburg, 1972) p. 182; TH, 'In the Small Hours'; EE to Mr and Mrs Edward Speyer, 15 December 1909, in Jerrold Northrop Moore (ed.), *Edward Elgar: Letters of a Lifetime* (Oxford: Clarendon Press, 1990) p. 215 (subsequently cited as *Letters of a Lifetime*).
19.   EE, *The Musical Times*, 1 September 1913; Alice Elgar, diary 27 June 1907, quoted in Moore, *Edward Elgar*, p. 514.
20.   EE to E. Newman, 23 November 1908, quoted in Moore, *Edward Elgar*, p. 529; ibid., p. 536.
21.   EE to E. Newman, 9 May 1911, in *Letters of a Lifetime*, p. 236.
22.   EE to Lady Stuart of Wortley (ASW), 15 August 1920, in *Windflower Letters*, p. 247.
23.   Moore, *Edward Elgar*, p. 787.
24.   Storr, *The Dynamics*, pp. 191, 178; *Life*, p. 251.
25.   EE to A. J. Jaeger, 30 July 1904, in *Nimrod*, p. 235; Fred Gaisberg, diary 28 August 1933, quoted in Jerrold Northrop Moore (ed.), *Elgar on Record: the Composer and the Gramophone* (Oxford: Oxford University Press, 1974) p. 214.
26.   Suzanne Langer, *Feeling and Form* (London: Routledge & Kegan Paul, 1953) p. 126, quoted in Storr, *The Dynamics*, p. 239; *Life*, p. 301.
27.   J. C. Brown, *A Journey into Thomas Hardy's Poetry* (London: Allison & Busby, 1989) p. 273; W. H. Reed, *Elgar as I Knew Him*, 2nd edn (London: Gollancz, 1973) pp. 131, 86.
28.   Storr, *The Dynamics*, p. 240; Reed, *Elgar as I Knew Him*, p. 129.
29.   Dennis Taylor, *Hardy's Poetry, 1860–1928*, 2nd edn (Basingstoke: Macmillan, 1989) p. xi; EE to ASW, 29 January 1911, in *Windflower Letters*, p. 75; R. L. Purdy, *Thomas Hardy: A Bibliographical Study* (Oxford: Clarendon Press, 1954) p. 166.
30.   Igor Stravinsky, *The Poetics of Music* (New York: Vintage Books, 1947) p. 33, quoted in A. Storr, *Music and the Mind* (London: Harper Collins, 1992) p. 185; Storr, *The Dynamics*, p. 239.
31.   'After the Last Breath'; 'Logs on the Hearth'; 'The Phantom Horsewoman'.
32.   21 February 1911, quoted in Moore, *Edward Elgar*, p. 610.
33.   EE to Dr A. Thomson, in ibid., p. 773.

34. *Life*, p. 57; EE to S. Colvin, 13 December 1921, in *Letters of a Lifetime*, p. 359.
35. EE to A. J. Jaeger, 5 February 1903, Novello archives, quoted in Moore, *Edward Elgar*, p. 391; W. H. Reed, *Elgar as I Knew Him*, p. 99.
36. EE to Lady Stuart of Wortley (ASW), 26 January 1919, in *Windflower Letters*, p. 221; legend, B. Maine, *Elgar: His Life and Works*, vol. II, p. 268 (footnote); Alice Elgar, diary 16 September 1918, in Moore, *Edward Elgar*, p. 726.
37. *The Woodlanders*, Ch. 41; 'If It's Ever Spring Again'; *Far from the Madding Crowd*, Ch. 2; W. Archer, *Real Conversations* (London: Heinemann, 1904) p. 32.
38. Robert John Buckley, *Sir Edward Elgar* (London: John Lane, The Bodley Head, 1905) p. 32; Lennart A. Björk (ed.), *The Literary Notebooks of Thomas Hardy* (London: Macmillan, 1985) vol. I, no. 1181.
39. TH to G. Putnam, 8 June 1911, in *Collected Letters*, vol. IV, p. 156; *Life*, p. 116; 'Lying Awake'.
40. *Tess of the d'Urbervilles*, Ch. 3 and *passim*; 'To an Unborn Pauper Child'; 'The Inquiry'; 'After a Journey'.
41. Ivon Hitchens, correspondence with Alan Bowness in *Ivon Hitchens* (London: Lund Humphries, 1973); TH, 'Rome: The Vatican: Sala delle Muse'. See also *The Well-Beloved*, and Proust: *A la Recherche du Temps Perdu*, for their ideas about the relation between love and art.
42. B. Whitelaw: *Billie Whitelaw: Who He?* (London: Hodder & Stoughton, 1995) pp. 126, 82, 117; Lyndall Gordon, *Eliot's New Life* (Oxford: Oxford University Press, 1989 pbk) pp. 169, 173; Miranda Seymour, *Robert Graves: Life on the Edge* (London: Doubleday, 1995) p. 331.
43. R. H. Taylor (ed.), *The Personal Notebooks of Thomas Hardy* (London: Macmillan, 1978) p. 240; 15 January 1894, 18 December 1893, in *Collected Letters*, vol. II, pp. 48, 44; 'Wessex Heights'.
44. W. H. Reed, *Elgar as I Knew Him*, p. 22; Mrs Gertrude Sutcliffe to Roger Fiske, in *The Gramophone*, July 1957, p. 54, quoted in Moore, *Edward Elgar*, p. 241.
45. EE to Walford Davies, 1 May 1920, quoted in Moore, *Edward Elgar*, p. 755; to Ivor Atkins, 30 December 1922, quoted in Moore, ibid., p. 762; ibid., Moore, p. 759, quoting Eugene Goossens, *Overture and Beginners* (London: Methuen, 1951).
46. EE to ASW, 23 June 1909, in *Windflower Letters*, p. 30; TH to Mrs Henniker, 13 July 1893, in *Collected Letters*, vol. II, p. 22; EE to ASW, 21 December 1909, in *Windflower Letters*, p. 34; to Mrs Colvin, 3 May 1910, in *Letters of a Lifetime*, p. 219.
47. EE to ASW, 10 February 1910, in *Windflower Letters*, p. 39; Moore, *Edward Elgar*, p. 569.
48. EE to ASW, 27 April 1910, in *Windflower Letters*, p. 46; 28 April 1910, in *Windflower Letters*, p. 47; to F.Schuster, 27 May 1910, quoted in Moore, *Edward Elgar*, p. 581.
49. EE to ASW, 25 October 1910, in *Windflower Letters*, p. 63; e.g. 'He Fears His Good Fortune', 'When I Set Out for Lyonnesse'.
50. EE to ASW, 24 March 1911, in *Windflower Letters*, p. 82; 25 October 1910, in *Windflower Letters*, p. 63; 7 November 1918, in *Windflower*

Letters, p. 215; EE to E. Newman, 29 January 1911, in *Letters of a Lifetime*, p. 229; to A. Littleton, 13 April 1911, Novello archives, quoted in Moore, *Edward Elgar*, p. 606.

51.   EE diary, 4 and 6 April 1910, in *Windflower Letters*, p. 43; *Life*, pp. 50, 120, 373.

52.   EE to ASW, 5 March 1917, in *Windflower Letters*, p. 176.

53.   EE to Lady Stuart of Wortley (ASW), 18 July 1920, in *Windflower Letters*, p. 244; V. Hockman, 'The Story of Nov 7, 1931', typescript at Elgar Birthplace, in Moore, *Edward Elgar*, p. 795.

10

Thomas Hardy, Epistolarian

RALPH W. V. ELLIOTT

'Letters are no matters of indifference; they are generally a very positive curse.'

'You are speaking of letters of business; mine are letters of friendship.'

'I have often thought them the worst of the two,' replied he coolly. 'Business, you know, may bring money, but friendship hardly ever does.'

Jane Austen, *Emma*, ch. 34

Mr John Knightley and Miss Jane Fairfax are exchanging views on the curse or the financial benefits of writing letters. Thomas Hardy was familiar with both the aspects of epistolary activity mentioned in this conversation and, indeed, with a third, the *'Lettres galantes*, I do not mean love letters, to fine women', which Lord Chesterfield commended in a letter to his godson, Philip Stanhope, in 1768.[1]

Hardy valued receiving 'letters that can really be called such in the old sense ... a pleasure I seldom experience nowadays' (VII, p. 153).[2] That was written in 1911. At the same time he was well aware that correspondence, especially 'my gale of correspondence' (V, p. 104), could be a burden, a sentiment which occasionally finds expression in his letters.

To consider Hardy as an 'epistolarian' – a rare nineteenth-century word – is to be aware of the immense debt we owe to the editors of his *Collected Letters*, the late Richard Little Purdy and Professor Michael Millgate, for the scholarly editing and meticulous annotating of the seven handsome Clarendon Press volumes, a debt which I here gratefully acknowledge. What the present paper attempts to do is to highlight or, if you prefer, to distil some of the less familiar aspects of Hardy's life and views, expressed in the first person, and

209

to indicate some stylistic and linguistic features to be found in his letters.

The first person is important, not only because as a novelist Hardy is a third-person narrator, because even his 'autobiography' is an impersonal narrative, albeit interspersed with personal letters and memoranda, but because Hardy frequently insisted that critics had no business to search for autobiographical elements in his fiction or for a philosophical system in, say, *The Dynasts*. That Hardy's poems are more directly personal, and that their 'I' and 'me' is often the poet speaking in his own voice about himself, needs no stressing. We need think only of, say, 'I Look Into My Glass' or 'Wessex Heights' or 'When I Set Out for Lyonnesse', to see the truth of this.

Dr Johnson is often credited with the comment that 'in a man's letters … his soul lies naked, his letters are only the mirrour of his breast', but in his *Life of Pope* he refutes this opinion:

> It has been so long said as to be commonly believed that the true characters of men may be found in their letters, and that he who writes to his friend lays his heart open before him. But the truth is that such were simple friendships of the *Golden Age*, and are now the friendships only of children … but a friendly letter is a calm and deliberate performance in the cool of leisure, in the stillness of solitude, and surely no man sits down to depreciate by design his own character.[3]

Not long after penning these words, Johnson commented to Boswell: 'It is now become so much the fashion to publish letters, that in order to avoid it, I put as little into mine as I can.'[4] Hardy, a very private person, probably felt much as Johnson did. Yet the glimpses into his domestic life, his health problems, and into his business dealings are as much worth lingering over as are the personal opinions and preoccupations which can be gleaned from reading his letters. It is here, perhaps more than anywhere else in his writings, that we can listen to the authentic voice of Thomas Hardy without the veil of his fiction or the deliberate obfuscation of his autobiography.

Hardy may not be baring his soul or laying his heart open before him, as Johnson put it, but he does draw back the curtains upon his heart and mind some little way when he writes, for example, to his friend Edward Clodd that 'Theological lumber is still allowed to discredit religion' (III, p. 5), or to Lytton Strachey that Queen

Victoria 'was a most uninteresting woman' (VI, p. 84), or to Florence Henniker 'I sincerely hope to number you all my life among the most valued of my friends' (II, p. 14). Cumulatively, the seven volumes of *The Collected Letters* mention recurrent themes that were clearly close to Hardy's heart.

His concern for the welfare of animals, for example, those 'mild creatures, despot-doomed, bewildered', was apparent for a very long time before he composed 'Compassion. An Ode' for the Centenary of the Royal Society for the Prevention of Cruelty to Animals in 1924, to which reference is made in the *Life*.[5] While writing *Jude the Obscure* it occurred to Hardy 'that one of the scenes might be useful in teaching mercy in the Slaughtering of Animals for the meat-market – the cruelties involved in the business having been a great grief to me for years' (II, p. 97). That this letter figures in the *Life*[6] only confirms its importance to Hardy, and this remained so throughout his life, witness his writing as late as July 1922 to the Duchess of Hamilton that slaughterhouse reform had his hearty support (VI, p. 144).

He returns to this topic in a letter to Florence Henniker: 'For my part, the world is so greatly out of joint that the question of vivisection looms rather small beside the *general* cruelty of man to the "lower" animals ... what an unfortunate result it was that *our* race acquired the upper hand, & not a more kindly one, in the development of the species' (III, p. 74). A few months later, in March 1904, he writes to an Anglican clergyman about the 'barbarism' of blood sports, wondering in the manner of Swift's *A Modest Proposal* 'why the children, say, of overcrowded families should not be used for sporting purposes. There would be no difference in principle' (III, p. 110).

Hardy is equally appalled by the use made of small animals, 'rabbits, pigeons, barn-fowls, ducks, & c.' in conjuring tricks; in one particular instance prompted to write to the Secretary of the RSPCA about it (III, p. 213), on another occasion to *The Times*. The mention of rabbits – coneys – recalls 'The Eve of Waterloo' from *The Dynasts* (Pt III, Act VI, Sc. 8), where his concern for helpless creatures, victims of human cruelty to its own species, was expressed with memorable compassion:

> Yea, the coneys are scared by the thud of hoofs,
> And their white scuts flash at their vanishing heels,
> And swallows abandon the hamlet-roofs.

'Looking back over the book,' he wrote to Edward Clodd in February 1908, 'the lyrical account of the fauna of Waterloo field on the eve of the battle is, curiously enough, the page that struck me ... as being the most original in it' (III, p. 298).

Hardy's sympathy for dumb creatures even extended to plants. Writing to Clodd he maintained that he had always known 'intuitively' that plants possessed consciousness, and that he hated 'maiming trees on that account' (III, p. 331).

There were other preoccupations and bêtes noires in Hardy's life, as revealed in the *Letters*. He disliked tobacco smoke: at the Royal Academy banquet in May 1914 it made his head ache, a condition with which today's non-smokers can readily sympathize. He increasingly disliked being pestered for autographs, especially by strangers, as he wrote to John Udal, a Dorset barrister and author, 'so many people being in the habit of sending me my own books for the purpose, & (as I regret to find) selling them afterwards for double the price they paid for them.' (V, p. 168).

Towards technological progress Hardy's attitude was at best ambivalent. One recalls the 'agricultural piano' in *The Mayor of Casterbridge* (Ch. 24), or the pulling down of the 'old moss-grown, mullioned Elizabethan cottages' at the end of *The Well-Beloved*, in order to build new ones 'with hollow walls, and full of ventilators' (Pt III, Ch. 8). But, as we know from the *Life*, he took readily to the bicycle, although not quite as recklessly as the young women in the midst of London's traffic, which he describes graphically with a touch of London dialect to his sister Katharine (II, p. 193), adding in another letter soon afterwards that 'the cycling here makes it dangerous to cross the streets' (ibid.).

Hardy's pride in undertaking strenuous cycling tours is obvious both from their mention in the *Life* and from fuller descriptions in such letters as one to Lady Grove in July 1898: 'I have just returned from a bicycle expedition to Bristol, Gloucester, & Cheltenham. The heat was tropical, & the backs of my hands, owing to my riding one day without gloves, were blistered, & are at present the colour of rusty iron' (II, p. 197). A modest reference to 'a few cycle rides' in the *Life* (p. 378) takes on a much more impressive colouring when he writes to Sir Frederick Macmillan in September 1910: 'I bicycled 24 miles over the hills yesterday, & the views were splendid' (IV, p. 118). Not bad for a septuagenarian who still manages at seventy-eight 'two or three short bicycle rides' to Egdon Heath and elsewhere in the neighbourhood (V, p. 283), although shortly before his eightieth birthday Hardy admits to the novelist Anthony Hope to not bicycling far nowadays, adding for good measure 'I ought to be a dignified figure sitting in a large arm-chair (gilded for choice) with a foot-stool' (VI, p. 18).

The motorcar did not entirely replace the bicycle in the life of the Hardys, although in his venerable years its conveniences offered opportunities to be mobile which Hardy appreciated. While still a keen cyclist, however, in his early sixties, he complained (as he no doubt would today) in a letter to Florence Henniker, 'the motor-cars are rather a nuisance to humble roadsters like me, one never knowing whether the comers are Hooligan-motorists or responsible drivers' (III, p. 33). What was equally obnoxious was 'Wessex being in a state of invasion by motor cars just now – which cover our apples with dust' (III, p. 266) – a typical August day in 1907, and a foretaste of what he might have had to endure by the end of the twentieth century, as 'trippers' and 'disconcerting invasion[s] by strangers' crowd into Dorset and there are even more accidents like the collision Hardy mentions in a letter to his wife, which took place near Max Gate in October 1924 (VI, p. 279).

The reference in the same letter to 'Wess' and 'Voss' – which has the attractive sound of a duo of television comedians – recalls not only the dog Wessex, with whom every student of Hardy is famil-iar, but also Harold Voss, the Hardys' chauffeur, one of the employees of Thomas Tilley, local garage proprietor and one-time mayor of Dorchester, who produced several of Hardy's plays. One hopes that Wess and Voss got on well together, although Wessex was not always overly friendly to outsiders.

If Wessex was the noisiest of the inhabitants of Max Gate, the succession of servants probably caused more problems to the Hardy ménage. There was 'a mutiny' amongst the servants in July 1886, forcing Emma to return to Max Gate from London to 'quell' it. On a previous visit Hardy had to remind Emma to 'caution the ser-vants about turning on & off the gas' (I, p. 133), which does not say much for their intelligence or sense of responsibility. Thirty-five years later Hardy writes to Florence Henniker that 'we have had of late great trouble with servants: they come & picnic for a month or two, & then leave, to picnic in somebody else's house' (VI, p. 10). On another occasion he apologizes to the critic Harold Child for their inability to put him up for a night, because 'unfortunately our servants are in rebellion, and we are largely dependent on char-women, added to which I am in a worse state of health than I have been in all the year' (VI, p. 222). Considering that there were never 'less than four servants to do the work of the premises', as Hardy wrote in 1926, he was justly incensed by the imputation in a newspaper article that Mrs Hardy 'runs the house at Max Gate by the help of a maid of all work (or words to that effect)' (VII, p. 27). This letter was addressed to a Dorchester solicitor, Hardy seeking 'absolute withdrawal of his statements' from the writer of the article, which appears to have been done. At the age of eighty-six Hardy ought to have been spared such annoyances.

Perhaps one of the reasons for having servant problems over so many years was, as Hardy once wrote to Florence Henniker, that 'the fresh air here gives them a colour & makes them attractive', so that 'a sort of hymeneal catastrophe' befalls the Max Gate establishment, as indeed it did in December 1904 when three of the servants left to get married on the same day, leaving the household sorely depleted (III, p. 151).

Hardy's ambivalence towards technological progress in agriculture and building and transport was matched by his hesitant acceptance of such innovations as the 'telegraph, telephone, & other modern inventions' (V, p. 9). 'By the way', the almost octogenarian writes to Edmund Gosse in January 1920, 'we have a telephone in this house, so should this [luncheon date] be inconvenient … you can ring us up – we are 43 Dorchester. (I ought to say that I personally am uncallable, not being able to hear what is said, but somebody would answer)' (VI, pp. 1–2). At the end of the same year he tells Edward Clodd about the telephone, adding 'I have nothing to do with it (except paying for it)', but he acknowledges the advantage for Florence of being able to talk to London people if necessary: 'This is not quite like seeing their faces, but makes the city seem curiously near us' (VI, p. 56). Hardy simply accepted the fact that he was 'bad at it' – and of course sometimes it did not work at all: 'The fault of the 'phone was at this end' (VI, p. 302). Considering how expeditious the postal services were almost a hundred years ago, Hardy was clearly at no great disadvantage being an epistolarian rather than a telephoner. After all, he could write a note from the Athenaeum in London to Bessie the parlour maid on Saturday evening, expecting it to arrive at Max Gate on Sunday morning (III, p. 64).

What Hardy might have made of faxes or today's even more impersonal electronic mail it is not difficult to imagine, especially in view of his frequent apologies in later life for having to send typewritten letters. 'Please excuse my being compelled nowadays to send a machine-written letter,' he wrote to J. S. Udal in March 1917 (V, p. 205), and elsewhere he referred to the typewriter as 'the universal printing-engine' (VI, p. 16). Many years later, in September 1927, he wished that he had 'learnt to use a typewriter when it was practicable years ago' (VII, p. 77). But it was too late; his eyes were now too weak.

Another modern invention that came late into Hardy's life was the radio. Writing to J. C. Squire on the day after his eighty-fourth birthday, he admits: 'I was inveigled into setting up Wireless, & did not know what was going to happen,' adding a PS: 'Our dog listened attentively.' What happened was that Hardy was able to listen to Squire broadcasting on the BBC 'An Appreciation of the Life and Work of Thomas Hardy – undoubtedly an extraordinary experience for the venerable gentleman (VI, pp. 252–3). Much the same 'great excitement' came two years later, in July 1926, when Hardy listened to his long-standing friend Edmund Gosse reading Wordsworth's 'Immortality' ode on the 'wireless' (VII, p. 33). Previously, in March 1924, Hardy had given permission for some of his own poems to be included in a broadcast lecture by a local lecturer, telling George Macmillan that 'Whatever effect broadcasting may have upon novels, it can do no harm to poems: it would in fact advertise them' (VI, p. 240). No fee was charged for the reading; as the businessman Hardy surmised, it was sound publicity – in every sense.

When Hardy wrote that letter of 11 November 1923 to Harold Child about the rebellious servants, he mentioned being 'in a worse state of health than I have been in all the year,' adding 'though it is nothing serious' (VI, p. 222). Part of this letter was included in the *Life* (p. 456), but without the reference to his health. Yet Hardy's letters do in fact frequently allude to the ailments which plagued him over the years. It is well known that the periodical publication of *A Laodicean* was threatened by Hardy's contracting a serious illness in late 1880, which at the time he referred to as 'a troublesome local irritation' (I, p. 82), but which he later admitted, both in the *Life* (p. 150) and in a letter to Florence Henniker, probably written in July 1893, had been much more serious: 'But think how I was handicapped afterwards. I had to lie with my feet higher than my head for some time of the 5 months. I forget what point I had reached when the illness began' (II, p. 25). He continued with the novel by dictating to Emma. This 'troublesome malady' kept him indoors and prevented his attending to 'many other little things' (I, p. 84), and it is quite characteristic of Hardy to gloss over it as if of slight importance, although Millgate's careful analysis points to a very serious, even life-threatening illness.[7]

Early in 1890, Hardy writes to an American acquaintance, Louise Chandler Moulton, 'I ... have been caught by the influenza' (I, p. 208), ascribing it to having 'caught cold – like everybody else' (I, p. 209). This probably alludes to the waves of influenza which affected many parts of the United Kingdom between 1889 and 1894, especially in the southern parts of England.[8] In June 1891 he complains to Edward Clodd of 'a disagreeable complication of neuralgia headache & influenza' (I, p. 236), and in January 1894 he explains to Dorothy Stanley that he has had to leave London prematurely, having 'got a violent attack of influenza, & feeling unable to attend to much in that state' (II, p. 48).

Although the peak of the so-called Russian influenza pandemic may have passed in 1894, Hardy continued to be plagued by further attacks of 'flu in subsequent years. In March 1895 he complained of 'a cold I caught on the chest' (II, p. 69); in May 1896 he wrote to Agnes Grove 'I have been unwell from a chill for the last two or three weeks' (II, p. 118), and in a letter to Florence Henniker, written about two weeks later, he blamed the 'malignant quality in the air of London' (II, p. 122). In April 1899, he writes, again to Florence Henniker: 'I had a visitation of the same complaint [an attack of influenza] about a fortnight ago, which has taken away all my energy, & left a slight cough, which I suppose will go. I do not know when we shall go to London; for myself I would rather go into a monastery' (II, p. 219). Hardy's quinquagenarian decade was clearly beset with recurrent bouts of ill health, although the same period witnessed the publication of his last three novels and his first volume of poetry, as well as two volumes of short stories.

However, more influenza was to follow, in May 1901, and almost exactly a year later he wrote to Edward Clodd, in May 1902: '[H]ere I am kept indoors over a large fire by a raging influenza, which seems to visit me in May as regularly as Schedule D [i.e. the income tax demand]' (III, p. 20). It happened again in May 1906 – certainly not a merry month for Thomas Hardy – although a decade later the 'flu came earlier, in March, when he wrote to John Galsworthy: 'It has been flirting with us off and on for the last three months. The conclusion I have come to about it is that people who live away from crowds get extraordinarily susceptible to the complaint – to infection, I mean. … One day in London is enough to give it to me at this time of the year' (V, p. 153).

Not surprisingly, as Hardy grew older, he became, if anything, even more susceptible to colds and coughs, at times being 'confined to the house … for a month or more' (V, p. 142), although his literary and, indeed, his epistolary activities continued steadily, and he was, as we have seen, still fit enough for a short bicycle ride now and then.

There were other ailments besides those I have mentioned; yet Hardy usually alludes to them uncomplainingly, even if his life was obviously made miserable at times and exceedingly so for so prolific and conscientious a writer. He asks Lady St Helier in April 1913: 'Do you know anything about varicose veins?' (IV, p. 265), which are preventing walks, excursions, and visits, and tells Edward Clodd a few days later that 'No relation of mine has ever suffered from such a malady. My mother was as lightfooted as a girl when she was over 80' (IV, p. 268).

A favoured liniment, Eliman's Embrocation, is recommended to Florence Henniker for sprains; and to Dorothy Allhusen he writes that the 'best preventive' against rheumatism is 'to make as little change as possible in underclothing all the year round', adding that while it is inconvenient in hot weather, it does save some suffering (III, p. 265). The air of London, as we saw, was considered by Hardy to be decidedly unhealthy, and 'London gardens *always* seem faded & dirty' (IV, p. 211), hence he advises Florence Henniker that 'chalk is the healthiest subsoil of any' (V, p. 11), albeit certainly not for growing onions, as he writes to an authority on agriculture, Lord Blyth, who had sent him a gift of Portuguese Onions in November 1919 (V, p. 339). Even a sip of brandy is not to be despised as a remedy for indigestion, he tells Florence, who had had the foresight to leave out a bottle for him to use while she was away from home. 'I think when I am in Dorchester I will bring home another bottle, in case of necessity' adds her thoughtful husband (V, p. 277).

These brief allusions to Hardy's domestic life and his health problems, all expressed as personal observations, are among the *obiter dicta* of a voluminous correspondence covering an astonishingly wide range of interests. That many of his letters are addressed to women comes as no surprise to his readers, nor does the affectionate tone of those addressed to Florence Henniker, Agnes Grove, and Florence Dugdale. That the letters to his first wife gradually lose some of their initial warmth is not surprising either: it was to be expected in a relationship in which 'Summer gave us sweets, but autumn wrought division,' as he wrote in 'After a Journey'. Yet, within a couple of months after Emma's death, he writes to Florence Dugdale 'If I once get you here again won't I clutch you tight' (IV, p. 255).

Such 'throbbings of noontide', as he calls them in one of his poems ('I Look Into My Glass'), are distinctly audible in some of Hardy's letters. He tells Florence Henniker of an amusing anecdote at an Academy 'crush', during which, while he was talking to a well-known society woman, she said 'Don't look at me so!' to which Hardy responded, 'Why? – because you feel I can see *too much of you*?' He explains in parentheses: 'she was excessively *décol-letée*' (II, p. 18). Years later, Hardy confessed to Edmund Gosse that on remembering Helen Paterson, the artist who illustrated *Far from the Madding Crowd*, he felt '"quite romantical" about her (as they say here)', adding ruefully that 'but for a stupid blunder of God Almighty' he might have married her instead of Emma, for they were both married at almost the same time 'but not to each other' (III, p. 218). This strong temptation to grow 'romantical' occurs in quite unexpected places. In a letter to Elspeth Grahame, wife of the author of *Wind in the Willows*, the 67-year-old Hardy confesses that when riding on top of an omnibus 'my attention is always too distracted by the young women around me in fluffy blouses to be able to concentrate on inner things' (III, p. 270).

Yet it is the 'inner things' which occupy Hardy in many of his letters. The horrors of the First World War called forth numerous comments about the pitiful state of the world, the European convulsion, the butchery, the atrocities, the 'gloomy time, in which the world, having like a spider climbed to a certain height, seems slipping back to where it was long ago' (V, p. 135). He was appalled at 'the cold scientific slaughter of hundreds of thousands' (V, p. 270), fearing, as he wrote in the 'Apology' prefaced to *Late Lyrics and Earlier*, that 'we seem threatened with a new Dark Age'.[9] From our vantage point at the end of a war-ravaged century we can but share Hardy's gloom that things are 'getting worse & worse. All development is of a material & scientific kind – & scarcely any addition to our knowledge is applied to objects philanthropic or ameliorative' (V, p. 309).

In his letters we can listen to Hardy talking about the years of war: the Zeppelin raids on London; the police in remote Wessex 'getting stricter here about illuminated windows' (V, p. 154); sub-marines about the shore of Portland; petrol rationing and other economies: 'We put on our coals as it were with sugartongs, drink cider only, in wineglasses, & send our ancient shoes to be mended instead of buying new ones' (V, p. 149). And in his capacity as a Justice of the Peace, Hardy had 'the tedious duty to perform of adjudicating on food profiteers' (V, p. 267).

Dorchester meanwhile was 'teeming with soldiers, mostly drunk' (V, p. 42) and German prisoners began to arrive, some of whom, 'amiable young Germans', were later sent to work in the garden at Max Gate (V, p. 203).

Hardy's despondency about modern warfare and his gloomy prognoses are hardly surprising. While working on the battle of Jena in *The Dynasts* (Pt II) he wrote to Florence Henniker in September 1904 that in that battle 'the combatants were *close* together; so differ-ent from modern war, in which distance & cold precision destroy those features which made the old wars throb with enthusiasm & romance' (III, p. 135). When he wrote these words, the Boer War had recently ended and 1914 was still ten years in the future. He agreed, in a letter to John Galsworthy in June 1911, that the use of aircraft 'will make war worse than ever', adding: 'However, of late years I have almost despaired of civilization making any big step forward. Possibly in the year 4000 we shall be nearly as barbarous as we are now in belligerency, marriage, treatment of animals, &c' (IV, pp. 161–2). To this we might respond that the world is still a very barbarous place as we approach the year 2000.

Despite such apparent despondency, Hardy disliked being accused of pessimism, and he repeatedly defends himself against the charge in his letters. A letter written to Alfred Noyes in 1920, which was included in the *Life* (pp. 439–40), cites a reviewer's comment, 'Truly this pessimism is insupportable. ... One marvels that Hardy is not in a madhouse.' He then goes on: 'Such is English criticism; and I repeat, Why did I ever write a line!', concluding that 'far from being the wicked personage they doubtless think me at present to be, I am a harmless old character' (VI, p. 55). Five years later, now aged eighty-five, Hardy published the little quatrain 'Epitaph on a Pessimist', of which we might remind ourselves in this context:

> I'm Smith of Stoke, aged sixty-odd,
> I've lived without a dame

From youth-time on; and would to God
My dad had done the same.

Fortunately, Hardy's dad hadn't, and despite hostile criticism, recurrent bouts of ill health, and the depressing state of the world, he
battled on, even if earlier pleasures palled. Thus, despite all the attractions of London and its social whirl – what Jane Austen neatly
summed up as 'the elegant stupidity of private parties' (*Persuasion*,
ch. 19) – Hardy grew increasingly to dislike the city. Already in
1896 he had told Florence Henniker, 'I have lately grown to feel
that I should not much care if I never set eyes on London again'
(II, p. 141), clearly put off by 'the turmoil of the streets' (VI, p. 261),
a sentiment extended to 'Paris and other noxious places' (VI, p.
291), especially in winter. Had the fluffy blouses on the omnibus
lost their charms? He did, however, relish exploring the English
cathedrals, sending picture postcards to relatives and friends, but
he was disappointed by the squalor of the city of Durham, which
'was not even clean enough to get a cup of tea in' (IV, p. 51). As for
England's two senior universities, Hardy concluded succinctly,
'Oxford being the romantic University, as Cambridge is the intellectual' (VI, p. 170).

Apart from numerous literary allusions and quotations in his
letters, Hardy occasionally writes at what J. I. M. Stewart called 'a
more substantially critical level'.[10] Writing to H. W. Massingham in
July 1907 on current tendencies in literature, Hardy believes 'there
may be a great reaction in favour of poetry before very long' (III,
p. 258). Yet, as he grew older, he patently did not care for what he
came to call 'the new ugly school of poetry (IV, p. 300), regretting,
as he wrote to Sydney Cockerell in 1918, 'that a fashion for obscurity rages among young poets, so that much good verse is lost by
the simple inability of readers to rack their brains to solve conun-
drums' (V, p. 275). Writing to Ezra Pound in March 1921, Hardy
admits: 'As I am old-fashioned, and think lucidity a virtue in
poetry, as in prose, I am at a disadvantage in criticizing recent poets
who apparently aim at obscurity. I do not mean that *you* do, but I
gather that at least you do not care whether the many understand
you or not' (VI, p. 77). Hardy may have been optimistic about the
great reaction in favour of poetry, but he obviously did not greatly
care for what he described to Robert Bridges as 'the woeful fogs of
free verse worship' (VI, p. 165). It is likely, as Millgate suggests,[11]
that Hardy was among the earliest English readers of Walt

Whitman, about whom he tells Florence Henniker in his 1916 Christmas letter, 'I always think, [he] wrote as he did, formlessly, because he could do no better' (V, p. 192).

'So much is hurriedly written nowadays', Hardy comments parenthetically to G. W. Foote in June 1910 (IV, p. 96), referring to one of his own recent 'hurried' letters to the Secretary of the Humanitarian League (printed in the *Life*, pp. 376–7). That he was not thinking solely of personal correspondence may be suggested by a comment to Galsworthy seven years later, that 'literature is getting too slovenly for words' (V, p. 221). Slovenliness, indeed, is one of the reasons why 'the English language is in danger of utter ruin, largely as it seems by the multiplication of half-illiterate publications' – this from the 82-year-old Hardy to a conference of Professors of English in America (VI, p. 147). He did not tell the American professors, however, that many years earlier, in 1906, he had told Sidney Lee that he was 'appalled at the ruin that threatens our fine old English tongue by the growth of American phraseology of the worst sort in our newspapers, which influence the speech of the people more than is realized' (III, p. 237). No doubt he included in this 'the rawest American', referred to in a letter to John Lane (IV, p. 131), and American spellings, which he did not care for either. But Hardy was not above using some 'raw' Americanisms himself, such as the phrase 'It is all fixed up', placing 'fixed up' in inverted commas and adding 'American language' in parentheses – and all this to his wife Florence (VI, p. 280). He quite unselfconsciously refers to 'the movies' in a letter to his publisher in 1922 (VI, p. 158), a word coined in North America a mere ten years previously, although elsewhere he speaks of 'a kinema production' and 'film rights'. As for the word 'cablegram', he brands it an 'illegitimate word!' in a letter to Florence Henniker (II, p. 110).

And yet Hardy's language is rich in words adopted, resurrected, coined in what Dennis Taylor has called his 'philological laboratory',[12] and the letters are no exception. He listened with amusement to the girlish slang of Lady Jeune's daughters at the theatre in 1894; he turns a reviewer's personal abuse back on to him, assuming that the reviewer is *himself* afflicted with 'sex mania', a word hardly of wide currency in 1897; he tells Hermann Lea: 'I was unknown to myself, Kodaked by some young men' while out on a private walk (III, p. 146), another word newly come into the language; he uses 'autumn' as a verb analogous to the verb 'to winter', and he revives the use of 'tennis' as a verb, writing to

Lady Keeble in 1927: 'why *did* you go tennising in such a wild way!' (VII, p. 77).

Hardy rejected the charge of writing in a patois, 'because', he explained to Edmund Gosse in February 1899, 'I used a dozen old English words which every true friend of the language is anxious to restore' (II, p. 214), a claim he repeated years later to Logan Pearsall Smith: 'I remember that in the 1st Edn of Wessex Poems I tried to popularize some good old English words, still living, down here, but I was met with opposition by the reviewers' (IV, p. 318). Hardy's letters must be regarded as part of his linguistic experiments, like coining the word 'flattites' to describe dwellers in flats in a letter to his sister Katharine (II, p. 222),[13] or punning on the double meaning of 'condescend', i.e. to act graciously, to deign, and to move down, when writing to Dorothy Bosanquet in Cambridge, 'If you ever condescend to Dorset, please come & see us' (VI, p. 87). The word recalls a curious slip of his pen, which he corrected with one of the shortest messages in all the seven volumes of *The Collected Letters*, addressed to the publisher Richard Bowker in November 1880: 'For "ascended" read "descended"' (I, p. 83), a correction to stand beside Eric Partridge's famous postcard, 'For "hell" read "heaven",' with its disturbing theological implications.

If we add the various comments on the vocabulary and pronunciation of dialect, as well as Hardy's own use of dialect words in his letters – as in all his other writings – we cannot but acknowledge the truth of William Archer's phrase 'seeing all the words of the dictionary on one plane', which Hardy deemed a 'happy phrase' (II, p. 207).[14] So he writes from London to the parlourmaid Bessie, at Max Gate, to 'get the gardener to chimp' the potatoes left in the cellar (III, p. 63), a word that found its way, via William Barnes's *Glossary of the Dorset Dialect*, into Joseph Wright's *English Dialect Dictionary*, to which Hardy was to contribute, in a postcard to Wright, the definition of another good Dorset word, 'trangleys', of which he says 'I have heard this used many times, but it may possibly be a nonce-word only' (III, p. 42). Wright prints only the one example, from *Two on a Tower* (Ch. 38).

Another dialect word, which Hardy shares with the Cheshire writer Alan Garner in his recent novel *Strandloper*, is 'sic-sac day' or '"shic-sac day" being what the peasantry call it' (I, p. 181), the 'Oak-apple day', which commemorates the future King Charles II hiding in an oak tree at Boscobel in 1651. Hardy was responding to some questions by Edmund Gosse, noted also in the *Life* (pp. 231–2), adding that the old English pronoun 'Ich' and kindred words were 'dying rapidly', although 'still used by old people in N. W. Dorset & Somerset'. Readers of *The Woodlanders* will recall Grammer Oliver's distinctive pronouns. Another expression '"good-now" is still much in use in the interior of this county though it is dying away hereabout', Hardy writes to Professor John Hales at King's College, London, in 1892 (I, p. 277); but the steady disappearance of dialect words is graphically illustrated by the words 'tranter' and 'to trant', which, some twenty years later, were to be heard only 'in the remote nooks of this county' (IV, p. 312). Here Hardy was writing to the editor of the *Oxford English Dictionary*, Sir James Murray, in October 1913. Hardy's use of the verb 'trant' in 'The Bride-Night Fire' is the only modern example of the word cited in the *Dictionary*.[15]

It is not entirely inappropriate that I have quoted Jane Austen in this paper, because Hardy, at the age of eighty, clearly enjoyed listening to his wife reading her novels, 'all six of them straight through – which I had not read since I was a young man', he tells John Middleton Murry (VI, p. 43). On the other hand, as for Spenser's *'Fairy Queen'*, he confessed years earlier to Mary Sheridan 'that, in common with so many English, I had never read it quite through' (I, p. 191). If Shelley is the 'greatest of our lyrists' (VI, p. 101), Shakespeare, Hardy writes to Harley Granville Barker of all people, 'is largely wasted in acting' (VI, p. 373), and he thought Iago 'the greatest failure in S's characters. ... I shouldn't wonder if he (Iago) didn't "slip idly from" S. just as a matter of potboiling' (V, pp. 173–4). This to J. W. Mackail who had just delivered the Annual Shakespeare Lecture of the British Academy, in 1916.

Goethe fares a little better with Hardy, although increasingly neglected 'over here', as he writes to Sir George Douglas after the end of the First World War (V, p. 303), adding in a subsequent letter, 'As to *Werther*, I have always had a sneaking liking for the tale, though that is morbidity, I suppose' (V, p. 323). Considering the fate of Goethe's novel, including an episcopal confiscation of the entire original Italian version and official bans in Denmark and parts of Germany, the author of *Jude the Obscure* probably could not help his sneaking liking. Such literary *obiter dicta* are to be met with frequently in Hardy's letters, as are quotations, and references to his own novels, stories, and poems. Many of these occur in his business correspondence; after all, as Mr John Knightley said to Miss Jane Fairfax in the quotation from *Emma* with which I began, 'business, you know, may bring money'. Hardy could be quite as canny in his dealings with publishers as Donald Farfrae in *The Mayor of Casterbridge* in his corn dealings, but his language, especially to Frederick Macmillan, whose judgement he trusted 'without hesitation' (VII, p. 14), was a model of courtesy and businesslike informality. Hardy would have hesitated to use an expression like 'Are you game to back up the idea?', as H. G. Wells, another Macmillan author, was liable to do.[16] Hardy's correspondence with the House of Macmillan, as the editors of *The Collected Letters* point out, is 'the most extensive, both quantitatively and chronologically' (I, p. x), the greater portion of it being the letters to (Sir) Frederick Macmillan, spanning more than forty years from March 1885 to December 1927.

One of the oddities of this correspondence is Hardy's epistolary vacillation in modes of address between 'Dear Mr Macmillan', 'My dear Macmillan', 'Dear Sir Frederick Macmillan' and 'Dear Sir Frederick'. In early 1916, to cite one example, Hardy uses three different modes of address to Sir Frederick Macmillan within less than three weeks. Perhaps Hardy had reasons for such stylistic variations, perhaps not. Some indecisiveness, at least some indifference, appears inescapable in Hardy's epistolary style.

As one reads through the seven volumes of the Purdy – Millgate edition of *The Collected Letters*, one becomes aware of differences in tone, in assuredness, between the earlier letters and later ones. It is as if the epistolary sequence reveals four ages of the man, which we might call the struggling Hardy, the successful Hardy, the eminent Hardy, and the venerable Hardy. Of course, they overlap and they are paralleled by his literary progress as novelist and poet. What distinguishes Hardy's letters is a basic courtesy. Even when 'so burdened with correspondence of late' as he was in August 1920 (VI, p. 37), including receiving a letter printed in the *Life* (p. 437) which ran: 'Dear Sir: / I am driven to wonder why the devil you don't answer letters that are written to you! / Very truly, A— M—'; or when irritated by insistent autograph hunters or unauthorized accounts of his life and work, Hardy's language remains forceful, but not offensive. Thus he refers to F. O. Saxelby's *A Thomas Hardy Dictionary* as 'rather a useless book' in a letter to Macmillan, adding that it is 'incomplete, ill-proportioned, erroneous, or what not' (VII, pp. 2–3). He might have been more favourably disposed to the Japanese *A Thomas Hardy Dictionary* of 1984,[17] a labour of love coming from a country where Hardy is studied and admired second only to his native England. That an unnamed 'Japanese gentleman' was puzzled about the expression 'green malt in floor', Hardy writes to Macmillan in 1926, is hardly surprising, 'as there is hardly anyone left in Dorset who would know the meaning of the saying, it having quite passed out of use' (VII, p. 8). But it lives on in the Japanese *Dictionary*,[18] and in *Tess of the d'Urbervilles* (Ch. 4).

Hardy concludes his letters with a considerable variety of phrases, ranging from the very formal 'yours obediently' and 'Your obedient Servant' to the intimate tone of letters to Emma and Florence Hardy, and to his closest friends, where he signs himself 'Ever yours affectionately', 'your affectionate friend', and the like. The customary conclusions to English letters are 'Yours sincerely', 'Yours faithfully', 'Yours truly', and 'Yours'. Hardy uses all of these, frequently modified by adverbs like 'most', 'very', 'always', or 'ever', and when his letters were drafted, dictated, or typewritten, and signed on his behalf by Florence or May O'Rourke, the secretarial help, the formula mostly used was 'Yours truly' or 'Yours very truly'.

The last letter in the final volume of the Purdy–Millgate edition was addressed to Hardy's long-standing friend Edmund Gosse and dated 'Xmas Day 1927'. It opens with the words 'Dear Edmund Gosse' and concludes with 'Best wishes to you & your house for the New Year – & believe m [sic] / Always your sincere / T. H' (VII, p. 89). Both the slightly formal mode of address and the warmhearted ending are, I suggest, wholly characteristic of Thomas Hardy, epistolarian.

Notes

1.   Quoted in Felix Pryor (ed.), *The Faber Book of Letters* (London: Faber and Faber, 1988) p. 71.

2.   Quotations from Hardy's letters are taken from *The Collected Letters of Thomas Hardy*, ed. Richard Little Purdy and Michael Millgate, 7 volumes (Oxford: Clarendon Press, 1978–88), citing volume and page. Quotations are published here by permission of the Miss E. A. Dugdale Will Trust.

3.   Samuel Johnson, *Lives of the English Poets*, ed. George Birkbeck Hill (Oxford: Clarendon Press, 1905) vol. III, pp. 206–7.

4.   James Boswell, *Life of Johnson*, ed. R. W. Chapman (Oxford: Oxford University Press, 1970) pp. 1443–4.

5.   Thomas Hardy, *The Life and Work of Thomas Hardy*, ed. Michael Millgate (London: Macmillan, 1984) p. 458, hereafter referred to as *Life* with page number.
6.   *Life*, p. 289.
7.   Michael Millgate, *Thomas Hardy: A Biography* (Oxford: Oxford University Press, 1982) pp. 214–16.
8.   See F. B. Smith, 'The Russian Influenza in the United Kingdom, 1889–1894', *Social History of Medicine*, 8:1 (1995) 55–73.
9.   *The Complete Poems of Thomas Hardy*, ed. James Gibson (London: Macmillan, 1976) p. 560.
10. J. I. M. Stewart, reviewing vol. III of the *Collected Letters* in the *Times Literary Supplement*, 10 September 1982, p. 968.
11. Millgate, *Thomas Hardy: A Biography*, p. 112n.
12. Dennis Taylor, *Hardy's Literary Language and Victorian Philology* (Oxford: Clarendon Press, 1993) p. 48.
13. Ralph W. V. Elliott, *Thomas Hardy's English* (Oxford: Basil Blackwell, 1984) p. 209.
14. See Ralph W. V. Elliott, 'Hardy's One-Plane Dictionary', *Thomas Hardy Journal*, 4:3 (1988) 29–48.
15. See Dennis Taylor, *Hardy's Literary Language*, p. 118.
16. See Lovat Dickson, *H. G. Wells: His Turbulent Life and Times* (Harmondsworth: Penguin, 1972) p. 195.
17. *A Thomas Hardy Dictionary*, ed. Mamoru Osawa and others. The Thomas Hardy Society of Japan (Tokyo: Meicho-Fukyu-Kai, 1984).
18. Ibid., p. 365.

11

Distracted Preacher: Thomas Hardy's Public Utterances

MICHAEL MILLGATE

I

I must begin with an urgent apology to Timothy Hands for stealing the title of his excellent book on Hardy and the church[1] – all except the question-mark. It seemed such a fine title for my purposes at that long-ago moment when it was unthinkingly chosen, and since it still seems a fine title now I've decided to make the delicate shift from theft to appropriation, rather along the lines of what the contemporary music business calls a 'tribute' album. Think of this then as 'Distracted Preacher 2' or 'Distracted Preacher: The Sequel'. And indeed, there may well emerge some suggestive parallels between Hardy's changing and often equivocal attitudes towards organized religion and his changing and often equivocal attitudes towards contemporary public issues.

This paper has been written on the basis of my experience with a project that had its beginnings back in the early 1970s and is now at last drawing to a conclusion. At the time when I started working with Richard Purdy on the edition of Hardy's *Collected Letters* we made the decision to exclude letters written to newspapers and magazines on the grounds that they should properly be considered not part of Hardy's personal correspondence but part of his published works. I'm perfectly certain that that was the right decision – that the destination and purpose of a transmitted document are far more important than the simple fact of its being cast in the form of a letter. But it does mean that every so often someone complains or claims or crows that such and such a letter to some editor or society or other is 'not in Purdy and Millgate' – making us sound in the process like some vast collective editorial stomach, not so much a Dead, perhaps, as a Digested Letter Office. In the light of that decision to omit public letters I shortly afterwards projected not just a friendly refuge for the items thus rendered homeless but an eventual scholarly edition that would collect all of Hardy's identifiable prose contributions to public discourse, print them in complete texts based on all the surviving evidence (manuscripts, corrected proofs, later revisions, relevant correspondence, etc.), annotate them fully, and organize them in a single chronological sequence that would facilitate perception of shifts in approach, emphasis, and direction at different stages of Hardy's career.

That edition, considerably expanded in size and scope and tentatively entitled *The Public Hardy*, is now approaching completion. Much of its bulk will of course be reassuringly comprised of the major and minor pieces of non-fiction prose with which students of Hardy are already familiar: for example, the three specifically literary essays ('The Profitable Reading of Fiction', 'Candour in English Fiction', and 'The Science of Fiction'), and the various comments on William Barnes; the almost political essay on 'The Dorsetshire Labourer' and the later observations on the same subject contributed to Rider Haggard's *Rural England*; and speeches such as 'Memories of Church Restoration', 'Some Romano-British Relics', and the words Hardy spoke when opening the Mellstock Clubroom and laying the dedication stone of the Dorchester Grammar School.

But *The Public Hardy* will also contain a great deal that is new – at least in the sense of being newly hunted down and rounded up and editorially corralled. Fresh material has steadily accumulated over the years, many items not listed in Purdy's bibliography have been identified and incorporated, and discussion of the edition and its problems during the first part of this paper should serve not only to reinforce existing knowledge of Hardy's non-fictional writings but also to expand and enlarge awareness of the ways in which Hardy operated as a literary professional and as a private individual within the public world of his day. The second part of the paper will then move on to offer some tentative summaries and assessments of Hardy's public performance over the course of his career and try to account for some of its apparent inconsistencies.

Although so much new material has become available for the edition it has not always been easy to apply consistent criteria for determining what should be included and what omitted. That basic definition of scope already offered – 'Hardy's identifiable prose contributions to public discourse' – may seem straightforward enough, but it can be problematic in practice. *The Collected Letters of Thomas Hardy*, for example, contains a good many items of personal correspondence that nevertheless found their way into print during Hardy's increasingly famous lifetime, and it's often impossible to be absolutely confident as to whether Hardy actively desired, retrospectively approved, or passively accepted publication of a particular item, or was simply never consulted in the matter. When one finds 'Not for publication' written across the top of a private letter the situation is straightforward enough. But when Hardy wrote in appreciation of the services he had received from the literary agent Alexander Watt or in polite acknowledgement of birthday greetings sent by the Mayor of Dorchester or the Vice-Chancellor of Cambridge University, did he know or suspect that his letter would subsequently appear in print? Or just not care? And in any case, was his permission ever sought? In most instances there is simply no evidence either way – inaction, after all, leaves remarkably few traces. But when it can clearly be established that an item of private correspondence was subsequently published with Hardy's knowledge and permission I would expect to include it in *The Public Hardy* – or at least those portions of it that actually appeared in print.

In December 1902, for example, Hardy in a personal letter to Theodore Watts-Dunton thanked him rather too warmly for the gift of his little fantasy called *Christmas at the Mermaid* and was promptly asked if his eulogistic phrases could be used in a newspaper advertisement for the book. Hardy said yes;[2] the advertisement has been found; and the quoted sentences will go into *The Public Hardy*. Sheer lack of evidence, on the other hand, seems likely to determine the omission of Hardy's well-known anti-cruel sports letter to the Reverend S. Whittell Key, suggesting in Swiftian vein that the children of overcrowded families might be used for sporting purposes. The letter sounds as though it might have been intended for publication; the original manuscript even carries markings suggestive of its being prepared for that purpose; but no actual publication has thus far been found. Fortunately the text is in this instance already available both in the *Life* and in *Collected Letters*.[3]

Hardy's speeches – in one sense his quintessential 'public utterances' – have also had to be considered individually rather than comprehensively included or excluded as a category. The *Life* speaks blithely of Hardy's entertaining his colleagues during slow afternoons in Blomfield's architectural office with 'short addresses or talks on poets and poetry',[4] but he certainly evaded almost all of the many invitations to speak that were thrust upon him in his later years. Lecturing, he declared in 1904, 'is beyond my powers & province',[5] and he always refused dinner engagements if there seemed any risk of his being asked to speak. It is true that occasional brief and even impromptu efforts are on record: according to the *Dorset Daily Echo* reporter, 'the tensest silence' followed Hardy's unexpectedly getting to his feet to say a few congratulatory words at the very end, or indeed *after* the very end, of a Dorchester Debating and Dramatic Society essay competition in March 1925.[6] But the problem for the editor is the frequent absence of any actual text for such utterances. A *Dorset County Chronicle* news item from early in 1918 reports Hardy as being thanked for entertaining the Hardy Players to tea following a performance of *The Mellstock Quire*, and then adds, sensationally enough: 'Mr. Hardy made a pleasant acknowledgement, and expressed his appreciation of the excellent manner in which the play had been performed.'[7] Sufficient unto that particular occasion, no doubt, was the report thereof, but it would be good to have more details of the speech at the July 1895 Omar Khayyám Club dinner in honour of George Meredith in which Hardy is said to have 'wittily and sweetly described his first meeting with Mr. Meredith in "a dusty back room at Chapman and Hall's"'.[8]

Although fuller accounts of Hardy's remarks on local occasions do sometimes exist, almost all of them are third-person summaries, so that the only speeches secure of a place in the edition are those for which Hardy's own scripts survive. All the important speeches come into that category, of course, although it seems somehow characteristic that the longest of them, 'Memories of Church Restoration', was actually delivered by someone else. Even more remarkably, perhaps, the second of the two speeches he wrote while President of the Society of Dorset Men in London was never delivered at all. William Watkins, the secretary of the Society, was supposed to read it out, as he had read out the first one a year previously, but he never got around to doing so, apparently because of the amount of time taken up by speakers who were personally present. The term 'filibuster' does not appear in reports of the occasion, but there's a palpable hint that the loyal

Dorset exiles were distinctly disgruntled at Hardy's absence from not just one but both of the annual meetings at which they had invited him to preside. Hardy, however, had only accepted the position on the understanding that he wouldn't be required to do anything, and he was considerably annoyed at having wasted time and effort on the speech – almost as annoyed as he had been when the publisher William Heinemann failed to make use of a Preface he had written for a posthumous volume of what he called the 'impassioned' poems of Violet Nicolson, who wrote under the name of Laurence Hope. It is to be hoped that Hardy's shade will be somewhat mollified by finding both these items included in *The Public Hardy*.

Publication of *The Public Hardy* will also release from bibliographical limbo a number of hitherto unrevealed examples of Hardy's skill at what might now be called manipulation of the media. Through genial encounters at the Society of Authors and the Savile Club and some of the many dining clubs of the day, Hardy established relationships of mutual convenience with several prominent journalists and editors – Moy Thomas, Edmund Yates, and Clement Shorter, for example, in the 1880s and 1890s, Arthur Symons, Harold Child, and others somewhat later on. So that when he had an item of news to make public, a book to promote, a criticism to counter, a minor score to settle, a log to roll, his preferred course was not to speak out directly in his own person but rather to nudge one of his journalist friends into speaking out on his behalf – generally in words that he had himself supplied.

Since the journalists for their part were always eager for items of literary gossip the relationship was happily reciprocal: James Milne of the *Daily Chronicle* is identified in Hardy's address book as a 'literary paragraphist', Lindsay Bashford of the *Daily Mail* as an 'enquirer for lit [erary] news'.[9] Asked by Hardy in 1890 to challenge another newspaper's negative comments on a charity performance by the American actress Ada Rehan and especially on the verses Hardy had written for her to speak at the end of the performance, Moy Thomas and Edmund Yates both responded in their respective columns with what might be called 'inspired' or 'instigated' paragraphs directly reflective of both the substance and the actual wording of Hardy's request. Over the years Clement Shorter, as editor of the *Sphere*, included in his regular 'Literary Letter' column, without attribution and often without rephrasing, numerous items that had in fact been supplied by

Hardy – among them an obituary of his friend Laurence Pike, a Dorset JP and animal-lover known nationally only as the author of letters to *The Times* about the sufferings of horses during the South African War.

It's true that Shorter was more eager than most to stay on good terms with Max Gate – to the point of printing one of Emma Hardy's poems and a photograph of one of her cats and getting her to judge a *Sphere* competition for photographs of beautiful babies. But when Jemima Hardy died in 1904 her son found no difficulty in silently supplying several newspapers and magazines with obituaries and portraits of her – loyally insisting that his sister Mary's painting (now in the Dorset County Museum) was the best likeness. Hardy, in short, was not above log-rolling and self-promotion – he may even have supplied Godwin's china-shop in Dorchester with the doggerel verses for its 'Wessexware'[10] – and there were plenty of people glad to be of service to so famous a figure.

Hardy was in fact rather given to action by indirection. As we know from Pamela Dalziel's splendid edition of *The Excluded and Collaborative Stories*, he became at different periods a concealed partner – a kind of Conradian 'secret sharer' – in some of the writings of Florence Henniker and Florence Dugdale. What *The Public Hardy* will more clearly bring out is the extent to which Hardy entered into similar – if differently motivated – partnerships with a series of commentators on his own writings and on the topography of Wessex. Secrecy was again an essential element. In August 1906 Hardy told Henry Woodd Nevinson:

> As to the article on my books that you contemplate writing, the only condition I make is that I do not personally appear in it as saying this or that: though I shall, of course, not mind giving any explanation of what may be obscure in them – that you may print it without saying how you arrived at your elucidations.[11]

Evidently such off-the-record briefings, as they might now be called, were perfectly acceptable not just to journalists such as Nevinson but to topographers such as Hermann Lea, whom Hardy supplied not just with information but with pre-fabricated paragraphs. They proved no less acceptable to literary critics such as Samuel Chew and Harold Child, who both published revised editions of their Hardy studies on the basis of corrections and guidance received directly from Hardy himself. It was another arrangement of mutual convenience: Hardy achieved his aim of silently setting right what he saw as damaging errors; the writers he assisted were glad to be corrected – and implicitly scolded – in private rather than in public, and gratified to be able to speak in print with a voice of borrowed authority.

Agnes Grove, Bertram Windle, Clive Holland, and the American critic Louis Untermeyer were among the other figures to whom Hardy supplied varying kinds and quantities of advice and correction, and while it would clearly be impractical for *The Public Hardy* to attempt any systematic identification and quotation of the textual results of Hardy's interventions, it does seem both useful and feasible to record his having taken such trouble and imposed such conditions. The edition will therefore include, within its overall chronological sequence, a series of briefly descriptive but non-textual entries devoted to recording Hardy's participation in acts of non-fictional publication of which he was neither the author nor the instigator. An obvious item for listing in this fashion is his assistance to Arthur Symons in the preparation of a new article on Thomas Hardy for the *Encyclopaedia Britannica*, but the same method will equally serve to record unacknowledged and even doubtfully attributed contributions of every kind. Hardy as a young architectural student, for instance, is said to have written up the details of John Hicks's church-restorations for use by 'the grateful reporter'[12] of the *Dorset County Chronicle*, and the edition will provide, duly framed by question-marks, the titles, dates of publication, and so forth for the published accounts of at least those restorations in which – thanks to the work of Claudius Beatty – Hardy is known to have been personally involved.

For purely practical reasons the edition may also have recourse to non-textual entries as a way of recording another category of public statements of which Hardy was in a peculiar sense the direct if unacknowledged author – namely, the many tombstones and memorials for which he was responsible. I have spoken vaingloriously on other academic platforms of breaking new bibliographical and editorial ground by including the texts of these interesting inscriptions in *The Public Hardy*, and indeed rich materials are available for such a purpose. Still surviving, mostly in the Dorset County Museum and the Frederick B. Adams collection, are Hardy's preliminary drawings and full-scale working plans for the tombstones of his parents, his grandparents, his sister, his first wife, and himself; also in existence are similar drawings for the memorials to Emma and himself that hang in St Juliot church, the brass plate in Stinsford Church in memory of the Hardys who once provided its music, the war memorial tablet visible at the Dorchester Post Office, and, best of all perhaps, the tombstone to Wessex in the pets' cemetery at Max Gate.

As providing a fascinating angle on Hardy's mortuary interests and devotion to family, the memorials represent a remarkable phenomenon, well worthy of record. At the same time, it has to be admitted that inspection of the drawings throws up only minor points of textual interest – for example, the stone to Wessex as carved does not exactly reproduce the punctuation in Hardy's drawing – and that the monuments themselves could be satisfactorily reproduced only by photographs, which would effectively be to leave them *un*edited. They will nevertheless achieve individual bibliographical status simply by being listed in the edition.

Entries of this kind will be further employed to record for the first time the many public petitions and letters to newspapers and magazines which Hardy did not write but which he agreed to sign in company with others. His fame and his reputation as a writer with a social conscience naturally exposed him to many requests of this nature, and it turns out that he co-signed a remarkable number and range of such communications over the course of his career. It is not surprising that he should have associated himself with messages of congratulation to Ibsen on his seventieth birthday, to Tolstoy on his eightieth and to Meredith at both seventy and eighty, and with appeals for the Keats–Shelley Memorial in Rome and the placement of a memorial to Byron in Poets' Corner. But it is more striking to find him co-signing letters that protest against the threatened execution of Maxim Gorky in 1905, deplore the laying of ritual murder charges against Jews in Russia, advocate the establishment of a Jewish state in Palestine, and express concern over the future of the British film industry. Despite his reputation for not having been swept away by patriotic fervour during the First World War, Hardy was also one of the fifty-two authors who signed an orthodox declaration in support of British war aims in September 1914, and one of the thousand so-called 'Representatives of the Brain-Power of the Nation' who in October 1916 put their names to the full-page launching in *The Times* of a campaign that deplored the damage being done by alcohol to the war-effort and urged the government to 'suspend all drink licences throughout the Kingdom for the period of the war'.[13]

These co-signed items (to repeat) will all be listed and briefly described in the edition but – because not written by Hardy – not reproduced as texts. There remain, however, some categories of Hardy-related material that *The Public Hardy* won't attempt to represent at all, or only very selectively. It will print, for instance, only a handful of items from among the large number of Thomas Hardy entries in contemporary biographical dictionaries. From an editor's point of view there are two major difficulties with such sources. In the first place, it is rarely possible to determine to what extent, or how often, the published information has been solicited from and/or verified with the biographical subject – to know, in short, how much or how little Hardy himself may have had to do with any given entry. The other, more purely practical, difficulty consists in the sheer proliferation of textually variant items, given that the relevant reference works typically appeared in a new edition every year or at least every other year. How many virtually identical lists of the titles and dates of Hardy's books can it be useful to reproduce?

The editorial response to this dilemma – as indeed to several others – has been partly principled, partly pragmatic. *The Public Hardy* will include the Thomas Hardy entry from the first modern edition of *Who's Who*, published in 1897, on the grounds that it was directly – and accurately – based on information supplied by Hardy himself: the form still survives on which he entered in his own hand the details requested – or most of them, since he failed to identify his parents.[14] Because he continued to keep his *Who's Who* entries up to date over the years the final revision made in his lifetime will also be included for purposes of comparison. The principal predecessor of *Who's Who, Men of the Time*, appears to have been less systematically authoritative, but there would seem to be some justification for including a specimen entry: first, because Hardy's initial appearance there dates from the 1880s and contains details later accounts omit; secondly, because evidence of his personally supplying the editors with at least some pieces of information is provided by the surviving note in which he sent in for a later edition the fact that he had become a Justice of the Peace not just for the Borough of Dorchester but for the County of Dorset as a whole.

The Public Hardy will also omit interviews as a category. Important as interviews undoubtedly are, especially for the indispensable glimpses they can provide of the personality and presence of men and women long dead, they are perhaps best considered as a genre unto themselves and treated together as a group – as James Gibson, indeed, is in the process of treating them. From an editorial standpoint the problem with interviews is always the basic irresolvable doubt as to the authenticity of what is represented as the direct speech of the interviewee.[15] This is a question not just of the Victorian and early twentieth-century lack of modern recording devices – such devices don't in any case entirely dispose of the problem – but also of the way in which the immense late-Victorian popularity of the journalistic interview so often led to extensive plagiarization of existing interviews and even to outright invention. Even a well-known interviewer such as Raymond Blathwayt, who did at least meet and talk with his subjects, might eke out from a single face-to-face encounter the material for several ostensibly separate interviews published in different newspapers and magazines.

Hardy wrote 'faked' or 'mostly faked' against several of the interviews he inserted into his 'Personal' scrapbook,[16] and he complained to newspaper editors on more than one occasion about interviews that had been obtained under what he considered to be false pretences. *The Public Hardy* will certainly print, however, the surviving draft of Hardy's prepared response to the journalist (James Milne) who came to interview him about the fate of Stonehenge in 1899,[17] and it may also include Hardy's lively conversation with William Archer, written down by the latter but made available to Hardy for correction and revision both before it went to the printer and when it was in proof.[18] What makes these two instances exceptional – what they have in common – is the clear evidence both of Hardy's acceptance of publication and of what he wished to be represented as saying.

Finally, I have decided not to reproduce Hardy's prefaces to his own works. There is clearly a case for their inclusion, but the counter argument can be made that they properly belong, as a matter of principle, with the books they introduce and that in these days they are in fact widely available and indeed generally familiar in those locations. Not entirely ruled out, even so, is the possibility of including the prefaces to the Osgood, McIlvaine edition of the novels as originally published – on the purely pragmatic grounds that editors generally, and understandably, prefer to reprint the revised and elaborated Wessex Edition prefaces of 1912–13, into which the texts of 1895–7 have for the most part been indistinguishably absorbed.

II

It will have become clear from these references to the number and variety of his public utterances that Hardy, at least in his later years, was rarely in want of a platform. Requests, invitations, and honorific gestures of every kind flooded in upon him simply by virtue of the fame and respect in which, as a writer of acknowledged greatness, he was increasingly held from the early 1890s to his death in January 1928. Inevitably, there were many requests that he refused or simply ignored. As I have remarked elsewhere, he did write in person to decline an invitation to write a poem supportive of the work of the Empire Marketing Board, but he got either his wife or his secretary to tell the Federation of Calico Printers that he could find no passages in his works descriptive of wall-paper.[19] He left entirely unanswered a request for comic poems that could be read out at a smoking concert in honour of recently elected Conservative Members of Parliament for Dorset. His instinct and policy, however, seem to have been to project a positive public image whenever it was feasible to do so, and when responding to requests that seemed essentially innocuous he tended to take the easy and comfortable course of compliance: as he said of his joining a Shakespeare Memorial Committee in 1905, while he often 'saw no great good' in such projects he generally 'saw no harm' in them either.[20]

But many of the individuals and groups who sought his support on larger and more controversial issues clearly did so not just because he was a famous writer but because he had written specific works – chiefly *Tess of the d'Urbervilles*, *Jude the Obscure*, and some of the early poems – in which they found assurance of a sensitive social and humanitarian conscience and a deeply pondered worldview, hence, they believed, a predisposition in favour of their own particular cause. When invited to venture into these more dangerous waters Hardy's responses could be complex, qualified, and even downright evasive. He told Florence Henniker, for instance, that when Dreyfus was found guilty in France by a second court-martial he had declined to sign an address of sympathy to Madame Dreyfus 'on the ground that English interference might do harm to her husband's cause, & wd do her no good'.[21]

When he was especially uncertain about an issue, indeed, or felt insufficiently informed, Hardy seems to have developed something of a habit of delaying his reply – deliberately or otherwise – until the moment for action had passed. In 1908 he failed to sign a statement on slavery in Angola, because (or so he told its sponsor) he put it aside 'to read up, & then forgot'.[22] In 1912 he was asked to join in a protest against the Lord Chamberlain's refusal to license Eden Phillpotts's play *The Secret Woman* unless specific changes were made,[23] but by the time he had quibbled over the wording of the document everybody else had signed it in its original form. The tactics of avoidance could sometimes prove embarrassing, however: when Hardy told a French journal in July 1899 that any remarks of his on the Dreyfus affair would be 'superfluous' to the active ongoing debate, its editors did not respect his obvious desire to stay silent but quoted him as thinking that too much had been said on the subject already.[24]

Hardy's response to the *Secret Woman* affair is particularly interesting in that censorship had long been one of his principal public themes. During the last two decades of the nineteenth century he had been an open supporter of Henry Vizetelly at the time of Vizetelly's imprisonment for publishing Zola's novels in England; he had complained strongly in his 'Candour in English Fiction' essay against the restrictive pressures exerted by the periodical press and the circulating libraries on the freedom of expression in the Victorian novel; he had written *Tess of the d'Urbervilles* and *Jude the Obscure*. His early twentieth-century record, on the other hand, seems distinctly less striking. He could be said to have dodged the *Secret Woman* protest; he failed to back up John Lane over the threatened suppression of a translation of Hermann Sudermann's *The Song of Songs*; and his letter supporting John Galsworthy's representations on stage censorship before a parliamentary committee in 1909 was rather ineffectually anecdotal – to the point that a commentator in the *Academy* could call it 'about the finest defence of the censorship that it would be possible to set up'.[25] It is true that in 1902 Hardy agreed to co-sign a letter to *The Times* protesting against the banning of Maeterlinck's play *Monna Vanna*, but even then he asked that 'some half a dozen names' should appear ahead of his in the list of signatures.[26] One of his conditions for signing the *Secret Woman* protest was to have been that the letter should also be signed by Henry James, A. E. Housman, Gilbert Murray, and Edmund Gosse, or by any three of them.

What is to be made of these apparent fallings from what we tend now to think of as grace? Why – in these as in so many other instances – did Hardy's personal courage, out in the practical world, seem so much less than the courage displayed by the author of *Tess* and *Jude* or, for that matter, *The Poor Man and the Lady*? It's necessary, first of all, to get a clearer sense of what Hardy saw as being at stake in these particular situations. In all but one of them the issue was stage censorship, and it was because he thought stage censorship primarily the province of dramatists and was anxious not to be perceived as claiming a place among the dramatists of the day that Hardy sought in the one instance to ensure that there would be other non-dramatists among the signatories and in the other that his name would not in any case appear too prominently. It's also clear that he thought neither *The Secret Woman* nor the particular translation of *The Song of Songs* provided sufficiently solid bases for serious challenges to the censorship laws.[27] He found *The Secret Woman* undistinguished as a play, the changes demanded by the Lord Chamberlain trivial, and the letter of protest overstated, while his criticism of the crudity of the Sudermann translation was subsequently endorsed by Lane's decision to bring out the book in an entirely new translation.

What seems to be operating in these instances is not just a cautious self-interested avoidance of direct confrontation but also a kind of quasi-puritanical truth-telling compulsion that Hardy sometimes compromised but never quite lost. Heinemann's decision not to use the preface to Laurence Hope's posthumous poems was surely influenced by Hardy's lukewarm praise of the poems themselves and his distinctly discordant insistence that it was always a mistake for women to use male pseudonyms – as of course Laurence Hope herself had done. Even his anonymously printed article on Florence Henniker must have left its adored subject somewhat underwhelmed by its observations on her novels and stories: of her latest novel Hardy observed that 'the growing strength in character-drawing makes the reader indifferent to the absence of a well-compacted plot'.[28]

Hardy, indeed, was always uncomfortable when commenting on the work of individual authors, especially other novelists. It is, on the face of it, remarkable that the author of three substantial critical essays and of significant prefaces to his own works should so consistently and unhesitatingly have turned down pressing invitations to write about such figures as Shakespeare, Fielding, Austen, Dickens, Thackeray, George Eliot, Zola, and Gissing. Hardy always maintained that he had neither a talent for literary criticism nor a method for its production, but he seems essentially to have felt, as he said when declining to supply an introduction to a novel of Zola's, 'that one novelist should not write on another except in eulogy'.[29] That this was something more than discreet avoidance of an uncongenial and indeed controversial subject is suggested by his response to a later invitation to write something about Dickens: '[I]t is almost impossible for me to criticize Dickens without, on the one hand, being considered invidious if I am as frank on his faults as on his genius; and, on the other hand, being considered to express eulogistic commonplace if I am indiscriminating.' The task, he suggested, should be taken on by those 'who stand in a more independent position'.[30]

The statement seems on the surface a curious mixture of self-effacement and self-assurance (Hardy was ready enough to see faults in Dickens even if not to talk about them), but that additional reference to not being in an 'independent position' helps to bring out the strong underlying sense of a quasi-personal relationship with Dickens (whom Hardy once heard read but never met) and of their interconnection along with other serious novelists within some ghostly literary confederation whose rules of decorum required that its members not speak ill of each other – 'that one novelist should not write on another except in eulogy'. Or, as Austen famously said to her fellow novelists through the pages of *Northanger Abbey*: 'Let us not desert one another; we are an injured body.'[31] If this interpretation is at all correct, it would seem to relate very suggestively to Hardy's extreme distress at criticism of his own work as well as to that fundamental truth-telling instinct spoken of just now.

That instinct – it might more generously be called a principle – was sometimes a source of difficulty to Hardy when responding to requests for action or comment on social and political issues. His long-standing lack of patience with Ireland and its politics – 'that unhappy & senseless country', as he once called it[32] – probably rendered almost automatic his refusal to sign a petition for the reprieve of Sir Roger Casement in 1916 or to support four years later Ford Madox Ford's initiation of a protest against government policy in Ireland. Conversely, his long-standing sympathy with the Zionist cause made him its strong and consistent supporter, whether writing on his own behalf (to a symposium in the *Fortnightly Review*, for instance) or co-signing the various public letters already mentioned. In general, however, major issues of this nature found him less than absolute in his judgements and less than wholehearted in his endorsements.

He has been criticized, for example, for giving so little public expression to his support for the women's suffrage cause: as late as 1916 he was still refusing to become publicly associated with the movement.[33] But it's important to remember Hardy's remarkable November 1906 letter to Millicent Fawcett, who had invited him to contribute to a pamphlet containing pro-suffrage statements by leading men of the day. His personal support of the cause, he explained, was real enough but grounded in the belief that the consequence of its success would be

> to break up the present pernicious conventions in respect of manners, customs, religion, illegitimacy, the stereotyped household (that it must be the unit of society), the father of a woman's child (that it is anybody's business but the woman's own, except in cases of disease or insanity), sport (that so-called educated men should be encouraged to harass & kill for pleasure feeble creatures by mean stratagems), slaughter-houses (that they should be dark dens of cruelty), & other matters which I got into hot water for touching on many years ago.[34]

Given the likely impact of such a programme if promulgated even now, ninety years later, it is scarcely surprising that Mrs Fawcett in 1906 felt that 'John Bull [was] not ripe for it at present'[35] – and omitted Hardy's letter from her pamphlet. Or that Hardy should tell Agnes Grove three years later of his fear 'that it would be really injuring the women's cause if I were to make known exactly what I think may be [the] result of their success – a result I don't object to, but which one half your supporters certainly would'.[36]

Hardy's standard plea was of course that his profession as a novelist required him to occupy in public a position of detachment, political neutrality, and non-involvement in organizations dedicated to social causes. He made the point with unusual specificity in 1897 when explaining to an American correspondent why he was unable to supply a magazine article on 'the marriage laws':

> The fact is that I am compelled by disposition, habit, & limitations to confine my writing to mere delineations of what I see, or fancy I see, in life, leaving to others the expression of views on

such spectacles, & the consideration of how to right, remedy, or prevent the wrongs which some of them undoubtedly are.[37]

Yet Hardy had in fact published a short article on the marriage laws in 1894, at the time of *Jude* and he was to publish another, rather unfortunately timed, in the year of Emma's death. Both are frank in their criticism of the existing legislation, but only up to a point well short of the profound radicalism revealed in the letter to Millicent Fawcett. What they jointly show is that while Hardy preferred to remain silent on such troublesome questions there were occasions when he felt impelled to speak out, if in subdued tones. It seems significant, in fact, that the symposium on divorce to which he contributed in 1912 was itself prompted by parliamentary proposals for revision of the current marriage laws – so that he was addressing a situation in which there seemed some possibility of practical change.

'But it is also clear that he saw, rightly or wrongly, some genuine risk for himself in speaking out, at least in the sense that any exposure of the extremity of his views on certain issues might indeed damage his public image and, potentially, his public sales. As he told a visitor in 1920, 'My views on life are so extreme that I do not usually state them.'[38] It can of course be argued that he should and could have been more vocal and forceful in advancing the causes in which he believed, and *The Public Hardy* will show that – especially as co-signatory to public letters – he was in fact more active than the current record would suggest. Because he neither initiated nor wrote the letters he co-signed,[39] they might be considered 'arm's-length' gestures, but they were none the less documents written precisely to attract attention and address current issues, hence likely to expose their signatories very nearly as much as an individual letter would have done.

Hardy's reluctance to enter too actively into the public arena is of course consistent with the other evidence we have of his personality and situation – his sense of privacy, his long-standing quietist tendencies, his lingering social insecurities, his deeply ingrained economic pessimism. We should perhaps not be especially surprised, therefore, at his preference for silence over speech, for suggestion over criticism, and for indirection over confrontation – nor even at his development of techniques for evading troublesome requests without refusing them outright. It was not, after all, as if there were no basis for Hardy's insecurities. We know something of

his early deprivations and difficulties; he certainly experienced confrontations enough at the time of the publication and reception of
his final novels; and it would be interesting to know how much
hostility he encountered when in the mid-1880s he ventured to
return to Dorchester as a man of modest fame and substance. His
appearing in public as an active Liberal on the stage of the Corn
Exchange in November 1885 may well have had social consequences which strongly influenced his subsequent disaffiliation
from all political movements and causes.

As Hardy grew older his appetite and energy for public debate
declined still further; its dangers and costs were all too clearly perceived. As he told Florence Henniker in 1904, 'when you begin a
newspaper correspondence there is no telling when you will end'.[40]
In turning down Ford Madox Ford's request in 1920 he explained
not just that he had despaired of Ireland but that he had grown
weary of the stresses of controversy: 'If one begins that sort of thing
he must be prepared to go on, or to get the worst of it, & at my age I
am not able to go on, apart from the fact that I have kept outside
politics all my life.'[41] Receiving a similar appeal from Walter de la
Mare some seven months later, Hardy returned the document
unsigned, 'believing such protests useless, &, in any event, my signature no help to them'.[42] When, in 1923, he refused a request made
by Dorothy Allhusen, one of his oldest friends, Florence Hardy
wrote back, in some embarrassment: 'I hope you will not be too
vexed with T. H. for his obstinacy. He is an old man, & was never
very easy to persuade I think.'[43] Wearying in his last years even of
his own most cherished issue, he instructed May O'Rourke, the
Max Gate secretary, to reply as follows to a request in early 1926
that he send a supportive message to a protest meeting against the
life-long caging of animals and birds: 'Mr Hardy wishes me to say
that he has already notified in public prints, &c, his opposition to
the practice of keeping animals & birds in captivity. A message
from him was therefore not necessary, & undesirable, since it is a
mistake to be over-emphatic even in a good cause.'[44]

'It is a mistake to be over-emphatic even in a good cause.' This
had always been Hardy's essential position – it has the ring of one
of his mother's minatory pronouncements – and its implied
tension, or perhaps compromise, between testifying and keeping
silent was finally, and characteristically, endorsed by his ghost-
writing much the most substantial of his non-fictional utterances
for publication after his own death. It has often been observed that

Hardy was extraordinarily adept at imagining himself as already dead, and in writing what he himself called *The Life and Work of Thomas Hardy* – what his widow published in somewhat sanitized form as *The Early Life* and *The Later Years* – he seized with avidity upon the possibilities offered by its posthumous perspective. Knowing that by the time the book was published he himself would be dead in fact and beyond further hurt, he not only presented the image of himself and his life that he wanted transmitted to posterity but took the opportunity to settle a few scores – above all to respond with long-brewed bitterness to the unforgotten hostile reviews of novels such as *Tess, Jude* and *The Well-Beloved* and verse volumes such as *Wessex Poems* and *The Dynasts*.

I have written in *Testamentary Acts* about the privileged status of last wills and testaments as providing an occasion for outspoken, truth-telling, quasi-posthumous speech without fear of responsive argument or anger. Which is why people in their wills sometimes feel able to espouse eccentric causes they would not have dreamed of publicly supporting in their lifetimes – or leave everything to a cats' home instead of to their expectant but unloved relatives. And I went on to suggest that Hardy may actually have seen *The Life and Work of Thomas Hardy* as a projective 'testament' from beyond the grave, 'a final uninterruptible and unanswerable contribution to that long dialogue between himself and his critics in which strategic and tactical advantage had seemed always to belong to the latter'.[45]

Very relevant here is what Keith Wilson has more recently said in *Thomas Hardy on Stage* about Hardy's relationship to the Hardy Players and their productions – that his essentially arm's-length encouragement of their activities allowed him to indulge his enthusiasm for the theatre while at the same time 'enjoying the luxury of being able to claim plausible non-involvement in the event of embarrassing publicity or adverse reviews'.[46] Activity by indirection. Exposition without exposure. Assertion without contradiction. These do indeed seem to have been Hardy's preferred positions for the conduct of his life as the public figure he so inevitably became. Eager as he was to see amelioration and reform of the multiple social and humanitarian wrongs he so clearly perceived, Hardy was in practice often distracted – deterred and at least partly silenced – by a shifting combination of personal, professional, social, and ethical considerations that may not seem especially substantial from our present position of comfortable distance and assumed superiority.

For Hardy himself, however, they were evidently distracting enough – even if they constituted, in their totality, a less overwhelming distraction than his preoccupation with the blank nonpurposiveness of the universe itself. In the spring of 1914 he could say: 'Altogether the world is such a bungled institution from a humane point of view that a grief more or less hardly counts.'[47] In confronting such larger, darker issues the question-mark absent from my title was for Hardy always implicitly present, as signifying hesitancy and doubt on the one hand and, on the other, that unresting, never-resolved interrogation of the meaning of things so wittily captured in Will Dyson's famous cartoon of the Immanent Will pathetically pleading, 'But Mr Hardy, Mr Hardy, if you only knew all the circumstances'.[48]

Notes

1.   Timothy Hands, *Thomas Hardy: Distracted Preacher? Hardy's Religious Biography and its Influence on his Novels* (Basingstoke: Macmillan Press, 1989).

2.   *The Collected Letters of Thomas Hardy*, ed. Richard L. Purdy and Michael Millgate, 7 volumes (Oxford: Clarendon Press, 1978–88) vol. II, p. 304 (subsequently cited as *Collected Letters*).

3.   Thomas Hardy, *The Life and Work of Thomas Hardy*, ed. Michael Millgate (London: Macmillan Press, 1984) p. 345 (subsequently cited as *Life and Work*); *Collected Letters*, vol. III, p. 110.

4.   *Life and Work*, p. 49.

5.   *Collected Letters*, vol. VII, p. 135.

6.   *Dorset Daily Echo*, 1 April 1925, p. 4.

7.   *Dorset County Chronicle*, 7 February 1918, p. 7.

8.   *Daily Chronicle*, 15 July 1895, p. 7.

9.   Address book in Dorset County Museum.

10.   See Pamela Dalziel's paper in the present volume, pp. 7–9, 19–21, and *Collected Letters*, vol. IV, p. 120, where TH acknowledges having made 'some suggestions' to Godwin's. The *Dorset County Chronicle*, 16 June 1910, p. 4, offered some samples, e.g.: 'No girl in Wessex rivalled Tess / In beauty, charm, and tenderness.'

11.   *Collected Letters*, vol. III, p. 223.

12.   *Life and Work*, p. 37.

13.   *The Times*, 27 October 1916, p. 6.

14.   In the *Who's Who* files still retained by the publisher, Adam and Charles Black.

15.   A recent article on the editing of Victorian interviews concludes that, at best, the filtering of everything through the interviewer makes it difficult to feel confidence in the validity of 'using such interviews as

if they convey the actual words of their nominal subjects': Patrick
G. Scott and William B. Thesing, 'Conversations with Victorian
Writers: Some Editorial Questions', *Documentary Editing*, 11, ii (June
1989) 38.

16. Scrapbook in the Dorset County Museum.
17. See Richard L. Purdy, *Thomas Hardy: A Bibliographical Study* (Oxford:
Clarendon Press, 1954) p. 306; the draft is in the Dorset County
Museum. Harold Orel's edition of *Thomas Hardy's Personal Writings*
(Lawrence: University of Kansas Press, 1966; London: Macmillan,
1967) pp. 196–200, usefully reproduces the interview as printed.
18. *Collected Letters*, vol. II, pp. 279, 280, 281; vol. III, p. 76; the 'conversation' itself is included in Archer's *Real Conversations* (London:
William Heinemann, 1904) pp. 29–50.
19. Michael Millgate, *Testamentary Acts: Browning, Tennyson, James, Hardy*
(Oxford: Clarendon Press, 1992) p. 128.
20. *Collected Letters*, vol. III, p. 156.
21. *Collected Letters*, vol. II, p. 229.
22. *Collected Letters*, vol. III, p. 363.
23. *Collected Letters*, vol. IV, pp. 200–1, 202–3.
24. *Collected Letters*, vol. II, p. 223.
25. *Academy*, 14 August 1909, p. 413.
26. *Collected Letters*, vol. III, p. 25.
27. Hardy told George Moore, who had challenged his position in
respect of Sudermann: 'If a protest over interference has to be made,
it would be a wiser policy to do it in connection with some safer
book' (*Collected Letters*, vol. IV, p. 133).
28. 'The Hon. Mrs. Henniker', *Illustrated London News*, 18 April 1894,
p. 195.
29. *Collected Letters*, vol. II, pp. 230–1.
30. *Collected Letters*, vol. VI, pp. 158–9.
31. *The Novels of Jane Austen*, ed. R. W. Chapman, 5 volumes, third
edition (London: Oxford University Press, 1933) vol. V, p. 37.
32. *Collected Letters*, vol. VI, p. 53.
33. *Collected Letters*, vol. V, p. 186.
34. *Collected Letters*, vol. III, p. 238.
35. M. Fawcett to T. Hardy, 4 December 1906 (Dorset County Museum).
36. *Collected Letters*, vol. IV, p. 3.
37. *Collected Letters*, vol. II, p. 154.
38. Marjorie Lilly, 'The Mr Hardy I Knew', *Thomas Hardy Society Review*,
1978, p. 102.
39. A possible exception was the joint Hardy, William Black, and Walter
Besant letter in defence of Harper & Brothers that James R. Osgood
seems to have drafted at Hardy's suggestion in November 1890
(*Collected Letters*, vol. I, pp. 218–20).
40. *Collected Letters*, vol. III, p. 113.
41. *Collected Letters*, vol. VI, p. 53.
42. *Collected Letters*, vol. VI, p. 94.
43. *Letters of Emma and Florence Hardy*, ed. Michael Millgate (Oxford:
Clarendon Press, 1996) p. 202.

44. *Collected Letters*, vol. VII, p. 12.
45. Millgate, *Testamentary Acts*, pp. 186–7.
46. Keith Wilson, *Thomas Hardy on Stage* (Basingstoke: Macmillan Press, 1995), p. 50.
47. *Collected Letters*, vol. V, p. 30.
48. The cartoon is reproduced in Michael Millgate, *Thomas Hardy: A Biography* (Oxford: Oxford University Press, 1982), following p. 400.

12

The Wit and Wisdom of Thomas Hardy

HAROLD OREL

I begin with an anecdote told by William Butler Yeats. It will sound familiar to many readers of the biographical trivia associated with Thomas Hardy. It has been repeated in various contexts, and most recently was retold by Anne Fadiman in the pages of *Civilization*, the magazine of the Library of Congress.[1] In the nineteenth century, and well into our own time, before most enthusiasts of a particular book went to an official book-signing ceremony in a bookshop or a department store, readers were accustomed to write to an author, asking him (or her) to inscribe a book with a signature, and possibly a dedication as well. They enclosed the necessary postage for a return trip of the book, and hoped that it would suffice. As Yeats recounted this particular incident, Hardy took Yeats upstairs to a large room that was filled from floor to ceiling with books – thousands of them: 'Yeats,' said Hardy, 'these are the books that were sent to me for signature.'

Quite apart from the fact that Yeats frequently embellished his stories to make a dramatic point, the anecdote itself does not ring quite true. It bespeaks a patronizing attitude toward readers who, after all, were guilty only of a desire to treasure something personal written by a writer who had touched their lives in some large or even small way. Hardy does not impress us as an author who would willingly or knowingly offend large numbers of his readers by refusing to sign copies of his books that they had taken the trouble to purchase and sent on to him. Indeed, Hardy respected the intelligence of his readers, and they in turn trusted him to be honest about his convictions.

My present concern is not with Hardy's place in the long tradition of English letters. Rather, I would like to deal with Hardy's wit and wisdom, both of which have impressed readers over a full century. The phrase 'wit and wisdom' deserves comment, though its antecedents are lost; it seems to have been in common use for centuries. Ralph Waldo Emerson was not the first to have used it when, on 21 July 1855, he responded to Walt Whitman's presentation copy of *Leaves of Grass*, 'I am not blind to the worth of the wonderful gift of *Leaves of Grass*. I find it the most extraordinary piece of wit and wisdom that America has yet contributed.'[2]

We can find examples dating back to the thirteenth century. Some of them are proverbs, a fact which means that several years must be added to the first dated citations. In the seventeenth century Sir Nicholas Bacon was called an 'arch-piece of Wit and Wisdom'. In the nineteenth century Nathaniel Hawthorne, in *Our Old Home* (1863), alluded to 'treasures of wit and wisdom ... still in the unwrought mines of human thought'. Only two years later R. F. Burton used the phrase as part of his title, *Wit and Wisdom from West Africa; or, A Book of Proverbial Philosophy, Idioms, Enigmas, and Laconisms.*[3]

Wit in this presentation is meant to be taken in its older sense of good or great mental capacity, of mental quickness or sharpness, of good judgement and discretion. I am not using it in its later meaning, that is to say, the utterance of brilliant or sparkling things in an amusing way – a natural way of referring to an individual who has a lively fancy and who possesses (and uses) a faculty for saying smart or brilliant things. Hardy illustrates wondrously well the familiar couplet of Alexander Pope,

> True Wit is Nature to advantage dress'd,
> What oft was thought, but ne'er so well express'd ...

Pope, of course, was thinking of wit in its original, broader meaning.[4] But when Charles Dickens described 'Uncle Bill' as 'evidently the wit of the party', he meant that Uncle Bill stood out because he could entertain his listeners with elegant turns of speech; with – what shall I call them? – witticisms.[5]

Thomas Hardy was not hostile to epigrammatic elegance. But there was a homeliness to his wit (as construed in this more limited sense) that probably debarred him from Uncle Bill's company. I have in mind such moments as when Sir Frederick Macmillan and Hardy, attending a social function in London, were approached by a lady who asked the novelist, 'Do tell me, Mr. Hardy, what did Tess mean to you?' and Hardy responded, 'Well I don't know what she meant to you, Sir Frederick, but to me she's been a very good milch-cow.' (As a caption in *Punch* might have added, 'The lady retires'.)[6]

Nevertheless, Hardy's wit and wisdom were not for all tastes, and probably contributed, to some extent, to his being misunderstood, or even disliked. Vere H. Collins, in the early 1920s, reproduced an exchange between himself and Hardy that doubtless made Collins feel uncomfortable. I reproduce the dialogue as Collins remembered it:

C.   Mr. Hardy, I hope I am not taking up too much of your time.
H.   Stay as long as you like. Do not think of us, but only of your train.
C.   Thank you very much.
H.   What train are you thinking of catching?[7]

Hardy was well aware of the way in which his life and character were impugned by some of his fellow-citizens in Dorchester. Most of these gossips did not know him personally, and their scandalous supposed 'truths' will not bear up under investigation. For example, a reporter for the *Independent* wrote, in February 1990, that Dorchester residents believed Thomas Hardy was a 'mean old bugger', tight-fisted and small-minded; but he certainly did not know how many of Hardy's contemporaries believed it, nor did anyone else who repeated the slander. Recently a reporter for the *Daily Telegraph* swore solemnly that Hardy had developed into a 'miserable old fellow' long before he died. This was not, and is not, true. Such stories, spread by members of the press and lately by television commentators, are designed to 'small' Hardy's reputation (to use one of Hardy's most characteristic rare words, an example of 'small' as a verb taken from Hardy, being the first one since 1665 listed in the *Oxford English Dictionary*), perhaps on the assumption that great men, looked at up close, are no better than most of us, and may be a good deal worse in their morals, ethics, and behaviour.

These characterizations of Hardy, these anecdotes, are almost all based on questionable evidence. They did not seriously diminish the high regard with which Victorian readers regarded one of their favourite authors, an author who, moreover, had gradually but unmistakably turned into a Grand Old Man of English Letters. The notion that 'most' citizens of Dorchester disliked Hardy for prizing his seclusion behind the walls of Max Gate, or for pretending to be better than his social class entitled him to be, is too sweeping a generalization to be credited. At any rate, such stories can be countered by anecdotes, supplied on equally good authority or better, which demonstrate a humaneness and largeness of vision that Hardy possessed throughout his very long lifetime.

More important, what biographers are frustratingly confronted by as they look into the enigma of Hardy's life is the *mysteriousness* of his personality. It has not been dissipated by the publication of a superb edition of his letters, nor by the accumulation of facts which have made the autobiographical substratum of his hundreds of poems more understandable to us at the end of the twentieth century than they ever were to Hardy's contemporaries. We have gained new insights from gender studies, from reviews of publishing practices and personalities, from connections established between Hardy and his literary and social contemporaries. What we do not have is a single key to Hardy's psyche, a simple explanation of his creative art. We know more about Thackeray or Trollope, and certainly a great deal more about Dickens, than we can ever be certain of as we consider the genius of Hardy's achievement.

Hence, I offer the following remarks about Hardy with some diffidence. Hardy should be remembered as a type of figure much more common in his own time than in the first half of the nineteenth century or in the second half of the twentieth, namely, as a writer who appreciated the complexities of human existence and wrote both his fiction and his poems with the intention of deepening his readers' sense of how difficult it was to see life clearly and in the round. He was, in brief, a Victorian sage comparable to Arnold or Carlyle. As John Holloway framed his critical thesis in his important 'Studies in Argument' (the subtitle of his book *The Victorian Sage*), logical and formal reasoning was not the strong point of books written by the truly wise men and women of the nineteenth century; a transcendent imagination coloured their perspectives (which could not be easily paraphrased by others); and if they wrote fiction rather than essays, in Holloway's words, 'we find illustrative incidents in a story instead of illustrative examples in an argument'.[8] If we ask *what* the incidents or examples illustrate, the answer must be: the general principles believed in by the sage.

Though many Victorian sages sought to persuade their readers as to the truth of those principles, they did not always seek to sway readers to the point of conversion. In his creative fiction, and even in most of his poems, Hardy was not engaged in the business of overt propagandizing. His stance, more often than not, was coolly analytical and critical. To protect himself, he lived so private a life that fully a score of his earliest biographers misunderstood and misreported a large number of important matters, such as the nature of his relationship to his first wife. Hardy was not trying to convert his public to his world-view. Rather, he was attempting to define what his world-view was through specific and particularized incident and example. In significant respects he differed from Ruskin, Morris, Mill, Newman, and Pater, as well as Arnold and Carlyle. He cherished his privacy at the same time that he dramatized a way of thinking about public issues that was peculiarly his own.

These generalizations are easily checked out against the personal experience of reading Hardy's novels, short stories, and poems. The overwhelming majority of Hardy's readers cannot – and would not – say that they are like the wedding guest who must stand transfixed while an ancient mariner, hypnotic-eyed, spins his yarn with an ever-insistent moral. (Coleridge, it must be remembered, apologized for there being too much of a moral in 'The Rime of the Ancient Mariner'.) We read Hardy for pleasure, and only afterwards does the shape of the narrator's intention become clear – if indeed it ever does.

Hardy rests content if a reader enjoys his story, knowingly or not knowingly conscious of an appreciation (however partial) of the artistic technique which shaped it. But a reader does not have to be illuminated by the truth of the general proposition that underlies the story, and indeed he or she may not be aware that there exists such a proposition.

The need for a just critical assessment of Hardy's creative output is thus poorly served by those who think they perceive a single figure in the carpet, and proceed to describe it in fulsome detail. Though Hardy believed strongly in many principles of private and public conduct, he did not choose to write as a didact pushing on others the truth of his own moral observations. On those relatively infrequent occasions when he chose to make public a personal position, he preferred to do it through a letter to *The Times*, a brief essay, or a poem in which the lyric voice spoke clearly. (Hardy's poems addressing issues of topical concern to a large number of his countrymen were written more frequently in the last third of his life than most readers appreciate.)

One may well ask, which issues provoked him into taking public stances? They are readily identified, and they illustrate a wide range of interests.

Hardy opposed blood sports at a time when such views were regarded as sheer crankiness. Animals and birds, he believed, had rights which blood sports trampled on. He rejoiced at the downfall of the Royal Buckhounds, and, admitting that his views on sport in general were 'what are called extreme', declared that it was 'immoral and unmanly to cultivate a pleasure in compassing the death of our weaker and simpler fellow-creatures by cunning, instead of learning to regard their destruction, if a necessity, as an odious task, akin to that, say, of the common hangman'. From this stance – recorded in *Humanity*, the Journal of the Humanitarian League (August 1901) – Hardy never deviated. He denounced vigorously the use of drugs on animals, the caging of birds, the keeping of tame rabbits in hutches, and any number of such 'cruelties' and 'useless inflictions'.

He was a strong champion of enlightened views on church restoration, and on the preservation of buildings with distinctive architectural features, in the face of wilful destruction of important elements of England's heritage. He knew whereof he spoke: he had been articled to John Hicks, a Dorchester architect and church-restorer, and he had worked for Arthur Blomfield, the eminent designer of churches and an architect who believed in restoration rather than destruction of still-viable structures, as well as G. R. Crickmay of Weymouth, who took over Hicks's trade, and T. Roger Smith, an architect who specialized in school design. Altogether Hardy worked full-time at the profession for a full sixteen years, from 1856 to 1872. When he served as consultant to the Society for the Protection of Ancient Buildings, he urged respect for the original craftsmanship to be found in oak pews, ancient stone work, and arches of the nave. His anger at indiscriminate tampering with chronicles in stone was expressed in any number of communications to interested parties as well as to the public.

He understood the true aims of the emerging science of archaeology long before most of his contemporaries. He was a good friend of General Pitt-Rivers, that extraordinary and vigorous champion of evolutionary change in museum displays (rather than the more widely adopted classifications of geography or nationality). Hardy wrote articles on the Maumbury Ring excavation of the early years of the twentieth century; the barrows of Dorset, and in particular

Conquer Barrow, opened only a few hundred yards east of Max Gate; and Stonehenge itself. (The major text of a famous 'interview' with Hardy, supposedly written by James Milne and published in the *Daily Chronicle* on 24 August 1899, was rigorously edited by Hardy, who wanted his views to be printed exactly in the form and language that he approved.) Archaeology, a developing science, helped to buttress his doctrine of the Immanent Will; its importance to Hardy cannot be over-stressed in biographical writings that seek to define his personal philosophy.

He knew that the divorce laws were repressive, and he fought for their liberalization. Hardy, we must remember, took a keen interest in the law, court proceedings, and the sentences handed down from the bench. In his later years he frequently dined with judges, even Lord Chancellors. As early as 1884, when he was in his mid-40s, he assumed the duties of a borough magistrate, serving in the Assizes until 1916, and as a judge in the Borough Petty Sessions until 1919. (Florence Emily Hardy served as a borough magistrate from 1924 on, and specialized in cases of girl offenders and cases of child welfare.) Hardy's stories and poems refer continually to legal issues, and his handling of such issues is both respectful and meticulously accurate. But the problems associated with the 'spectacles' of bitterly incompatible marriages, were, surprisingly often, the theme of his writings. The 'Postscript' to his Preface to *Jude the Obscure*, for example, stressed the importance of the role that the divorce laws of England had played in his devising of the 'tragic machinery of the tale', and he knew that the wrongs of an unhappy marriage needed to be righted, remedied, or prevented by an evolving social conscience: if not in his time, then, he hoped, within the near future.

He correctly judged the need of the Church of England to modernize its texts in order to appeal to a younger generation. In the early 1920s he awaited eagerly the publication of the new Prayer Book of the Church of England, and hoped for the development of some scheme to make 'the Established Church comprehensive enough to include the majority of thinkers of the previous hundred years who had lost all belief in the supernatural'. The dashing of his hopes – after he discovered that the revisions of the *Book of Common Prayer* had not been carried out 'in a rationalistic direction' – caused him to lose 'all expectation of seeing the Church representative of modern thinking minds'.[9] In his too-sanguine expectations as well as in his subsequent disillusionment, Hardy was representative of thousands of would-be reformers of Church doctrine.

He accurately measured the futility of the millions of sacrifices in the Great War, and he prophesied the coming of an even bloodier conflict. Although he wrote and published several patriotic poems designed to help the Allied cause, he became increasingly depressed by the senselessness of trench warfare, and the death of Lt Frank George of the 5th Dorsetshire Regiment (called by both Hardys their 'only decent relation',[10] Lt George was probably destined to become the Hardys' heir) and the structural weaknesses of the Versailles Treaty helped to reinforce older views that he held about the futility of war as a means of settling international conflicts, views which had been given most eloquent voice in *The Dynasts*.

Hardy's understanding of the self-destructive tendencies of late nineteenth-century farm management, and of government policies affecting agriculture, was dead on target. He was never more explicit than in his extended essay 'The Dorsetshire Labourer', published in *Longman's Magazine* (July 1883), and important recastings of the ideas contained therein may be found in *Tess of the d'Urbervilles* and *The Mayor of Casterbridge*. Hardy was not nostalgic for an agricultural past that he knew would never come again; he did not think of farm conditions in the first half of the century as a Golden Age, despite what some contemporary reviewers believed. He agreed with the mordant point of view recorded in Rider Haggard's probing analyses of England's agricultural crisis, a crisis that began in 1885 and continued right up until 1914, when the Government was forced to move vigorously to help the farmer.[11]

On all these matters, Hardy spoke from the heart. His was a remarkably unclouded crystal ball. And when he spoke on these issues, readers paid attention.

Nevertheless, we should not misrepresent the kind of Victorian sage that Hardy became in his final decades by saying that, as he aged, he fought more overtly to see his views prevail. It is more precise to say that Hardy stated his opinions on all these matters with a somewhat dry-toned rationality; he was never less than lucid in outlining the reasons why he believed as he did; and his sincerity in wishing for an amelioration of conditions that he personally abhorred is apparent in every communication that he addressed to the public. But he detested the passion of social reformers who always sought the limelight, and he shrank from confrontations that might destroy his deeply cherished privacy.

Keith Thomas has written, in his capacity as General Editor of the Past Masters series published by Oxford University Press, that the typical Victorian sage 'denounced the industrial civilisation in which [he] lived for its social injustices, its aesthetic shoddiness and its moral and cultural emptiness', and for his pains was often regarded by many contemporaries as 'unsound' or even mad.[12]

Hardy, like Ruskin, Morris, Carlyle, and Arnold, took an 'heroic and hopeless stand against the inadequate ideals dominant in their time' and 'kept open their communications with the future'; but Hardy, unlike them, couched his denunciations in less vitriolic and sarcastic language, and spoke more quietly, if no less eloquently, about the elements of Victorian culture that offended him. Marjorie Lilly, a visitor to Max Gate in 1920, told Hardy that he seemed to have pulled out 'all the stops' in *Jude the Obscure*. Hardy's quiet response was, 'Do you think so? My views on life are so extreme that I do not usually state them.'[13]

It is useful to argue, as David J. DeLaura did in his groundbreaking study *Hebrew and Hellene in Victorian England*, that 'The public statements of Victorian critics and essayists (and sometimes of poets and novelists) are often best regarded as refutation, qualification, or approval of some other writer's views.'[14] Hardy's fascination with tradition need not be denied, and the quickness of his response to a number of the fatuities infecting public discourse in England need not be minimized; but Hardy was not attempting to respond to what has been called, in a still fashionable phrase, the anxiety of influence. His views on the rightness and wrongness of human behaviour were hedged round with qualifications. He was guarded and circumspect in stating these qualifications; for the most part they yield their full meaning only when his technique of indirection is carefully analysed. Many readers assumed, during Hardy's lifetime, that they understood what Hardy meant to say at a time when Hardy provided little assistance to those who – reading between the lines – wanted to paraphrase his meaning in unequivocal language.

As a consequence, the storm about Hardy's 'pessimism' began to swirl at an early stage in his career, and it interfered directly, for a significant fraction of his audience, with reading enjoyment. It led to charges of nihilism, of brooding negation of civilized values; and the hostility deepened after the publication of *Jude the Obscure*, when unfriendly reviews appeared in the London *World*, the *Pall*

Mall Gazette, and the *Guardian*. Edmund Gosse wrote an impassioned critique in the *St James's Gazette* (8 November 1895):

> It is a very gloomy, it is even a grimy, story that Mr. Hardy has at last presented to his admirers. ... The genius of this writer is too widely acknowledged to permit us to question his right to take us into what scenes he pleases; but, of course, we are at liberty to say whether we enjoy them or no. Plainly, we do not enjoy them. We think the fortunes, even of the poorest, are more variegated with pleasures, or at least with alleviations, than Mr. Hardy chooses to admit. Whether that be so or no, we have been accustomed to find him more sensible to beauty than he shows himself in 'Jude the Obscure'. ... We rise from the perusal of it stunned with a sense of the hollowness of existence.

Gosse's friendship had begun in 1874; it was fortified by numerous meetings at the Savile Club; Gosse was the first visitor to be entertained by Hardy at his home in Shire-Hall Lane (also known as Glyde Path Road). Hence, Gosse's strong reaction to *Jude* was not something that Gosse enjoyed experiencing or, for that matter, writing about. When we recall how personally Hardy reacted to criticism, it is astonishing that the friendship between Gosse and Hardy was not permanently damaged.

Gosse was not alone in believing that Hardy's narrative bespoke a twisted doctrine. The problem had begun (for many) with the publication of an earlier novel. Far away in Samoa Robert Louis Stevenson had been appalled by *Tess*, and wrote to Henry James, who shared his low opinion of the 'message' in Hardy's masterpiece. (Stevenson, as the *Letters*, newly edited by Bradford A. Booth and Ernest Mehew [1994–5], reveal, was so displeased by what he interpreted as Hardy's fall from grace that he wrote grim attacks on *Tess* to a much wider circle of friends than Hardy ever knew.)

If close friends like Gosse and Mrs Henniker could misinterpret Hardy's cast of mind in the 1890s, it is perhaps not surprising that Hardy's intention in *Jude* – 'to show the contrast between the ideal life a man wished to lead, & the squalid real life he was fated to lead',[15] a contrast that Hardy believed might be discovered in *everybody's* life – was misread by Mrs Oliphant, casual acquaintances, and complete strangers who thought of *Jude* as a 'purpose novel', as some kind of manifesto on the marriage question.

Hardy's determination to exact a full look at the Worst in order to discover the possible existence of a way to the Better may have led to an unsettling ambiguity in his presentation of Jude's unhappy lot in life; if so, that would explain why there is no consensus as to whether Hardy's last novel succeeded as art or failed as too programmatic a performance. (I personally believe that *Jude* is one the the great novels of the nineteenth century, and that Hardy's anger at the hostile reviews, which led to his renouncing the novel as an art-form, ended prematurely the career of England's best story-teller. He had many more stories to tell, and indeed abbreviated versions of these stories appear in the poems he wrote in the last third of his life. The consequence of Hardy's decision to turn to poetry as a full-time writing responsibility was nothing less than a tragedy in the unfolding history of the English novel.)

Nevertheless, Hardy was expected, by readers at all levels of society, to point their lives in a direction they wished to go. If *Jude* failed in this regard for some of them, that momentary failure still did not destroy the moral leadership Hardy had assumed, over a period of two decades, as a Victorian sage. In his restrained and quiet way, Hardy had seemed to echo Carlyle's message in the 'Everlasting Yea' section of *Sartor Resartus*, a message which implored readers to 'Be no longer a Chaos, but a World, or even Worldkin. Produce! Produce! Were it but the pitifullest infinitesimal fraction of a Product, produce it, in God's name!' As Wendell V. Harris put it, in *The Omnipresent Debate: Empiricism and Transcendentalism in Nineteenth-Century English Prose*, Victorians took to heart Carlyle's definition of work as 'the manufacturing of a world, a cosmos, out of chaos', and hoped for order in an emerging world-to-be that sages such as Hardy might describe to them.[16]

The majority of Hardy's readers appreciated, during the full run of his novel-writing days, that he was not prescribing courses of conduct for his fictional creations but describing the difficult, and at times impossible, dilemmas that even the best of intentions might encounter in an implacably indifferent universe. That is to say, Hardy stated the terms of the paradox, and allowed readers to draw their own conclusions. If his statement (couched always in dramatic terms) ran counter to conventional doctrines of how men and women were supposed to behave (and children, too, as in the notorious case of Little Father Time in *Jude*), he shied away from any admission that he was responsible for the philosophical statements expressed by his characters. For example, he denied that anything in *Jude* had been taken from his own life, and claimed, with justice, that the novel should not be construed as autobiographical. It was only when he became convinced that not enough 'finely-touched spirits' existed to support his novel-writing endeavours – to protect him against the harsh winds of hostile reviews – that he turned to his first and most enduring love, the writing of poetry.

I have mentioned by name only two of Hardy's fourteen novels because the mid-1890s constituted his most critical decade, the period in which he decided to ignore as much as possible the over-tender sensibilities of readers corrupted by lending-library standards of decorum, morality, and what we call, in the late twentieth century, politically correct thought, speech, and behaviour. Perhaps, he wrote on 17 October 1896, he could express more fully in verse ideas and emotions which ran 'counter to the inert crystallized opinion – hard as a rock – which the vast body of men have vested interests in supporting'. In this private moment of meditation (the note was not intended for publication) he drew a distinction between potentially subversive theological opinions in a novel which would cause critics to 'sneer, or foam, and set all the literary contortionists jumping' upon him, 'a harmless agnostic', and the same opinions expressed in a poem, which would lead merely to a shake of the head as if such opinions did not matter in the real world. 'If Galileo had said in verse that the world moved, the Inquisition might have let him alone.'[17]

Even as late as 1901, in his Preface to *Poems of the Past and the Present*, he still felt obligated to defend the subject matter of his poems as largely 'dramatic or impersonative even where not explicitly so', and to argue that 'unadjusted impressions' in his poems, written down in 'widely differing moods and circumstances', recorded 'diverse readings' on the road to a true philosophy of life – as if he, in his sixth decade, had not already defined for himself such a philosophy.

The sales of Hardy's books of poetry, including *The Dynasts*, were consistently smaller than those of his novels; but Hardy's satisfaction that he was writing to please himself rather than editors of magazines or book-publishers or women-readers grew exponentially with the years. Perhaps more important, his remoteness in the rural world of a Wessex that most Englishmen had never visited, his unwillingness to compromise his opinions (theological and otherwise) for the sake of easy popularity, and his faithfulness to an honourable craft that endured long past the life-span of practically all the great Victorian poets (including Swinburne), contributed to the public's sense of Hardy's *gravitas*.

Hardy refused to court the general public with pronouncements that would flatter their prejudices. Less appreciated by modern critics is the fact that the general public admired his taciturnity and independence of opinion. He aimed his books at those who respected his right to have opinions, though theirs might differ. Once, writing to Mrs Henniker shortly before the Great War broke out, he mused wistfully, 'Altogether the world is such a bungled institution from a humane point of view that a grief more or less hardly counts. Wishing one had never come into it or shared in its degrading organizations is but a selfish thought ...'.[18]

But he never wholly gave up hope that conditions would improve (he described himself as an evolutionary meliorist), even after the Treaty of Versailles proved that large dreams for the comity of nations would have to be abandoned. He held fast, rather surprisingly, to old-fashioned virtues, as if faith in them would help to cancel 'the rages of the ages'. Brigadier-General J. H. Morgan, walking with Hardy to Stinsford Churchyard in October 1922, was pleased to hear Hardy say that he believed in going to church. 'It is a moral drill,' Hardy said quietly, 'and people must have something. If there is no church in a country village, there is nothing.' After laying his flowers on Emma's grave, he added that people needed and should have the liturgy of the Church of England ('a noble thing') and the Psalms of Tate and Brady: 'These are the things that people need and should have.'[19]

As we consider Hardy's relationship to his respectful readers, we should acknowledge the fact of Thomas Hardy's essential conservatism, even though several of his opinions – such as those on the realities governing both marriage and divorce – were well in advance of popular opinion. By and large, he was able to reconcile himself to the conventions of Victorian society. Many, if not most, of the Victorian sages who seem to us today to have dominated the discourse of the nineteenth century entertained strongly reformist, and occasionally radical, views as to what needed to be done to solve the Condition-of-England question, a question that they unanimously agreed was parlous. Because Hardy's opinions were not delivered in oracular fashion, they may well have been listened to more attentively as a consequence.

Finally, John Holloway's three most important guidelines for our understanding in the late twentieth century of all the Victorian sages, should be cited: they sought to see old things in a new way; their extraordinary influence over their contemporaries was explainable not in terms of the novelty of their ideas (many of which, when paraphrased, may disappoint us because they come so close to being platitudes), but rather in the magnificence of the language, that appealed to imagination as well as intelligence; and these sages may be fruitfully studied as writers of literature.[20] Hardy's achievement, like that of Carlyle, Mill, and Arnold, may be accurately characterized in these terms.

Thomas Hardy's professionalism as an author may rank him above all the other sages who pontificated, exhorted, and challenged their readers to improve their moral and ethical sensibilities. Many of their writings have dated, perhaps badly so, in part because their primary interest was not the production of literature as such. For Thomas Hardy it was, and never more so than after he turned from the writing of novels to the writing of *The Dynasts* and some 950 poems.

Notes

1. Anne Fadiman, 'Words on a Flyleaf', *Civilization*, III, 1 (January–February 1996) 82–3.
2. 'Emerson to Walt Whitman', in *Twelve American Writers*, ed. William M. Gibson and George Arms (New York: Macmillan, 1962) p. 57.
3. It is perhaps worth noting that the last word of Burton's title is indeed 'Laconisms', notwithstanding that the *Oxford English Dictionary* gives this book title as one of its illustrative quotations for the allied word 'Laconicisms'. Ed.
4. Alexander Pope, 'An Essay on Criticism'.
5. Charles Dickens, 'London Recreations', in *Sketches by Boz*.
6. Quoted by James Gibson in 'The Editor's Notes and News', *The Thomas Hardy Journal*, III, 2 (May 1987) 10.
7. Vere H. Collins, *Talks with Thomas Hardy at Max Gate, 1920–1922* (London: Duckworth, 1928) p. 9.
8. John Holloway, *The Victorian Sage: Studies in Argument* (London: Macmillan, 1953) p. 12.
9. Thomas Hardy, *The Life and Work of Thomas Hardy*, ed. Michael Millgate (London: Macmillan Press, 1984) pp. 448–9 (cited hereafter as *Life and Work*).
10. See Robert Gittings, *The Older Hardy* (London: Heinemann, 1978) p. 168.

11. See Rider Haggard's books on the agricultural crisis (all of which Hardy read): *Rural England* (1902), *The Poor and the Land* (1905) and *Regeneration* (1910).
12. Keith Thomas, 'Foreword' to *Victorian Thinkers: Carlyle, Ruskin, Arnold, Morris* (Oxford: Oxford University Press, 1993) pp. v, vii.
13. 'The Mr. Hardy I Knew', *The Thomas Hardy Society Review*, I, 4 (1978) 102.
14. David J. DeLaura, *Hebrew and Hellene in Victorian England: Newman, Arnold, and Pater* (Austin, Texas: University of Texas Press, 1969) p. xi.
15. *The Collected Letters of Thomas Hardy*, ed. Richard Little Purdy and Michael Millgate (Oxford: Clarendon Press, 1978–88) vol. II, p. 93. Letter, dated 10 November 1895, is to Edmund Gosse.
16. Cf. Wendell V. Harris, *The Omnipresent Debate: Empiricism and Transcendentalism in Nineteenth-Century English Prose* (DeKalb, Ill.: Northern Illinois University Press, 1981) p. 207.
17. *Life and Work*, p. 302.
18. *One Rare Fair Woman: Thomas Hardy's Letters to Florence Henniker 1893–1922*, ed. Evelyn Hardy and F. B. Pinion (London: Macmillan Press, 1972) p. 162.
19. Edmund Blunden, *Thomas Hardy* (London: Macmillan, 1958) p. 165.
20. Holloway, *The Victorian Sage*, pp. 9–11.

Index

Picasso